P9-DCR-365

A SECOND CHANCE

"A sweet little girl told me you went to Magdelena's for supper. Were you on your way to tell me so I wouldn't hear from someone else you were going to pursue her?" Ellie asked.

"Are you talking about Charity, Magdelena's little schweschder?"

"Jah, she and her mamm came in the bakery to purchase some goodies. She mentioned you."

Her worried eyes and fidgeting hands endeared her more to him. Her sweet nature and soft expression didn't show any anger on her part over his harsh judgment of her during their previous meeting, just concern he might be severing their relationship for good. He wasn't proud of the harshness he'd shown her. He wouldn't cause her another minute of doubt.

"Mamm accepted the supper invitation, and she insisted I go. I made it clear to Magdelena and my parents I wasn't over you." He inched closer to her. "I reacted horribly to what you had to tell me about your past. I'm sorry, Ellie. Really sorry . . ."

Books by Molly Jebber

The Keepsake Pocket Quilt series
CHANGE OF HEART
GRACE'S FORGIVENESS
TWO SUITORS FOR ANNA

The Amish Charm Bakery series
LIZA'S SECOND CHANCE
ELLIE'S REDEMPTION

Collections
THE AMISH CHRISTMAS SLEIGH
(with Kelly Long and Amy Lillard)
AMISH BRIDES
(with Jennifer Beckstrand and Amy Lillard)

Published by Kensington Publishing Corporation

Ellie's Redemption

MOLLY JEBBER

ZEBRA BOOKS
KENSINGTON PUBLISHING CORP.
www.kensingtonbooks.com

ZEBRA BOOKS are published by

Kensington Publishing Corp.
119 West 40th Street
New York, NY 10018

Copyright © 2019 by Molly Jebber

All rights reserved. No part of this book may be reproduced in any form or by any means without the prior written consent of the Publisher, excepting brief quotes used in reviews.

To the extent that the image or images on the cover of this book depict a person or persons, such person or persons are merely models, and are not intended to portray any character or characters featured in the book.

If you purchased this book without a cover you should be aware that this book is stolen property. It was reported as "unsold and destroyed" to the Publisher and neither the Author nor the Publisher has received any payment for this "stripped book."

All Kensington titles, imprints, and distributed lines are available at special quantity discounts for bulk purchases for sales promotion, premiums, fund-raising, educational, or institutional use.

Special book excerpts or customized printings can also be created to fit specific needs. For details, write or phone the office of the Kensington Sales Manager: Attn.: Sales Department. Kensington Publishing Corp., 119 West 40th Street, New York, NY 10018. Phone: 1-800-221-2647.

Zebra and the Z logo Reg. U.S. Pat. & TM Off.
BOUQUET Reg. U.S. Pat. & TM Off.

First Printing: February 2019
ISBN-13: 978-1-4201-4485-7
ISBN-10: 1-4201-4485-5

ISBN-13: 978-1-4201-4486-4 (eBook)
ISBN-10: 1-4201-4486-3 (eBook)

10 9 8 7 6 5 4 3 2 1

Printed in the United States of America

To my loving husband, Ed

ACKNOWLEDGMENTS

Thank you to:

Dawn Dowdle, my agent, and John Scognamiglio, editor-in-chief, for all their expertise and support.

Misty, my beautiful, talented, and smart daughter who lights up my life and helps me in so many ways.

Mitch Morris, the best brother, friend, encourager, and someone I admire.

Sue Morris, my mother. A beautiful, elegant, and amazing woman.

To Debbie Bugezia, Lee Granza, Mary Byrnes, Connie Melaik, Elaine Saltsgaver, Kelly Hildreth, Ginny Gilmore, Melanie Fogel, Donna Snyder, Linda Schultz, Lynn Smith, Darla Landgren, Ann Wright, Doris Kerr, Cyndee Perkins, Sigrid Davies, and many other friends. You know who you are and how much you mean to me.

Aunt Sharon Sanders and Aunt Sheila Walters for their encouragement, love, and memories.

Patricia Campbell, Diana Welker, and Marie Coutu and the Southwest Florida Romance Writers group for your advice, love, and friendship.

To Marilyn and Carolyn Ridgway: You've both lifted me up more times than I can count! You're both such a blessing!

To Connie Lynch: You are so good to me. Love your blog and you.

To Sandra and Denise Barela, Celebratelit.com: Thank you for your expertise, friendship, advice, and encouragement!

To my readers: I couldn't do this without your support and prayers. Thank you so much.

Chapter One

1912, Charm, Ohio

Ellie Graber glanced at Joel Wenger across the room. Her heart raced, and her cheeks warmed. His blue eyes and pleasant voice had popped into her mind often since they'd met at Liza's marriage to her daed four weeks ago. Since Joel's family was new to the community, she was glad Joel's parents had been present at the last service and heard about the wedding and attended. He was tall and confident but not arrogant. He'd missed the last worship service, and she hadn't run into him in town. Worship every other Sunday had made for a long wait but worth it to speak to him again. She wanted to learn all she could about him.

She bowed her head. The bishop prayed for the after-service meal and dismissed them from the Yoders' front room. She jumped up from the hardwood bench, stretched, and walked outside with Hannah.

Hannah nudged her. "I caught Joel looking at you several times. You and he had a very short conversation the first time you met. Maybe today you'll have a chance to get to know him better."

Ellie heaved a big sigh. "Hannah, I'm afraid."

Hannah quirked her brow. "Of what?"

"He's the first man in a while I've been interested in. I might be setting myself up for heartbreak if he finds out about what I've done. I'm sure the other available Amish men have avoided me because of it."

"Ellie, God forgave you. Now, forgive yourself." Hannah whispered, "Joel's headed in your direction. I'll sit with Eva and Leah." Hannah gave her a sweet nod and hurried to the long tables filled with food dishes.

Joel reached her. "Ellie, would you mind joining me in the shade under the oak trees near the pond? I've got a blanket already spread, and I found a stack of firewood and used a couple of pieces to hold it down."

Her heart raced. Of course she'd sit with him. She'd waited for this moment for weeks. "Danki, I'd be happy to."

She went to the tables displayed with dishes filled with food and scanned the many selections. A bowl of enticing uncooked carrots, celery, and broccoli cut in bite-size pieces made her mouth water. She scooped a helping onto her plate, then selected a ham-spread sandwich out of the basket beside it. Smiling, she waited for Joel to fill his plate. He stood at least six feet tall, and his muscles threatened to rip his sleeves. The word *handsome* didn't do him justice.

"Do you have everything you need?"

Ellie nodded. She'd add *thoughtful gentleman* to the list of why she found him attractive. She strolled with him to the blanket, sat and balanced her plate on her lap. The abnormally warm breeze for this time of year brushed her cheeks. Orange and brown leaves fluttered from the trees.

"I love summer." She sighed. "It's September twenty-second already. This may be the last day we'll go without jackets and shawls. I'm sad to have the season end."

"Summer is my favorite time of year too. We've been fortunate to have the higher temperatures this long. The rest of my family loves snow. I can't understand it." Joel exaggerated a shiver. "I dread the cold. If Mamm hadn't told me silly stories about my child-hood, I'd think I was adopted." He laughed.

She chuckled. He had a sense of humor. Another plus to add to the list of reasons she cared about Joel. "We didn't have a chance to talk much at my parents' wedding. Are you happy in Charm?"

"My parents and I have been busy getting things in order, and we haven't had time to socialize or explore the town. I'm anxious to do both. I also had an upset stomach and missed the last service. I haven't had a chance to get out and about much to get to know people."

Ellie smiled. "I'm sorry you were sick. I'm glad you're here today."

A woman approached them. She narrowed her light blue eyes and crossed her bony arms. "Joel, I expect you to socialize with all our new friends and not spend your time with one person."

Joel stood. "Mamm, this is Ellie Graber. Liza Graber is her stepmamm, and Ellie works for her at the bakery in town." He offered Ellie a hand to help her stand.

Ellie clasped Joel's fingers and balanced her plate in her other hand. She steadied herself and froze. The tall woman's pinched lips and hands on hips unnerved her.

Mrs. Wenger scanned Ellie from head to toe. "Ellie,

I'm sure you'll understand if I take Joel to speak with his other friends. Joel, kumme with me. Let me introduce you to someone."

Ellie swallowed the lump in her throat. Why was this woman set on separating her from Joel? "Nice to meet you, Mrs. Wenger."

Red-faced, Joel sighed. "Ellie, I apologize for leaving you. I'll speak to you again before I leave."

Ellie nodded. "I enjoyed our talk." She set her plate on the grass, then helped him fold the blanket.

"I did too." Joel gave her a regretful sigh, tucked the blanket under his arm, and followed his mamm.

Hannah, Leah, and Eva rushed to her.

Hannah crossed her arms over her chest. "You and Joel were smiling until Mrs. Wenger interrupted you. What happened?" Hannah rested a hand on Ellie's shoulder.

She glanced at her friends. "We were having a pleasant conversation, and then Mrs. Wenger insisted he go with her. She was rude and scolded him for not conversing with their other friends. I just turned eighteen, and she treated me like I was a child. I don't understand her cold demeanor toward me."

Leah ran her shoe over a stray dry leaf. "I overheard my mamm talking to her about you. Mamm has a wagging tongue, and she loves to tell the past and present gossip to the newcomers first. It frustrates Daed and me."

Ellie squinted. "She's been good to me when I've been to your haus. I'm surprised she'd share the worst about me with them."

Leah waved a dismissive hand. "She likes you, and she approves of us being friends. However, she believes you should wait for two years to marry, considering your history."

Hannah huffed and drew her head back. "Your mamm is too opinionated and eager to win friends the wrong way. Do you agree with her about Ellie, Leah?"

She held up her palms. "Nah, I do not."

Eva wrung her hands. "Ellie, Mamm agrees with anything Leah's mamm says. I hope you won't allow their views to interfere with our friendship."

"I understand how difficult it must have been for you both to share this information with me. I'm glad you told me. I cherish our closeness, and this won't change anything between us. I feared there would be consequences."

Eva gestured to the parked buggies and wagons. "Leah, your parents and mine are walking to the buggies. We'd better go."

Ellie and Hannah bid them farewell.

Hannah clasped her hand. "Don't let what you were told today upset you."

Ellie couldn't shake off the heavy sadness in her heart. Joel had captivated her from their first meeting. She might as well put her silly notion to grow a friendship with him out of her head. Mrs. Wenger would make sure it didn't happen. "I doubt God would want Joel to go against his mamm's wishes. The woman made it apparent she doesn't approve of me."

"She hasn't gotten acquainted with the sweet, smart, and adorable Ellie yet. Be patient. You will run into her at social gatherings and church. Engage her in conversation, and I'm sure she'll warm up to you." Hannah walked over to her basket on the table, reached in, and pulled out two cookies and handed one to Ellie.

Ellie held the molasses cookie. "Your friendship

means so much to me. You always lift me up." She sighed. "I'll give it a try." She took a bite and hugged herself. "These are exceptional."

She glanced at Joel. Abigail Fisher had his attention. Petite and attractive, she had a distracting habit of talking with her hands. Her smile so big, Ellie waited for her face to crack. Guilt shot through her. She shouldn't be judgmental. She didn't know much about Abigail. Jealousy had gotten the best of her.

Ellie frowned. Mrs. Wenger laughed with Joel and Abigail. Joel's mamm approved of this girl. Ellie's chances of Joel giving her another thought or his mamm warming up to her were growing slimmer by the minute.

Hannah passed her another cookie. "Quit frowning at Joel and Abigail. We stay away from her for a reason. She's cunning and not your typical Amish girl. Her parents have spoiled her, and she is used to getting her way."

"She's always avoided me. I don't know anything about her."

"The Fishers moved here three years ago. I wilkomed Abigail to Charm. She's our age. At first she was nice, then she turned her nose up at me for no reason. She's strange. Be glad she avoids you. I doubt Joel will be attracted to her. Her parents treat her like a princess, and she isn't afraid to speak her mind. Joel's talking to her means nothing. He was dragged over to her. He sought *you* out." Hannah shot a glance at Joel and darted her face back to Ellie. "Glance at him this instant."

Ellie met Joel's gaze.

He exchanged an endearing glance with her before returning his attention back to Abigail.

A spark of hope welled in her. Maybe Hannah had a point. She might have a chance with him after all.

Mrs. Wenger stared approvingly at Abigail. "Joel, this sweetheart brought us rhubarb tarts when we first moved in, and we had a nice chat. You had gone to town to buy a new saw blade and missed meeting her. You two should make plans and get to know each other. Her family owns the fifth farm to our left."

Joel listened to Abigail and stole glances at Ellie. Unlike Abigail, Ellie had a pleasing voice and the prettiest sky-blue eyes. Her honey-blond hair showed through her sheer white kapp. She came to his shoulder and had the daintiest hands and slender fingers. He was intrigued by her, and he longed to ask more about her life. He swallowed the frustration with his mamm intruding into his conversation with Ellie.

He didn't have any interest in Abigail. The annoying girl wouldn't stop prattling on about her favorite barn cat. Standing next to Mamm, he dared not escape, or she would be unbearable to live with the rest of the day.

Daed approached them. He tipped his hat to Abigail. "I'm Mr. Wenger."

Mamm held out her palm. "Meet Abigail Fisher. She and Joel are getting better acquainted." She put her hand on Abigail's back. "She's a charming girl."

Abigail blushed. "Pleasure to meet you, Mr. Wenger. Your fraa is the one who is charming."

Mr. Wenger gave her a curt nod. "Pleased to make your acquaintance, miss. Enjoy the rest of your day. We must be going."

Abigail asked Mr. Wenger, "Do you mind if I steal Joel away for another minute?"

"Not at all. Take your time."

Mrs. Wenger gave her son a gentle push. "You can meet us at the buggy. I need to gather my things, so don't rush." She waved to Abigail and joined Daed.

Abigail pulled Joel aside. "I've lived in Charm for about three years, and I plan to stay and raise a family here someday. It's a pleasant little town. You're going to enjoy life here. Kumme to my haus tomorrow around six. We'll have supper with my family then take a walk or buggy ride. I'll be glad to show you some good fishing and canoeing spots."

The last thing he wanted to do was spend more time with Abigail. "I have a lot of work to do. I'm going to have to decline, but danki for the invitation."

Abigail rolled her eyes. "Don't be silly. Your mamm approves of our getting together. I'm sure your family will understand. You have to have a little fun, and you will have supper at home. I make the best corn-bread. You don't want to miss it."

This girl was pushy, and it annoyed him she'd called him silly. An unusual trait for an Amish girl. One he didn't want in the girl he would choose to pursue. "I'm sorry. I'm going to decline. We haven't got everything the way we want it. It's going to take time."

"I wonder if you would turn down Ellie's invitation to supper."

Joel's stomach clenched. He suspected this girl hid the forward side of her personality from his mamm. "Ellie and I met at her daed's wedding. This is the second time we've run into each other."

"You should stay away from her."

Joel narrowed his eyes. "Why?"

Abigail kicked a small stone to the side. "It's no

secret. Her daed brought her to Charm for a fresh start."

"I'm not comfortable discussing Ellie with you."

"Someone has to tell you before you get yourself in trouble. She's not a nice girl."

Heat rose to his cheeks. He had to ask two important questions. "Has she committed her life to God? Has she joined the church?"

"Jah to both your questions, but it doesn't matter. I wouldn't trust her."

He'd learned firsthand how gossips could tarnish one's reputation. His family had suffered from embellished stories about his schweschder, Maryann. He'd hoped taking Mamm out of the home they'd once shared with his schweschder in Lancaster and bringing her to a new location would help heal her heart from the hurt they'd suffered as a result of Maryann's actions. He hoped never to experience such pain again.

Abigail lowered her chin and gazed up at him. "I hope you won't judge me for warning you about Ellie. I'm trying to protect you. You're new in town, and I don't want you to waste your time on someone who may hurt you."

He didn't believe her. She had an ulterior motive, to shift his focus from Ellie to her. It wouldn't work. She was forceful, driven, and rude. "Let's change the subject. I'm sure there's something else we can discuss."

"Kumme to my haus for supper." She raised her shoulders. "No harm in friends sharing a meal together. I'll expect you at my haus tomorrow evening around six."

Joel gritted his teeth. This girl had the determination of a beaver taking down a tree. Mamm would never let him live it down if he didn't say jah to her request. He was certain Mamm wouldn't be convinced he'd given Abigail a fair chance unless he accepted her invitation. The minute he got home, he'd make his disinterest in Abigail known. Then maybe Mamm would quit playing matchmaker when he told her he wasn't interested in Abigail. "I'll be there."

Abigail swayed from side to side and curled her lips in a satisfied grin. "I hope this will be the first of many visits you'll make to my haus."

He gave her a curt nod and left. Abigail would be hard to avoid at social gatherings and church. Going to her haus for supper to prove to Mamm and to Abigail he'd given the girl a chance might be a mistake. The girl wouldn't be easy to deter. He shook his head. He'd be polite but direct with her tomorrow evening.

Joel listened to the crunch of dry brown leaves with each step and gazed at the gray clouds. Hot summer weather had left, and the temperature turned cool this twenty-third day of September. Questions about Ellie swirled in his head. Ellie's answers to Abigail's warning could ruin any chance of friendship, or perhaps more, with her. He'd hope for the best. First, he had to go to supper at Abigail's and tell her the truth.

He worked hard until five thirty and then freshened up, changed clothes, threw his pole and dinted metal box he used to store what he needed in the back of his wagon, and headed to Abigail's. On the way, he admired the big barns, white homes, and pristine fields. Charm, a quaint small town, had the necessary businesses to supply whatever he needed. He didn't miss the larger and busy town of Lancaster.

Joel guided his horse to the hitching post, jumped down, and secured the animal.

Abigail opened the door and came skipping in his direction.

"You're here! Kumme on in."

He approached her. Her enthusiasm would make his planned conversation with her after supper awkward. Guilt shuddered through him. Kumming here was a bad idea. "Good evening. Lead the way."

She took him inside to the sitting room. "I'll hang up your coat."

He handed it to her. "Danki."

Her daed stood and offered his hand. "Call me Ben."

A cheerful, round-as-she-was-tall woman appeared. "Joel, I'm glad you could join us for supper. Would you care for some water, coffee, or tea?"

"Danki. Water would be fine."

Abigail gestured for him to sit. "I'll bring you a glass. You stay and chat with Daed."

Mrs. Fisher left the room, wiping her hands on a dish towel. "I'll be in the kitchen. Ham and beans and cornbread will be ready in a few minutes."

Ben settled back in a maple chair with stuffed blue cushions on the back and seat, stretching his long arms. "My dochder tells me you moved here from Lancaster, Pennsylvania. What brought your family to Charm?"

Abigail returned, handed him a glass of water, and sat a respectable distance from him on the settee. She flashed him a cheerful grin.

Joel held up his water. "Danki, Abigail." He then focused on Mr. Fisher. "My grossmudder and grossdaadi died in a haus fire not far from us. My parents wanted a fresh start, and a good friend offered to buy

both properties and suggested we consider Charm.
He'd visited here a time or two and said the location
and smaller size appealed to him."

"We love living in Charm. I'm sure you will too."
Ben relaxed and crossed his legs.

Mrs. Fisher stuck her head in the room. "Time for
supper. Take your seats at the table."

Joel followed Abigail and her daed. Steam escaped
from the large white porcelain bowl centered on the
table. The scent of yellow cornbread drifted from
the woven basket covered with a thin white cloth. His
stomach grumbled. "Mrs. Fisher, danki for preparing
this meal. It looks scrumptious."

Ben offered a prayer of thanks to God for the food.

"Call me Lovina. Sit and dig in. We've got plenty for
two or three additional servings. And Abigail made
her special cornbread just for you." Mrs. Fisher's rosy
cheeks beamed as she handed him the ladle with her
calloused hands. "Abigail gushes about your mamm,
and I can understand why. I met her at the service, and
she is lovely."

"She's fond of Abigail too." He glanced at the breadbasket. "Abigail, danki for making the cornbread."
Joel passed the ladle to Ben, and then accepted the
breadbasket from Lovina. He wished Mamm didn't
like Abigail quite as much as she did. He slathered his
cornbread with apple butter. Mamm put on a good
front when she chose to. The Fishers would be shocked
to learn Mamm had a temper and battled sadness
often.

Ben held a spoonful of ham and bean soup. "Your
daed and I had a pleasant conversation before the service Sunday. He said you are a hardworking farmer
and he's blessed to have you working alongside him."

"Daed has set a good example for me. He has taught

and continues to teach me how to manage crops, livestock, and many other things. I'm grateful to him. We're close."

Daed was his best friend, confidant, and teacher. He admired his patience and devotion to Mamm, in spite of her dismissiveness and lack of interest in him.

Joel and Ben discussed farming, and Abigail and Lovina listened. He waited for a pause in the conversation and then nodded to Abigail. "Would you like to take a walk?"

Abigail rested her hand on her mamm's shoulder. "I'll help with the dishes first."

"You and Joel enjoy your walk. I don't mind taking care of the dishes. Your daed will help."

Ben nodded. "I'd be happy to."

Abigail snatched a blanket from the quilt rack and her shawl from the knotty-pine coatrack.

Joel followed her outside. "Do you want to fish? I brought my pole." He shrugged into his coat.

"Bring it. I'll sit and watch you. We can chat while you fish." She threw her shawl around her shoulders.

They walked to the pond across the road and waved to families enjoying the evening sharing picnic suppers and fishing. She spread the blanket, and he pulled a small container out of his tackle box and removed a worm. He readied his pole and cast his line. He felt an immediate tug and reeled in a small bluegill and then released it. "Your parents are easy to talk to, and I enjoyed their hospitality."

"I could tell they had a good time with you."

His heart pounded in his chest. He set his pole down and sat next to her. "Abigail, danki for inviting me over. I appreciate your friendship."

"Friendship?" She crossed her arms and stared at him.

"I'm sorry, Abigail. I don't foresee anything more for us."

"After what I said about Ellie, you still want to pursue her, don't you?"

His shoulders tensed. "Please don't bring up Ellie again."

"I don't understand, Joel. Your parents and my parents are happy about our getting together." She swiped the tear trailing down her cheek.

"I don't want to leave you with the wrong impression. I'm sorry, Abigail." He stood and offered her his hand.

She didn't take it. "I'll get the blanket."

He grabbed his fishing pole and waited on her.

She joined him with the blanket folded in her arms. "I'm going to wait on you, Joel. I believe you'll find out Ellie isn't the kind of fraa any Amish man would pursue. Then you'll kumme back to me."

"Please, Abigail, don't wait for me."

They walked back in silence. She stopped by his wagon. "I'll be here for you if you change your mind."

He got in the wagon. The girl was exasperating. "Good day, Abigail."

He headed home. Glad each of the five farms between his home and Abigail's had a lot of acreage, so she didn't live too close to him. Girls in Lancaster had talked to him, but none had caught his attention the same as Ellie. No sparks flew with Abigail. She insisted on leaving the door open, and she didn't take no for an answer. He wanted the girl he would consider for a potential fraa to listen to him and for them to solve problems together. Abigail left him with the impression she would always insist on being in charge. To have a fraa speak unkindly of others wouldn't suit him either.

He glanced behind him in the wagon bed and moaned. He'd left his tackle box by the pond. Turning his wagon around, he went to retrieve it. Families were gathering their things and getting in their wagons. Ellie and her young brother Peter were walking toward the pond. They must've just arrived.

Ellie waved and motioned for him. "Kumme and join us." She waited for him to reach them. "Peter, this is Joel Wenger. You probably noticed him at Liza and Daed's wedding and at the service this past Sunday."

Peter looked at him. "I do." He held up his fishing pole to Joel. "Do you wanna fish with me?"

"I left my pole in my wagon. Why don't you fish, and I'll talk to Ellie and watch you. If you catch a big fish, I'll gladly help you reel it in."

Peter nodded and skipped to the pond. He cast his line.

"Ellie, please excuse me a minute. I left my tackle box earlier." He strolled over to get it and returned to her side.

Ellie patted the spot next to her on the tattered patchwork quilt, then pulled her thin shawl around her shoulders. "Were you fishing earlier? Did you catch anything?"

He didn't want her to find out from the gossips about him joining Abigail and her parents for supper and assume he was pursuing the annoying girl. He'd rather she found out what happened from him. "Abigail and I were here earlier after we finished having supper with her parents. We visited more than I fished."

Ellie stared at Peter, her eyes sad. "It's getting cooler outside. Maybe I should take Peter home."

Joel noticed her expression was full of disappointment. He'd given her the wrong impression. He wasn't good at this. "Ellie, please don't leave. I'm not interested in Abigail. I went to supper to prove to Mamm I had spent enough time with her to know she isn't for me. Abigail has impressed Mamm, and it's been difficult for me to not upset her or Abigail."

Ellie stared at the pond. "Have you been honest with Abigail?"

"Jah. I told her I didn't foresee anything more than friendship with us. She insisted she'll wait on me. She's sure I'll change my mind. The girl is determined."

Ellie chuckled. "If you keep your distance, maybe she'll give up."

"I hope you're right."

Peter skipped to them. "Can I play ball with my friends? They're right over there." He pointed to the kinner.

"Go ahead, but we'll have to leave soon. Stay where I can watch you."

"I will." Peter cupped his mouth to Joel's ear. "Talk all you want, and then I'll get more time to play."

Joel laughed. "I'll do my best."

Ellie rolled her eyes. "Peter, I can hear you."

Peter shrugged, kissed Ellie on the cheek, and then hurried to join the kinner.

"He's a sweet child. You're good with him."

"I'm blessed to have him as a bruder. I went through a difficult time in my life after my mamm passed. His schweschder had passed a short time before we met, and he had been sad and spoke only when necessary. When we met, I reminded him of her in age and appearance. We became fast friends. His mamm died, and she left a letter giving Daed legal guardianship of Peter should anything happen to her. Peter and I shared the deep hurt and loss kumming from losing our mamms. We are helping each other heal."

Joel's heart thumped in his chest. He would be grief-stricken if anything happened to his mamm. He loved her, and she took care of their home. He knew she loved them, even if she didn't show it in words or hugs. "I'm sorry you both suffered such a painful loss."

"Peter has adjusted better than I had anticipated, especially for just being six. Liza and Daed are wonderful with him. I'm sure he reminisces about his mamm and schweschder now and then. My mamm kummes to mind often. She and I were close."

He wished he and Mamm were closer. Mamm had been sad and not herself for a while.

Peter returned. "My friends are leaving. Joel, will you fish with me?"

"I've got to get home, Peter. It was a pleasure to meet you." He tousled the boy's hair.

"You'll have to kumme to our haus and meet Snuggles, my rabbit."

Joel knelt on one knee. "I'd like to meet Snuggles. You picked a good name for your pet. I wouldn't have thought of it."

"Danki." Peter stood a little straighter.

"We should head home, Peter. I don't want you getting sick in this cooler air." She gathered their things and bid Joel farewell.

"Be careful going home." Joel carried his tackle box and hurried to his wagon.

He glanced over his shoulder. Peter held Ellie's hand as they got in their buggy. She and Peter had a special bond. He and Maryann had once shared a similar bond. He envied his friends who had strong relationships with their siblings.

He went home and took his time taking care of his horse, then went inside. "Good evening."

Mamm held her threaded needle and sock. "Did you have a pleasant time with Abigail and her parents?"

Joel stood tall, feet apart. "Abigail isn't the girl for me, and I told her we should remain friends."

"Joel Wenger, are you mad? The girl is delightful. Why wouldn't you give her a chance? Is it her parents?"

"Her parents are kind and gracious. But she's not the kind of girl I would want to consider for a potential fraa. She makes me uncomfortable with her pushy behavior."

Mamm glared at him. "You sure were chummy with Ellie Graber. Mrs. Keim warned me to keep you away from Ellie. She said the girl shouldn't be trusted. Stay away from her."

He was shocked at her outburst, but he wouldn't take the word of rumormongers. "Ellie's a sweet girl. We shouldn't believe the unkind words of others about someone until we know them better ourselves."

Daed gave him an understanding nod. "You're right, Son, and choosing a partner is an important decision. Take your time. The right one will kumme along. One look at your mamm, and I had to get acquainted with her. The more we talked and got together at social functions, the more I fell in love with her."

Mamm blushed and kept silent.

Daed was a gentle soul, and he always came to Joel's aid.

"I want what you describe, Daed." Joel rolled his shoulders and yawned. "It's been a long day. I'm off to bed." He left and went to his room.

Leaving his parents alone might generate a loving conversation between them after Daed's compliment to Mamm. Daed had loneliness written on his face often, and Joel prayed they would rekindle the love and laughter in their marriage. His schwescher's bad decision had changed his mamm, and not for the better. She was worried, frustrated, and brokenhearted. She'd withdrawn from them, and the happy mamm he once knew had changed to a sad and bitter woman. He missed the endearing exchanges, touch of the hand, and closeness they'd shown to one another in the past.

He wanted to marry a woman who would bring out the best in him and he'd do the same for her. Ellie had lifted his mood the minute he met her. She listened intently and appeared to have a caring heart. Easy to talk to, he enjoyed her company. He was curious to find out more. She was someone he would pursue. He'd deal with whether the gossip about her was true and Mamm's disapproval much later.

He knelt and said a prayer to God, undressed, and got in bed. Opening his Bible, he turned to Deuteronomy 31:8. *And the Lord, he it is that doth go before thee; he will be with thee, he will not fail thee, neither forsake thee: fear not, neither be dismayed.*

He put his Bible on the side table, slid flat on his back, put his head on the pillow, and stared at the ceiling. He hoped Abigail wouldn't cause any trouble. He had an inkling she was good at misleading people into believing she was someone she was not. Brash with him, she was kind to Mamm. With her parents, she was sweet and obedient. He didn't understand her behavior. He was sure she wouldn't take no for an answer.

Chapter Two

Ellie worked to concentrate on Peter's chatter about playing with his friends on the way home, but her mind drifted to Joel. He listened to her, and he'd expressed compassion about the loss of her mamm. Each time they spoke, he impressed her more. She gazed at the horses frolicking in the field as they drove past. Joel hadn't mentioned anything negative he might have heard about her. She had time to show him she was the kind of girl he'd want to consider. She might get her heart broken when the time came to spill about her transgressions, but she'd take the risk.

She pulled up next to Daed inside the open barn. "Good evening."

Peter jumped out and hugged him. "I fished and played with my friends. Ellie has a new beau. His name's Joel." He cupped his hand to his mouth and giggled.

Daed took the reins. "Joel?"

"Joel Wenger. His family recently moved here from Lancaster, and they attended your wedding. He and I are getting better acquainted."

"You'll have to ask him to supper. I need to meet this young man if my dochder is interested in him." He gave her an impish grin.

Peter looked at Daed. "He's kumming to our haus soon to meet Snuggles. I already asked him."

Daed laughed. "Good for you."

Ellie and Peter walked to the haus and went inside. "Time to wash your hands, feed you, and play one game of checkers before you go to bed."

Liza held her arms open, and Peter ran and hugged her. "Guess what? Ellie and I met Joel at our fishing spot, and he kept staring at her." He moved his eyeballs from side to side and chuckled.

"Peter, remind me never to tell you a secret." Ellie crossed her arms.

He wrinkled his nose. "Why?"

Liza handed him a wet rag. "Because you couldn't keep it inside. You'd tell. Now wipe your hands."

He stuck out his bottom lip. "Nah, I wouldn't." He pouted, wiped his hands, and handed the rag back to Liza.

Liza had dishes on the table filled with pot roast and vegetables. "You're a good boy. We have no complaints."

Daed came inside and took his usual chair at the table.

Peter entertained them with stories of playing with his friends at the pond throughout supper. He pushed his empty plate aside. "Time for checkers."

"Not until after your bath. I have pots of warm water on the stove. I'll do the dishes first."

"I'll take care of Peter." Ellie took the pots of warm

water Liza had prepared off the stove and carried them to the tub.

Peter bathed, changed into his nightclothes, and snatched the checkers game off the shelf. "I'm gonna win!"

Ellie played two games of checkers, took Peter to bed, had him say his prayers, tucked him under the covers, and then joined Liza and Daed. "He talks me into another game each time, and he beats me. He's a smart child."

Liza quirked her brow. "Tell us more about Joel."

Ellie smiled and joined them for coffee at the table. "He's a gentleman, and his eyes don't stray when he talks to me. He pays attention to what I'm saying. I told him about the loss of Mamm, and he was understanding."

Daed settled back in his seat. "Peter didn't mention a specific date Joel was to kumme over. Maybe the next time you run into him or after Sunday service you can ask him." He teased her, "Or let Peter ask him."

"Daed, don't ask Joel a lot of questions and scare him away."

"I want to learn all I can about this young man if my dochder is entertaining thoughts of him."

"Liza, talk sense into him."

Liza squeezed Ellie's fingers. "You'll get no help here. I'm all for your daed finding out about Joel. And I may have a few questions."

"I don't have a chance with any man. You'll both ruin it for me before the relationship has a tiny thread of a chance to begin."

Jacob stretched his long arms across the table and folded his hands. "We'll be gentle."

Ellie yawned and stretched. "Mrs. Wenger is a bit difficult. She didn't crack a smile when I met her. Leah said her mamm prattled on about me in a negative way. I'm sure she would prefer that Joel not have anything to do with me."

Liza held her hand and rubbed her thumb across Ellie's hand. "Ignore them. They're wrong to talk about you, and she may have been having a bad day. She shouldn't judge you based on gossip."

"I am. So far, Joel hasn't asked me about it. I'm going to wait to bring it up until we've had time to build our friendship."

"You're taking a big risk not telling him right away." Liza stood and removed her apron.

Ellie grinned from ear to ear. "I want to show him I've changed before I tell him about my past." She yawned again. "Time for bed." She padded to her room.

Her stomach fluttered with excitement about Joel. Would he accept her once he found out the truth? He'd ask at some point. Would his mamm learn to accept her if she and Joel grew serious? She wouldn't want in-laws who wouldn't accept her. The Wengers' attitudes could cause tension between them. Joel had a mamm she wasn't sure she could win over. She wouldn't go against God's will for her life again. And causing discord in the Wenger family would definitely not be God's will.

Ellie woke early Tuesday morning. She milked the cows and fed the horses. Stepping inside, she sniffed the aroma of eggs and bacon frying in the two cast-iron skillets. "I could devour a bear, I'm so hungry." She poured coffee for the three of them and sat.

Daed patted her arm and gazed at her with his kind brown eyes. "I'd have milked the cows. You have the bakery to tend to."

"Sometimes I take pleasure in milking and find it a peaceful place to have a chat with God."

Liza served them and took her seat. "You are cheerful most of the time, but you have a little extra happy skip in your step since meeting Joel. I'm anxious to find out where this leads."

"I'm not in any hurry for you to get serious with anyone. I prefer having you right here with us." Daed gave her a loving pat on the arm.

"I love you both for supporting me. Who knows? You may be stuck with me for a very long time if these gossips have anything to do with it!"

Liza swiped the air. "You'll find someone. I still have butterflies when I set eyes on your daed. Look at Jacob and me. I never thought I'd marry again, and then he came to town and changed my life. I'm so glad he did."

Daed beamed. "Me too."

"Ellie, you have a habit of ignoring the unpleasant. Be careful." Liza sighed. "Please understand. I don't want to squelch your joy over Joel. I just don't want you to get hurt. He's bound to hear more about you. On another note, do you mind handling the bakery today with Hannah? Abe came by early this morning and told me Esther's not well. She should rest, and I'll do her chores. My dear schweschder will fight me on keeping off her feet, but I'm going to insist she stay put. She's got a sick stomach."

"Not at all, and give Aunt Esther a hug for me." Ellie kissed Liza's cheek and hurried to devour her eggs and take two bites of her bacon. "Liza, I appreciate your advice, but I'm still going to wait to tell Joel about my past." She headed down the hallway. "I'm going to my room to change and then head to the bakery. Hannah's picking me up."

Liza stood. "I'll give Peter another few minutes, and then I'll get him up for breakfast and school."

Daed opened the door. "I'll be in the barn."

Ellie rushed outside and got in Hannah's buggy. "Greetings, best friend. Liza's taking the day off to help your mamm. We're on our own at the bakery."

Hannah frowned. "Mamm was up all night with an upset stomach. I'm glad Liza offered to stay with her. She won't listen to me or Daed. Liza has a way with her."

Ellie leaned her head on Hannah's shoulder for a moment. "Liza has a way with all of us. I can't believe I gave her such a hard time when we first met. She's always got our best interests at heart."

Ellie and Hannah waved to Daed and left. Ellie was glad she lived close to town and Hannah.

Dr. Harrison passed in his buggy and tipped his hat. The girls smiled.

Ellie enjoyed the fresh air, yellow leaves on the maple trees, and the lush green pastures along the way.

Hannah wrinkled her nose. "You look as if you found money on the side of the road."

Ellie recounted her conversation with Joel. "It's ridiculous. My mind races with thoughts of Joel. I can't control it."

Hannah flicked the reins to urge the mare to pick up her pace. "I'm glad. Enjoy it."

"What about you, Hannah? Hasn't anyone caught your attention?"

"Not yet."

"What about Timothy Barkman?"

Hannah rolled her eyes. "He's a flirt, and he doesn't have a serious bone in his body. Everything is fun to him, and he lives one day at a time."

"You'll find someone irresistible one day."

"Jah, God has a plan for all of us. I'll wait until He introduces me to the right one. If not, when you have kinner, I'll borrow them to spoil."

Ellie admired Hannah's wisdom. Her friend was an old soul in a young woman's body. She gave the best advice, had patience, and was the most loyal friend Ellie had ever had. "I have noticed Timothy with several different girls at the socials. He keeps them laughing, but some girls stay away from him."

"He's broken a few hearts. I doubt he means any harm, but his flirting gets him in trouble. Some girls fawn over him, and when he concentrates on one, even though this doesn't last long, the others get perturbed." Hannah drove to the livery and handed the reins to the owner.

Ellie got out of the buggy the same time as Hannah, and they walked outside. "You're smart to recognize these things about Timothy. He might surprise you one day and be ready to settle down. Maybe then you'll reconsider."

"I'm not in any hurry. And someone else might kumme along before then." She shrugged and playfully bumped Ellie's arm, then glanced at the people milling about the town.

Ellie overheard two men discussing the election for president taking place on November fifth. The short one was for William Howard Taft, and the taller man argued Woodrow Wilson would be a better choice. She was glad the Amish didn't get involved with politics. She would imagine the Englischers, who had differences of opinion on the matter, could get into some heated debates.

Ellie stood on her tiptoes to glance over the two

Ford motorcars and buggies on the road in front of the bakery. "Hannah, what is Abigail doing here?"

"If her scowl is any indication, I'd say she's up to no good."

"She wouldn't be here to discuss Joel, would she?"

"Probably. She's rude and bold. Just stand your ground."

They approached her.

Ellie folded her hands behind her. "Abigail, we don't open for another two hours. If there's something you need, I'll be happy to let you in and get it for you."

Abigail raised her chin and glowered at Ellie. "I'm not here to shop. I came to speak with you in private before your customers arrive." She glanced at Hannah. "Greetings, Hannah. Do you mind giving us a few minutes?"

Hannah met Ellie's gaze. "Ellie, I can stay."

"I appreciate it, but I'll be all right. I'm going to walk her around to the back. I'll be inside in a bit."

Hannah nodded, got out her key, and unlocked the door. She hesitated before going inside.

Ellie chose the path between the bakery and furniture store. She kept her head down to avoid eye contact with any passersby. She didn't care to make idle chitchat with anyone right now. Her goal was to listen to Abigail, remain short on answers, and start work as soon as possible.

Abigail followed her in silence.

Ellie faced her and waited.

Abigail stood, feet apart, arms crossed. "Joel is of interest to me. We had a pleasant supper together with my parents, and his parents adore me. Don't waste your time with him."

"What gives you the idea I'm *wasting* time with Joel,

as you put it?" This girl was obnoxious. She and Joel were no business of Abigail's.

"I noticed you flirting with him on Sunday."

She took in an exasperated breath. "I'm not going to discuss Joel with you. Our friendship isn't any of your concern."

"Listen to me, Ellie Graber. You're not fit for any Amish man. You can't be trusted. Stay away from Joel. He's mine."

Ellie narrowed her eyes. The old brash Ellie threatened to tell the girl what she really thought of her, but she'd worked too hard to prove she had changed, nor did she want to give Abigail more gossip to spread. "My friends and family have forgiven me for my mistakes. I'm disheartened you choose not to."

"I have a right to my opinion." She scowled. "You're not the kind of girl I'd want to befriend."

Ellie stared into Abigail's eyes. "I doubt Joel would appreciate your visit here today, and furthermore, he can make his own decisions." She turned on her heel and walked the narrow way to the front door of the bakery, hoping Hannah had left it unlocked. She turned the handle and stepped inside. Closing the door, she held her breath for a moment. *Good.* Abigail wasn't going to pursue the matter. *At least not anymore today.*

Hannah bustled over. "I should've unlocked the back door. I didn't give it a thought. I'm glad you came to the front. Your face is as red as a beet, and it's not hot outside. What did she say to you?"

"She told me to stay away from Joel. The girl brought out the worst in me. I could hardly control my temper."

"Uh-oh. How did you respond?"

"Don't worry, I didn't let the conversation escalate, but I told her Joel could make up his own mind."

"I'm shocked she let you get away with such an answer without insisting again you stay away from him."

Ellie sucked in her top lip. "I didn't wait for her response."

Hannah shook her head. "She is unbelievable."

"Abigail's brashness reminds me of the old me." She sighed at the irony.

"You and Abigail are opposites. You're kind and loving. You'd never obsess over a man or threaten another woman. Raised Amish, Abigail has no excuse for her callous behavior."

Ellie sighed. She'd listen to her friend's advice. She'd set her sights on Joel, and she'd concentrate on her life, family, and friends. "I've got about two hours before we open, so I'll help you bake until it's time to take care of customers."

Hannah folded her hands. "I've put the ingredients together for molasses cookies. Maybe you can pull what you need off the shelves for peach tarts."

Ellie baked cookies and tarts with Hannah until time to open. She changed her apron, turned the window sign, and went to the counter to wait on customers.

At the end of the day, she poked her head in the back room. "It's five, and I've locked the door."

"I've baked ahead molasses and butter cookies and three sugar cream pies. I'm ready to go."

Ellie wondered if she'd run into Joel before the next Sunday service. She wished she could crawl into his head and find out if she was on his mind as often as he was on hers, or was his mamm chirping in his ear?

* * *

Joel hit a rut in the road on his way back from helping the bishop repair his porch steps Wednesday morning, and he struggled to guide the wagon. He got out and studied the damage.

A young man he recognized from Sunday services pulled his wagon behind his and got out.

Joel couldn't remember his name. "Greetings, I'm Joel Wenger. I believe we met at the Sunday service."

"I'm Timothy Barkman. We were introduced at one of the Sunday services. We got interrupted before we had a chance to talk." He bent to check the wheel. "Do you have a spare wheel at home?"

"Jah, nice to meet you again, and I do have a spare wheel. I can walk home and get it. I live close."

"Climb in my wagon. I'll take you and bring you back. The repair will be easier if the two of us fix it. We'll take your horse with us."

"I appreciate the help." Joel and Timothy tied the mare to the back of Timothy's wagon. He got better acquainted with his new friend on the short trip to his haus.

Timothy halted in front of Joel's barn. "You've done good work with your property. It looks nice. Where are you from?"

"Lancaster, Pennsylvania. It's a larger town than Charm. I prefer a smaller town. Did you grow up in Charm?" Joel faced Timothy.

"I've been in Charm all my life. I love it. The people are kind, the town is big enough to have everything we need, and the scenery is beautiful, including the women." He scanned the area. "A perfect place to raise a family someday. Although, I'm not in a hurry for marriage. I make it a point to talk to all the available pretty girls." Timothy jumped down. "Do you fish or target shoot? We have a big pond where I've caught some good-sized fish. To target shoot, I put up empty tin cans on tree stumps or whatever I can find in the woods to prop them up."

"I do both." Joel was glad he'd met Timothy. He had an impish way about him, red hair and freckles, and a cheerful attitude. The young men he'd met had been friendly, but he hadn't had the time to cultivate a friendship.

"Why don't you kumme to my place tomorrow evening?" Timothy said. "My family has a lot of land. We've got plenty of room to shoot and not bother anyone. Our haus is the second one on the left on Brown Road if you go straight from here." He pointed in the direction of his family's farm.

He'd wanted to make friends, but he'd not had time to socialize, what with getting the property in shape. He and Daed had almost accomplished the task. They were ready to work into a regular routine maintaining it and caring for the animals. He could spare time to meet new friends. Timothy's offer had kumme at the right time. "Danki. I'll take you up on your offer."

Daed met them. "Joel, where's the wagon?" He nodded to Timothy. "Excuse my manners. I'm Joel's daed, Shem Wenger."

Timothy nodded. "I'm Timothy Barkman. Joel needed a new wheel, and I offered to help."

Joel crossed his arms. "I'm thankful Timothy came along. We had a chance to talk on the way over here. He's invited me to go target shooting tomorrow."

"You've been working hard. I'm glad you're taking some time for yourself." Daed patted his back. "I'll get the wheel. You boys help yourselves to a cold drink from the pump."

Joel and Timothy each got a drink of water and then stepped in the wagon, and Daed returned with the wheel and placed it in the back for them.

"Good to meet you, Timothy. Stop by anytime."

"Danki, sir." Timothy snapped the reins. "It was a pleasure to meet your daed. Do you have siblings?"

"A schweschder. She's no longer with us." He didn't want to get into the story about Maryann. He hoped Timothy wouldn't question him further. "Do you have siblings?"

"Aaron. He's ten and a handful. When he was five, our mare kicked him in the head and caused him to act younger than others his age. To accept the result of the accident for Aaron has been hard for my parents. They're not as patient with him as I am."

"Peter, Ellie Graber's little bruder, might be good for Aaron. He has a big heart and a gentle soul. He's smart but not arrogant."

"I'd really appreciate it if you could bring Ellie and Peter to my haus. They know Aaron from being at the socials and at services, but they haven't had a chance to really get to know him."

Timothy had provided Joel with a good reason for him and Ellie to talk more. And he would like to include Peter too. He had chosen to shut out any gossip and Mamm's disapproval. Maybe it was a mistake, but it was one he was willing to make. He had a knack for ignoring his problems.

"When?"

"Daed wants our family to spend all day Sunday together, since we don't have a worship service. We usually always have company. How about the next Sunday? You can all kumme after we finish our after-service meal.

We can play horseshoes. I have smaller ones for Peter and Aaron."

Joel chatted with Timothy about how much they enjoyed playing horseshoes, target shooting, and fishing, and then they arrived at his wagon on the road, repaired the wheel, and harnessed the mare again to Joel's wagon.

"Danki, Timothy. I'm glad we met. I'll kumme to your haus tomorrow for target shooting. What time is good?"

"Five thirty. And please talk to Ellie and Peter. Ask them to plan on Sunday a week out, at my haus at two. Aaron needs a friend."

"All right." Joel waved, traveled home, and pulled up in front of the barn.

Daed met him. "You made a new friend. I'm glad. Timothy's a cheerful young man with a playful glint in his eye."

"I've noticed him at the Sunday services, but we hadn't had a conversation. I'm looking forward to doing things with him."

Daed put a hand on his shoulder. "Son, Abigail was here again. She's not giving up."

Joel's mouth gaped open. "Daed, she is persistent. What should I do?"

"Ignore her. She'll get the message eventually."

Maybe he'd ask Timothy about Abigail and ask for his advice. He wondered if he'd had any issues with the obnoxious girl.

Joel walked inside the haus. "How are you, Mamm?"

"I've had a pleasant day. Abigail brought me this beautiful rose from her garden. Isn't it lovely?"

He didn't want to upset his mamm. She did look happy. He'd let her delight in her time with Abigail. What harm could it cause? The hairs on his neck prickled. Abigail had ulterior motives. How far would she go to interfere with him and Ellie? He pushed the concerns out of his mind. Another problem he refused to face. A fault he knew might lead to trouble later, but it was easier to ignore his concerns and concentrate on his beautiful Ellie.

Chapter Three

Ellie walked with Hannah and Liza to the bakery Monday morning. "I'm glad you said Esther was doing better this past week, Hannah. She still looked a little pale when you all came over for dinner Sunday afternoon. I missed having Sunday service, although I enjoyed our leisurely day together as a family at our haus." She'd missed not speaking with Joel this past week, and she had to wait another week until she'd lay eyes on him again.

"It's good we have services every other week to give us more time with our families and friends. It was fun. Dr. Harrison suggested it may be certain vegetables not agreeing with Mamm. She is stubborn and doesn't watch her diet. It takes her a while to get better if she's eaten a lot of what doesn't agree with her. She has been at the stove each morning since Liza stayed with her, making Daed his crispy bacon and planning what work she wants to do, instead of resting."

Liza chuckled. "She loves taking care of people. It's always been her nature. I'm relieved she's much better."

Hannah hooked her arm through Ellie's. "Too bad

Joel hasn't kumme to the bakery. You must miss him.
Since we didn't have a Sunday service this past week,
I was hoping you'd run into him in town."

"I suspect Mrs. Wenger is keeping him from me. I
wish I could show her I am the kind of woman she
would want her son to be interested in. She's so opposed."

"She's a mystery." Hannah frowned.

Ellie sighed. "I'm afraid his mamm's disapproval
will prevent us from growing into anything serious. He
wouldn't want to upset his parents, and neither do I."

Liza crossed the street with them. "I haven't had an
opportunity to talk with her much. Maybe you and I
can visit her when we have time."

"Danki, Liza. Maybe if you're with me she'll be more
be open to speaking with me." Her stepmamm supported her whenever she needed it. Mrs. Wenger was
certain to befriend Liza. Her mood lifted.

Ellie scanned the street and storefronts. The town
buzzed with activity. Motorcars honked their horns at
slow-moving buggies and wagons. Englisch men wore
a variety of colorful clothes. Some with suit jackets and
matching creased pants and others with flannel shirts
and work pants with big buckle belts. The ladies wore
printed skirts with blouses or dresses with buttons and
rounded collars. She did think the dresses with simple
ribbon and trim were pretty.

The short paperboy stood on his toes and waved
the latest edition. "Extra! Extra! Read all about it!
It's confirmed on this fine day of September twenty-
sixth! Three days ago, President Taft issued an executive
order barring foreign ships, whether commercial or
military, from the waters of Hawaii's Pearl Harbor,

Cuba's Guantanamo Bay, and the Philippines' Subic Bay."

Ellie shivered. "I avoid any news dealing with politics. The president issuing these types of orders scares me."

"I agree with you. President Taft sure does have to make a lot of important decisions. He's under tremendous pressure." Hannah pointed to the bakery. "Joel's waiting for you."

"Must be important this early hour of the morning." Liza hooked her arm through Ellie's.

Ellie's stomach fluttered. "I hope he has good news."

"Joel, would you like to kumme inside?" Liza pushed her key in the lock and opened the door.

Hannah gave him a shy look and went inside.

He shook his head. "Mrs. Graber, good morning. Danki for asking. I've got to get home and help Daed. Do you mind if I speak with Ellie outside a few minutes?"

"Of course not. Take your time." Liza gave them an approving nod, stepped into the bakery, and shut the door.

Ellie gazed at him. "Is anything wrong?"

Joel took off his hat and held it to his side. "Nah. I came to ask you something. I met Timothy Barkman on Wednesday, and we went target shooting together Thursday. In conversation, Timothy mentioned Aaron, his bruder, could use a friend. I suggested Peter. He asked me to talk to you about having them play together Sunday at his haus after we finish our after-service meal. Would you consider joining us?" He looked at her sheepishly. "I planned to get with you earlier this week, but Daed and I have been busy building a new fence. Sunday, Mamm asked if I would stay home and spend time with her and Daed."

"I'm glad you're here now." She beamed. "We'd

love to go to the Barkmans' with you." She'd jump at the chance to spend time with him for whatever reason.

"I feel sorry for Aaron. It probably isn't easy for him—being ten and acting much younger due to his injury, getting kicked in the head a few years ago—to make a really good friend. Do you think Peter will mind playing with him?"

Ellie waved a dismissive hand. "I'm sure Peter is aware of him. They just haven't been encouraged to be friends. Peter will be fine. I'm certain they'll have a good time together."

"I'll tell Timothy to expect us. I'll take you and Peter in my buggy when we've finished our meals after the service on Sunday, and then take you both home afterward." He plopped his hat on his head. "I'm looking forward to it."

"I am too." Should she tell him about Abigail? Nah, she didn't want to spoil their special moment. She waved and watched his back until he got in his wagon and disappeared down the road. Would Joel be upset she kept Abigail's visit from him? She dismissed the thought and went inside.

Hannah stopped putting a tray of cookies on the counter. "What did he say?"

Liza leaned on the counter with her elbows, fists under her chin. "Jah, tell us."

"He's taking Peter and me to Timothy Barkman's haus after the service and meal on Sunday. Joel thought it would be a good idea to encourage a friendship between Peter and Aaron, and Timothy agreed."

"It's a grand idea. The kinner will be good for each other." Liza winked. "And it gives you and Joel an excuse to talk more."

Hannah grabbed a towel and gave it a playful snap.

"I can't wait for you to tell me every detail Monday morning when I pick you up for work."

Ellie helped Liza and Hannah stack the shelves with cookies, tarts, pies, and breads, then she opened the bakery for customers.

Dr. Harrison pushed open the door. "Good morning, Ellie. I'm ready for some hot coffee." He sniffed the air. "Do I smell molasses cookies baking? If so, I'll take two, please."

Sheriff Williams followed him inside, newspaper tucked under his arm, and took his usual seat at the counter. "I'll also take a cup. Thank you." He nodded and concentrated on the paper.

"Wilkom, gentlemen. And jah, you're just in time for some fresh molasses cookies." Ellie held up the coffeepot. "I've got coffee ready for both of you." She poured two cups and set them in front of the men. Then she ran to the back and returned and served them the cookies.

Sheriff Williams slid half the newspaper pages to Dr. Harrison. "Danki, Ellie." He concentrated on his paper. "My mouth is watering for Whitman's Sampler to come to the general store. The company is producing them, but they aren't sure when the new sampler will be sent to stores. The little boxes contain samples of the most popular chocolate pieces sold."

Ellie stifled her chuckle. The sheriff didn't need to add any inches to his belly overlapping his belt. She loved Whitman's candy, and she might have to try the sample box. "The man who started the Whitman candy sure has made his company a big success. Whitman's has been around for as long as I can remember."

Dr. Harrison focused on his paper. "I was fascinated with Stephen Whitman and how he made his company successful, so I researched his life. I often thought it would've been fun to run a candy company but didn't imagine you could make a good living from it. He proved me wrong. And my ambition to become a doctor won out."

Ellie leaned back and crossed her arms. "What did you find out about him?"

"He was a Quaker and, at the age of nineteen, he opened his first confectionery shop in Philadelphia in 1842, and came up with lots of ideas to market his candy and attract customers."

The sheriff shifted his gaze from the paper to Dr. Harrison. "Who runs it now, and has he done anything different to keep the company growing?"

"Walter Sharp has carried on the same strategy with enticing people to buy the candy. He's the current president, and he offers a money-back guarantee if you aren't satisfied with the candy. A bold decision, but a good one."

"I doubt he gets many disgruntled customers. Their chocolates are delicious." The sheriff went back to reading his paper.

Dr. Harrison glanced at his friend's stomach. "Yes, we can tell you're very satisfied with the company's confections."

"You mind your own business and leave me alone." The sheriff harrumphed and stuck his nose inches from the paper.

Dr. Harrison elbowed his arm. "If I did, you'd come knocking on my door wondering why I wasn't at Liza's to meet you every morning the bakery is open." Dr. Harrison gently slapped the sheriff's back.

"I suppose I would." The sheriff's cheeks pinked, and he addressed Ellie. "I'll take another molasses cookie, and give him one."

Ellie smiled. The two men had been friends for

years, and she enjoyed their ribbing and talk about current events when they frequented the bakery. Sometimes they bantered as if they were kinner, and she had a difficult time stifling her chuckle. She was glad Liza had switched positions with her. Waiting on customers gave her the opportunity to learn what was going on in the community and outside world.

Maybe when Joel had time, he'd visit her at the bakery. She rolled her eyes. She shouldn't be acting like a silly schoolgirl pining after this man she hardly knew, but she couldn't help herself.

Liza stuck her head out the open doorway between the bakery and kitchen. "Gentlemen, what a pleasure."

"Liza, what are you baking today?" Dr. Harrison looked at her.

"I'm trying out a new recipe for peach cinnamon and nut bread. I'm afraid the peaches might make it too soggy or heavy."

"Sounds tasty to me. I'd be glad to sample it for you." Sheriff Williams beamed.

Dr. Harrison rolled his eyes. "Of course you would."

Liza disappeared and returned with a sample for each of the men. "I need your honest opinions."

The men devoured the samples.

Sheriff Williams gave the table a gentle slap. "It's a winner, Liza!"

"I must agree with my friend here. Very good."

"Danki." She put a hand on Ellie's arm. "Isn't Ellie doing a good job at the counter?"

"Excellent. You should be proud of her."

"I am. Off to work I go." Liza went to the kitchen.

Ellie served the men each a sugar cookie. "These are on the haus. It's the least I can do for your complimenting me to my boss." After Abigail's confrontation and the gossips still prattling on about her, it was refreshing to receive compliments from others.

They all laughed.

Dr. Harrison snapped his fingers and swiveled in his chair to face the sheriff. "I forgot to tell you Norman bought a used Model T Ford motorcar from a man in Canton. It's in mint condition. You've got to go take a look at it."

"Good for him. I'll take a gander at Norman's motorcar later this afternoon. The paper had an article about the problems owners encounter with those crank cars. Didn't sound good."

"I doubt he'll encounter any problem he can't fix. He's got a knack for repairing motorcars."

Ellie pulled a container of butter cookies from under the shelf and arranged them under the glass dome on the counter. Motorcars fascinated her. No horses to harness, and you could travel to places in less time. She understood why the Englischers desired them, although she had no desire to change. She loved the horses, wagons, and buggies. They held a soft spot in her heart for tradition.

A boy pushed the door hard until it banged against the wall. He ran in and jumped up and down. "Timothy! Timothy! I want an oatmeal cookie!"

Timothy followed him in. "Calm down, Aaron, and lower your voice." He gave Ellie a sheepish wince. "I'm sorry for his outburst. When he gets excited, his voice gets loud sometimes."

Ellie grabbed an oatmeal cookie and came around to face Aaron. She bent and handed him the cookie. "Aaron, we love it when customers get excited about kumming to the bakery."

He tilted his head. "I like all your cookies."

"Danki, Aaron." Ellie tousled Aaron's soft brown hair, her eyes on Timothy. "What can I get you?"

"I'll take a loaf of nut bread. Joel said you've agreed to bring Peter to play with Aaron on Sunday."

"Jah, danki for inviting us."

Hannah came from the kitchen to the counter. "Ellie, here's a rhubarb pie for the counter shelves." She glanced at Timothy and gasped. "Oh, I didn't know you were here. Greetings."

"Hannah, kumme join me, Joel, Ellie, and the boys on Sunday. We'll play games and have a relaxing time." Timothy's cheeks dimpled.

Aaron tugged on Timothy's hand. "She's pretty."

"Jah, everytime you see her, you say she's pretty. And I agree. She is, Aaron." Timothy smiled at Hannah. "What do you say about Sunday, Hannah?"

Hannah blushed. "I . . . um . . ."

"She'll be there." Ellie avoided Hannah's gaze.

"Great! We better go, Aaron. We've got chores to do. It's been a pleasure, ladies."

Aaron waved.

Ellie waited until the door shut. "Hannah, Timothy likes you. He beamed when you walked in."

Hannah whispered, "I'm not going Sunday. He makes me uncomfortable."

"You're interested in him. I could tell by the way you couldn't put two words together when your gaze met his."

"He is handsome. All the girls agree. The problem is when he speaks. The man's mischievous grin and compliments are too forward. He's not ready for a serious girl like me."

"Kumme with me, please. If you don't, I'll be the only girl. We can have fun together."

"I'll ponder it."

A woman swayed into the bakery with an air of authority, her hair fashioned in the popular bob Ellie had noticed among the Englisch women. The customer wore a light pink high-necked silk blouse with a long cream-colored skirt. The soft wool shawl around her shoulders looked expensive.

Ellie gestured to the shelves in the counter. "How may I help you?"

"I'm passing through town, and I can't pass up sweets. I had to stop in your bakery." She studied Ellie's face. "Darling, you have such a dainty nose, and those blue eyes of yours would melt any man's heart. What I wouldn't do to dress you in some of my designer clothes."

Ellie blushed. "Danki." The emerald ring on the woman's hand was hard to miss. "Your ring is exquisite."

"Thank you, darling. My husband, Hubert, bought it for me in Paris last year."

Ellie froze. Abigail stood behind the woman. When had she snuck in?

Abigail chimed in. "She'd probably be thrilled to have you dress her in clothes such as yours. She's quite adventurous. Right, Ellie?"

The woman narrowed her eyes at Abigail. "Young lady, it's impolite to interrupt."

Abigail opened her mouth then shut it. She pinched her lips and pretended to study the contents of the display case.

Ellie stiffened, and, dismayed, her temper flared. She fought to control it and ignored Abigail. "Madam, I'm flattered, but I'm Amish and my dress is part of our tradition. What can I interest you in today?" She gestured at the baked goods.

"I apologize. My husband tells me I'm too impulsive

sometimes. I'm not familiar with the Amish traditions and lifestyle."

Ellie said, "No need to apologize."

"I'll buy an apple pie and a dozen molasses cookies."

Ellie accepted her coins and wrapped her choices. "Danki for kumming in. I hope you'll visit us again."

"It was a pleasure to meet you, and if we pass through this town again, I will."

Abigail stared at Ellie until the door shut and the customer had gone. She jutted her chin and scowled. "Even Englischers can sniff out your desire for beautiful things, Ellie."

"What do you want, Abigail?"

An elderly man made his way into the bakery and stood behind Abigail.

Abigail scrunched her face. "Two loaves of cranberry bread."

Ellie slid the wrapped package to her. "Here you go."

Abigail paid for her purchase and left.

Ellie held a hand to her stomach. She had a bad feeling about Abigail's visit today. Now what did the girl want? She was positive she hadn't kumme to the bakery only to buy bread. She was glad the troublemaker left and refrained from saying anything more to frustrate her further.

Ellie pressed her lips tight to stifle a yawn during the bishop's message Sunday morning at the Kanagys'. The days had dragged by this past week as she'd waited to see Joel. She had tossed and turned all night, excited about her afternoon with him. She stole a glimpse of him. Her gaze met his, and she thought her heart would melt.

Ellie cringed as she listened to the bishop talk about

loving your enemies. Ellie prayed Abigail would stop antagonizing her. The girl had worked hard at being her enemy. Distance between them would be best, but Abigail sought her out. She didn't know how much more she could take before lashing out at her adversary. The girl had tested her patience to the limit.

The bishop read Matthew 5:44, "'But I say unto you, Love your enemies, bless them that curse you, do good to them that hate you, and pray for them who despitefully use you, and persecute you . . .'"

A pang of guilt stabbed at Ellie's heart. She couldn't imagine liking Abigail, let alone loving her. She bowed her head and prayed silently. *Dear Heavenly Father, forgive me for my wrongs, and soften my hardened heart toward Abigail. Amen.*

The bishop finished his sermon, led them in a hymn from the *Ausbund*, prayed over the bountiful food, and dismissed them.

Hannah walked outside with her. "I'm not going to Timothy's."

Aaron came from behind Hannah and clasped her hand. "Pretty girl, you're kumming to my haus today. Timothy said so."

"How can you disappoint his sweet face?" Ellie chuckled.

Hannah and Timothy had red hair and green eyes. If they did get married one day, their kinner were sure to have the same. She better not tease Hannah about this. She was prickly where Timothy was concerned. Hannah might get upset with her.

Hannah sighed and playfully tapped his nose. "I'll be there, sweetheart."

"Yippee!"

Peter joined them. "Ellie, Aaron asked me to sit with him. We were first in line and have our plates at the table over there. I can't find Mamm and Daed. Will you tell them?"

"Jah, you go ahead."

Peter dashed to Aaron.

Joel approached them. "Ellie, Hannah, sit with Timothy and me and the boys at the picnic table to the left of the barn."

"Danki. We'll get our plates and be right there." Ellie gave him a warm grin.

Ellie followed Hannah and filled her plate. "The message this morning pricked my conscience."

"Because of Abigail's poking at you?"

"Jah. The girl won't leave me alone."

"There are some people we forgive but we stay away from for our own good. Abigail's one of them. I'm upset she's provoking you. I wish I'd been there when she interrupted your conversation with the Englischer the other day."

"It's probably better you weren't. I don't want her to treat you mean." She overheard Abigail's laugh and avoided looking in her direction. "Let's not let her spoil our day." She squeezed Hannah's hand while holding her plate with the other. She and Hannah joined the boys.

Joel slid and patted the spot next to him. "Sit by me, Ellie."

She squeezed her elbows to her sides and sat. "Danki."

Aaron motioned to Hannah. "I saved you a seat next to me, pretty girl."

"Her name is Hannah." Timothy gave him a stern look.

"I know. I just like calling her pretty girl. You called her a pretty girl to Joel." Aaron shrugged his shoulders and took a bite of his buttered white bread.

Peter huffed. "Don't pick on Aaron."

Ellie loved Peter's protective stance with his new friend, but she couldn't sit still. She had to rescue her friend. "We should address Hannah by her name. We don't want to embarrass her."

"I'll call you Hannah from now on. All right?" Aaron gave Hannah puppy-dog eyes.

Ellie surveyed her friends. All were stifling their chuckles at the innocent boy.

Hannah nodded. "No harm done." She tapped him gently on the nose. "You're a charmer, like your bruder."

Timothy blushed and gave her an impish shrug.

Ellie and the others didn't comment and finished their meals.

Joel stood. "Ellie, I brought the wagon so you and Peter can go to the Barkmans' with me."

Timothy pointed to his buggy. "Hannah, you can ride with Aaron and me. Peter, you can ride with us too."

"May I?" Peter folded his hands and held them under his chin.

"Please let him." Aaron stared at her.

Ellie and Peter waved good-bye to her parents in the distance. "It's all right with me. Go ahead."

Hannah stared at her shoes. "Timothy, if you don't mind, I'll go with Ellie and Joel."

He crossed his arms. "I do mind. I may need help with these two ornery boys. And Joel and Ellie may enjoy time alone to talk on the way."

Hannah winced. "I suppose they would. All right, Timothy. I'll go with you."

Ellie hugged her and whispered in her ear. "He won't bite. Relax." She strode alongside Joel to his buggy and got inside. "Danki for taking me."

He waited for a moment to flick the reins, and

met her gaze. "My pleasure. I've looked forward to this day."

"I have too." Her heart fluttered with delight.

"Are you happy working at the bakery?" Joel waved to their friends passing them.

"I love it. Liza is a talented baker and creative with her recipes. It's fun working with my best friend and stepmamm. Do you have any interests other than farming?" She loved watching the blond bunny hopping in the lush green grass on the side of the road.

"I tinker with wood when I have time."

She shifted in her seat to focus on him. "What do you make?"

"Tables and chairs. I sold quite a few in our previous hometown."

Ellie hesitated to ask her next question. She wasn't sure how she'd handle the disappointment if he didn't have a positive answer. "Are you glad you moved to Charm?"

"I am. How about you?"

She rested easier. Their family had no plans to leave. "I lived in Nappanee, Indiana, before moving here, and I enjoy both towns. Daed marrying Liza, and having Hannah as my best friend, has made Charm special to me. I don't plan to move again." Maybe she shouldn't have mentioned Nappanee. He might ask questions. Questions she wasn't prepared to answer. She held her breath a moment.

His shoulders slumped a little. "I've had close friends. Here I am twenty-two, and there's no one I'd call a best friend. I envy you."

She'd had a difficult time winning over some of the Amish girls in the community. The gossips had shed a bad light on her past behavior. She understood it could be a challenge to make new friends, let alone a best friend. She was grateful for Hannah. "It takes time to nurture relationships with others, and it's not easy with our work schedules. Timothy will probably introduce you to other young men." She hoped he would leave time for her. "You're always wilkom to kumme over to my haus."

Joel waggled his brows. "When?"

She jerked her head in surprise. Her heart skipped with excitement. "How about tomorrow night at six?"

"I'd be honored." He pulled back the reins to slow the horse.

Ellie pointed to a small pond. "Look at those two beautiful geese paddling beside each other. They're lovely. This property stretches far and wide. Much like ours. It's got plenty of room for the boys to run and play."

"It's quite a place."

She jumped to the ground. "They've got two porch swings and enough room for rocking chairs. We have the same. Our porch is my favorite place to have some quiet time and watch the squirrels hunt and bury nuts, the fireflies light up in the summer, and butterflies fluttering around the flower bushes. I miss those things in the winter."

"I appreciate all those things too." Joel stepped out of the buggy and tied the horse to the post.

Ellie walked with him to join Hannah, Timothy, and the boys.

Timothy led them to the backyard, where he already had wooden pegs in the ground and horseshoes in different weights and sizes.

Peter picked one up. "This is heavy!"

Aaron passed him a lighter one. "Try this one."

"Much better. Danki."

Ellie stood next to Hannah and watched Timothy and Joel instruct the boys on how to play the game. Joel had a more serious side to him than Timothy. A sign of his maturity she found attractive. Joel would make a good daed someday. Patient, firm, and kind.

Aaron stomped to Joel. "Will you show me the right way to throw? My bruder won't let me try." He crossed his arms and stuck out his bottom lip.

Timothy's cheeks reddened. "I'm sorry, little bruder. Kumme back. I'll let you play."

Peter threw one and bounced on his toes. "I did it! I did it!"

Aaron ran to Joel. "Will you help me, Joel?"

Joel handed him the horseshoe then put his hand over the boy's. He guided his throw.

Aaron clapped and jumped up and down. "I made it! I made it!" He hugged Joel. "Danki!" He wrinkled his nose at Timothy.

Timothy removed his hat and scratched his head. "You sure have a way with kinner, Joel." He put his hand on Aaron's head. "Kumme on, bruder. I've put checkers out for you and Aaron."

Hannah whispered close to Ellie's ear. "Timothy has a big heart. He just needs more time to mature."

Ellie nodded. "I understand what you mean."

Timothy acted as if he didn't have a care in the world. He was fun-loving and didn't appear to have a serious bone in his body. She was sure he did have his serious moments, but Hannah was smart to not consider him for now. She walked with the group to the picnic table.

Timothy had checkers arranged on top of the table. "Would you like to play checkers while the four of us play horseshoes?"

Aaron faced Peter. "Do you? I'm kinda bored with horseshoes."

"I wouldn't mind playing checkers." Peter followed his new friend and squirmed onto the seat across from him.

Ellie went with her friends to the horseshoes. She and Hannah played together, while Timothy and Joel played a couple of yards away from them. Ellie rounded the peg with each throw on her turns.

Hannah threw and missed each time. "Ellie, how do you do it?" She laughed and rested her hands on her hips.

She shrugged. "I've played the game a lot with Daed over the years. Let me show you." She took Hannah's hand and guided her throw.

The shoe swung around the peg. Hannah clasped her hands and held them to her chin. "Finally! Danki, friend."

"Want to watch Joel and Timothy?" Ellie gestured to them.

Hannah nodded.

"All right, here I go." Timothy took a moment to stare at the peg, made a show of holding the horse-shoe, and then threw it. The horseshoe landed over the peg. "Three in a row!"

"Well done, Timothy." Joel lobbed his horseshoe with ease and made it.

Timothy held up his palms. "Do you ever miss?"

Joel shrugged. "I do."

Ellie observed Joel. He didn't boast like Timothy. His humbleness was apparent, confident he didn't have the need to prove himself. "You both had a good game."

Mrs. Barkman brought out a tray of cold sandwiches and lemonade. "Take a break and have some supper."

Ellie and the others thanked her, relaxed on the seat at the table, and enjoyed the food.

Peter rounded the table and sat across from Aaron. "Why do you have a dent on the side of your head?"

Ellie gasped. Heat rose to her cheeks, and she opened her mouth to speak.

Joel gently gripped her arm under the table. He whispered, "Let Aaron explain. If you scold Peter, it may embarrass them. If Aaron answers, it will show Peter has gained his trust, and it will be a natural conversation between them."

She bit her tongue and nodded.

Aaron shrugged and tapped the indentation on his head. "Our mare kicked me right here. I got too close and touched a sore spot on her leg. It makes me sad when schoolmates call me slow and won't play with me."

Batting the air with his hand, Peter sighed. "I'll be your friend."

Aaron sat up straighter and held his spoon in midair. "Let's hurry and eat. Then we can play with the kittens."

Ellie's eyes pooled with tears. She was proud of Peter for his compassion and understanding. Kinner could be intolerant and impatient with others who weren't like them. Joel had been right. If she'd interfered, it would have made everyone at the table ill at ease. "Danki for stopping me from making a mistake. It was best to let the boys talk it out." Ellie raised grateful eyes to him.

"Peter is easy to love. His innocence is refreshing, and his acceptance of Aaron shows his big heart."

She winced. "I should've forewarned him about Aaron's accident. I didn't find the time."

Joel shook his head. "Nah, their conversation turned out perfect. They have an understanding between them."

Ellie folded her hands tight. Did she and Joel have a silent understanding between them not to broach the subject of what he'd been told about her? She held the thought close to her heart. She didn't want anything to ruin her time with him today.

Timothy loaded the dirty plates on the wooden tray his mamm had left at the end of the table. "I'll carry these inside, and then we can play checkers or other board games."

Hannah stood and gathered the empty glasses. "I'll follow you inside with these." She faced Ellie. "Shouldn't we get going soon?"

Joel stood. "Jah, we should head home. Hannah, I'll be glad to take you, Ellie, and Peter home."

"Nah, I'll take her." Timothy raised his brows.

"Danki, Timothy, but I'll go with the others." She bustled into the haus carrying the glasses.

Timothy didn't move. "I'm afraid she can't stand me. I wanted us to be friends."

Ellie was certain Hannah didn't mean to offend him. "She does care about you."

"Are you sure?"

"I am." She hoped she hadn't overstepped by giving some assurance.

He beamed and went inside.

Hannah returned wearing a baffled expression. She leaned close to Ellie's ear. "Did you give him the impression I was interested in him? He resembled a puppy the way he was on my heels in the kitchen."

Ellie opened her mouth but shut it.

Timothy stepped between them. "I'm glad you came today, Hannah. I hope we'll get together again soon."

Hannah turned on her heel. "Timothy, I consider you a friend. Frankly, I don't believe you're ready to pursue anything serious with a woman."

He bent and plucked a long blade of grass and tied it in a knot. "You pegged me right, Hannah, but we don't know what the future holds." He met her gaze. "We had fun, didn't we?"

"We did."

"Friends?"

Hannah sighed and stared at her hands. "Jah, friends would be nice."

Ellie listened to Hannah and Timothy's exchange, and then she gave Joel a knowing look and chuckled.

Joel whispered to Ellie, "I'm curious to find out where our friendship leads. Are you?"

She blushed and nodded. "I am too."

"Good." Joel held her gaze for a moment then called to Peter. "Time to go home!"

Peter skipped to them with Aaron by his side.

Aaron stared at the ground and kicked a small stone. "Will you kumme back sometime?"

Peter hopped from one foot to the other and peeked through his lashes. "Sure, I will. You can visit me too. I'll show you Snuggles, my rabbit."

"I can't wait. Danki."

Timothy rested his hand on Aaron's shoulder. "All of you kumme back anytime. I doubt anyone could wipe the smile off my bruder's face, and I credit Peter for putting it there."

Ellie nodded. "We'll get them together again soon."

The Barkmans came outside and everyone said their farewells.

Joel guided the mare down the lane onto the narrow dirt road to Hannah's.

Hannah bumped Ellie's shoulder. "What did you say to Timothy?"

"He was disappointed you wouldn't let him take you home. He didn't think you wanted his friendship. I assured him you did."

"What! Why would you say such a thing?"

"Settle down. I said *friend*. Anyway, you made your position clear with him, and he understood and agreed with what you said."

Joel chimed in. "It may take a long time, but I suspect someday you and he will have a special bond and maybe something more."

Hannah scoffed. "You're a romantic, Joel. Timothy's a little boy in a man's body. Not a characteristic I find appealing."

"He's fun-loving, a tease, and lighthearted. All good qualities. He's just taking longer than most to grow up."

Ellie admired Joel. He didn't have anything to prove, and he said what was on his mind, but in a kind way. She noticed some Amish men at socials were too quiet and kept to themselves. Other men, such as her daed, had to encourage them to get involved in conversations or activities.

Joel listened to Peter tell about his visit with Aaron. The boys had not wasted any time in becoming friends. Ellie had been good with the boys, and she hadn't hesitated to take his advice. He could relax and be himself around Ellie, and he took special note when she was quiet and listened to him. The kind of girl he would consider a potential fraa if they didn't run into any insurmountable problems. He was very interested in her.

They arrived at the Grabers' home.

From the back seat, Peter wrapped his arms around Joel's neck. "I had fun today."

"I'm glad you had a good time."

Peter stepped out, waved, and ran inside the haus.

"Ellie, I'm glad we had this time together." He hopped out of the buggy and gave her his hand. "Do you want to ask Liza about my kumming to supper tomorrow at six?"

She shook her head. "Liza loves a full haus, and she'll be delighted to meet you, so will Daed."

"Until tomorrow then." He tipped his hat and got in his buggy. At the end of the lane, he glanced over his shoulder. She was still in the same spot and waved to him. Jah, the spark between them was evident. Tomorrow night he'd meet her parents. Maybe he'd learn more about Ellie from them. What was she like at Peter's age and growing up? He wanted details. He hadn't told her about his schweschder. Amish didn't speak about such things, but he must be honest with her. He wasn't sure how she would react, and he'd put off the conversation a little longer.

Chapter Four

Ellie pressed a hand to her chest. She hadn't wanted the day to end. She was sad to leave Joel's side. Tomorrow night couldn't kumme soon enough. Liza and her daed sat in the sitting room drinking coffee.

"Did you have a peaceful afternoon without us here?"

"It's too quiet when you and Peter aren't with us." Liza hugged Peter, sitting on the other side of her. "And this one hasn't stopped going on about his new friend, Aaron."

Peter pointed to the side of his head. "Poor Aaron. He got kicked in the head by a horse, and he has a big dent right here."

Daed clasped his hands and rested his elbows on his knees. "Peter, some kinner may treat Aaron unkindly because of it. I'm proud of you for being his friend."

"He said kinner had been mean to him." He puffed out his chest. "I told him I'd be his friend."

"Good boy." Jacob kissed Peter's forehead. "Invite Aaron here. You can swing on the tree swings and play with the dog."

"What dog?" Peter's mouth dropped open.

Liza laughed.

Ellie raised her eyebrows. "A dog?"

"I'm afraid so." Liza rolled her eyes.

"Kumme with me." Daed opened the back door and gestured to a dog tied to a wooden peg with plenty of rope to roam. He untied the rope, held on to it, and walked toward them.

The animal rushed to Peter, jumped up, and licked his face.

Peter giggled and petted the dog. "What should we call him?"

Hand on her hip, Ellie scratched the dog's ear. "He's the color of cinnamon."

"Let's call him Cinnamon!" Peter hugged the dog's neck. "Where did you get him?"

"Englischers dropped him out of their motorcar. I waited until they were gone, and then I brought him home. I was afraid he'd get hurt. Some people are so thoughtless when it kummes to God's creatures. Cinnamon can't be more than a year old."

Ellie ran her hand along his back. "He's so loving. How could anyone abandon him?"

"Maybe they could no longer care for him, and they could find no one to take him." Liza sighed.

"Now I have two new friends, Aaron and Cinnamon."

Cinnamon ran around the yard in excited circles then back to Peter.

Ellie watched Peter play with his new pet. She came alongside Liza. "Are you in favor of this new addition to the family?"

"How could I refuse my very persuasive husband? And you must admit, Cinnamon is adorable."

"You're a good mamm." She cleared her throat. "I invited Joel over for supper tomorrow at six. Do you mind?"

"Mind? Of course not. I take it your time with him grew your interest in this young man?"

"Jah. I'm always thinking about him. And he keeps giving me more reasons to care about him." She held her hands to her cheeks and beamed. "Liza, he's so wise and kind. I could listen to him talk all day. He's interesting, and he's a good listener. I can't wait for you and Daed to get to know him."

"I've got some ham. I'll fry it up with some potatoes, and we'll have green beans to go with it."

"He can meet Snuggles and Cinnamon." Peter wrinkled his nose and rubbed Cinnamon's wet kiss from his cheek.

Daed came alongside Ellie. "Don't worry. I will ask him a few hundred questions. I'll try not to make it too awkward."

Ellie pretended an exasperated look. "Please don't embarrass me, Daed." She knocked his arm with hers.

"I won't promise any such thing."

"You're impossible."

"Liza tells me the same thing." He darted her a mischievous grin.

"Don't mind him. I'm sure Joel and he will do just fine together." Liza squeezed Ellie's hand.

Ellie played checkers with Peter and then put him to bed. She went to her room. Would her family like him? She couldn't think of any reason why not. She was anxious for tomorrow night to get here. She liked where things were going with her and Joel.

Ellie stared off as the bakery cleared of customers Monday afternoon. She'd found it hard to concentrate on work in anticipation of Joel kumming to supper. No doubt her family would ask him a lot of questions. She hoped they didn't annoy him. She was sure her family would redeem themselves by also being kind and wilkoming.

Hannah tapped her shoulder. "I can guess what's on your mind."

"Aren't I being ridiculous? I'm so happy about him kumming over this evening." She hugged a towel to her chest. "This must've been what Liza and Daed experienced the first time they saw each other. They often mention the spark they had the minute they met."

"I'm tickled you and Joel are getting along so well. Have you told him yet?"

Ellie shook her head.

"No rush, but you shouldn't avoid the topic for too long." Hannah reached for Ellie's hand.

"You're right. I'm afraid of what he'll say." She would delay it for as long as she could, but she wouldn't tell Hannah. "You'll have to kumme over and meet Cinnamon. The dog is obedient. Peter's crazy about his new pet."

Hannah heaved a big sigh. "I'm jealous. Mamm refuses to let us have a dog. She says when I have my own haus, then I can have a dog." She gently tucked a stray hair back in Ellie's kapp. "You'll have a good time at supper with Joel and your family. I'm sure of it."

Liza came to the front room. "Abigail, the girls must not have noticed you. What can we offer you today?"

Ellie and Hannah whirled around with open mouths. Speechless, Ellie stared at Abigail.

Liza sniffed the air. "I'll have to let Ellie help you. Hannah, can you help me? I may have left the white bread in too long, and the cookies I left on the hot metal tray need to be put on a plate before they burn."

Hannah nodded and followed Liza to the kitchen.

Abigail narrowed her eyes and twisted her mouth in

a sinister grin. "I went past your haus, and you have a new family pet. You must've found my precious dog. I wondered where she'd been. I'll be over to pick her up this evening after six. Did I hear you say Joel was kumming to supper? Maybe I'll stay for supper along with Joel. I'm sure Liza won't mind."

Ellie's cheeks grew warm. "First of all, the dog isn't yours. It's a male, and an Englischer dropped him off on the road near our haus."

"The Englischer must've found him. And I meant to say him. Silly me. Of course I meant to say him."

A man walked in and used his cane for support. A woman came in with him, holding his elbow.

Abigail moved closer to the couple. "I was just leaving. You go right up to the counter, and I'm sure Ellie will be glad to help you. I'll be over later, Ellie."

"Abigail, wait!" Her stomach clenched as she watched the door close. She forced a smile and concentrated on her customers. "We have molasses, butter, and oatmeal cookies, or peach, apple, and blueberry tarts, an assortment of breads, and many other offerings."

The feeble gray-haired woman tapped the counter with her long nail. "I'm having a hard time choosing. Henry, what would you like?"

Ellie swallowed the bile rising in her throat. She wanted to run after Abigail and tell her not to intrude on their supper or even consider taking Cinnamon. The girl was lying, and she was cunning, devious, and mean. There'd been a time when some might've accused Ellie of these same bad behaviors. Although she would never have forced herself on others to get her way or threatened to take a pet away from a family. Abigail must've overheard everything Hannah and she had said before Liza discovered her. The girl moved in and out of places like noxious air.

Ellie returned her attention to the couple scrutinizing the pies, cookies, tarts, and breads on the counter shelves.

The husband clasped his fraa's hand. "You love blueberry pie. Let's get one of those and a dozen molasses cookies. Our friends who shop here claim they're the best."

Ellie loved the tenderness between the two. A tenderness she wanted to share with the man she would marry when the time was right. She packaged their selections, accepted payment, and bid them farewell.

Hannah peeked out the open door between the main room and kitchen. "Why was Abigail here? The snarl on her face leads me to believe it wasn't to buy anything."

Ellie huffed. "She's pushed me too far this time. She's claiming Cinnamon is her dog. She slipped and called her missing dog a *she*. And she's invited herself to supper tonight at my haus to take the dog home."

"Isn't Cinnamon a male?"

"Jah." Ellie untied and threw her apron over the hook. "Can you watch the counter for a few minutes? I've got to find her. I don't want her showing up and ruining our evening, and I won't let her break Peter's heart over this dog. I've had enough."

"I will, but be cautious. I don't trust her. We Amish avoid confrontation. She's a conniver. She'll want to antagonize you in front of others to make you look bad."

"I'll do my best. No promises." Ellie took a deep breath and left. She searched the general store, post office, and apothecary, weaving in and out of the shoppers crowding the town. Pausing outside, she scanned the storefronts and the patrons entering and exiting each one.

Abigail passed in her buggy.

Ellie ran after her and waved frantically. "Abigail, I need to speak with you."

Abigail pulled her buggy to the side of the road. "Get in."

Ellie stepped in and took a seat next to her. "Abigail, Cinnamon is not yours."

"Why, Ellie, are you calling me a liar?"

Ellie tightened her grip on the side of the buggy. A storm of anger welled in her throat. She swallowed hard to suppress it. "I don't want to argue with you, Abigail. I just want you to stop making my life miserable."

Abigail smirked. "If I kumme to your haus this evening and claim the dog is mine, your parents won't argue with me. They'll relent because Amish don't like to argue. And it's my word against yours."

The girl was relentless. "What do you want?"

"Joel. Make an excuse as to why he's uninvited for supper and stay away from him. His mamm loves me. Now all I have to do is convince him. But as long as you're in the way, he won't give me a chance."

"Joel told me he made it clear to you he's not interested. I doubt I have anything to do with his reasons." She had to convince Abigail to drop her claim on the dog. Peter would be devastated. "My bruder loves his pet. You'll crush his heart if you stake a claim on the dog."

Abigail leaned closer to her. "Do what I say, and Peter can keep the mutt. It's up to you, Ellie. Now, get out."

Frustration like a downpour of rain on a hot tin roof ignited within her. She jumped down and whirled on her heel toward the buggy to tell Abigail it would be easy to find out she was lying by asking her parents and friends about the dog, but Abigail was already heading out of town.

Joel mucked the stall. At the Grabers' he'd get better acquainted with Ellie's parents. He cared about her, and his mind raced with thoughts of her. Time with her was never enough.

Hours later, Joel washed and shaved. The wooden holder nailed to the wall held his brush, razor, and a small circle of tin to use as a mirror. A mirror would've been better for this task, but he didn't want to do anything to appear prideful and understood why the Amish avoided such things.

Bathed and dressed, he bid his parents farewell and headed to Ellie's. He waved to Amish men passing him in buggies, whom he recognized from the Sunday services.

Brown and yellow leaves covered the grass, and the cool, crisp air brushed against his face. Three white and black speckled cottontails hopped into the woods as he drove by. September was warmer than usual. They hadn't had a threat of frost. Crops were thriving in all the fields of his neighbors and friends along the way. The harvest would be good this year.

Joel secured his buggy at Ellie and Peter's haus and met them on the porch. "Who are you holding?" He smiled at Ellie and nodded to Peter, who was holding a dog. He scratched the pet's ear.

Peter nuzzled his nose in the dog's fur and then looked at Joel. "Cinnamon." He put the pet down and opened the door.

Ellie chuckled. "The mutt took to Peter right away.

They've been inseparable. We have all fallen in love with Cinnamon."

The dog jumped down and ran, tongue hanging out of his mouth, and tail wagging.

"He's a playful dog."

"Would you prefer to sit inside or outside? Supper will be ready in about twenty minutes."

Mrs. Graber opened the door. "Joel, I'm so glad you could join us. May I offer you some hot tea or coffee?"

"Hot tea, please, and danki for the invitation, Mrs. Graber."

Mrs. Graber had a calmness about her. Her soft voice and cheerful mood put him at ease. In his home, he cherished the rare moments free of tension. He never knew when Mamm's temper would flare, and he didn't remember the last time she'd actually relaxed. She did everything in a hurry or with nervous energy.

"Call me Liza."

Mr. Graber came outside and offered his hand. "And I'm Jacob. Why don't you and Ellie sit on the porch, and I'll help Liza. We can chat during supper, and after, we'll build a fire outside and have dessert."

Peter jumped up and down and clapped his hands. "I love when we have a fire outside! Let's make apple pies with our pie irons."

"Good idea, Peter. We have enough bread, and I've got some leftover baked apples with cinnamon from this afternoon. I'll get the hot tea and be right back." Liza went to the kitchen.

"I'll help." Jacob followed her.

Ellie gestured for Joel and Peter to follow her to the rocking chairs and bench. She slid one chair across from Joel and plopped in it.

Something was wrong. Ellie kept darting her eyes

to the lane from the road leading to the haus and
fidgeted her hands. Maybe she was nervous about him
meeting her parents.

Peter left the porch and returned with Snuggles.
"Here's my other friend."

Joel slid to the edge of his seat and rubbed the soft
ears of the rabbit. "You're blessed to have such good
pets. Snuggles is docile and hasn't tried to bite my
fingers."

Ellie leaned in and buried her fingers in the white
fluffy fur, looking to the lane with concern and not at
him or the pet. "This furry little bunny is so gentle.
Snuggles doesn't bite or scratch."

Peter held Snuggles close, with Cinnamon right up
against his leg. "I'm going to play with them until
supper." He left holding Snuggles, and Cinnamon ran
after him.

Joel scanned the property. "I was amazed at the size
of this place when I first passed by. This is the largest
Amish haus in this community, and the fields are too.
It's quite impressive with the oversized barn, smokehaus, ice haus, and large workshop. Very well done."

"Liza was a widow. Her husband had family wealth,
and he was blessed to make money selling his crops,
and her bakery is successful. She's thankful for Abe,
her bruder-in-law, for taking care of it and managing
the field hands. Abe is Hannah's Daed, and I love
having him, her, and her mamm, Esther, nearby."

Joel set his glass on the small wooden table beside
his high-backed rocking chair. "Ellie, are you anxious
about me meeting your parents? You aren't yourself."

Ellie paled and jumped to her feet.

Liza came to the door. "Supper's ready." She yelled

to Peter, "Please put Snuggles and Cinnamon away and kumme inside."

Joel noticed Ellie sighed with relief at her stepmamm's interruption.

Peter hurried to the cage. "May I bring in Cinnamon?"

"Jah, I suppose."

Joel snatched his glass and followed Ellie inside and to the supper table. "Where should I sit?"

Ellie pointed to a chair and avoided his gaze. She helped Liza arrange plates of sliced ham, green beans with bacon pieces, and fried potatoes on the table. She grabbed the basket of bread and a small dish of butter and set them in the center before taking her seat.

Peter slid onto his chair. "I'm starved. This food smells good."

Cinnamon darted under the table and lay near Peter's feet.

"This does look delicious, sweetheart." Jacob took Liza's hand in his. "Let's bow our heads." Jacob offered a prayer.

Ellie passed Joel the beans. Her hands shook. "There's more on the stove. Take as much as you want."

Joel thanked her and took the plate. It was unfortunate Liza had interrupted and called them to supper when she did. He was curious to find out what had Ellie upset.

Jacob buttered his bread. "What plans do you have for the future, Joel?"

Ellie choked on the food in her mouth. "Daed!"

Joel held up his palm. "It's all right, Ellie. I tend to the farm and handcraft things when I have time."

Jacob sipped his water. "I tinker in the workshop now and then. I made Liza a hope chest. What do you build?"

"And you did a beautiful job on it." Liza squeezed his arm.

"I've made storage boxes, benches, tables, and chairs. The furniture store owner in Lancaster sold some pieces for me. I've put the money aside for building a haus someday. I may try the same arrangement with the store in Charm."

Jacob jerked his head back in surprise. "What a grand idea."

Peter chatted about his pets, and they all discussed how well the crops were doing.

Joel enjoyed the banter, laughter, ease of conversation, and obvious love this family had for each other. Ellie was quiet most of the evening. He'd pull her aside after supper and ask her what was on her mind. Whatever it was, he wanted to help her resolve it.

Ellie drank the last of her water. "I couldn't fit another bite into my stomach. This food was so good."

Liza covered Ellie's hand. "Danki, honey." Liza got up from her seat and stretched her neck to see out the window. "Someone's kumming to visit." She moved to the window.

Ellie jumped up, her eyes wide. "It's Abigail." She fisted her palms. "I should've told you about her visit to the bakery today. I was hoping she wouldn't follow through with her threat."

Joel wiped his mouth and stood next to her. He didn't like the dread in her voice.

"What threat?" Jacob narrowed his eyes and crossed his arms.

Knock. Knock.

They all went to the door.

Ellie opened it. "Abigail."

Abigail stepped inside. "Have you told everyone,

Ellie, how happy I am you found my dog? Something smells good. I hope I haven't interrupted your supper. Joel, what a surprise to find you here."

Peter looked up at Ellie. "Cinnamon is my dog." His eyes pooled with tears as he scooped his pet in his arms.

Joel narrowed his eyes. Abigail's implications were unbelievable. She'd never mentioned having a pet. "Jacob, do you mind if Abigail, Ellie, and I go outside to discuss this?"

Jacob circled an arm around Peter. "You go ahead. I'll be here if you need me."

Liza stood with her mouth open and hands to her cheeks.

Ellie led them outside, away from the haus to the weeping willow tree by the pond. "Abigail, I won't let you take the dog. You're lying."

Abigail's hand flew to her lips. "Ellie, I'm upset you'd think I'd hurt Peter on purpose. I'm equally distraught about losing my dog. I'm sure he'll understand."

Joel didn't trust Abigail's word on this. She was up to something. Her voice was sickeningly sweet and her gestures forced. She was the strangest girl he'd ever met. "Why haven't you mentioned having a dog? And when I went to your haus, there was no sign of one."

"She's been missing."

Ellie glared at Abigail. "There, you did it again. You called Cinnamon a she, and the dog's a male."

Joel stared at Abigail. "Why would you set out to torment Peter? Why are you doing this?" He wouldn't let this girl hurt Ellie or Peter. He had grown fond of them, and he would protect them.

"I was upset and confused. I meant to say him."
She sniffled.

Ellie huffed and put her hands on her hips. "Joel,
Abigail was angry when she overheard you were kumming to supper. She said if I didn't stay away from you,
she'd claim the dog was hers and it would be her word
against mine."

"Abigail, how could you?" Joel couldn't understand
why Abigail would go to such great lengths to pursue
him. To lie and to hurt other people after he'd made
it plain he was not interested in her. She must not be
right in the head to threaten Ellie this way. "You should
leave, and I don't want you to bother this family again.
If you do, Mr. Graber and I will meet with your parents
and the bishop and tell them what you've done."

"What?!" Abigail heaved a big breath and snarled
at him.

"You heard me. You've put me in the position of
being firm with you. I tried being polite, and you didn't
listen."

Jacob approached them. "Abigail, if we ask your
parents, friends, and neighbors if this dog is yours,
what will their answer be?"

Lips pinched and flustered, she ignored him and
ran to her buggy, untied her mare, and left in a hurry.

Liza and Peter joined them.

Peter swiped wet tears from his cheeks. "Is she
kumming back to take Cinnamon? Is he her dog?"

Joel bent and put his hands on Peter's arms. "Cinnamon is your dog. Abigail won't bother you anymore.
I'll see to it."

Peter wrapped his arms around Joel's neck. "Danki.
I couldn't stand to give him up."

Ellie hugged Peter. "You and Joel build the fire for

the pies, and I'll go inside and help Liza with the dirty dishes."

Liza pointed to the front door. "Peter, would you mind getting some lap blankets for us?"

He shook his head. "I'll go get them." He scampered to the haus.

Liza squeezed Ellie's shoulder. "Jacob and I cleaned the dishes, and Peter pitched in too. Why don't you and Joel sit by the pond? We'll build the fire and get things ready. I'm sure both of you would like some privacy to discuss what happened. We can learn the details about Abigail after Peter goes to bed."

"Danki. I should share with Joel what's been going on with Abigail." She turned to him. "Do you mind going by the pond for a few minutes to talk?"

"I'd be glad to." He strolled with her to another bench not far from the edge of the water. Two fat robins flew overhead and perched themselves on a branch in the maple tree near them.

Ellie picked a piece of lint off her dress then looked at the pond. "Abigail has bullied me about you on several occasions. She blames me for your disinterest in her. I tried to convince her I had nothing to do with you and her, but she wouldn't listen. Tonight was a good example."

Joel let out a long sigh. "She's frequented our haus and befriended Mamm. I suspect to try and get closer to me. She won't leave me alone. Mamm has honored my request not to encourage her where I'm concerned, but she said Abigail won't stop prattling on about me. Mamm overlooks it, and she'd like me to change my mind about Abigail, but I won't."

"She has gone too far this time by involving Peter."

"Jah, she has. I suggest we go to the bishop and have

her parents there too. I doubt this is the first time she's bullied someone. We have to put an end to this."

Ellie nodded. "Part of me is furious with her, and the other part of me is sorry for her. She wants to be loved, and she goes about it the wrong way."

Joel fought to not put his arms around her and hold her. "I'm responsible. If it wasn't for me, she wouldn't have involved you. Let's schedule a meeting with Abigail, her parents, the bishop, and you and me. I'd rather not involve our parents."

"My parents are reasonable. I'm sure they'll agree. Danki."

She gazed at him with her big blue eyes, looking vulnerable. He thought his heart would soar right out of his chest. He'd do anything to shield her from harm.

He reached out and brushed her hand with his. "I don't like you upset. I've grown to care about you a lot in such a short time."

"I care about you too, Joel."

Her heart-shaped face and stiff shoulders relaxed. She had lifted her fingers to his when he brushed over them. "You should've told me Abigail was threatening you. How terrible you had to endure this on your own."

"I had hoped she wouldn't follow through with her threat. I didn't want to burden you with my troubles. We're enjoying getting to know each other, and I didn't want to complain about her." She stared at the grass. "I prefer to handle things on my own."

"Now you don't have to. I'm here." He covered her hand with his for a moment. Her skin was soft.

She blushed. "I like having you in my life."

Peter raced to them. "Here are the blankets." He

handed them each one. "Fire's ready, and I have the pie irons for us." He had them tucked under his arm and held them up.

"Good boy." Ellie smiled at him.

They all crossed the yard to the big tree logs next to the fire pit and sat on them.

They made apple pies, laughed, and had a good time.

Ellie led them in hymns, and they sang around the flickering flames.

Joel could listen to her melodious voice all night. She sang with such clarity.

Two hours later, Liza wrapped her shawl closer. "Peter, it's time for prayers and bed. Say good night to Joel, and let's head inside."

"Kumme back real soon, Joel." He hugged him.

Joel loved this child. He was innocent and a fun little boy. "I will."

Liza waved to Joel. "Kumme by anytime, Joel."

"Danki for the meal. I appreciate your hospitality. I'll take you up on the offer and be back soon."

"Good." Liza took Peter's hand and walked inside.

Cinnamon barked, ran in circles around them, and finally padded next to Peter to the haus.

Joel talked to Jacob about farming until Liza returned.

Ellie shared with her parents the conversation she had with Abigail and the meetings they'd had prior. She explained the plan to meet with the bishop and Abigail's parents.

Joel rested his elbows on his knees and clasped his hands. "Jacob, do you mind if Ellie and I handle this?"

Jacob remained silent for a moment, then rubbed his chin. "You're not responsible for Abigail's behavior,

Joel, but I appreciate your helping Ellie with this. It's hard for me to stay out of it, but having less people involved is probably best. If it doesn't go well, I will arrange a visit with her parents and the bishop again."

"Danki. I agree with you. We will need your support if things go awry, but I trust the bishop will want this behavior squelched, and maybe her parents will as well. I doubt they know what she's up to. Abigail's a chameleon and able to change her demeanor on demand. She's quite deceitful."

"We Amish are not without our troublemakers. Hopefully, the bishop and Abigail's parents can appeal to her good side and she'll show some remorse and back down. She obviously craves attention and love. It's sad."

"I agree. I'll set up a meeting tomorrow."

"Danki, Joel."

Jacob stood and kissed Ellie on the forehead. "I'm going inside. Ellie, please douse the fire before you kumme in the haus."

"I'll be happy to."

"You're always wilkom in our home, Joel." Jacob put a hand on Joel's shoulder and strode to the front door. Liza joined him.

Joel stared at the orange hue of the flames and enjoyed the warmth on his face. The peaceful flicker of the fire and crackle of the burning wood was warm and cozy. "I could sit here for hours with you. It's such a peaceful evening."

"In spite of Abigail's antics, the night has been such a pleasant one. Each time we are together, I grow fonder of you." She reddened. "Oh my, I shouldn't have been so forward."

Joel grinned. Ellie had made him very happy

confirming what he'd hoped she was feeling about him. "Don't apologize. I'm glad you speak your mind."

She chuckled. "You may not be at some point. I have to watch what I say and how I say it. Abigail tested my ability to do this more than once. I did raise my voice to her a time or two."

"Now and then when people try to take advantage, it's understandable." Joel had been surprised at Ellie's blunt statements to Abigail earlier, but he didn't blame her for her reaction. Abigail had tried to hurt someone she loved, and Ellie would do her best to make sure it didn't happen. He admired her for it. He admired a strong woman, and Ellie had both a soft and hard temperament. "I'm going to have to light my lantern to go home. Night is approaching, and I should be going."

Ellie stood. "I'm not ready for this night to end."

"Me either." He rose, and they crossed the yard to his buggy. He scanned the haus. Everyone was inside and no one was watching. He pulled her close and gently kissed her soft lips. Ellie didn't step away. She lifted her head to him. His heart sang with delight. He hoped as they went forward, nothing would interfere with their relationship progressing. He stepped back and held her arms. "You've made quite an impression on me, Ellie Graber."

"I'm going to remember this kiss forever, Joel."

He caressed her cheek. "I don't want to leave you, but I must. I'll stop by the bakery tomorrow and tell you when the bishop and Abigail's parents have agreed to meet with us. And don't worry, everything will work out fine." He got into his buggy, drove down the path, and glanced over his shoulder. She stood waving to him. His beautiful Ellie. The first girl he'd ever considered wanting to pursue for his fraa. They were already handling a problem together. He was confident they could solve anything together.

A snake slithered across the road and his mare reared. "Whoa, girl, it's all right." He calmed the horse and flicked the reins. He and Ellie had a lot to learn about each other. He didn't think anything would halt their blossoming relationship, but his stomach knotted. He had a secret he had to tell her. One the Amish forbade him to tell. One her family might not overlook.

He rubbed the stubble on his chin. Abigail insinuated Ellie had a questionable past. Was she lying about Ellie? Abigail had a boldness he didn't like, and her smile and words didn't seem genuine. They'd just got acquainted, and she wanted to discredit Ellie. But was there any truth to what Abigail said? Could Ellie be holding back a secret from him? One he couldn't overlook?

Chapter Five

Ellie touched her lips. Joel's kiss lingered on them. Her heart full of joy, she went inside. She savored the warm fuzziness filling her from head to toe. Her and Joel's spark was powerful, but their time together was effortless. He'd defended her against Abigail's accusations and suggested the solution to solve the problem by meeting with the bishop and the girl's parents.

She had held her breath when Joel asked her daed to let him arrange and speak at the meeting. Daed had understood and approved Joel's request, although she knew he would swoop in and arrange a second meeting if the outcome wasn't to his satisfaction.

Her parents sat by the fire in the sitting room.

Liza rested her knitting needles in her lap. "I'm impressed with Joel, and he's definitely smitten with you."

Daed put his sock feet on the footstool. "He's a gentleman, and I respect how he wants to show his loyalty to you. Peter's quite taken with him too."

"He had a good time. Whenever we're together, our relationship grows." She chatted a few more minutes with them and then padded to her room.

Tomorrow, Joel would probably tell her when

they'd sit down with the bishop and Abigail's parents. She'd be nervous, but she trusted Joel.

Ellie worked the counter Tuesday serving customers until three. She put a hand to her growling stomach and poked her head in the kitchen. "Have the two of you taken a break to have a snack? I haven't had a minute to myself out here. I've got to have the sandwich I brought."

Hannah opened the cabinet and passed Ellie her bag. "Here you go. Take a seat. We managed to steal a few minutes to scarf down our sandwiches. Sit and enjoy yours. If anyone wants to buy goodies, I'll wait on them. Liza told me about Abigail. I pray all goes well with the bishop and her parents."

"I'm appreciative of Joel stepping in. I'm certain the bishop won't approve of her behavior, and he has a gentle but firm way of getting his point across. I'm ready for some help with Abigail. Otherwise, our encounters are going to escalate, and I'll be as bad as she is, spouting off at her." Ellie gobbled up her ham sandwich and drank a full glass of water. "The salt in the ham makes me thirsty, but it's so yummy. I'm much better."

"No good kummes from losing your temper. Remain calm, and your discussion will go much better." Liza nodded to the window. "Joel's crossing the road, and he's headed in this direction."

Ellie rushed to the door and opened it. "Liza noticed you out the window, and I wanted to surprise you."

"You succeeded." He chuckled and came inside. "The bishop will ask Abigail and her parents to meet us at his haus at six. Is this agreeable with you?"

She nodded. "Of course. Whatever time you say."

"I'll pick you up at your haus, and we'll go together."

"Would you join us for supper tonight?" She wanted to spend as much time with him as possible.

"I would, but I'm going to decline. I need to tell my parents about Abigail and deter Mamm from getting closer with her. I'm protective of Mamm, and I don't want Abigail to cause her any heartache. She likes Abigail, and she doesn't realize Abigail may not have good motives for befriending her. If Abigail got frustrated with Mamm for some reason, I'm afraid she'd retaliate. I want to avoid any more confrontations with Abigail after this."

A distinguished gentleman entered the bakery. He perused the dessert shelves.

"I should let you get back to work. I'll be at your place a little before six." Joel held her gaze a moment then left.

She would be with him again at six. She'd count the minutes until then. Smiling, she went behind the counter. "Did you have any particular dessert in mind today?"

The man tipped his black top hat. "The peach tarts, rhubarb pie, and nut cookies all appeal to me. Which one do you suggest? If I take them all home, I'll add ten pounds to my already round middle. I must show some restraint." He laughed, and his handlebar mustache waggled when he spoke.

A woman in a beautiful gray wool coat, trimmed in black velvet, entered. She had her hair swooped in a tight bun.

"I'll be with you in a moment."

The woman hooked her arm through the gentleman's. "I'm with this handsome man. He's my wonderful husband of forty years." She lay her head on his shoulder for a second. "What are you going to choose for us, dear?"

"I'm glad you came in. I can't decide." He tapped his finger on his lip.

"You love nut cookies. Let's buy them and the rhubarb pie."

"Perfect." He smiled and gave her a curt nod.

Ellie wrapped their purchases and accepted payment. She bid them farewell. What a lovely couple. Forty years was a long time to live together. Their adoration for each other was evident in their exchanged endearing looks. She hoped she'd marry one day and have forty glorious years with her husband. Would Joel be the one for her? She hoped so.

Five came, and Ellie waited for Liza to lock the door and take them home. She pulled her heavy wool shawl about her. The clouds blocked the heat of the sun and the afternoon breeze chilled her. She listened to Liza and Hannah chat about what cookies they'd made ahead for the next day and what they planned to bake in the morning, nodding her head at the right times.

She had grown more anxious about the outcome of the discussion she and Joel were headed to. "I'm uncomfortable about meeting with Abigail and her parents. Joel's picking me up in about forty-five minutes."

Hannah clasped Ellie's hand. "Don't worry. The bishop's a wise man. I'm sure the meeting will be fine."

She could count on Hannah to calm her nerves. "Danki. I'll tell you the details tomorrow."

Liza bid Hannah farewell, headed home, and darted a glance at Ellie. "Amish avoid confrontation, especially in our community, where we strive for peace, but sometimes we have to face unpleasant circumstances.

This is one of those times. I'm proud of you and Joel for taking a stand in a humble way."

Ellie tightened her grip on the side of the buggy. "I'm not sure how humble I'll be, but I'll do my best to behave."

"You'll regret it if you don't." Liza glowered at her.

Ellie shrunk in her seat. "I've worked hard to soften my words and keep the fire low on my temperament."

"Jah, and I'm proud of you. I'll pray for you while you're gone." She pulled in front of the barn. "You go in and fix yourself some eggs before Joel gets here."

"Danki, Liza. I'll send Daed out to help you."

Liza nodded.

Ellie went inside and met Daed kumming out of the kitchen with his mouth full. She grinned and tilted her head. "What have you been up to?"

"I stuffed a cookie in my mouth. Liza doesn't let me have dessert before supper, but I couldn't pass up her maple sugar cookies." He rubbed his stomach. "I've had five today."

"You better chew and swallow it before you hit the door." She gestured to the door. "Liza's waiting on you to help her with the buggy. Joel is picking me up soon to go to our meeting."

"Good, then you can put this problem behind you. I'll help Liza. Peter is out back playing with Cinnamon and Snuggles. It tickles me how those two animals have become the best of friends."

"Peter is a good teacher. He works at making them friends. I'm impressed with my bruder's guidance skills."

She poured herself a cup of leftover coffee and chose bread and apple butter for her snack, instead of the eggs Liza suggested. She went to the back porch and watched Peter cuddle and love on his animals.

"Ellie, watch Cinnamon sit when I tell him to." He instructed the dog to sit, and the pet obeyed.

"What are you giving him for a reward?" Ellie took another chunk of her bread and put it in her mouth.

"I'm breaking off pieces of one of Mamm's maple sugar cookies."

"No more than one or the poor thing will never sleep. He'll have too much spunk from the sugar."

"All right."

Joel met her halfway across the yard. "Looks like Peter is putting on quite a show with Snuggles and Cinnamon. Liza and Jacob told me you two were back here. We're running late. Are you ready?" He waved to Peter. "Hi, buddy!"

Peter scampered to him. "Can you play with me?"

Joel shook his head. "We have to leave. I will some other time."

Peter pouted his lips. "When?"

"Soon, I promise."

He beamed. "Don't forget."

Joel waved good-bye. "I won't."

Ellie got in the buggy next to Joel and bid her family farewell, and they went to the bishop's. She pointed to a large black bear. "Look at its size!" She hadn't encountered bears up close, and she hoped she never would.

"I've seen a couple of large bears kumming out of the dense woods there."

She edged closer to Joel. "Are you nervous about the outcome of our get-together this evening?"

"I asked God to give me the right attitude and words to say, because I'm frustrated with Abigail.

She's different than any other girl I've met. I'm hoping she and her parents will respond to the bishop in a positive way."

Ellie nodded. "I gave Daed a rough time when Mamm passed. Stubborn and angry at the world, I took my frustration out on him. He forgave me over and over again." She'd been forgiven by her friends and parents during her rebellious time, and she should do the same for Abigail. She dug her nails into her palms. Abigail had made it so difficult. She bowed her head and prayed silently. *Dear Heavenly Father, dissolve my bitterness against Abigail and please give me the compassion I need to forgive her. Amen.*

"Ellie, are you all right?"

"I prayed for God to give me the compassion I need to forgive her. She has a tendency to make my blood boil, and I struggle not to get angry with her."

"Luke 6:36 kummes to mind for times like this. 'Be ye therefore merciful, as your Father also is merciful.'" He halted the horse and stepped down. "Abigail and her parents are here. Let's go in."

Ellie waited until he had secured the mare, and they approached the porch together.

Joel rapped on the door.

The bishop, somber, held it wide. "Make yourselves at home. May I offer you anything?"

Ellie shook her head and nodded to the bishop and guests. "Good evening." She chose a chair by the fireplace.

Joel chose the one next to her. "Not for me, danki." He nodded to Abigail and her parents.

Abigail stared at her hands folded in her lap. Her parents had slumped shoulders and worried faces.

The bishop settled back in a chair where he could

address the group. "Let's bow our heads for a word of prayer. Dear Heavenly Father, open our hearts and help us to approach this discussion with your scriptures in mind. Let us conduct ourselves in a way that is pleasing to you. Amen." He opened his Bible. "I've turned to Mark 12:31, 'Love thy neighbor as thyself.' We should keep this verse in mind this evening."

The bishop closed the Bible and set it on the side table next to his chair. "Ellie and Joel, I've asked the Fishers not to tell me anything about why we're gathered here until you both arrived. Abigail, you go first."

She slumped her shoulders and tilted her head in meek stance. "Joel came to supper and left me with the impression he was interested in me, and then I noticed he was speaking a lot with Ellie. I overheard Ellie at the bakery say Joel was kumming to her haus for supper. He betrayed me, and I'm brokenhearted."

Joel gripped the arms on the chair. He'd been accused unjustly, and it was her word against his and Ellie's. His schweschder had tarnished their reputation by her actions and caused damage to their family. He couldn't afford for their fresh start here to be ruined for no good reason. He'd have to think hard before he spoke. Waiting on the bishop, he kept his mouth closed. He glanced at Ellie, and she sat stiff. This was difficult for both of them.

The bishop nodded to Joel. "Please tell me how you view what Abigail has shared."

Joel met the bishop's gaze. "I had a pleasant evening with the Fishers. Then Abigail and I went to the pond near their home, where I told her I wasn't interested in a relationship with her. She said she would wait on me, and I asked her not to. I don't understand why she has persisted in pursuing me."

Mr. Fisher, holding his hat in his lap, scooted to the edge of his seat. He held out his palms. "Abigail, why do you do this?" He frowned and shook his head. "Since moving here, two other men have kumme to me about your relentless pursuit of them, and I have told you this is unacceptable behavior and to stop. Have you done the same to Joel?"

Mrs. Fisher dropped her chin to her chest and concentrated on the floor.

"Nah! He's a liar!" Abigail jumped up with fire in her eyes.

The bishop rose. "Young lady, please control yourself."

"Sit down, dochder, right now." Mr. Fisher stood and crossed his arms.

Abigail frowned and plopped in the chair. "You must believe me."

Ellie cleared her throat. "Abigail, you've threatened me and done everything you could to destroy my friendship with Joel, knowing he has made it clear he's not the one for you. Please, don't make us give these details to your parents and the bishop."

"Go ahead. No one's going to believe you after what you've done."

Ellie winced and caught her breath. "Hurting me isn't going to make you feel better."

Mr. Fisher quirked his brow. "What details?"

Joel said, "Abigail came to the Grabers' and insisted the abandoned dog they took into their home was hers. She also called the dog 'she' and the animal is a male."

Mrs. Fisher dropped her small wrinkled hands from her worried face. "What dog?"

"Jah, Abigail, what dog?" Mr. Fisher narrowed his eyes.

Abigail's eyes pooled with tears. "I'm sorry, Daed. I found out Ellie invited Joel to supper. She mentioned a stray dog, and I told her I would claim it was mine if she didn't stay away from Joel. I shouldn't have been so foolish. I'm so ashamed." She covered her face with her hands.

Joel couldn't tell if Abigail was sorry or pretending. Her daed shook his head.

The bishop peered over his spectacles. "Abigail, from what's been discussed, am I to understand you've been rude and lying to Joel and Ellie on different occasions to get your way?"

She pleaded, "Jah, and I don't want to cause any more trouble for them or my parents. Please don't order a shunning as punishment for my family because of what I've done. I'm truly sorry, Joel and Ellie, bishop, and Mamm and Daed. I hope you'll forgive me."

Joel uncrossed his arms. Abigail cared what the bishop thought of her. It was evident in her plea. This meeting had been a good idea. He was ready for this meeting to end. He and Ellie had made their point. He could only hope Abigail was being truthful. "I forgive you."

Ellie said, "I do too. I just want to put this behind us."

The bishop gave Abigail a stern look. "Young lady, you've joined the church. If I hear you have hounded Joel, Ellie, or anyone in our community, I will impose a shunning for a period of time. Do you understand?"

She bobbed her head. "I do." Her face pinked, and

she swiped a tear from her cheek. "It won't happen again."

Mr. Fisher stood and shook the bishop's hand then Joel's. "I'm sorry for my dochder's behavior."

"No hard feelings, Mr. Fisher. I wish you the very best."

The slender man held his hat with calloused hands. "You're a good man, Joel. And Ellie, danki for your forgiving heart."

Ellie blushed. "I harbor no grudge against Abigail, and I pray you and your family will have peace after this."

Abigail gave Ellie and Joel a weak wave and left.

Mrs. Fisher took Ellie's hands in hers. "Danki for showing Abigail mercy. Should I visit your mamm and explain? We've passed by them at church, but we haven't actually gotten acquainted."

"Nah, she and Daed will be happy we've resolved the problem, and it's not necessary. I can assure you they will be fine."

Mr. Fisher plopped his hat on his head. "I should tell you, we'll be moving soon. We've accepted my bruder's offer to help him farm his land and move into the haus in Sugarcreek he has available since his in-laws have passed."

The bishop patted the man's back. "I'm sad you're leaving. If you need help loading your belongings, I'll be glad to help. Have you found someone to take your home?"

"Our neighbor, Emmanuel Wittmer, is buying it. He'll move his in-laws into his haus and occupy mine. With six kinner, he needs more room."

"I'm glad you and he worked out an agreement."

The Fishers said farewell and left.

Joel and Ellie thanked the bishop and headed to the buggy.

Joel tensed as guilt gripped him. He was glad the family was moving. He'd pray Abigail truly had a change of heart. Her parents were kind, and it was evident they didn't want any trouble. Abigail wasn't anything like them. They must find her bad choices disappointing. He helped Ellie into the buggy. "I'm glad we were able to resolve this problem." He got in and headed to Ellie's.

"I don't understand Abigail." She clicked her tongue. "She can change her mood in an instant. I did appreciate how the bishop conducted the meeting. He follows the scriptures, and he is a good leader for our community."

"I am also pleased how the bishop handled everything. Listen, we have done our part by forgiving her. We can put this behind us and move on with our lives. I'm glad they're moving. I would've been cordial and kind had the family planned to stay in Charm, but I would've suggested we keep our distance until we were sure she was true to her word to not cause us any more trouble." He gave her a shy grin. "Here we are already solving problems together. We're off to a good start in our relationship, Ellie Graber."

"Abigail and your mamm have become friends. Did you tell her what Abigail has been doing or about going to the bishop's?"

He hadn't wanted to upset Mamm. Not sure of the outcome, he had decided to wait to mention anything to Mamm until he had all the information. He didn't want to cause her any pain, and she would miss Abigail. The girl had been good to her, even if she'd done it under false pretenses. "Nah, I'll tell her when I get home."

She inhaled a deep breath. "Hopefully she'll not be too hurt to learn about Abigail's intentions to win you over." She fidgeted with her kapp ribbon. "I'd like to get better acquainted with your mamm."

"Let's give her time to adjust to losing Abigail, and then we'll warm up to having you befriend her." Mamm had believed whatever lies Abigail had told her about Ellie. He would invite Ellie to their haus to show Mamm that Ellie was a delightful girl.

Ellie nodded. "I hope this is the last problem we have to solve for quite a while."

"I hope so too." He pulled the buggy down a side path behind tall trees, where they'd be hidden. He pulled her to him and kissed her soft petal lips. "Ellie, we've known each other for such a short time, but I'm very fond of you. We've got much to learn about each other, but I'm awestruck by you already." He smiled, reluctant to end the moment. "We'd better get going. Getting caught kissing is all we need." He flicked the reins and headed for the main road.

She giggled and then grew serious. "My heart feels the same, Joel. Tonight, as hard as it's been, I was happy to have you by my side." She hesitated, lowered her eyes, and then looked at him. "I am upset your mamm is against you having anything to do with me. We have to work together to change her mind."

"Don't worry. She'll kumme around when she gets better acquainted with you." They arrived at her haus. "Do you want me to kumme in with you and tell your folks what happened?"

She shook her head. "I'm sure you're anxious to tell your mamm the story. My parents will be glad the whole mess is over. I'll say a prayer all goes well for you when you tell your parents." She jumped out and waved.

"Danki, sweetheart. Get a peaceful night's sleep." He headed toward home and shivered. Night was descending, and the air was getting cooler. He halted, grabbed the lantern, and turned it up, glad he had a short distance to go. He'd been proud of Ellie showing kindness to Abigail. They'd weathered this storm, and he was certain they could handle many more if need be. Jah, she was the one for him. He'd pray his mamm would soften her hardened heart toward Ellie.

He arrived home, unharnessed his mare and put her in the barn, fed her, and offered her water then went inside. His parents sat by the fire, chatting.

Mamm whipped her head in his direction and narrowed her eyes. "Where have you been?"

Joel plopped on the settee and struggled to relax. "Ellie, the Fishers, and I all met with the bishop."

Daed edged to the end of his seat and set his hot tea mug on the side table. "Why?"

"Jah, why?" Mamm stopped darning a hole in a wool blanket.

Joel tensed. "Abigail approached Ellie more than once and told her to stay away from me."

Mamm slammed her needles on her lap. "Ellie must be lying!"

Mamm jumped to the wrong conclusions about Ellie at every turn.

"She's not lying." Joel recounted what Abigail had been up to and about the meeting. He had hoped Mamm would understand Ellie had handled this situation with grace.

"I find it hard to believe Abigail would threaten to do something so heartless." Mamm stared at him.

"Abigail is a complicated girl. She's been pushy and obsessive over other men in the past, according to her daed."

"She had me fooled. I enjoyed her company. I hope our friendship was genuine. I'd like to think so." Mamm frowned.

Daed sat back in his chair. "She's troubled. We should pray for her and her parents."

Joel got up and knelt by her chair. "I agree, Daed." He covered his mamm's hand with his. "I dreaded disappointing you by telling you about what has been happening. You've been good for Abigail, and you obviously brought out the best in her. I believe she genuinely cared about you."

"I hope you're right. She filled a void for me with your schweschder gone. We laughed and shared precious memories. I'm fortunate to know a different side of her. I'll miss her." Mamm wiped her moist eyes. "I wish her family much happiness in Sugarcreek. Maybe the fresh start is what they need."

Joel rose, stretched, and nodded to his parents. He didn't want to discuss Abigail anymore. He could use some quiet time. "I'm going to get ready for bed and read awhile."

"Get some rest. You've had a long day." Daed smiled.

"I'm making grits with your eggs tomorrow for breakfast." Mamm picked up her needles.

"One of my favorites. Danki, Mamm." He padded to his room and shut the door. He sat in the hardwood spindled chair next to his bedside table and lantern. The meeting with the bishop earlier and the reaction of his parents to it had turned out much better than he'd anticipated.

Mamm hadn't revisited the topic of Ellie. Maybe she would give Ellie a chance, with Abigail out of their lives. He would need them to get along if he was going to consider her for a fraa. It was necessary for them to follow God's will for their lives, their kinner, and his and Ellie's overall happiness. The hairs on the back of his neck prickled. Mamm's approval would be a challenge. He didn't want anyone or anything to destroy his new relationship with Ellie. He hadn't made plans with her again, but he'd schedule something with her tomorrow.

Chapter Six

Ellie told her parents about the meeting with the Fishers and the bishop. "The family is moving to Sugarcreek." She couldn't help but be relieved. She didn't want any more interference by Abigail in her relationship with Joel. They had enough opposition from Mrs. Wenger.

Liza held a cup of tea. "I wish them the best, and I'm relieved the girl won't be interfering any longer with you and Joel. He's a gentleman and Jacob and I enjoyed his company. I'm impressed with his maturity, goals, and manner."

Daed chuckled. "I can't stand the thought of you leaving this haus one day to get married. I guess it's inevitable, and if so, I do approve of Joel, too."

Ellie hugged Daed's neck and then settled in the old oak rocker her late mamm had used often during her childhood. "He has a big heart, and he's strong and firm at the same time. His wisdom showed in his words and actions this evening."

"Now you can move on with him without looking over your shoulder wondering if Abigail will interfere.

Do you have plans with him anytime soon?" Liza set her cup of tea on the side table and lifted Cinnamon off her lap to the floor.

The pet scampered to Peter's room.

Daed got up and went after him. "I'll open Peter's door. I don't want the mutt to wake him up scratching at the door to get in. I'll leave you girls to talk, and I'll head on to bed."

The women nodded.

Ellie held up her palms in question. "Nah. I'm hoping he'll show up at the bakery sometime this week."

"I'm anxious to spend some time with Mrs. Wenger. I'm not happy about her dismissing you over gossip. Let's you and I visit her one day soon and shower her with kindness. We'll take an assortment of our cookies to her for a gift."

"I'm nervous about speaking with her. If you go with me, maybe she'll at least be civil." Ellie twisted her hands together. She didn't want to address any concerns Joel's mamm might have gleaned through gossip. She had moved on with her life, and there was no need to look back. She would have a serious discussion with Joel at some point, but not until the time was right.

"You should have the conversation with Joel about your adventures before we chat with Mrs. Wenger. The ultimate decision is up to you. Be careful you don't make things worse by avoiding what you must do."

"I'm going to wait. We'll visit Mrs. Wenger and have a light conversation and avoid any difficult questions. Joel and I are having such a good time together. I don't want to spoil it." She kissed Liza on the forehead. "Get a good night's sleep."

In her room, Ellie dressed in her nightclothes and

got in bed. She pulled the covers to her chin and stared at the ceiling, wide-awake. She rehearsed the conversation she'd have with Joel. Her hands gripped the sheet. Men, Amish or otherwise, wanted a potential fraa with a good reputation in the community. Not one with a tarnished past full of rebellion and wrongdoings. The repercussions of her bad behavior could destroy any chance with not only Joel, but of any future as an Amish man's fraa.

She didn't want anyone but Joel. She had justified her actions in her head at the time, but confessing the story to Joel sounded terrible to her, as if she were talking about someone else. She had been naïve to assume he or any Amish man would overlook the way she spent her time in the outside world. Joel might sever ties with her. Her heart plummeted. A crack of bright lightning lit up the room, and thunder boomed, rattling the lantern. She shivered and pulled the covers closer.

Ellie accepted a plate of assorted pies from Hannah Wednesday morning at the bakery counter. "The cinnamon and sugar juices are oozing out of the apple pie, and it smells so delicious. You must've just taken this one out of the oven."

"I did." She pointed to the other pie. "And I added extra cinnamon to this one."

Two tall men ducked under the doorframe and approached the counter. They sported thick mustaches and mirrored each other.

One of the men snarled and waved his hand. "George, stop annoying me. I love the Yanks, so don't go putting 'em down. They made a big win at Hilltop Stadium. I'm proud of 'em."

George rolled his eyes. "Sports is a waste of time, Nub. You should be farmin' instead of wastin' your time readin' and keepin' up with 'em in the newspaper."

"You have your nose in the paper most days."

George stepped back and huffed. "I read the important news and then get to work."

Ellie swallowed the chuckle threatening to escape. These men, she guessed around sixty, bantered worse than Dr. Harrison and the sheriff. Their long faces with large noses, narrow eyes, and small, thin lips looked similar. "May I help you?"

"I'm Nub, and this here is my brother, George. We're passin' through and thought we'd stop in and get us some treats." He waved George over. "What do ya want, George?"

George bent and scanned the shelves. "How 'bout a loaf of oat bread and some cherry tarts, and I'll take some of those butter cookies."

Nub read the sign for prices and set coins on the counter. "We'll take what he said and add an apple pastry. Thank you, darlin'."

George smacked his lips. "Now don't go callin' her darlin'. It's rude."

"I'm bein' neighborly, not fresh. Stop tryin' to embarrass me, you ol' goat."

Nub gave a sheepish shrug. "I didn't mean no disrespect."

"Ever since our wives died and we moved in together ten years ago, I've had to get on him about his manners." George waved a dismissive hand at his bruder. "Don't pay him no mind. He means well."

"None taken. Danki for kumming in." She handed him his packaged purchases.

The men bid her farewell and left.

She laughed and held her stomach. The men had added to her already cheerful day. How wonderful the two men were close and had each other after their wives had passed. If Peter hadn't kumme along, she wouldn't have had a sibling to share life with, like these two men. Meeting them had reminded her how fortunate she was to have a little bruder.

Joel rushed in. "The clouds are dark. Rain is kumming. I should've waited until a better time, but I couldn't wait to speak to you. Will you kumme to supper tonight?"

Her stomach churned. She would be nervous around Mrs. Wenger. She'd engage her in conversation and attempt to nurture a friendship with her. "Danki for the invitation. You don't have to pick me up. I'll drive my buggy over."

"Nah, I'd rather we travel together. It will be dark earlier, and I don't want you going home by yourself."

"I appreciate it." She passed him a ginger cookie. "How did your mamm take the news about Abigail?"

Joel's smile faded. "She was hurt and shocked. Abigail had shown her a more compassionate side. She'll miss her. Abigail and Mamm might have had a special bond. Although Abigail never seemed to do anything without motive."

"Abigail is hard to figure out."

He took off his hat and rubbed the back of his neck. "I'll warn you. She's been tainted by Abigail, so it won't be easy. I've been as positive as I can about you, and it's important to me that you and she get along."

"It's important to me as well." Her cheeks heated and her heart thudded in her chest. She was tired of having to defend herself. "Your mamm is being unfair to judge me so harshly based on gossip and Abigail's tales." She dug her nails into her hands. She stopped short. Her last sentence could bring up the very conversation she wanted to avoid. She tightened her lips.

Joel held his hat to his side and lifted her chin with his forefinger. "I'm praying about Mamm and you. I'm confident God has a plan, and he'll work this out."

She gave him a weak grin. "I'll pray about this too."

"I'd better get ahead of this rain. I'll be at your haus at five thirty." He hurried out the door.

Hannah and Liza burst into the room and faced her.

"We confess." Hannah held up her hands. "We listened to your conversation with Joel. You were a little defensive with him about his mamm. Why? He can't control her behavior."

Ellie put her elbows on the counter and fists under her chin. "The woman has been told the worst about me from the tattletales and Abigail. She pinches her lips and squints each time we meet, but I'm determined to befriend her and show her I am a good fit for Joel and their family." She shook her head. "No doubt I'll need God to perform a miracle in Mrs. Wenger's heart."

"You could've asked me to watch the counter, taken Joel outside, and addressed what the gossips are saying about you." Hands on Ellie's shoulders, Liza looked directly into her eyes. "Again, you put it off. The gossips don't have the details. You do. He should be told, Ellie."

"I don't want to talk about it." Ellie darted her eyes to the window. "I'll put my best smile on and work hard to befriend his parents. Then I'll tell him."

Hannah wiped a dab of flour off Ellie's hand. "You'll do fine."

"I'm rooting for you and Joel. I just know how important it is to both of you to have both sets of parents blessing your relationship. If you marry, you're tied to his family too. God doesn't want dissention." Liza moved to the kitchen's open doorway.

Hannah gave her friend's arm a squeeze. "Remember, with God all things are possible." She followed Liza to the kitchen.

Ellie loved Hannah. Leah and Eva were her friends, but Hannah was her true best friend. She could trust her to keep her secrets, and Hannah understood her. The door opened, and Ellie went back behind the counter, ready to serve the customers. An older woman dressed in a smart red hat matching her thick wool coat and a girl about Ellie's age in a green, heavy, wool shawl studied the shelves. They both stood frowning.

"Did you have something in mind today?"

The older woman's dark eyes glared at the young woman next to her. "I'm Mrs. Jackson, and this is my daughter-in-law, Julia. The girl hardly opens her mouth. It's no wonder. She doesn't like to make decisions, cook, or sew."

Ellie, red-faced, bristled at Mrs. Jackson's outburst about Julia. She wanted to wrap protective arms around the thin girl. Her heart broke for the girl with worried green eyes and quivering lips. "I'm not good at sewing either. My stepmamm and my best friend are doing their best to teach me, and I'm getting better. Maybe Julia just needs more time."

Mrs. Jackson glared at Ellie. "Listen here, young lady. I am out of patience with her. She ran off from one husband and talked my son into marrying her."

Tears trickled down Julia's face. "You're embarrassing me."

Mrs. Jackson scoffed. "I'm sure your poor decisions in life are the talk of the town and this isn't news to anyone." She pressed a hand to her temple. "I brought you here to get you out of the haus and to buy my son some wonderful surprise desserts. Now pick out what he'd want."

"Oatmeal cookies are his favorite."

Ellie removed Julia's selection. "Will there be anything else for you?"

Mrs. Jackson frowned. "Trade the oatmeal cookies for the butter ones. I'm sure he'd like those better."

Ellie struggled to remain cordial. "Take both. The oatmeal cookies are our gift." She winked at Julia as Mrs. Jackson dug in her reticule for coins.

Julia mouthed, "Thank you."

Mrs. Jackson paid for their purchases. "You have a lovely bakery. I love the aroma of fresh cookies, tarts, pastries, and breads. I'll be back. Now come along, Julia."

Ellie bid them farewell. Mrs. Jackson was horribly rude to Julia. How did Julia stand listening to the woman berate her? There would be no escaping the miserable woman since she was married to Mrs. Jackson's son. A shiver ran through her. She'd be upset if she had to give up Joel for this reason. Her conversation tonight with his parents would be a telling indicator of their future.

Hannah came to Ellie holding a cookie. "Try this."

Ellie grinned and eyed Liza and Hannah as she took a bite. The cookie melted in her mouth. Sugar, cinnamon, and strawberry juice rolled over her tongue. "I love the addition of the strawberry flavor with the cinnamon, but I wouldn't have thought to put them together."

Liza waved her hands. "I worked hard to get just the right amount of each ingredient to create a good strawberry cookie. We've got plenty of strawberry jam."

"The fluffiness of the cookie is appealing, and the flavor is light and refreshing."

"I agree." Hannah accepted the rest of Ellie's cookie and plopped it in her mouth. "Maybe you should take some of these to Joel's parents. The gift might give your evening a pleasant start." She winked.

Liza clapped the flour dust from her hands. "I'll put a plate of them together for you."

"Danki!" Ellie would do all she could to change Mrs. Wenger's opinion of her. Strawberry cookies couldn't hurt. She couldn't wait to talk to Joel again. They never ran out of topics to discuss, and she could gaze into his big blue eyes forever. The thought of letting him go for any reason made her heart heavy.

Joel went to Daed in the pigpen. "I've invited Ellie to supper. I'm interested in her as a potential fraa. Of course, it depends on how things progress between all of us. I'd appreciate your effort to befriend her."

Daed stopped filling the pigs' feed trough. "Have you told Mamm?"

Joel shook his head. "I wanted to tell you first."

"She may not approve of the idea."

"I really care about Ellie, Daed. Will you help me out with Mamm? Ellie's important to me."

Daed kept his head down and tiptoed around his mamm to avoid any arguments. Joel needed his daed to stand firm with him on inviting Ellie to their home and treating her with kindness and respect.

"All right, Son. Let's go find your mamm." He set

the bucket down and draped his arm around Joel's shoulders.

They went inside the haus and found Mamm sweeping out the mudroom.

"Is everything all right? You both look serious." The broom upright, she rested her hand on the top of the handle.

"I asked Ellie for supper this evening."

"You're not giving me much notice, young man."

"Please don't make this difficult for me. Ellie doesn't care what we serve." He sighed. "I realize you don't care for her, but you've not given her a fair chance."

Daed stood next to him. "We should extend a warm wilkom to any of Joel's friends he brings home. Let's get better acquainted with Ellie and put what the gossips have told you aside."

Joel wrinkled his brow. "Has Mamm told you what the gossips have said about Ellie?"

"Nah. She understands I don't have any interest in rumors."

Mamm sneered. "There's always an ounce of truth in what they say. *Trouble* is the word they use when they mention her name. The gossips say not to trust her."

"Enough talk about Ellie." Daed tilted his head and crossed his arms.

Mamm narrowed her eyes. "Joel, has she told you about her past?"

"Not yet. If there's something notable to tell, I'm sure she will discuss it with me at some point. We're looking forward to the future, and I don't necessarily care about her past."

"I'm not promising you I'll accept her with open arms." Mamm gripped the broom and swept the dirt from the mud floor, stirring up dust.

Daed motioned him outside, and they walked to the barn. "Son, let's leave your mamm alone until Ellie arrives. She's informed Ellie is kumming this evening, and let's not give her an opportunity to ask you to get out of it."

"What about the place she sets for Maryann? Will she abide by your wishes to not set a place setting for Maryann when we have company?"

"You haven't told Ellie about your schweschder?"

"Nah. I would rather not. She would probably want nothing to do with me if she learned of Mamm's fixation and the shame Maryann has put on our family by running off with an Englischer."

"You're wrong to keep it from her, and you may be underestimating her." He patted Joel's back. "I trust Mamm will honor my request."

Hours later, Joel sniffed the aromas of chicken and vegetable stew and fresh baked bread filling the haus. Maybe Mamm had had time to reflect on her bad attitude and she was going to make a positive effort to wilkom Ellie.

He called out to his parents, "I'm going to get Ellie. I'll be right back."

Daed came from the hallway. "All right. We'll be ready."

"Danki, Daed." Joel waited for Mamm's response. *Nothing.* He tensed, got his buggy ready, and headed to Ellie's haus.

She was waiting on the porch. Beautiful with her flawless pale skin and sweet smile. His heart skipped a beat each time he encountered her.

He got down and tied his horse to the post. "I should speak to your parents before we leave."

"They're in the kitchen. Let's go in." She went in and waited for him to follow her. "Mamm, Daed, Joel is here."

Her parents came to the front room. "Joel, it's so nice of you and your parents to have Ellie over." Liza handed Ellie a plate. "Here's your cookies."

Joel put his nose inches above the plate. "Strawberry?"

"Jah, and they are delicious. They're made with strawberry jam. I hope your parents like them."

He chuckled. "They both love strawberries, so I'm sure they will. Danki."

Joel and Ellie bid the Grabers farewell and left.

Joel coaxed the mare to a fast trot. "Are you nervous?"

"Very."

"Don't be. I'll be right by your side. My daed is easier to talk to than Mamm, but I'm confident she'll kumme around." He pulled the buggy into the woods out of sight. "I need to talk to you in private before we join my parents." He had to tell her about his schweschder. He couldn't trust Mamm not to mention Maryann or what happened. It would be best kumming from him. He hoped it wouldn't discourage her from wanting to associate with him or his family. Amish were kind to the families who suffered such a loss, but most parents didn't want their sons or dochders to marry into such a family, as if rebellion and desertion were contagious. He stared at her sweet lips and couldn't stand it another minute. He pulled her to him and kissed her gently.

She didn't discourage him but rested her hands on his arms. He loved her. He hadn't believed his friends who claimed to have fallen for their fraas at first sight, but now he understood. He couldn't deny the strong connection he had with Ellie the first time they'd met, and it had grown each time they were together.

She gazed at him with her sky-blue eyes. "You can tell me anything, Joel."

"My schweschder, Maryann, and I were close growing up. It broke my parents' and my hearts when she left the Amish life to marry an Englischer. Mamm hasn't given up she'll return. She keeps her room the same, sets a place for her at supper, and makes blankets, bonnets, and dresses for her. Mamm's carefree, loving, and kind mood most of the time has turned bitter, angry, and sad. Daed and I have tried to help her adjust, but to no avail. She insists Maryann wouldn't have left if it wasn't for the smooth talk of her husband. She blames him rather than Maryann."

Ellie dabbed the tears pooling in her eyes with the back of her hand. "I'm sorry for the pain your mamm is going through."

Joel hadn't expected such an emotional reaction from Ellie. She understood and truly cared. "I was afraid you wouldn't want to associate with our family after I told you about Maryann."

"Maryann's decision has no bearing on us. I understand completely."

Joel noticed two hunters in the distance. He didn't want to leave, but he didn't want to tarnish Ellie's reputation and give the men the impression they were doing anything wrong. He urged the horse to go toward home. "Danki for understanding, Ellie. Mamm may be hard to befriend at first. She's taken to heart all the gossip she's been told about not trusting you for some reason."

Ellie stiffened. "Our Amish teaching states we aren't to listen to gossip. Gossips can be cruel, as I'm sure you've learned from when your schweschder left. We aren't to pay them any mind."

"Don't worry. I don't."

Joel drove home and halted the buggy near Daed, who was waiting outside, and hopped out.

Daed approached the buggy and nodded a wilkom. "Ellie, I'm glad you're joining us this evening for supper."

"Danki, Mr. Wenger. It's a pleasure to be here." She stepped out and onto the ground.

"You call me Shem." He gestured to the front door. "You two go on in. I'll take care of the mare and be right behind you." Daed hurried to take the reins from him.

"I appreciate your help with the buggy, Daed."

"No problem. You enjoy your time with this lovely young lady." He winked.

Ellie blushed. "Your daed is a sweetheart. He's got your same sandy blond hair and kind blue eyes."

"He does, and we're close. He is patient with Mamm, but he asks her not to discuss Maryann when we have company and to abstain from setting a place for her at mealtimes. He shuts my schweschder's bedroom door whenever anyone is kumming so they don't notice the clothes Mamm's made for her on the bed."

"Does he believe Maryann will return?"

"Nah, he and I accept she's married and made her choice. We practice shunning her as the Amish law dictates. Mamm's refusal to follow the law puts us at risk. The bishop and most Amish folk wouldn't be happy with what's she's doing. I pray she'll accept Maryann's departure, heal her broken heart, and return to the kind and sweet woman my daed married."

Ellie gave him a tight-lipped smile and turned her head.

Joel frowned. Ellie had been distant since he'd told her about Maryann. It was strange. She'd been compassionate and hadn't hesitated to say she understood about Maryann. A fast response to a sticky situation. Not one most Amish would give. They might have even scolded him for bringing up the subject. He wrinkled his forehead. Something was wrong. "You've changed since leaving your haus. Is it my story about Maryann?"

Ellie's face paled, and she opened her mouth to speak, but Mrs. Wenger met them at the door. "Ellie, kumme in."

"Mrs. Wenger, your supper smells good. Danki for having me."

Joel bit his tongue. A hard glint appeared in his mamm's eyes as she examined Ellie from head to toe. Her mouth set in a grim line didn't bode well either. This would be a long night. "Would you like something to drink, Ellie, while we wait for supper?"

"Water, please."

Joel waited for his mamm to offer to fetch it. He didn't want to leave the women alone. He didn't trust what his mamm might say.

Mamm waved her hand at him. "What are you waiting for, Joel? I'll stay with Ellie while you go to the kitchen. There's a pitcher on the counter."

He hurried to pour the water into a glass and crossed to the open doorway.

Mamm had her hands folded in her lap, and her back straight. "Joel's busy helping us get settled. He doesn't have much time for socializing with you. I'm sure you understand."

Joel hurried into the room and fought to control

the scolding rising in him. Before Ellie could answer, he went in and handed Ellie a glass of water. "Mamm, your stew might be overheating or burning."

"Oh no!" His mamm bustled into the kitchen. "I'll be right back."

Ellie gave him a doubtful look and chuckled. "Was the stew really overheating?"

"I may have exaggerated a bit, but I had to rescue you. I apologize for her insinuation I don't have time for you. Let me be clear. I do and want to have time with you."

There it was again. Her smile turned into a frown.

"What's bothering you, besides my mamm's rudeness? You started to say something earlier until Mamm interrupted."

"Supper's ready." Mamm rushed into the room. "Joel, call Shem. Ellie can go ahead and sit at the table."

"We'll kumme to the table together." Joel glanced at Ellie, and she had a look of relief. She'd acted quiet and reserved before they'd encountered his mamm. Something was on her mind. He'd find out before the night's end. He didn't want anything to kumme between them. He nodded and went to the door. He called for his daed, and the man smiled and pointed to the pump. "I'll wash my hands and be right in."

Joel returned and peeked around the open doorway. His mamm and Ellie were setting the stew, bread, and butter on the table.

"Mrs. Wenger, your stew looks wonderful."

Mamm gave Ellie a curt nod. "It's quite good. Now sit, and the men should join us in a minute."

Joel cringed. Ellie was trying hard to please her, and his mamm remained belligerent. He glanced at the table. She hadn't set a plate and utensils for Maryann.

Daed would be pleased. He needed all the help he could get from his daed.

"The table looks beautiful, Mamm. Is there anything you need?"

She waved him to the chair. "Nah. Sit yourself down before the food gets cold."

Daed came in and took his seat. "I'm hungry, and you've made a fine meal, my dear."

Mamm rolled her eyes, ladled stew on their plates, and then sat. She bowed her head and closed her eyes. "Shem, say a prayer for the food."

Daed thanked God for the food and raised his head. He slathered a thick layer of butter on his bread. "I prefer a little bread with my butter, Ellie. How about you?"

She accepted the breadbasket from him. "I love butter too."

Joel sipped his water and then set his glass in front of his plate. "Ellie brought some strawberry cookies for us. I put them on the counter by the hutch."

"Strawberry cookies? I've never tried them." Mamm raised her brows.

Ellie straightened the blue quilted napkin on her lap. "Liza loves to create new recipes. This one is now my favorite cookie. The strawberries were good this year, and we made more jam than usual from them. I hope you like them."

"You can count on me to try them." Daed patted his stomach. "I'll leave plenty of room."

Joel let the tension roll out of his body. The supper was going well. Daed had lightened the mood.

"I've made a sugar cream pie for dessert. The cookies will keep for another day." Mamm stared hard at Ellie.

Joel's face heated. Mamm would grasp at anything to embarrass Ellie. Her attempt to run Ellie out of here and away from him was obvious. "I'm sure Daed and I will have room for both."

Ellie, red-faced, set her spoon on her plate. "Mrs. Wenger, I didn't mean to offend you."

Daed waved his hand. "No need to apologize, Ellie. Your gift is much appreciated by all of us. And call my fraa Naomi. You don't mind, do you, sweetheart?"

She looked at her plate. "I suppose not."

"Ellie, Joel told us how Peter joined your family. He's told us the boy is smart, sweet, and kind."

"He has brought so much joy to our lives. I don't remember what life was like without him."

Joel was thankful Daed was making up for Mamm's behavior. Ellie beamed when she talked to him. And he could tell from Daed's happy demeanor that he approved of Ellie.

"That speaks highly of your family for taking him in when his mamm died."

"Peter also lost a schweschder. He'd become reclusive until we met. I reminded him of her, and we bonded. Our friendship helped with his transition into our family when his mamm passed."

Joel darted a look to his mamm. Would she be impressed at the generosity of Ellie's family taking this little boy into their home? "Peter is an obedient child. I love being around him." He hoped his Mamm would let her guard down.

"We had a dochder. Did Joel tell you about her?" Naomi glared at Ellie.

Shem raised his palm to stop her from talking. "We aren't going to speak about her. I'm sorry, Ellie. My dochder ran away with an Englischer. I realize we shouldn't talk about her. It's been difficult for my fraa."

"I understand, and I'm sorry this happened to you."

Mamm splayed her hand on the table. "Maryann

never gave me any trouble. She was a good girl and loved by many until a persuasive Englischer whisked her away from us. I understand you went on a jaunt without any word to your daed while you lived in Nappanee and then had the nerve to brag about your adventure."

Ellie shot up from the table and pushed her chair back. "I'm not comfortable discussing this. I should go."

Joel and his daed stood.

Joel rushed to her side. "Please stay, Ellie. We'll take our dessert outside. I'll get us some blankets to put around us and build a fire."

"Please listen to Joel, Ellie. My fraa isn't herself. We don't want you to talk about anything you don't want to. Take some time with Joel. He's been looking forward to you kumming, and I've enjoyed your company too." He stared at his fraa. "Apologize for your outburst."

She stared at her plate with her arms crossed and jaw tight. "I'm sorry, Ellie."

Joel held his breath a moment. The apology was insincere. Reminded him of when Mamm scolded him for sneaking a cookie from the jar. He'd apologized for getting caught but not for taking the cookie. Time to separate her from his mamm.

He grabbed wool blankets from a hall cabinet, took a small box of matches, and headed outside with her. "Let's get out of earshot, where we can talk in private."

The trees were losing their leaves and daylight had become shorter. He stacked some wood in the fire pit and kept one blanket and handed her the other. They covered themselves and gazed at the scattered puffy clouds. The air was cool, but not too cold to be outside.

"Tonight was a disaster. I'm sorry, Ellie." He breathed deep and let out a heavy sigh.

Ellie's misery was palpable. She hadn't uttered a word since leaving the haus. What could he say to get her to open up to him?

Ellie wanted to run home, but she didn't have her buggy. The dreaded moment had kumme to tell Joel the truth. She had put off this conversation in hopes Joel would fall in love with her and it would be easier to accept and dismiss her wrongful decisions. *Why tell him?* Even if he could forgive and forget her past, his mamm would never give her a chance. Why was his mamm so unforgiving?

Joel touched her shoulder. "I understand if you want me to take you home, but I would appreciate it if you'd stay and talk to me."

She had fallen in love with him. He had become an important part of her life. She dreaded being apart from him. She couldn't hide behind any more excuses. "I had hoped to postpone this conversation with you until we'd had more time together. Before I tell you my story, please understand I'm faithful to God and committed to live the Amish life for the rest of my days on this earth."

Joel covered her hand with his. "Ellie, what are you talking about?"

She ran her tongue over her teeth and sighed. He didn't realize she was about to shatter both their worlds.

"After Mamm passed, I was angry and upset with everyone and everything. Nothing made sense anymore. Mamm and I were close, and I was devastated without her. The pain of losing her grew worse each day. Jane and her bruder, both Englischers, introduced themselves to me in downtown Nappanee. Jane was sweet, interesting, and caring."

Joel removed his hand from hers. "What was your relationship with Jane's bruder?"

"I didn't have any romantic notions for him. He left Jane and me alone most of the time." Maybe she shouldn't blurt out her story all at once. She'd stay silent and let him ask questions.

"Did you tell your daed about meeting the Englischers?"

"He wouldn't have approved." She held the blanket tight. Her heart pounded in her chest. "I told Jane I was curious about the world, and she coaxed me to try it. Jane understood my loss, since her parents had passed a few years before. She and Duke still lived in the family haus. Duke managed the farm and animals, and she made a good living altering clothes for townsfolk. She invited me to stay with them and learn more about the outside world. We formed a friendship, and I longed for the escape. One day, I left with Jane and Duke and didn't tell Daed where I was going."

Joel's mouth opened, as his eyes grew wide. "Your daed is one of the most easygoing and kindest men I've met. He must have been worried sick about you. How could you do such a thing?"

Her chest tightened. His judgment hurt worse than she'd imagined. The realization of what Daed must've gone through came rushing back, and the ugly guilt she'd fought to forget slithered through her.

She'd delayed her confession to Joel for selfish reasons. She cringed. She didn't want to relive this part of her life and have to vomit out the details of the pain and hurt she'd caused her daed and friends. "I lashed out from grief by trying to escape the Amish life and Daed and anything reminding me of Mamm. Going with Jane and Duke provided a different location and type of living. Somewhere I wouldn't be reminded of the life Mamm and I shared."

"Did you wear Englischer clothes?" He rose and paced. "What did you do to participate in the outside world?"

She swiped her tearstained cheeks with the backs of her hands. His agitation and stern voice were expected but hard to face.

She didn't want to divulge any more information than she had to. "I did wear the clothes. Jane provided them. I'm not sure how much I'm comfortable sharing with you. I have a hard time reliving this again. The grief over Mamm and shame of what I've done is rushing back."

Joel gazed at her, his jaw set. "You need to tell me everything if we're going to continue our relationship."

She flexed her hands and folded them tight until her knuckles turned white. She couldn't stand to lose him, but she feared the worst. She groaned. "Please, Joel. Let's leave the past where it belongs."

He stopped pacing and looked at her. "Ellie, tell me everything."

"I went to a dance, listened to piano music, and read the newspaper often." She focused on the dead, dry leaves near the blanket, not far from her feet. Like them, her relationship with Joel was dying.

He huffed. "Did you dance with strangers?"

Her breath caught in her throat. This conversation was going from bad to worse. "I did, but nothing happened. I didn't go anywhere with them. They were all gentlemen."

"What changed your mind to kumme back to your daed?"

"Duke had kumme home in a bad mood one evening. He grabbed my arm to pull me to him. I pushed him away. Jane rescued me from him and told him to leave me alone. He did, and he went to bed. Jane took me home the next day. I wasn't safe there any longer."

"So you didn't kumme home to ask forgiveness?"

She hadn't been ready to ask for forgiveness when she returned. How could she make him understand the horrible grief that had made her angry, frustrated, sad, and in so much pain? She couldn't reconcile it in her own mind. She'd justified her actions at the time. Now, she understood she'd been sinful and irresponsible. "Nah. I was still upset about Mamm and losing my close friendship with Jane once I'd returned to my Amish community. I boasted about my time in the world, and I proved a challenge for Daed. I regret all of it." She stole a glance at Joel and ached at the shock reflected in his face. "I'm remorseful about all my dreadful actions."

He threw his hat on the ground and combed his fingers through his sandy blond hair. "I am stunned at what you've told me. You're not the girl I imagined. You as a rebellious, disobedient, and somewhat wild girl is far from the Ellie I know."

She stood. He'd been faithful to God as he mourned the loss of Maryann from his life. Would he ever really grasp why she may have reacted in this way?

She gazed at him. "I promise you, Joel, you can trust me."

"Ellie, I'm confused and disappointed." He sat back on the blanket and stared at the fire.

She pressed her hands to her cheeks. She had to

tell him everything. She wanted to erase the tension between them, but she had to tell him the rest. She cringed. "My rebellion didn't stop there." She studied her shaking hands. "Bill Phillips befriended me in town. We met and talked without Daed's knowledge. He was a good listener and empathetic, and we became friends. He had a horrible daed, and I hadn't overcome my need to rebel. We planned to run away. He took me to his aunt and uncle's haus." She met his gaze. "We stayed in separate rooms, and nothing inappropriate happened. We were never more than friends."

"You left twice!" He stood and backed away from her. "Did you tell your daed where you were going this time?"

She kept her head down. "Nah. I didn't tell Daed a thing. And jah, I left the Amish life twice." Joel's disappointment sent chills through her body.

"Were you falling in love with him?"

He glared at her, and she knew a wrong answer could sever their relationship for good. Not one doubt could be left in his mind about Bill. She'd never been so glad than at this moment that she'd not thought of Bill as anything more than a friend. "Nah!" She shook her head. "He wanted more than friendship, but I didn't care for him as more than a friend. He understood."

"How did his aunt and uncle receive you?"

"They wilkomed me, and his aunt took me under her wing. She loves God and her family. I'll always be grateful to her. She helped me heal. I asked Bill to bring me home, and by this time, I had changed. I desired to follow God and the Amish life. God, my family, and friends forgave me, and I will remain forever thankful."

"Is there anything you've left out?"

"There is more. Bill's daed passed our haus soon after he'd brought me home. He threatened Bill and Daed with a rifle. He was angry at Bill and blamed me for our leaving Charm. Mr. Phillips isn't fond of the Amish. He has a reputation in town as a bully and troublemaker. He held Daed responsible for raising such a rebellious dochder and blamed me for taking Bill away from him. He set fire to our fence, which could've destroyed much of our property had Daed not caught it in time. Another time, Mr. Phillips threatened to harm Daed when he went looking for me at their home before I came back." Her stomach churned. She'd have held herself as responsible as the troublemaker if he'd ended her daed's life. "I'm remorseful about it to this day."

She sighed and clutched her arms. She wouldn't blame Joel if he ran as fast as he could away from her. But she prayed he would stay and give her the chance she didn't deserve.

"What did Bill do?"

"Mr. Phillips left in a huff. The sheriff stopped by later and told us Mr. Phillips had gone to the saloon and gotten in a brawl, injuring a man. The sheriff had locked him in jail. Daed didn't approve of Bill taking me away, but he and Bill talked. Daed trusted me when I told him Bill had not been dishonorable to me in any way and he had remained a friend. Daed listened to Bill, and he had empathy for him and his mamm. He offered Bill money to help him out. Bill went home and asked his mamm to leave with him, and she agreed. They fled town and went to live with his aunt and uncle."

"You went to great lengths to ruin your reputation and hurt your daed." He glowered at her and shook his head. "You not only brought danger to yourself but others. The opposite of what Amish are taught from the time they are kinner. We abhor trouble and violence. Didn't you realize the effect your actions would have on your family?"

"Stop, Joel. Please stop. I have to live with what I did, and repeating it to you makes me sick about it all over again. God's and my family's and friends' unconditional love helped me to get through the pain and discover happiness again. I've told you everything. I can't talk about this anymore. You have to decide if you can put this behind you and move forward with me." She shifted her gaze to her shoes.

"I've never understood kinner practicing rumspringa. Kinner running off to explore their selfish desires and turning their backs on God and their parents. Going against everything they've been taught and what's proven to be the best for them. What you did was worse. You left no word as to your whereabouts, and you returned with the same obstinate attitude and then left again. This time almost getting your daed murdered."

He backed up to the large oak tree trunk and leaned against it, crossing his arms. "I don't understand you or Maryann. I don't believe she was curious about the world. She was gullible, and I think this Englischer husband of hers made a big impression and she fell in love with him. I doubt she would've left if it wasn't for him, but not because she wanted to explore what the world had to offer. I'm still frustrated with her for leaving. She was foolish." He narrowed his eyes. "You sought out an escape. No one pushed you to leave with them."

Her face heated, and her mind raced. She fought to control her tongue. "No one is without sin, Joel Wenger. Not even you. I imagine you'll regret some of your harsh words to me as you ponder our conversation later. I don't recognize this side of you." She understood this information might have shocked him, but there was no need to let him go on and on with his scolding.

She went to him. "I've learned from my mistakes. I can't change my past, and I can't speak for Maryann, but you shouldn't judge either of us. I reacted to grief over my mamm by running away from my life and everything familiar, but I returned and repented." Her lips quivered. "Love is powerful. And I do believe God never leaves or forsakes us if we truly believe in him, whether we're Amish or not."

He huffed. "Ellie, even if I agree to work toward a future with you, regardless of what you've told me, I have my family to consider. Maryann has caused such great pain to my parents. What if my parents accept and love you, and we marry one day, and then we suffer a tragedy? How do I know you won't react by running away and breaking our hearts? I can't take the risk."

Her heart plummeted, and tears pooled in her eyes. "Joel, what are you saying?"

"I'm saying you've shattered any chance of a future for us with this tale."

She wrung her hands and didn't touch the tears wetting her cheeks. "But, Joel, what about forgiveness?"

He held her gaze, and his voice softened. "I forgive you, Ellie. I just can't forget it."

She didn't care if the gesture was improper, she had to connect with him. She reached out to touch his arm but dropped her hand to her side. Her heart couldn't withstand his rejection if he jerked away. "Please, Joel. I don't want our chance for a future to end." She was certain she'd never love anyone like she did him. His schweschder's leaving the Amish life had tainted his view and made her revelation much worse for him to take in. She was sure of it. She had to convince him he had nothing to worry about. "I promise you, no matter what happens in our lives, I would never leave you if our relationship leads to marriage."

His face reddened. "Love means being honest. You kept your past from me, knowing the gossips were right about you. How could you?" He raked fingers through his thick, sandy blond hair. "I refused to believe Abigail or what Mamm had been told about you. I wouldn't even let them speak about it to me. You should have told me right away about your past. Instead, you were deceitful."

She stood erect. "Deceitful!"

"Jah. You should've told me sooner. Instead, you waited in the hopes I'd fall for you, to make it harder for me to leave if I couldn't accept what you've told me today. Well done. You succeeded. It is hard to walk away from you, but I won't live a life wondering if you'll revert back to your old ways." He walked away from her, then glanced over his shoulder. "I'll take you home. I don't have anything more to say." He untied his mare and waited for her to get in, and they left.

She fisted her hands under her chin. The silent and short ride home was long. She couldn't shake the sadness and ache of regret filling her from head to toe. Liza had warned her more than once to tell Joel sooner

rather than later about her abrupt exits from Nappanee and Charm. The cost of her delay in telling him
had been him leaving her. His set jaw and accusations
of deceit didn't lend much hope for a reconciliation.

He halted the buggy. "Please give your parents my
regards."

She got out of the buggy and turned to ask him if
he'd stay and talk more. She didn't want to let him go.
Especially not like this.

He tugged on the reins and left in haste.

Tears wet her cheeks. She swiped them from her
face and swallowed. She'd steal a few minutes before
going inside the haus. She paced back and forth in
front of the smokehaus. She had lost him for good. It
hurt so much.

Liza came outside. She patted the bench close by.
"Kumme sit."

Ellie plopped next to her.

Liza circled her shoulders in a hug. "I noticed you
alone and pacing. What's wrong?"

Ellie wrapped her arms around Liza and rested her
head on her stepmamm's shoulder. "You were right.
Delaying telling Joel about what I'd done was the
wrong thing to do." She cried and clung to Liza in the
silence.

Liza kissed Ellie's hair. "I'm sorry you're suffering.
I'd do anything to take this pain from you. Would it
help if Jacob spoke to him on your behalf?"

Ellie separated from Liza and shook her head. She
swiped her cheeks with the backs of her hands. "He
has a good relationship with you and Daed. I'd rather
not involve you." Ellie told Liza about Maryann. "He's
been scarred by his schweschder's leaving. They were
close. He and I had grown serious about each other.

Now he doesn't trust me. I brought this on myself. I should've been honest. I knew deep in my heart this might happen."

Liza reached for Ellie's hand. "Your confession was a lot for him to absorb. His heart may not let him walk away for good. If God intends for you and Joel to marry one day, it will happen. If not, God will carry you through this difficult time, and your family and friends will too."

"One of the best decisions I ever made was letting go of my fears about you and telling Daed to marry you." She gently squeezed Liza's hand.

"I love you, Ellie. Everything will be all right. The hard part is having patience."

"Patient, I'm not." She managed a weak half-grin. "Do you mind telling Daed? I don't relish rehashing this again right now."

"I'll tell him. Why don't you go to your room and rest?"

Liza rose and pulled Ellie up by her hands. "It's getting chilly. Kumme on. We'll walk inside the haus together."

She nodded and went inside. Daed snored on the settee, and Peter was asleep curled up on a blanket on the floor next to his wooden animals. She grinned at Liza and tiptoed to her room and closed the door. Falling back on her bed, she stared at the ceiling. Tears pooled in her eyes. She loved Joel so much. She never expected her past actions to inflict such heartache. She closed her eyes. "Dear Heavenly Father, forgive me for deceiving Joel. Please bring us back together if it is your will. If not, please give me the strength to get through this. Amen."

She pressed a fist to her heart. The future looked

bleak for her and Joel. Mrs. Wenger didn't approve of her, and now Joel wanted nothing to do with her. If Amish allowed dancing, Mrs. Wenger would be dancing in the streets over their relationship ending.

The future with Joel appeared impossible, but with God, everything was possible. What did God have in mind for them, and would it be together or apart?

"Danki, Daed." She respected Daed for not skirting around Joel and her having parted ways. He'd been good to communicate with her and create their close relationship.

Peter heaved a heavy sigh. "I'm going to miss him around here!"

"I will too." She couldn't stand the thought of food. She drank her coffee and rinsed the mug. "May I fix the two of you more breakfast?"

"Nah, I'm full." Peter slid off his seat and handed her his plate.

Daed waved a hand. "You go pick up Hannah." He tousled Peter's hair. "I'll drop you at the schoolhaus after I clean the kitchen."

"I'll help you, Daed." Ellie picked up a dishrag.

He took it from her. "Nah. You go on. I can handle things here. Hannah will be waiting for you. Your horse and buggy are ready."

She kissed his cheek and Peter's. "Danki. Tell Liza I hope she's better soon."

Her daed opened the kitchen cabinet door. "Will do."

"Have a good day, Ellie!" Peter opened the door for her.

Not long ago, she'd been alone with her daed. She never would've imagined Peter or Liza being in their lives. Her heart was full of love for them, and her life was happier with them in it. She'd miss Liza at the bakery today and hoped she was better by the time she got home. Not knowing what was wrong with her stepmamm concerned her.

She wished her future would include Joel. She'd fantasized what being married to him would entail. He'd farm, and she'd take care of their haus. They'd

Chapter Seven

Ellie went to the kitchen. Peter and Daed were at the table devouring eggs and bacon. She didn't want to ruin their morning with her sadness. She'd put on a good front. "Good morning, you two." She poured herself a cup of coffee. "Where's Liza this fine Thursday morning?"

"She's sick with a tummy ache." Peter smiled at her with milk covering his top lip.

"I insisted she stay home today. She was fine when she came to bed. Around midnight, I woke and went to the outhaus to find her. I knocked on the door, and she told me she'd been making frequent visits there for a couple of hours. She's finally sleeping." Daed reached over and tousled Peter's hair.

Peter giggled and forked another piece of egg.

Ellie sipped her coffee. "I'm concerned about Liza. Should I ask the doctor to kumme and check on her? She hardly ever gets sick."

"Nah. She won't hear of it. She insists she'll be fine. Let's give her a day or so. Might be something she ate." He put his mug in the sink. "I'm sorry about Joel. Liza told us." He rose and kissed her forehead.

laugh, plan for kinner, and have picnics and long walks discussing their days.

She snatched her brown crocheted shawl from the hook by the door and went to her buggy. Breathing in the cool refreshing air, she admired the beautiful pitch-black colt grazing in the neighbor's yard. Anything to take her mind off Joel for a second was good.

She readied her buggy, enjoyed her ride on the way to Hannah's. She arrived and halted the buggy where Hannah stood outside. "Good morning."

Hannah slid in on the bench next to her. "Where's Liza?"

"Sick with an upset stomach. I offered to get the doctor, but Daed said to give her a day or so."

Hannah frowned. "I hope she gets over it soon. She's always so caring about all of us. Is there anything we can do?"

"Nah. I'll run home to check on her and kumme back this afternoon, if you don't mind managing the store. Hopefully, she'll be over her sickness. If not, I'll insist on taking her to the doctor."

"I'll be glad to wait on customers while you go to her. I'm sure your daed will keep an eye on her, but I'll rest easier when she's better and not worse."

"Me too." She frowned. "I've got more bad news."

Hannah slapped her legs and shifted to Ellie. "What?"

"I told Joel about my leaving the Amish life twice, and he was none too happy. He severed ties with me."

Hannah's hands flew to her open mouth. "I'm speechless. I'm so sorry, Ellie."

"It's my fault. I should've listened to your and Liza's advice and told him sooner. Although, I'm not sure it would've mattered. He abhors rumspringa and, let's face it, I didn't practice rumspringa. I left without telling Daed, I came back and boasted about my adventures to you and our friends, and I didn't ask for forgiveness from anyone. I continued to rebel. Then I left again, and both times, with Englisch men."

"But you were friends and nothing inappropriate happened with either of them. There was no romance. Does he understand this?"

"He does, but even when I told Joel the story, I cringed. Just the fact I left with Jane and her bruder, and then with Bill, sounded bad."

"You've changed." Hannah clasped Ellie's fingers and gave them a gentle squeeze.

"My choices were awful. I'm fortunate that when I went to the dance hall with Jane, the men I danced with didn't touch me inappropriately and were gentlemen. She was a good girl, and the owners insisted the patrons be respectful of one another. Jane said they didn't tolerate bad behavior. They kept a sharp eye out while we were there."

"How much did you tell Joel?"

Her shoulders slumped. "Everything."

Hannah blew out a breath. "Even about Mr. Phillips threatening your daed when he found you and Bill?"

She grimaced and nodded. "The entire mess." Joel's disappointed and disgusted expression sickened her. He'd stared at her as if she were a stranger. Had their positions been reversed, she would've been hurt and suspicious about him. She'd have asked the same questions.

"Are you hurt, angry, what?"

"I'm numb and in a fog." She didn't approve of his harsh judgment, but part of her understood it. In time, she prayed he would realize he'd gotten well enough acquainted with her to trust her word. The problem was she had left twice. A hard point to swallow for anyone, let alone Joel. He'd been contemplating a future with a woman who'd committed the very thing he was so against. "I may grow frustrated later."

Ellie and Hannah left the buggy at the livery and crossed Main Street to the bakery.

Ellie unlocked the door, stepped inside, and held it open for Hannah. "I've lost him."

"Not yet. Let him digest all this. You've built up a solid friendship which has blossomed into love. Am I right?"

"Jah, but love isn't enough. You must have trust and dedication. I destroyed his confidence in me. I broke his heart." She ached at his disappointment in her. She'd do anything to fix this. "What can I do, Hannah?"

"Wait. Anything you say or do now would fall on deaf ears. Emotions are high for both of you. Let the dust settle."

She snatched her apron off the hook and tied it behind her neck and waist. "Danki for listening to my woes."

"I'm always here for you." Hannah rubbed Ellie's back. "This will pass, one way or another."

"It's *another* I'm worried about."

"Take one day at a time or one hour at a time to get through it. Whichever is easier, and remember, I'm always available to listen. God has a plan. Joel may be a part of it. Just be patient."

"Liza suggested the same. I'm as patient as a caged bear, but I'm making an effort to remain calm."

Until eight, she mixed flour, sugar, and spices to create cookies across from Hannah on the worktable. "I love to dig my hands in the dough, beat together the ingredients, and breathe in the delicious scents of baked goods."

"Consider baking a good remedy for what ails you." Hannah threw her ball of dough in the air and caught it. "It's fun to use our old recipes and create new ones."

"My favorite is leftover pie crust layered with cinnamon, butter, and sugar. Rolled up and then sliced and baked in the oven." She kissed her floured fingertips. "Delicious!"

"Me too. I'll make some this afternoon to cheer you up."

"Good idea." Hannah had been a surprise gift in her life. Her friend had lifted her mood more times than she could count. She was a good friend to Hannah too, but Hannah had exercised a lot of patience when they first met, putting up with her obnoxious attitude before she'd kumme to her senses.

She glanced at the clock. "Time to open. I'll unlock the door and exchange this dirty apron for a clean one." She switched aprons and opened the door. She gasped. "*Mrs. Wenger.*" She took a breath. "I wasn't expecting to find someone kumming in at the same time I opened the door. Please, kumme in."

"You caught me off guard too." She shook her head, lifted her chin, and brushed by Ellie to the counter. "I'll take three apple tarts and two loaves of nut bread."

Ellie wrapped her purchases. "The apple tarts are no charge today, Mrs. Wenger. A gift to you and your family."

Red-faced, Mrs. Wenger pressed her coins on the counter for full payment for her purchases. She scoffed. "Don't try and butter me up to get in our good graces. I want nothing to do with you. Stay away from Joel." Her lips tight, she hurried out of the store and shut the door behind her.

Ellie fell back against the wall and hung her head. The woman had added to her sadness and frustration

over departing from Joel. Mrs. Wenger was closed off
to Ellie. The woman couldn't even manage a smile
in her direction. Why couldn't she give her credit for
returning to the Amish life? Ellie gripped her apron
and blinked back tears. She had work to do and pon-
dering this any further wouldn't change a thing. She
didn't want to appear sad in front of customers.

Two women came in the bakery.

She grinned at them. "Wilkom."

The women smiled at her.

"Patricia, look at these cherry jam sugar cookies!
I've never thought of using cherry jam in cookies." She
tapped on the glass. "I'll take a dozen, please."

"Diana, I love the flavor of cherry jam. Thank you
for pointing them out." Patricia studied the shelves. "I
must have a dozen of those." She perused the walls
then grinned at Ellie. "Your bakery is lovely." She took
a deep breath. "And is so inviting with all the fresh
bread, cinnamon, and sugar aromas."

"Danki for stopping in. I hope you'll visit us again
soon." She accepted their payment and handed them
their wrapped selections.

She watched the kind Englischers leave. They had
lifted her mood and brightened her day. *A breath of
fresh air would be good.* She opened the door and scanned
the crowded street. Store owners were opening their
doors, sweeping their doorsteps, and waving to each
other.

She tensed. Joel was across the street chatting with
Magdelena Beachy. She groaned. The woman's beauty
had caught her attention the first time she'd gone to
Sunday service in Charm. Under her thin white kapp,
her coal-black hair complimented her flawless skin
and dark brown eyes. She closed the door and ran to

the kitchen. "Hannah, kumme here! Kumme to the window with me."

Hannah followed her. "What's happened?"

She nodded in Joel's direction. "Across the street, Joel is talking with Magdelena. Her smile stretches from here to Nappanee as she talks to him. I can't stand the possibility of him eventually marrying another woman. The terrible thought hadn't entered my mind until now."

"Don't jump to conclusions."

She toyed with her kapp ribbon. "We met the same way. Then next came friendship and, from there, we were falling in love."

Hannah chuckled and covered her mouth. "I'm sorry to laugh, but you're going overboard with your imagination. Joel isn't going to get over you in one day and take up with another woman the next."

"Magdelena is available, beautiful, smart, and the ideal Amish woman for him."

"Everybody's got habits and opinions others may find annoying. She's sweet, but she's too perfect."

"What do you mean?"

"She's picked something from his sleeve three times since I've been watching them, and she's adjusted the pins in her kapp twice. The woman is a perfectionist."

"You're attempting to make me laugh. I appreciate it, but it's not working."

"She is sweet, but you've captured Joel's heart. I doubt he's ready to consider someone new."

"Joel's somewhat of a perfectionist, although I find the trait attractive. They're probably *perfect* for each other." She rolled her eyes. "I'm going to go mad if I don't stop letting my mind go there." She quirked the corner of her mouth. "Earlier, Mrs. Wenger came in and bought tarts and bread. I offered her the tarts at no cost to show kindness. She was nasty to me. I get in trouble by breathing around her."

"The woman frustrates me with the way she treats you. It's uncalled for and ridiculous. Ignore her. Maybe with her being so against you and Joel, you're better off if you aren't considering a future with him. It's important for families to get along."

"I just don't understand her."

Hannah guided her from the window to behind the counter. She reached inside the kitchen door and handed Ellie a plate of cookies. "Dwelling on Mrs. Wenger will add to your sadness over Joel, and it won't accomplish anything. I want to help put some cheer into those bones of yours." She darted around the corner and presented Ellie with a heart-shaped butter cookie. "Just for you."

She accepted the gift. "You're the best, Hannah."

Hannah nudged her. "So are you." She handed her a tray of assorted cookies. "Here are more goodies to fill your shelves." She gasped. "I left white bread in the oven. Maybe for too long!" She dashed to the back room.

The door opened, and Ellie dropped the cookies. She swallowed to wet her dry throat and breathed deep to recover. "Magdelena, um . . . are you looking for anything special?" She hadn't expected to face the girl so soon after watching her with Joel.

"I came in to get molasses cookies, but I'd better help you first." She rounded the corner and stooped to pick up the broken cookies. "I'm sorry if I startled you."

"You're kind to lend me a hand, but I'll clean this mess up after you leave."

Magdelena shook her head. "Nonsense. I'm not in any hurry."

Ellie dragged over a wooden trash bin, and she and Magdelena threw the pieces in it. "I'll sweep and get the rest later. Danki. I appreciate your help."

"Happy to oblige. I'll take a dozen molasses cookies, if you have enough. Liza's recipe is the best." She paid for her purchases. "Ellie, I noticed you and Joel talking a lot after the Sunday service meals. Are you and he planning a future or are you just friends? I ran into him in town, and I plan to ask him to supper unless he's taken."

Ellie struggled to answer her. She wanted to tell Magdelena she loved Joel and to please stay away from him. She wouldn't do such a thing. She had no hold on him. Joel was clear he wouldn't plan a future with her. She hoped in time he would return to her. She bit her bottom lip. Joel wouldn't appreciate her pushing Magdelena away from him. She wouldn't risk being perceived as controlling or unfair. She'd tell her the truth. She swallowed the hurt. "We're friends."

Magdelena's smile couldn't get any wider. "Danki, Ellie."

Ellie fell back against the wall behind the counter after Magdelena departed. Magdelena was a perfectionist, all right. The annoying woman had even cleaned up Ellie's mess. And it was thoughtful of her. The woman couldn't be friendlier, which made it harder to resent her for being interested in Joel.

Hannah passed through the open doorway from the kitchen. "I had my hands full in the kitchen when I heard you drop the tray of cookies, or I would've thrown them away for you. I recognized Magdelena's voice? Am I right?"

"I'm afraid so."

"What do you mean?"

"She asked if Joel was available. I had to tell her jah,

but I almost choked on my answer. She's perfect for him. No ugly past, beautiful, smart, polite, and probably for a boatload of other reasons. I find her very likeable. I'm sure he will too."

"He could've pursued her, but he chose you." Hannah squeezed Ellie's arm. "Why don't you go and check on Liza. The trip home might be the distraction you need from Joel."

"Danki, Hannah. I promise I won't be long." She lifted her shawl off the metal hook by the door and crossed the road to the livery. She greeted friends and customers going in and out of the stores, got her buggy, and went home. She waved to her daed working in the garden, and then went inside to the sitting room. "Liza, you're dressed and up. I'm surprised. How are you?"

Liza sipped her hot tea. "I'm doing much better. Nothing to worry about. I'm sure whatever it was, I'm over it. I kept a biscuit and this tea in my stomach, and I'll be back to work tomorrow. I'm sorry to leave you and Hannah to run the bakery by yourselves today."

Ellie batted the air. "Don't be silly. We're worried about you. You take it easy. I'll make supper tonight."

"Your daed said he'd make eggs, pancakes, and bacon. I believe the man would live on breakfast food for all three meals a day if we'd let him." She chuckled.

"Jah, he would."

"How are you doing?" Liza leaned forward and brushed Ellie's cheek with the back of her fingers.

"I'm heartsick over Joel. I'd give anything to make the pain go away." She kept her chin down but looked up at Liza. "Magdelena and Joel were laughing and talking in town. I happened to look outside the bakery window and caught them. I can't stand the thought of him being interested in another woman. And she's a lovely person."

"Ellie, he's going to need time to get over you too. And maybe he'll find you're the one for him. These days apart will be sad and upsetting, but you will heal or you'll get back together. God will make sure of it. In the meantime, we love you and I'm always here to listen."

"Having you listen and give me advice does help." She glanced at the clock. "I should get back to the bakery. Hannah might be swamped with customers." She stood. "I'm relieved you're better." She kissed Liza's cheek.

"Hug Hannah for me."

"I will. Love you." Ellie rushed out and went back to work.

Hannah had a line of four customers. "Ellie, I'll help you wait on customers until I go to the kitchen. We're almost out of oatmeal cookies."

"All right. Danki." Ellie hung up her shawl.

They waited on the customers until the store emptied. Hannah had worried eyes. "How's Liza?"

"She's drinking hot tea, and she had a biscuit. Both agreed with her. She's on the mend and plans to join us tomorrow."

Hannah grinned. "I'm thankful it's nothing serious."

"I'm sorry you got bombarded while I was away."

"I had one customer at a time until the last few minutes before you came in. Being alone does make me appreciate having you and Liza with me."

"We make a good crew. I didn't imagine working at a bakery. I really love it. The aromas, creating new recipes, and, best of all, working with you and Liza. The sheriff and Dr. Harrison keep me entertained each morning, and it's fun to talk with the customers.

Most of them, I should say. Some can be rude." She pushed a stray hair back in her kapp. "Being here also helps ease the agony of Joel and me parting."

"I love digging my hands in dough, forming cookie balls, and selling goods people enjoy. I find working here rewarding and fun. Devouring our creations ourselves is even better!" She laughed. "But I've got to stop." She patted her middle. "Or I'm not going to fit in my dresses."

"Me too!"

"I'm going to the kitchen to bake. You're much better at the counter than I am. I'm too slow!"

"You do fine." She watched Hannah go to the back. She couldn't get her mind off Mrs. Wenger's earlier visit to the bakery. The woman was like a herd of cows standing in the road. She'd like to grow a civil relationship with Mrs. Wenger. She didn't relish having ill feelings with anyone. But how could she go about it?

Joel bought long nails from the hardware store and avoided the bakery. Ellie had revealed difficult news for him to swallow. She'd been obstinate, disobedient, and rebellious for a while after her mamm's death. Had he met her then, he wouldn't have given her any consideration as a potential fraa. The Ellie he knew was sweet, compassionate, kind, and faithful to God. She spoke her mind but in an appropriate manner. The Ellie she'd told him about was the opposite of this.

Right or wrong, she'd accomplished having him fall in love with her before she spilled her true history. He couldn't shake the fact she'd made bad decisions. No coaxing or prodding. She'd sought to flee to the outside world. The Englischers provided her a way out. She claimed she'd not done anything inappropriate with the men she left with both times. He believed her. She could've omitted some of what she'd told him to make it easier on herself, but she'd been honest. He'd asked direct questions, and she'd answered them. He respected her for her honesty, but it was too late . . . or was it? He rubbed his forehead. She wasn't easy to forget. She still had a hold on his heart.

He ached and couldn't think straight since their troubling discussion. To pursue her would mean he was ready to accept her past. His family would know it too, reminding him of the pain of what they went through in Lancaster when Maryann left. No wonder his mamm didn't approve of Ellie, and he was sure she didn't have all the details. She'd never give him her blessing to pursue Ellie, even if he chose to.

Daed had shown his support of them. He might change his mind once he found out about Ellie's bad choices. Joel's happiness with Ellie had been shattered. He'd found women attractive and befriended them but, until Ellie, he hadn't been interested in any of them enough to pursue them. Ellie was the first woman to capture his heart. She would attend Sunday services and social events. The sight of her would make his heart spin. He dreaded not talking to her and having to work hard to move on. He'd wait a while before telling his parents. He wasn't sure he could truly let her go.

He went home. His mamm approached him. "You missed Magdelena Beachy and her parents. They've invited us to supper Monday evening."

Magdelena was a pleasant and cheerful woman. She had a slender frame and beautiful dainty features, but he wasn't interested in anyone but Ellie. He needed time to get over her before he could even think about pursuing another woman. "I'll decline. I don't want to give Magdelena the impression I'd be interested in her."

"She went to the bakery and spoke with Ellie. She left us with six of Liza's molasses cookies. She said she asked Ellie if you and she were interested in each other. Ellie said you were available." She squinted and tilted her head. "What happened between you two?"

Daed had joined them. "You were quiet and gloomy this morning. I planned to ask you when you came back from town if everything was all right."

So much for waiting to tell them about Ellie. "She told me she had left the Amish life twice. Once in Nappanee, Indiana, and again, when she and her daed moved to Charm. I won't go into the details, but I will not be going to her haus, and she won't be kumming here."

Mamm scoffed. "I told you so. The gossips were right about her. You must be angry she deceived you and didn't tell you earlier."

"I'm sad more than anything. And, in all fairness, she said she was lost over the grief of her mamm. They were close, and she had a difficult time being reminded of her at every turn. She met a woman in the outside world who helped her heal. She returned to Charm and asked God, the church, family, and friends to forgive her. She's changed, and she reaffirmed she will never leave the Amish life again."

Daed wiped his brow with a worn handkerchief. "Joel, I don't understand. Don't you believe her? What's the problem?"

Mamm shifted in her chair to face her husband. "Are you out of your mind? The girl left the Amish life not once, but twice. How could he be sure she would never leave if tragedy struck or for any other reason?"

"She didn't strike me as a person who would lie.

Besides, she told him the truth. It must be difficult for her to expose her past to him. She's put it behind her and changed."

Eyes wide, Joel turned to Daed. His revelation shouldn't surprise him. He had no doubt Daed would receive Maryann with open arms if she returned. He had a forgiving heart and sought the best in everyone until they gave him reason to do otherwise. "I'm hurt she kept it from me this long. I didn't believe what the gossips and Abigail had insinuated about her. It's a lot for me to digest. Right now, I won't be pursuing her."

"I'll be upset if you change your mind about Ellie." Mamm pointed a finger at him. "You'd be dragging us into the gossips' conversations if you were to resume your pursuit of her. I had enough of the gossips talking about us when Maryann left. Surely, you wouldn't put us through it again. There are plenty of other women available, such as Magdelena."

Daed wagged a finger. "The gossips are wrong to prattle on about townsfolks' mistakes. The bishop has spoken on this subject, targeted at those who participate in such discussions, asking them to stop. I don't pay the gossips any mind."

"You may not, but I do. You're gullible." Her forehead furrowed. "I'm protecting our son from future heartache. You should agree with my counsel. I wish you'd told me this before I went to the bakery today. I was hoping I wouldn't have to lay eyes on Ellie, but she waited on me. She offered me free tarts, and I turned them down. She can't do anything to get in my good graces. I'm glad you came to your senses, Joel." She whisked away from them and left the front room.

Joel opened the door for Daed, and they stepped outside onto the porch.

Joel crossed his arms against his chest. "Mamm shouldn't be rude to Ellie. Ellie was kind to offer her free desserts. Mamm is going overboard to show her dislike for her." He shook his head. "She's never going to accept Ellie, and maybe my ending things with her is best for all concerned."

Daed rested a hand on his shoulder. "Mamm is angry at the world over Maryann's leaving. She thinks of Maryann as vulnerable and needing her. She excuses her leaving and blames the Englischer Maryann married."

"I understand Mamm rationalizes Maryann's faults because she's her dochder. I don't have patience for her criticizing Ellie at every turn."

"Ellie is the easiest target for her to focus her anger on." He placed a hand on Joel's arm. "I can tell by your demeanor you're struggling to stand by your decision to distance yourself from Ellie. I believe she has a stronghold on your heart. Pray and seek God's guidance. Maryann didn't return to us. Ellie repented and came back to her family and the Amish life. Take her at her word." He left Joel and stepped inside the barn.

Joel walked the fields and checked the status of the crops. His happy life had turned to one of turmoil and distress. Mamm would no doubt become his matchmaker again if Magdelena's supper invitation was any indication, and it was the last thing he wanted her to do.

Daed's opinion had shocked him into questioning his abrupt response to sever ties with Ellie.

Hours later, he joined his parents for supper. Steam rose off the bowl of fried potatoes, and the scent of cinnamon on hot apples on top of the ham made his mouth water. He'd lost his appetite until now. "Mamm, I'm hungry. This meal looks good."

"Danki. Now I expect you to join us at the Beachys' Monday evening. Understood?"

He chose not to argue. "Understood, but please don't encourage Magdelena or her parents about me and her."

"You don't have any idea what's good for you. Sometimes a mamm has to intervene on her child's behalf and nudge them along a bit. Don't worry. I've got your best interest at heart."

"Mamm, please. I mean it. I'm confused. I may choose to pursue Ellie again, and if I do, it's my decision and not yours. I'm taking time to sort everything out in my mind. Please honor my request."

"You need my advice, whether you like it or not. Now, don't give her another thought. Listen to your mamm." She put up a hand. "Enough said on the matter."

Daed shook his head. "Let's have a peaceful supper. And, Fraa, don't disregard what Joel is telling you. He's a grown man."

She scoffed but didn't comment.

Joel hurried to empty his plate, bid his parents good night, and went to his room. Ellie's laugh and the way she gazed into his eyes and hung on his every word made him feel like the most attractive man on earth. He loved her slender fingers, dainty hands, and the softness of her lips on his when he kissed her. He missed her.

He'd assumed she'd been innocent and followed the Amish rules. It was the impression he'd construed from her kind attitudes and compassion for him, her family, and their friends. Guilt, foolishness, and love mixed together confused him. He could forgive her, but could he really let go of her past and trust her?

He'd avoid her as much as possible until he'd had time to kumme to a definite conclusion. This Sunday was their off day from a service. He'd stay at home and rest. The next Sunday would present a challenge not to stare at Ellie's beautiful face and overcome the need to speak to her.

His next dilemma would be making sure he didn't give Magdelena the wrong idea about why he would attend supper with her family.

Joel built a new chicken coop and outhaus and tended to the animals for the rest of the week. No service yesterday had forced him to rest and forestalled an awkward encounter with Ellie, but he longed to talk to her. He rolled his tense shoulders back. He'd dreaded Monday kumming, but here it was, and he was going to supper at Magdelena's. He blew out a frustrated breath. Ellie's face was ever present on his mind. He'd give anything to have a moment's peace from his tormented heart.

Mamm called out to him. "Joel, time to get washed up and ready to go. Husband of mine, you too."

Joel accompanied his daed to the haus. "I'm not happy about this."

"There's no getting out of it now. We'll have a pleasant time. I'm looking forward to getting to know them. They've been friendly at the Sunday services. You can be cordial to Magdelena, and if she presses you, tell her in polite terms you aren't interested."

He nodded and got ready to go. An hour later, they traveled to the Beachys'.

Magdelena met them at the door, along with a little redheaded girl.

"Kumme in." She introduced him to her schweschder, Charity, and her parents. "Please sit and make yourselves comfortable."

Charity stared at him with her big green eyes and held a forefinger to her lips. Her shy smile added to her charm. He guessed her age around five.

Mamm stood. "Let me help."

Magdelena hooked her arm through Mamm's. "You can help me set the table."

Charity padded behind them.

Joel listened to the men discuss their work on the farms. He nodded when it was appropriate. He couldn't shake his frustration and sadness over Ellie. She had raised grave concerns. She suffered a great loss, went through a rebellious time to overcome her grief, and then returned to God. He clasped his hands tight. He couldn't make a mistake in who he chose for a fraa. Divorce wasn't an option for him if Ellie should leave if they experienced a traumatic incident.

"Joel, Son, I asked you a question." Daed shook his arm.

His cheeks heated. He sat up straight. "I'm sorry. My thoughts drifted elsewhere for a minute."

"It's all right." Daed rubbed his back. "Tell Mr. Beachy about the things you build in the workshop."

He leaned forward. "When time permits, I like to handcraft wooden boxes of various shapes and sizes to store potatoes, vegetables, or other items."

"Call me Mark, and I admire your talent. I repair things, but I don't have the knack for woodworking."

Mrs. Beachy came in. "Supper's ready."

"Let's go, men. I'm hungry." Mark ushered them to the kitchen.

Charity tugged on Joel's pant leg. "Will you sit by me?"

He grinned and took the seat next to her. "I'd be honored."

She beamed. "Danki."

Magdelena pulled out the chair and sat on his other side. "I hope you'll stay long enough for us to take a walk and chat later."

Mamm spread her napkin on her lap. "Of course we will."

Joel's stomach churned. Magdelena was beautiful and charming, but Ellie had a firm grip on his heart.

Daed darted a glance at Joel and back to Magdelena. "We don't want to overstay our wilkom, and Joel and I have to get up earlier than usual to start our day tomorrow on the farm." Daed took an exaggerated deep breath. "Mrs. Beachy, you have cooked enough food for a king, and it all looks delicious."

"Call me Bernice."

Joel could've bolted over the table and kissed his daed. He had done his best to rescue him. He didn't miss Mamm's pinched lips and hard stare at her husband. Joel didn't want to cause trouble, but he was glad to have his daed's support.

Mark said a prayer for the food and passed his fraa the first plate. "Joel, my dochder is a fine cook, and she'll make a good fraa to a man one day. I suggest you consider her before some other gentleman snatches her up."

Bernice bobbed her head and took a bite of the chicken she'd prepared in a light broth.

Joel struggled to swallow the sip of water he'd taken.

The man was forthright in why they'd been invited. The reason he shouldn't have kumme. Why had he let his mamm talk him into this? "This meal is delicious." He cleared his throat and took a drink of water.

Magdelena blushed and gave him a bashful smile.

Charity giggled and held a hand to her mouth.

Daed scooped another helping of stewed tomatoes onto his plate. "Mark, please tell us about raising cattle. I've thought about it, but I'd have a lot to learn first."

Again, his daed had intervened on his behalf. He was blessed to have such a thoughtful man for a daed.

Joel nodded. "Jah, I'm interested too."

"I'd love to share my experience with you. It is quite a process."

Joel listened to the man during supper give details about how to raise cattle. He enjoyed Mark's talk and was relieved he didn't push Joel any further about his intentions toward his dochder.

Bernice rose and removed an empty serving plate from the table. "You men take your discussion to the sitting room, and, Magdelena, grab your shawl and show Joel the property."

"Can I go?" Charity stared at her mamm with pleading eyes.

"You stay in the kitchen or sitting room. You can play with your dolls."

Joel shrugged. "I don't mind if she joins us."

Charity would provide a wilkom distraction from having any serious discussion with Magdelena.

Magdelena gave him a curt shake of the head. "Charity, you stay here."

"Please. Joel said he wants me to go."

Bernice turned on her heel. "Charity, you are not going with them."

"Oh, all right." She pouted and lifted her doll out of the wooden cradle in the corner of the room. "Is Peter your friend, Joel?"

Joel grinned at the child. "Jah, he's a good friend."

"I like him. I like his schweschder too. She's pretty. Is she your friend too?"

Joel froze. All eyes were on him. Charity's question about Peter hadn't phased him. Her inquiry about Ellie had prickled the hairs on his arms. "Jah, I'm friends with the Graber family."

Magdelena pulled her shawl tight around her shoulders. "Let's go. Shall we?"

He rose.

Charity waved to them and wore a pitiful look of rejection.

He was half tempted to reach for her hand and take her with them. *Not a good idea.* He shouldn't disrespect Magdelena or her mamm. He waved back to the sweet little girl and dragged his feet to the door and opened it. He followed her outside. The fall evening air was cool but not uncomfortable in his heavier wool shirt. "Are you warm enough with your shawl?"

"I'm fine. Danki." She scanned the land. "Daed and his men do a good job managing our property, and raising cattle was a good decision." She sat on the weathered hardwood bench outside the barn. "Sit with me."

Joel picked up a stick from the ground and toyed with it. He wasn't in the mood for any serious conversation, and she no doubt had questions. She'd had to have noticed him with Ellie at the after-service meals.

"You've not paid me any attention, and you appear

to have other things on your mind. I had hoped this might be the first of many times we'd spend together. Tell me what's bothering you. Maybe I can help."

Beautiful and caring, she would be a wonderful woman for him to consider pursuing, but he wasn't the one for her. Until he could reconcile what to do about Ellie, he wouldn't open himself up to Magdelena or any other woman.

"I don't want to give you the wrong impression as to why I came to supper. I came to encourage a friendship between our parents." He held up his palms. "It's not you. You're everything any man would be blessed to consider for a potential fraa." He looked away. "It's no secret Ellie and I were getting acquainted and our friendship was growing." He diverted his gaze to the horse grazing in the corral. "She told me something upsetting, and our relationship ended. I need more time before I can move on with another woman."

She frowned and folded her hands in her lap. "Ellie and I talked. She said you were friends." She sighed. "It's obvious by the way you're acting, you two are more than friends."

Joel dropped the stick and stood. He rubbed the back of his neck. "Our parting was recent. It's been hard since we had our difficult conversation. I'm not sure where things with Ellie and me will end up."

Magdelena nodded and rose. She crossed her arms. "Was this her decision or yours?"

"Mine. I'm not sure I did the right thing." He shuffled his feet. "I shouldn't be discussing Ellie with you."

"I've heard from the gossips about her past, but I've also witnessed her change of heart to commit to the Amish life and God. If you're judging her based on her mistakes, I'd be disappointed in you."

Magdelena was straightforward in her support of Ellie. Not at all what he'd expected in a woman he thought was interested in him.

He kicked the stick he'd dropped and flexed his hands. "It's not easy for me."

She narrowed her eyes and moved her hands to her hips. "It shouldn't be hard for you, Joel. You still care about her, don't you?"

He closed his eyes and nodded.

"Then don't let her go. Leah has told me Ellie isn't the same girl she met when her family first moved here. She's serious about her decision to obey God and Amish law, and she's been as good as her word. I trust Leah and Ellie. You should too."

His throat constricted. Magdelena, Leah, and others were accepting and happy about Ellie's change. She was defending the woman he loved, and he'd pushed Ellie away. Magdelena's wise advice had penetrated his heart. He had been thinking about this all wrong.

"You surprise me, Magdelena."

"I don't want a man who's in love with another woman, and I like Ellie. I invited you here to find out where the two of you really stood. I'd like nothing better than the two of you reconciling your differences."

He smiled. "You're going to make a man very happy one day. If I didn't care about Ellie, I'd have been interested to find out if I was that man."

"Danki, Joel." She hugged herself. "Let's go inside. I'm chilly, and Charity will never forgive me if I don't let her have time with you."

The little girl had startled him with her comments about Ellie. Kinner said whatever was on their minds.

He guessed he shouldn't be surprised. He liked Charity's dimpled cheeks and the impish gleam she had in her eyes. "She's adorable."

Magdelena laughed. "Most of the time."

They went inside and played checkers with Charity.

Daed tapped him on the shoulder a half hour later. "Is your game about over? It's time for us to go home."

"Do you have to go?" Charity stuck out her bottom lip.

"We do. I've enjoyed your company. Danki for playing checkers with me."

Charity got up and hugged his neck.

He stood, and he and his family thanked them for their hospitality, got in their buggy, and headed home.

Mamm glanced at him in the back seat. "How did you and Magdelena get along?"

"She's a woman I admire, but I'm not interested in anyone but Ellie. I've got to heal over our parting."

"I wouldn't waste another minute on Ellie. Magdelena will have other offers. She's quite a catch with her beauty and charm."

Daed halted the horse in front of the haus. "What a pleasant evening. I really enjoyed myself." He grinned. "Why don't you both go in and get settled. I'll take care of putting the mare in the barn."

"I'll help you." Joel got out.

"Nah. I'm sure you're anxious to have some time to yourself. I can handle it."

Mamm stepped out of the buggy and headed for the haus. "I'm going in before I catch a cold."

Joel waited for Mamm to go inside and shut the door behind her. "Danki for everything you did for me tonight."

Daed winked. "I'm proud of you. You handled yourself well. And we men have to stick together, right?

"Jah, but you go the extra mile to help me out. Your support means a lot."

"I enjoyed our visit with the Beachy family, but I didn't approve of Mamm pushing you in Magdelena's direction without your consent."

"She means well, but she's ruthless in her attempt to steer me away from Ellie."

"Ignore her. She's in a hurry for you to get married and have kinner."

Joel laughed. "She's relentless."

"Of course. She can't help herself." Daed gave him a rueful grin. "Go inside. I'll be in soon."

He nodded, went inside, and hurried to his room, hoping to avoid Mamm. He didn't run into her. She must be in her room or the kitchen. He slumped in his bedroom chair. He didn't know how to get across to Mamm to stop interfering in his life. He was glad he'd gone to the Beachys'. Magdelena had made good points about Ellie. He'd been foolish to judge her. He'd talk to her tomorrow and make things right.

Chapter Eight

Ellie cleared everything from the counter. She swiped the glass shelves with a damp rag and then dried them with a dry towel on this quiet Tuesday morning. She refilled the shelves again with the day-old pastries, tarts, and Liza's famous molasses cookies. She'd offer them for a reduced price. Since the last time she'd seen Joel, the days had dragged by slower than dripping molasses in January. She wished they'd had a service this past Sunday so she could at least have found an excuse to ask how he was doing.

She'd been foolish to sit on the porch and hope he'd tell her and show her that she was the only woman for him. Her stance on his negative reaction to her news shifted back and forth like a clock pendulum from sad to angry and back again. She wasn't surprised to once again suffer the consequences of her behavior. Her story was hard for any Amish man or woman to hear and accept, considering she'd outdone herself on disobeying most of what she'd been taught. Anger fired in her stomach. He should forgive her and love her enough to trust her. She slumped her shoulders. Sadness eased out the anger as she reminded herself she'd waited too long to reveal what she knew he would find repulsive, or worse, unforgiveable.

She'd take him back in a moment, but each day he didn't contact her, her hope waned. She heaved a sigh. There was also the problem of his mamm's rejection of her. Even if Joel could put what she told him about her past behind him, God would have to perform a miracle before Mrs. Wenger would agree to them planning a future together. She'd caused enough damage to her family and disregarded God's will for her life too often to make the mistake twice. She wouldn't marry any man without his family's blessing. It was asking for trouble.

She popped her head in the kitchen. "Liza and Hannah, are there any new goodies to add to the shelves today?"

Hannah held up a big metal bowl. "I'm experimenting with adding blueberry jam to butter cookies."

"Interesting combination. I'll be anxious to sample your new creation."

Liza picked up her rolling pin. "I'm mixing peaches and cherries together for a pie. It's a good thing we canned a lot of fruit."

"Those will sell fast. Put one aside to take home."

"Good idea. I have enough fruit to make eight." Liza rolled the large wooden pin back and forth.

"Good morning, Ellie. Do you have some hot coffee for us?" The sheriff slid the paper from under his arm.

"I sure do. I didn't hear you kumme in. How are you both today?"

Dr. Harrison accepted a portion of the pages from the sheriff. "My knees are sore, but overall, I'm in good shape."

The sheriff gasped. "President Roosevelt was shot yesterday!"

"What? Where?" Dr. Harrison peered over his friend's shoulder at the article.

Ellie stopped to listen.

"Says here President Roosevelt was on his campaign trail greeting attendees in Milwaukee, Wisconsin, when a saloonkeeper, John Schrank, shot him at close range."

Ellie gulped. "What's his condition? Is he in the hospital?"

The sheriff wrinkled his nose and pulled the paper closer. "Pages of his speech and a glasses case slowed the force of the bullet and saved his life. He went ahead and gave his speech and went to the hospital after he was finished. They're calling his injury a flesh wound."

Dr. Harrison shook his head. "Why did the man shoot him?"

"He didn't approve of Roosevelt running for a third term."

"What a silly reason to pull a gun." Dr. Harrison harrumphed.

Ellie finished wiping the counter. "Maybe he's touched in the head."

"You're right." The sheriff read on. "The paper is reporting he's mentally ill. He'll probably end up in the mental institution."

Ellie straightened two chairs and Abigail's face came to mind. She was glad her encounters with the disturbed girl hadn't been violent like President Roosevelt's encounter with the saloonkeeper who shot him. What a relief the bullet was slowed by the glasses case and papers. He could've been killed. Her daed had kumme much too close to something like that when Mr. Phillips shot him and grazed his shoulder. People could surprise you, and not in a good way. She was glad the president survived.

Dr. Harrison and the sheriff finished their coffee and food and left for work. Ellie watched the door each time it opened. *No sign of Joel.* She couldn't help it. She wanted him to burst into the bakery and declare her past didn't matter and he couldn't imagine his life without her. Almost a week had gone by without a word from him. Was he thinking about her? Did his heart hurt like hers? Or was he set on letting her go for good? She'd have to talk to him soon. She couldn't let him go without an attempt to reconcile.

Hannah skipped to her, holding a pastry. "Try this."

Ellie tore off a piece and plopped it in her mouth. "Blueberry and strawberry filling with lots of sugar?"

Liza poked her head in. "And a bit of lemon and maple syrup."

"I love it!" Ellie tore off another piece and set it on her tongue.

Hannah smiled. "Liza and I made them together."

Liza shrugged. "Our customers will be the true test. Here's a plateful to put in the case, Ellie."

Ellie accepted the plate and bent to place it on the glass shelf. "Let's call them red and blue tartlets, shall we? I'm sure they'll be a new favorite."

Hannah approached Ellie. "What a wonderful idea!" She untied her apron and put on her thick cape. "Do you mind if Liza and I go to the general store? They got in a new shipment of small, medium, and large wooden spoons, and I'd like to show them to Liza. We could use some new ones in the kitchen."

"Good idea. Sure, go ahead."

Liza and Hannah bundled up in their capes, bid her farewell, and left.

The door swung open, and Ellie gasped. "Bill Phillips, what a nice surprise! How are you?"

He picked her up and twirled her around.

Dizzy, she laughed. Then froze. *Joel.* When had he kumme in? His timing couldn't have been worse. "Bill, please put me down."

Joel, red-faced, bristled, and slammed the door.

"Bill, I'll be right back." She hurried outside and searched. Where did he go so fast? He'd probably never speak to her again. She'd have to find him and explain later. She had a store to run and a friend to talk to. Hands on hips, she glanced in both directions and then went back inside the bakery.

"The man left in a huff. A friend of yours?"

"Joel is his name. Until last week, I had hoped he and I were developing our friendship into something more serious."

"I can explain to him this was harmless." He brushed her fingers with his. "Although I've missed you, and I did stop in to find out if I had a chance with you."

"You're a good friend, Bill." She folded her hands behind her. "But I'm committed to the Amish life in Charm, and this is where I will stay. I love being back with my family and friends. The Englisch life isn't for me."

He smiled. "I understand. Would you like me to meet Joel and explain? I don't want to cause you any trouble."

She threw up her hands. "I'm not sure what to do. I appreciate your offer, but I'll tell him our meeting here today was innocent. I'm hoping he'll understand. I told him a few days ago about my time in the outside world with you and your aunt and uncle. He was shocked, and he hasn't spoken to me since then. This didn't help matters."

"I'm sorry, Ellie."

"You didn't mean any harm. Enough about me. How are you and your family?"

Bill had been patient and good to her. His aunt had been instrumental in helping her heal during her stay with Bill and his relatives. His aunt helped her sort out her confusion and supported her decision to go home to Charm.

"Mother and my aunt and uncle are doing fine. Mother and I live in the house behind theirs, and we're happy we're near them. Mother's been altering clothes and making dresses for the women in the community."

"Has your daed written to you? I've been praying he'd have a change of heart."

"He's written Mother and me several times from prison." He grinned. "He said he's had time to reflect on his life, and he isn't proud of his actions. He's asked us for forgiveness."

She believed God could work a miracle in Mr. Phillips's life, and she was happy for their family. Mrs. Phillips had lived with his bad temperament a long time. She could understand if the woman might not believe him. "Is your mamm skeptical of him?"

"Yes, but the more he writes to us and shows his emotions, the more she believes him. We wouldn't move in with him again right away, but we might permit him to visit us when he gets out. He could get released early for good behavior and showing remorse. I plan to stay in our house on my aunt and uncle's property. There's enough work for both of us to make a good living, and I'm content there." He winked. "I'd be happier if you'd agreed to consider me a suitor."

She blushed. "I'm sorry, Bill. You're a good man, but my place is here with my Amish community and family."

"I understand." He grinned. "The sweet, sugary aroma of this place makes me hungry." He eyed the desserts displayed on the glass shelves.

She rounded the counter and selected pastries and an assortment of cookies, packaged them, and handed them to him. "These are yours free of charge. Give your family hugs for me."

He lingered at the door in silence for a moment. "I wish you the very best, Ellie."

She smiled and watched him shut the door behind him. Bill had been a good friend, and if she hadn't met his aunt, she might have stayed in the outside world longer and gotten into more trouble before she listened to God. Bill would make any woman a wonderful husband in every way, just not her. She had her sights set on Joel. What could she say to Joel to assure him Bill's swinging her around with such familiarity had been harmless? She groaned. The shocked expression on his face and picturing what she and Bill must have looked like to him put her nerves on edge. He might refuse to give her a chance to explain.

What if customers had kumme into the bakery? His picking her up had surprised her and made her laugh. She'd been flustered and it was over in a matter of seconds. She hadn't thought fast enough to tell him to put her down right away. Lesson learned. She'd be more careful if Bill ever came in again, but she sensed his good-bye was final this time.

Hannah came inside and opened her package. "Look at this dark blue fabric I found on sale for half price." She held it up to her cheek. "The material is soft."

Liza nodded. "I bought two large wooden spoons to replace our cracked ones." She held them up, then stuffed them back in the bag. "Ellie, you're not listening to us. What's on your mind?"

Hannah took a step closer to her friend. "Jah, Ellie, did something happen while we were gone?"

Ellie told them about Bill and Joel.

Hannah gasped and put a hand to her mouth. "Oh dear!"

"I should've told Bill to set me on my feet right away, but he caught me off guard. His visit was a surprise. I didn't react the way I should've. For a second, I stepped back with him to the outside world."

Liza brushed Ellie's cheek with the back of her fingers. "Sweetheart, did Bill swing you around often to surprise you when you stayed at his aunt and uncle's?"

Ellie shook her head. "Nah. This was the first time." She shrugged. "Englischers are more carefree with their harmless touching as male and female friends. Such as a hug or pat on the shoulder or holding hands for a moment. Bill didn't do those things, but Jane explained she had male friends who greeted her with a hug." She let out a regretful sigh. "I realize it's not proper anywhere, but he whisked me up in his arms fast. I should've protested."

Liza tucked her bag of spoons under her arm. "You can't change what's happened, but you can attempt to repair the damage with Joel. Go to his home after work. Pull him aside and tell him the truth."

"Liza's right. You should explain to him about

Bill's visit as soon as possible. We'll take care of the customers."

"Danki to you both." She untied her apron and hung it on the wooden hook. "I'll meet you at home, Liza. Hannah, I'll tell you what happens in the morning."

Liza grabbed Ellie's hand. "Let's pray before you go."

They held hands.

Liza bowed her head. "Dear Heavenly Father, forgive us for anything we've said or done that is not pleasing to you. Give Ellie the right words to explain herself to Joel to mend this misunderstanding and for both of them to be at peace. If your plan is for them to be together, please give Joel the assurance Ellie is the right woman for him and open his mamm's heart to accept and wilkom Ellie into their family. Amen."

Ellie dabbed her damp eyes with the pads of her slender fingers. "I'm blessed to have such a loving family and friends who love and support me. Here I go. I'm shaking I'm so nervous."

"You'll do fine. No matter the outcome, you need to do this for your sake." Hannah stepped behind the counter and tied her apron on.

Ellie waved at them, crossed the road to the livery to pick up her horse and buggy, and headed to Joel's. Her hands shook as she held the reins. Would he talk to her? Maybe he would be outside and she wouldn't have to speak to his mamm. The woman might answer the door and refuse to tell Joel she was there. She scooted back on the bench and sat up straighter. She could do this.

Arriving at Joel's haus, she gulped. Her heart pounded in her chest. *Joel.* Handsome as ever, staring right at her. She hurried to get down.

He took long strides to her. "Ellie, what are you doing here?"

She held the reins and waited. He didn't take them from her. She hurried to tie them to the hitching post. "Please, Joel. Give me five minutes to explain."

His lips pinched in a grim line and his arms crossed, he glared at her. "What is there to explain? You were in a man's arms while you laughed. Very inappropriate for an Amish girl. The Ellie I thought I knew would never do such a thing. Nah, you don't have anything to say I need to listen to." He swiveled away from her.

She touched his arm. "I'm in love with you and only you. Bill, the Englischer I told you about in my past, a good man who remained a friend, came in and lifted me off my feet before I could utter a word. He meant no harm and neither did I. I should've told him to put me down right away, but he took me by surprise. I told him about you, and that I am here to stay. Please, Joel, understand the act was innocent. I wouldn't let it happen again, given how it looks."

"Ellie, how would you have reacted had you found me in the same predicament?"

She bowed her head. "Startled and upset. But if you explained, as I'm doing, I would've understood."

He took off his hat and raked fingers through his thick sandy-blond hair. "You don't mind your actions, and I can't be with a woman who doesn't respect me enough to consider me when she's out in public. Had Leah's mamm walked in on you and Bill, she would have spread the news all over town in five minutes. I don't want to damage my family or friendships with someone who doesn't value them or the Amish life as I do."

She had a glimmer of hope. Joel hadn't disputed

her explanation about Bill, but he *was* upset about their greeting he witnessed. She noticed his face had softened when she'd said she loved him. He'd turned and given her his full attention again, instead of walking away from her.

"Joel, I've made mistakes. Today, I made another one, pushing you farther away from me. I pray you'll believe I'm sincere in staying here and hopefully building a future with you. I am the woman who will honor you, respect you, and make you happy. I'm willing to do my best to show your mamm all of this too."

"I wish things were different, but I can't forgive and forget right now. What you've told me about your time in the outside world, and your actions with Bill, make me question whether you could be lured back there at some point." He held her gaze for a moment, then gestured to the barn. "I should get back to work."

Tears streamed onto her cheeks. "Joel, I'm going to pray and wait. I'm not giving up on us." She untied the mare, got in the buggy, and drove down the lane.

The love in his gaze gave her hope. They'd built a strong foundation for a future together. There was no denying their friendship had blossomed into a serious relationship. She wouldn't make it easy for him to ignore her. She'd speak to him at social events and church services, until he asked her to stop.

Joel struggled not to whisk Ellie to the side of the barn out of sight and press his lips on hers. Her explanation about Bill had been enough for him. Had she wanted to have a relationship with Bill, she would've stayed with him and not returned to Charm. He was jealous and disappointed at her interaction with Bill.

But she'd told him he was the one she loved. Should he trust her? He scratched his head. But did her experience in the outside world taint her ability to discern what was right or wrong in living the Amish life? No other Amish woman he knew would allow such a thing to happen. Innocent or not, she shouldn't have acted in such an irresponsible way.

What other things would she do to embarrass him even if he chose to put her past aside and move forward with her? He slammed the shovel into the hay, ashamed he'd had such stringent thoughts about how Ellie should behave. He'd made mistakes too. Kissing her hadn't been proper, but he'd done it anyway. She claimed she would do her best to monitor her behavior in the future. What more did he want from her?

He finished his chores, washed his hands, and went inside.

Mamm glowered at him and stood at the stove over a pot of boiling homemade noodles. "Why was Ellie here?"

He'd hoped his mamm hadn't noticed Ellie. He wouldn't give her details. "She and I needed to have a discussion about something."

"What?"

"I'd rather keep our conversation private."

Mamm harrumphed and poured the noodles in a large strainer. "I don't like secrets kept in this family. Must be bad if you can't share it."

His dander raised, he fought to control his voice. "Why is it so easy for you to dismiss Maryann's behavior in leaving the Amish life, but it's out of the question for you to accept Ellie's mistake, even though she's returned and asked forgiveness?" The question penetrated his brain like a finger held to a hot flame. Hadn't he done the same?

She whirled around and pointed at his chest. "Her no-good husband dragged her away and filled her with lies. She's sweet and innocent and not used to slick-tongued Englisch men."

Daed entered the kitchen. "What is going on in here? Why are you raising your voices?"

He touched his fraa's face. "Your cheeks are as red as fire. Why?"

Joel relaxed his clenched jaw. "Mamm and I were discussing Ellie. I asked her why she could forgive Maryann for her actions and not Ellie."

Daed tilted his head and scratched his bearded chin. "I find your question valid, and I disagree with what I heard as your mamm's answer. Maryann was an adult. She made her decision. No one dragged her off our property."

Glaring at them, Mamm scowled. "I didn't mean literally, but figuratively. Maryann never would've left if he hadn't wooed her into falling in love with him. Shy and lacking confidence, she fell prey to him. Ellie kummes across confident, and she left out of curiosity." She faced Joel. "Has she told you the details about her leaving the Amish life, not once, but twice, mind you?"

Joel's chest tightened. He would never share what Ellie had told him. He'd protect her no matter what. "She's told me what happened."

She crossed her arms, lips in a firm line. "Tell us."

"Nah." Daed waved his hand. "Ellie's explanation is for Joel's ears only. We should trust our son. She shouldn't be judged for her past mistakes when she's asked for forgiveness and changed. I find her pleasant, kind, and genuine."

Mamm transferred the noodles to a bowl and added a spoonful of butter to them. "You're wrong about Maryann and Ellie, but I'll let the matter go for now. Sit, supper's ready."

Out of sight from her, Daed put a finger to his lips.

Joel nodded, relieved she'd dropped the conversation. Daed needn't worry. The heated discussion with his mamm had pricked his guilt for judging Ellie. He'd thought he could dismiss her from his mind and heart, but he loved her deeply.

When she'd gotten out of the buggy, his heart betrayed him and swelled with joy at the sight of her. The past few days, he'd missed her so much. The first time they'd met, he'd felt a connection he couldn't explain. Love at first sight hadn't made sense to him until he'd met Ellie. With each passing day that he'd left her alone, he'd jeopardized her faith in him to protect her and love her, and trust him with her thoughts and fears. She'd confided in him. He'd thought only of himself. Love meant putting the one you cared for first. He'd fix this, and soon.

He listened to his parents discuss the sick cow and what they might do to help it heal. He finished his food and excused himself. "I'll be back later. I've got something I need to do."

Daed pushed his plate aside and rose. "Do you mind taking care of whatever it is tomorrow? I'd like help with the cow. I've got some ideas on what to feed old Bertha to help her stomach, and then I need your muscles to lift the heavy trunk I have in the barn to the other side."

Joel knew Daed would think of other things when he

was on a roll to get organized. He'd wait until tomorrow morning to speak to Ellie. "Nah. I'll stay home and help you. It can wait."

He and Daed moved the trunk, fed the concoction to Bertha that the neighbor suggested, and stacked the wood Joel had cut earlier in the day.

"We'll have to work by lantern if we don't quit soon."

Daed chuckled. "I'm tuckered out. Danki for your help. Let's go inside."

"Before we do, can we sit for a minute?" He motioned to two bales of hay.

Daed sat across from him. "What's on your mind?"

"Ellie told me where she went, what happened, and why she came back when she left home twice. She admits she was angry over the loss of her mamm. She disrespected her daed by leaving town without writing a note to him. And she had a bad attitude toward the Amish life the first time she returned. I was shocked and upset. I wanted nothing to do with her, but, at the same time, I was hurt."

"What changed her mind? She's back and, at supper the other night, she acted like a very proper girl, fit for any Amish man to consider for a fraa. We all do things we're not proud of. Do you think her commitment to God and the Amish life is genuine?" Daed stared at him.

"I do. Grief-stricken over her mamm's passing, she lashed out and ran from the memories they shared together. She came home the first time and still had unresolved grief over the loss of her mamm, and she left again. She overcame her grief with the help of a loving woman she met while away the second time. She came home and asked forgiveness from God, friends, and family. She claims this is where she'll stay."

"Do you love her?"

He nodded. "What she told me is hard to grasp. The fear she'd run from me at the first sign of trouble put me off. But she assures me this isn't so."

"Did Ellie run off because she was in love with an Englischer?"

"Nah. She made friends, but nothing romantic with anyone."

"Then her situation isn't the same as Maryann's. Don't judge her based on your schweschder's decision. You fell in love with this Ellie. The Ellie who poured out her transgressions, in the hope you'd understand and trust her. Pray about this and seek God's will for your life. But be careful you don't make a decision you may regret. Love means being there when things are good and when they're difficult."

"You always look at the bright side of every situation. You've even dealt with Maryann's departure better than Mamm and me. How do you do it?" Joel admired his daed's compassion and patience in hard times and when others were going through turmoil. He didn't sit in judgment of anyone. He'd not said a harsh word about Maryann.

"No one is without sin. I'll always love Maryann, and I pray for her to return to us. I don't like what she did, but she's still my little girl. I pray she's safe and healthy. I have you and your mamm to care for, and I can't let the pain of Maryann's decision make me bitter or rob me of the life God intends for me to live. What hurts most is watching your mamm suffer."

Joel prayed he'd be as good a husband and daed to his fraa and kinner. Daed had provided a good example of a daed's love and devotion to his family. Mamm had let his schweschder's rejection of the Amish life overshadow her marriage. He'd walked in on Daed holding Mamm several times as she wept. Daed had a sparkle in his eye when he looked at Mamm, and he didn't hesitate to tell her he loved her or share an endearing moment from their history together. He never stopped trying to make her happy.

"Danki, Daed. I just needed to talk it out."

"I'm always here for you, Joel." He rose.

They walked across the yard and into the haus. The sitting room was empty. He shrugged. Mamm must have retired for the evening. He bid Daed good night and went to his bedroom. Tomorrow morning he'd go to the bakery and ask if Ellie could spare a few minutes in private outside. Liza and Hannah had never hesitated to give them a few minutes alone to talk. Ellie had a loving family and good friends. He'd missed them too these last few days. They were a cheerful group and easygoing and added joy to his life. Jah, he didn't want to go another day with her thinking he didn't want anything more to do with her.

He'd done what he'd been afraid she'd do by running away from her and dismissing her when she'd poured her heart out to him. He hoped she would forgive him for not being the man he aspired to be in making her feel loved. He wouldn't blame her if she turned him away. He pressed a hand to his stomach. He was positive he'd never find another Ellie.

Chapter Nine

Ellie swept dirt off the bakery floor, which the customers had tracked in on their shoes Wednesday morning. The door swung open, and she leaned the broom against the wall. *Magdelena's mamm and little schweschder, Charity.* The woman mirrored Magdelena's beauty. The two could be schweschders rather than mamm and dochder. Charity skipped to the display. She had a round face, and freckles decorated her nose and cheeks. She was adorable but didn't resemble her mamm or Magdelena.

"Good morning. Are you after anything special?"

Charity pressed her little nose to the glass. "How about some ginger cookies!"

Ellie reached for one. "You can have one now, if it's all right with your mamm."

"You're too kind, Ellie. Jah, you can have one, Charity."

Ellie came around the counter and passed the cookie to the sweet little girl. "There you go."

Charity gave Ellie a shy smile. "Danki." She held it in her pudgy fingers. "Your friend came to our haus last night. He says he's friends with Peter too."

Ellie cocked her head. "You've got me curious. Which of my friends visited you?"

Mrs. Beachy perused the counter. "Joel Wenger. Magdelena invited him. He's such a kind man. We had an enjoyable time with him and his parents."

"Jah, he is an exceptional man." Ellie rounded the corner and stood behind the counter. She pressed a hand to her tense stomach.

"Is Peter here?" Charity brushed crumbs from her upper lip.

"He's in school, but I'll tell him you asked about him."

She swayed from side to side and glanced at Ellie with a grin. "I like Peter. I get to go to school next year."

Ellie fought to not chuckle. "You'll enjoy it. Peter does."

"Maybe Peter and I can both be Joel's friends. My schweschder smiled a lot at Joel last night. I hope Joel kummes to our haus lots. Maybe he can bring Peter sometime."

Mrs. Beachy made her selections and paid Ellie for them. "Danki, Ellie. I can't wait to try all these delicious desserts. We love kumming here. The aroma alone is worth the visit."

Ellie waved to them and waited until the door closed. She leaned against the wall and gulped a breath. Joel had gone to Magdelena's. So much for taking time to heal. He must've shut the door on them for good. She had held out hope he'd miss her and find it easier to forgive and trust her again. He'd already moved on. Would this ache ever go away? Would she ever open her heart to another man? Right now, she doubted it. The door opened, and she straightened and forced a smile. "Esther and Peter, what a nice surprise!"

Peter ran to her and hugged her waist. "I don't have school today. Miss Mast sent us all home about an hour after we got there. She didn't look so good. She kept holding her stomach and running outside. Daed took me to Esther's because he promised the neighbor he'd help dig a new well."

Esther kissed Ellie's cheek. "We thought we'd drop in and get some of Liza's molasses cookies. I've been itching to get back here for a visit. The place looks and smells good."

Liza and Hannah ran into Peter as they came out of the kitchen, and the women circled him in a hug.

"I'm glad you came in, Esther." Ellie pointed to an apron on the worn wooden peg. "Haven't moved yours. I remember our times together here every time I look at it."

Esther held it out. "I should take the dirty thing home and wash it."

"Nah, the flour and sugar give it character." Liza rested her head against Esther's for a moment.

Hand on her hip, Hannah swiveled to Peter. "I overheard you say you got out of school today. Are you glad?"

Peter tilted his head. "I like school, but I'm glad to kumme here too." He gasped. "I almost forgot. I drew you a picture of a flower, Mamm. I'll go get it."

"Maybe I should go with you." Ellie opened the door.

He shook his head. "Nah, our buggy is right outside. I'm a big boy now. I'll be right back."

The women laughed.

Liza held her cheeks. "He's growing up too fast."

Ellie strolled to the window. A woman paced outside and she was talking to herself. The woman disappeared out of her view. She sighed and dismissed the strange passerby. "He keeps us on our toes with all his questions. He asked me if fish have lips the other day, and I laughed so hard, tears ran down my face."

"He's inquisitive." Liza chuckled.

Ellie turned on her heel back to the window. *Where is Peter?* The hairs on her neck prickled. Something wasn't right. "Peter should've been back by now. I should check on him." She opened the door and stepped out. She yelled, "Peter!" The strange woman had tied Peter to the bench in her wagon. The deranged woman took off, and a rooster tail of dust whirled up off Main Street. She was taking off with him! She couldn't let her get away!

A man stopped and stared. "What is going on?"

A woman waved her hands. "She snatched him! He cried for help! He doesn't know her! It all happened so fast!"

"Peter!" Joel jumped in his wagon. "Ellie, get in. We'll go after them."

What was Joel doing here? It didn't matter. She'd find out later, and she needed his help. She jumped in next to him. "Let's go now!"

Liza came out. "Ellie! Our Peter! She's getting away with Peter!"

Esther threw her arms in the air. "We've got to run after them!"

Hannah held her cheeks. "We have to do something!"

"Esther, the sheriff's kumming into town. Tell him to catch up with us." She gestured to him. "He's too far away for us to wait. I'm going with Joel."

Joel took off. "Ellie, don't worry. We'll get Peter back." He slapped the reins. "Kumme on, girl, go!"

The horse galloped fast, kicking up dust.

Ellie's heart thumped hard. A wagon wheel hit a rut in the road. She lost her grip and her body lifted off the seat. She clasped the side rail. "Whoa! We almost tipped over!"

"I've got it! We're all right." He stared straight ahead. "Don't let me down, girl. Gallop as fast as your legs will go!"

The horse shook its head and gained speed.

"Where is she taking him?" Ellie stretched her neck to watch Peter's back.

"We'll soon find out."

Peter screamed in the distance. "Help me!" He struggled on the bench seat to wrangle free.

"We're getting a little closer." Ellie leaned forward, stiff. She fisted her hand and fought the helplessness creeping in her. She wouldn't give in to it. They'd reach them, and they'd bring Peter home.

Ellie held on to the side of the buggy. "She keeps on going! Your horse can't keep this pace forever."

"I doubt she lives too far from town. I doubt she'd travel far alone." Joel snapped the reins. "Go, girl, go!"

Ellie swallowed the bile rising in her throat. She should've gone with Peter. She'd never forgive herself if something happened to him. Why hadn't she gone outside with him?

She glanced over her shoulder. "It's the sheriff and his deputies. They're kumming."

"Good. We'll keep going since we're closer to the kidnapper. We'll lead them right to her." He nodded to a big white haus on a hill in the distance. "She might be headed for the haus up there."

"You were right. She hadn't traveled far to get to town."

The kidnapper's brown hair flapped in the wind. She was tall with broad shoulders. The kidnapper's larger horse gave her the advantage over Joel's mare.

Ellie stared straight ahead at the kidnapper and Peter. "I've gone by this haus before, but I've never noticed anyone outside."

Joel darted his gaze to the sheriff. "The sheriff is way back behind us. We'll keep leading him to the kidnapper, and then once he catches up to us, we'll stay back and let him and his lawmen take over. There may be dangerous men living with her."

Ellie nodded. The rumble of the horse's hooves shook the ground. "Poor Peter! We have to get him away from her. She couldn't have good intentions. I noticed her out the window. She paced and talked to herself. I sensed something was wrong. I never should have left Peter alone." She gripped the side of the fast-moving buggy. "Peter, we're kumming! We're kumming!"

Peter didn't attempt to turn around. She groaned. The horse's hooves pounding the dirt and the distance between them must've drowned out the sound of her voice.

The kidnapper jumped out of the wagon, untied Peter, and snatched him in both her arms, and dragged him inside the haus.

Joel and Ellie looked back at the sheriff.

Joel said, "The sheriff will catch up to us soon. He's getting closer."

"Who are you? Let me go!" Peter cried. "Joel! Ellie!"

Ellie swayed next to Joel. The wagon wheel had hit another rut and slowed the horse. She regained her balance and sat on the edge of the seat. "Peter!" She kept her eyes on him in the distance. Her heart ached. She wanted to run after him.

Joel flicked the reins again. "Kumme on, girl. You're all right. Let's go!"

The horse picked up momentum.

The sheriff caught up to them. "Esther pointed us in the right direction. I'm glad you followed the kidnapper. It helped me spot you and kept us on track. I was just kumming into town on my horse. My deputies must've noticed me barreling through town and followed. They're close behind." He went ahead of them, dismounted, and hurried to tie off his horse.

Joel pulled up next to him. "I'd like to help, Sheriff."

The sheriff got off his horse and secured it to a worn hitching post. "You two stay in your wagon. We'll take care of this." The deputies arrived, and he motioned for his men to go with him after Peter and the stranger. He rushed to the door and rapped hard with his fist. "This is the sheriff. Open this door, and let the boy go."

Ellie held her fists to her quivering lips. "I'm afraid for Peter."

"Shut up and go away, Sheriff. I won't let you take my Leroy. Ya hear?"

Ellie shivered. The defiant woman wasn't budging. She wouldn't give in easily.

The sheriff held his rifle to his side. "I'll break this door down if you don't cooperate."

"Go away, or I'll shoot you where you stand."

Ellie looked at Joel. "She's loud and mean. No telling what she'll do." She prayed for Peter's and the men's safety.

Another woman with auburn hair and average height and weight pulled her wagon next to them in front of the haus. "What is going on?"

Ellie pointed to the haus. "The deranged woman in this haus kidnapped my bruder from town. She's got him inside."

The woman didn't respond and took one big jump out of her wagon and ran to the sheriff. "I'm her sister, Pamela Myers. Harriett's not right in the head. Let me try. Harriett, open this door right now."

"Pamela? I found Leroy and brought him home."

"Harriett, Leroy went to Heaven. Remember, he got ill and passed."

"No! You're wrong. You're lying! He's our Leroy."

Pamela turned to them. "I'm sorry. My sister had a child who died last year. Her husband ran off with another woman before the funeral." She shook her head. "Anyway, the child passed away at the age of five from an unknown illness. The child never enjoyed good health. She is replacing her boy with yours." She pounded harder on the door then dropped her fist to her side. "Let me in, Harriett. I want to meet him."

Joel and Ellie stared in disbelief.

"The woman is troubled. This is dangerous." Ellie let tears fall onto her cheeks. "I feel so helpless."

"She wouldn't hurt her child. I doubt she'd harm Peter. This will all be over soon, and we'll take Peter home." He covered her hand.

Ellie loved Joel so much. He protected her and comforted her, and she was relieved he was with her. He gave her the reassurance and calm she needed in this storm. She prayed God would work a miracle in his mamm's heart so she didn't have to live her life without him. "Joel, I'll never forgive myself if Peter gets hurt."

"Don't go there. Everything will be fine. The sheriff will take charge, and he won't put Peter in danger. If we're quiet, we'll hear their conversation."

Ellie nodded.

"Would she injure the boy?" Sheriff Williams stared at Pamela.

Ellie pressed a hand to her throat.

"I doubt it." Pamela turned the nob. "Unlock the door, Harriett. I need to kumme inside."

"You kumme in alone."

Pamela motioned for them to step back. "She's unstable. You have to let me reason with her. She's desperate and anxious, which makes her very aggressive. She won't hesitate to shoot you. I don't want anyone injured, or worse. Give me a few minutes."

The sheriff said, "From what you've said, she may harm you."

"I'll be all right. She won't do anything to me." She wrung her hands. "We've only been here a week. Leroy passed right before we left Akron. She was taking a nap when I left. I went to the neighbor's to buy eggs. I stayed longer than I should have. The change in location has upset her, and she's still grieving over her son. She's been a handful, and unpredictable."

Ellie fidgeted her hands. "Peter must be terrified."

Joel raked a hand through his hair. "He'll be in your arms in no time."

"Madam. Step aside. You're facing a mad woman. Now time's a wastin'." The sheriff motioned for the deputies to get ready to go in.

"Harriett, please! Let me in!" Pamela screamed, as a deputy subdued her.

The door creaked open a few inches.

The sheriff forced it open. His deputies ran in with him. "Put your gun down now!"

The woman ranted and raved and waved the rifle at them. "I'm his mother. Get out of this house now! You touch Leroy, and it will be your last day on this earth. You got it!"

Ellie eyed the sheriff through the open door. She held her breath and exhaled, shaking her hands. "She's in full view over there." Ellie pointed to the window. "Where's Peter?"

Joel gasped. "He'll be all right. The sheriff's got this under control."

His pale face didn't convince her. She loved him for attempting to keep her calm, but she didn't trust this crazed woman.

"Don't harm my sister!" Pamela struggled to get away from the deputy's grasp on the porch.

The sheriff took Harriett by surprise and grabbed the rifle. His other deputy pulled Harriet outside, dragged her hands behind her back, and handcuffed her. He had a tight grip on her arm.

Another deputy grabbed her other arm.

"Let go of me!" Harriett jerked her arm to no avail.

Pamela wagged a finger at Harriett. "I'm ashamed of you! You can't take a child. You're being ridiculous." She narrowed her eyes. "You were not to go anywhere without me."

Harriett's shoulders slumped and tears dampened her cheeks. "Please don't make me give Leroy up. He's mine."

The sheriff waved his hand. "Peter, you can kumme out now."

Peter bolted out the door. "Ellie! Joel!"

Joel and Ellie got out of the wagon and ran to him. Joel lifted him up, and they hugged him.

Peter shivered and swiped his tears. He'd wet his pants. "I was so scared. She kept calling me Leroy."

"She had a little boy named Leroy who got ill and passed. She wanted to believe you are him. She's not right in the head."

"I just want to go home. I don't ever want to see her

again." He buried his head in Joel's shoulder and had a tight grip on his shirt.

The sheriff handed the disturbed woman off to his deputies and approached Joel and Ellie. "I'll take care of the woman, and you take Peter home."

"Danki, Sheriff." Joel carried Peter and waited for Ellie to get seated. He slid her bruder on her lap.

Peter snuggled close to Ellie and held a fist of the fabric on her sleeve. He pressed his head against her. "She's so scary, Ellie." He wept and his body trembled.

Joel headed to Ellie's haus. "You're safe and the woman can't hurt you anymore." He rested a hand on Peter's leg.

Ellie tightened her arm around Peter and her hand gently held his head against her. "We'll be home in a few minutes, and you'll be with Snuggles and Cinnamon, safe and sound."

Peter had mashed his body so close to hers, she was uncomfortable. But she didn't move an inch. She'd do anything to make him feel safe again.

Joel had risked his life for them. He'd been close to the bakery at the time. Kumming to talk to her? His timing couldn't have been better.

She ached for their problems to dissolve so they could go back to the way things were between them before she told him about her past. His part in rescuing Peter made it even harder to accept they might never plan a future together and hurt worse than ever. She glanced at him. Maybe he'd changed his mind.

Joel pulled the buggy up at Liza and Jacob's. They were outside pacing across the yard with Abe and Esther. Jacob had his arm around Liza.

They came running to the buggy. "Peter!"

Jacob stepped up and scooped Peter in his arms. He put the boy on the ground, and Liza, Esther, and Abe circled them in a hug, then stepped back.

Liza's eyes damp, she wrapped her arms around her husband and Peter and turned her head to Joel and Ellie. "I'm glad you're both all right. I prayed and prayed for your safe return. I've been beside myself with worry. Jacob and Abe wanted to go and find you, but I begged them to stay here."

Jacob faced Joel. "We're so thankful you were there to help."

"She lived in the big white haus on the outskirts of town. It's an out of the way place. Liza's right. There was nothing you could do. We let the sheriff handle the situation, and he did a fine job." Joel gave them a reassuring smile.

"Danki for everything, Joel." Liza held Peter's hand. "Would you like to go inside?"

He hung his head and nodded.

"Esther, do you want to join us?" Liza waved her over. "I would love to."

"Abe and I paced and fretted." Jacob rubbed his arms. "We couldn't sit still. At least we would've been doing something. It took everything I had in me to stay put."

"I was as bad as he was, fidgeting and worrying." Abe clasped Joel's shoulder. "We did say a prayer for everyone's safety. We might never have found Peter if you hadn't followed them."

Ellie stood next to Joel and rolled her tense shoulders back. "Everything happened so fast. The woman grabbed Peter and practically threw him in her buggy, tied him up, then she took off with him. I ran out. Joel was near the bakery and saw what she was doing. He hurried and got in his wagon, and I did too. Esther ran to the sheriff as he was kumming into town. We took off after them. The mad woman dragged Peter inside her house before we could get to them. Her schweschder arrived and said the woman was not right in the head, had lost a son, and probably thought she could replace him with Peter."

Abe blew out a breath. "Did she have a gun? Were you in danger?"

Joel moved his boot across dry leaves, then met Abe's gaze. "A rifle. We stayed back at the sheriff's request and watched them through an open door and window. The hardest part was staying out of the way. I wanted to help, but I knew it was best to adhere to the sheriff's advice and stay in the wagon."

Jacob reared his head back. "You did the right thing. Did she surrender to the sheriff?"

Ellie held up her hands and let out an exasperated breath. "We watched and listened to the whole thing. Her schweschder, Pamela, begged the sheriff to let her reason with the mad woman, who we heard her call Harriett. The sheriff didn't trust Harriett not to harm Pamela. He burst in and wrestled the weapon from Harriett and subdued her, and Peter ran to us. I thought I was going to go mad before it was over. I was a mess. Without Joel, I'd have been at my wits' end. He was patient and calming."

Jacob clasped Joel's arm. "Danki for everything, Joel. We're blessed you were there."

He would do it all over again if necessary. The bond he had with this family had become important to him. The days he'd stayed away from Ellie and her family had left him with a sense of loss and sadness. He not only loved Ellie, but them too. "I wouldn't hesitate to do it again. You're all important to me."

"You've found a place in our hearts as well, Joel."
Abe patted his arm.

Jacob circled an arm around Ellie. "Hannah stayed
back to manage the bakery. She must be beside herself
with worry. Will you go and help her? Liza can then
stay with Peter the rest of the day. I'll tell her later the
details of what happened."

"I'd be glad to." She motioned for Joel to follow her
away from her family. "Danki. You gave me strength
today, just being with you. You said all the right things.
I fell apart."

"I may have appeared calm, but I was worried. You
did well under the circumstances." He wanted to tell
her how important she was to him, no matter what
they were going through. But he noticed the sheriff
headed in their direction. "The sheriff's here."

The sheriff halted his mare and dismounted. "We
have the woman in custody, but I'm sure the judge
will deem she go to the mental institution, where she
can't hurt anyone again. Pamela, the schweschder,
said she realizes she can no longer properly watch and
take care of her."

Jacob and Abe thanked the sheriff for his help.

"Such an unusual and frightening situation. I'm just
glad everyone was left unharmed." Jacob shook his head.

They all agreed.

"I've got to get back. You take care." The sheriff bid
them farewell and headed toward town.

Abe scratched his neck. "I should get back to work,
but I'll go in and ask Esther if she wants to stay or go
with me." He clapped Joel's back. "Danki, Joel, for what
you did. Ellie, sweetheart, I'm glad you're all right."
He winked at her.

Jacob hugged her. "Ellie, I'm glad you're home safe."
He stepped to Abe. "I'll go inside with you."

Ellie waved to them. "Love you both."

Jacob walked next to Abe to the haus, then stopped. "Kumming in with us, you two?"

Ellie waved them ahead. "I'd like to talk to Joel a few more minutes before I return to the bakery and help Hannah."

Jacob and Abe nodded and went inside.

She motioned to the bench near the pond. She clutched her heavy wool shawl, sat, and waited for him to sit next to her. "Let's get our minds off what happened today. I've got a question."

"What is it?" He rubbed his hands together and blew to warm them.

"A sweet little girl told me you went to Magdelena's for supper. Were you on your way to tell me so I wouldn't hear from someone else you were going to pursue her?" She sucked in her lips and stared at the ground.

His tightened chest eased. "Are you talking about Charity, Magdelena's little schweschder?"

She squinted and spoke soft. "Jah, she and her mamm came in the bakery to purchase some goodies. She mentioned you."

Her worried eyes and fidgeting hands endeared her more to him. Her sweet nature and soft expression didn't show any anger on her part over his harsh judgment of her during their previous meeting, just concern he might be severing their relationship for good. He wasn't proud of the harshness he'd shown her. He wouldn't cause her another minute of doubt.

"Mamm accepted the supper invitation, and she insisted I go. I made it clear to Magdelena and my parents I wasn't over you." He inched closer to her. "I reacted horribly to what you had to tell me about your past. I'm sorry, Ellie. Really sorry."

Ellie didn't respond right away. She watched a hawk fly over the water. "You've avoided me for days. What changed your mind and why now?"

He frowned. She'd taken a minute to gather her thoughts before commenting. He hoped she'd understand he was truly remorseful. He crossed his ankles. "Maryann's leaving tainted my view, and I made an unfair comparison. She left for a man she loved. You did not. She hasn't returned. You did. I have to choose to trust you, and I do."

Joel picked up a small stone and threw it in the water. Ripples moved across the pond. "I needed time to sort this all out. And I had an enlightening discussion with Daed. He and Mamm's relationship remains strained since Maryann left. Mamm's positive outlook and happy demeanor has all but disappeared, and she lets her grief overshadow the joy she could still have with Daed, me, and friends."

"He's the opposite of her. I feel bad for him." Ellie frowned.

Joel covered her hand with his. "He accepts the things he can't change, and he trusts God completely. He has the best attitude. He likes you and advised me to not make the worst mistake of my life if I love you. We all grieve differently. Who am I to judge?" He raised her hand to his lips and kissed it. "Forgive me?

"I do forgive you. But do you still have a sliver of doubt about me?"

"Nah, I promise."

"Good." She grinned. "I express my opinions more than the average Amish woman. I hope you can contend with that trait."

"I can manage. I may even wilkom it. I prefer a partner from whom I can ask advice."

He took her in his arms and kissed her tenderly on

the lips. His stomach danced and his heart soared. "I love you so much, Ellie."

"I love you too, Joel. I've missed you. Those were the longest days after we'd had our difficult conversation. I wondered what you had on your mind or if you'd ever speak to me again. It kept me up most nights. Maybe I'll get a decent night's sleep now."

"I didn't sleep peacefully either. Maybe we'll both get a good night's rest now we've reconciled." He stretched his arms over his head. "I should go home and explain why I've been gone so long."

"I understand. I can't danki you enough." She squinted and stared at her hands. "Joel, we still have to put off any plans for a future until your mamm softens her heart about me."

"God has turned bad into good. I trust God will take care of Mamm's disposition. We can put it behind us, and your family will help Peter overcome any fears he has left about this experience."

"Peter's been through a lot of turmoil and sad times. I'm impressed with how he overcomes adversity for someone so young."

"If folks aren't told that you and he aren't really bruder and schweschder by birth, they would never believe it, considering you both have so much in common. You're both strong-willed, are determined, speak your minds, and are brave."

"I'm not sure if you're complimenting us or not." She laughed.

"Compliments, for sure. All right, maybe not on the strong-willed trait." He touched her nose with his forefinger. "You're a beauty, Ellie Graber. How could I not fall in love with you?"

She blushed. "I'm glad you did."

He kissed her on the cheek and bid her farewell. "Give your family my regards."

"I will." She waved to him, went inside and checked on her family, and then left for the bakery. She left the horse and buggy at the livery and hurried across the street and inside the shop.

Hannah threw up her hands. "What happened? Is Peter all right? Are you all right?"

"Jah. Everyone's fine." She recounted the details to Hannah.

"How horrible!"

"It's been quite a day. After having such a terrible experience, Joel and I had a good talk before he left my haus. I just wish his mamm wasn't a problem."

"I'm sorry she's being so obstinate toward you. I'm happy you and Joel made up."

Customers entered and gathered around the counter.

"Will you man the counter? I'll go back to baking."

"Jah. I'll be fine." Ellie turned to the women. "What may I take off the shelves for you?"

The women each gave her their requests and paid for the purchases. They took seats at the tables and praised their desserts.

Ellie was glad the bakery was profitable and popular among the townsfolk. She had found solace, love, and peace working here.

She dragged a stool behind the counter and sat. Would Peter escape this unscathed? She'd be sad if he let it dampen his gift of looking on the bright side of things. His positive attitude was one of his best traits. They'd all help him get through the days ahead until this horrific event faded.

Joel had become close with her family, and they loved him. She was happy he wasn't interested in Magdelena. He loved her! What could she do to persuade Mrs. Wenger to really talk to her? She couldn't think of a thing. She'd depend on God to intervene.

Joel slumped his tired shoulders. The tension of Peter's rescue had depleted his strength. He didn't care. Ellie and he had reconciled, and they would pick up where they'd left off. She'd been quick to forgive him, and she hadn't made him grovel. He wouldn't have blamed her if she had. He'd thrown one question after another at her during her confession, and not in a kind way. Rehashing in his mind their talk, he was ashamed of himself. Proud of her to have withstood his tongue-lashing. She'd been humble and caring.

He secured the wagon and horse and went inside. His parents sat at the kitchen table having corn and potato soup.

"I was away for longer than I'd intended. I'm sorry."

"Where have you been?" His mamm got up, scooped soup into a bowl, poured him a glass of water, and then set both before him.

He sat on the hardwood chair and recounted what happened in town while he ate.

Daed sat upright. "Son, I'm relieved everyone came out of this all right." He rested his elbows on the table and held his palms out. "What are the odds something so horrible would happen in Charm? Our little sleepy community. I'm glad this woman will be prevented from harming anyone else, but I feel sorry for her. She's not well."

Mamm swiveled her head to her husband. "The woman is a menace. She deserves punishment for her actions, mad or not. Taking a child and putting him in harm's way. I have a hard time stirring up empathy for her."

Joel was sure she would've said the opposite before Maryann's leaving. She'd have empathy for most anyone. How could she change so much? He'd prayed to God and asked forgiveness for resenting Maryann and blaming her for Mamm's drastic personality change. "I have some work to do outside. I'll be in the barn." He put his hand on the doorknob.

Daed rose. "I'll go with you."

They strolled together to the barn. Daed rubbed Joel's back. "I'm proud of how you helped the Grabers, and I'm relieved you all survived unharmed. How about we grab our tools and hang the new shelves I made for the wall inside the barn?"

"Good idea." Daed, for the umpteenth time, was there for him. He'd calmed his nerves and stayed next to him while they worked. Daed's attempt to take Joel's mind off his problems was thoughtful, but it wasn't working. Ellie had a hold on his heart, and he had to talk to her about the importance of their future and not allowing anyone to stand in their way, and soon.

Chapter Ten

Ellie hugged Peter. "Are you sure you're all right to go to school today? You can kumme with Liza and me to the bakery."

"Nah. Daed said the sheriff will make sure the mean woman is in a special place where she can't get out and take me again." He grinned. "And this is Thursday, when we get two treats if we memorize a longer verse than usual. I memorized my Bible verse, so I'll get a piece of candy from the teacher."

Ellie smiled and tapped him on the top of the head. "What is it?"

Peter licked his lips and, feet apart, stood straight. "'And be kind to one another, tenderhearted, forgiving one another, even as God in Christ forgave you.'"

"Where's it found?"

Peter gave her a curt nod. "Ephesians 4:32."

"I'm impressed, little bruder. The verse isn't an easy one to recite. Very good." She rested her hand on his shoulder. "Do you forgive the woman who took you?"

He nodded. "I forgive her, but I don't *ever* want to see her again. She's scary, and she said really bad words." He put fingers to his mouth.

"What did she say?" Ellie would rather explain to him what they meant instead of him bringing them up to his teacher or friends.

"Shut up." His eyes widened and his shoulders raised.

Bad but could be worse. She didn't need to explain what those words meant, and Peter understood by his big-eyed expression and hand over his open mouth they were wrong to say. "Jah. We shouldn't use those words."

He shook his head. "Nah. We'd be in big trouble if we said what she did." He tilted his head. "I knew you'd kumme and get me."

She loved her little bruder. They were blessed he'd kumme to live with them after his mamm passed. Mae must've suspected her illness was serious. Ellie was thankful the woman had written a letter asking them to take Peter should anything happen to her. She remembered the day the sheriff brought Peter and the letter he found the day Mae passed. She'd liked Mae, and she had formed a bond with Peter and his mamm when she watched Peter while Mae worked in town.

He'd been through so much, and he hadn't allowed the grief over the passing of his mamm, daed, or schweschder to taint his desire to love, show compassion, and be kind to others. He loved life and trusted everyone until they gave him a reason not to. He had kumme through this most recent nightmare like a brave little soul.

She gazed in wonder at him. She'd learned much by his example. "You have a good heart, little bruder." She kissed his temple and then glanced out the window. "You better go. You'll be late. Daed's getting in the wagon to take you to school."

He hugged her, carried his dinner bag, and skipped out the door.

Liza came out of the bedroom minutes later. "Has Peter left? I couldn't find my list I'd written out before I went to bed last night. I found it on the floor under the nightstand. We had breakfast together, but I wanted to bid him farewell."

"He did leave, but don't worry, he'll be fine."

"Should we have kept him with us today to make sure he's really all right after having such a frightful experience?"

"I asked him, and he was confident in his decision to go to school. Getting him back into his routine may be the best medicine. Peter's tough. All his trauma has definitely made him stronger."

"He bounces back from all the difficult situations he's been through. He never ceases to surprise me." She squeezed Ellie's fingers. "You've been through your share of tragedy and hardships. The latest being your upset with Joel. Are you stronger because of it?" Liza tucked her list in the clean flour sack and hoisted it over her shoulder.

"I leaned on Mamm and Daed too much before she died. The good thing kumming from what I've been through is I'm stronger and better prepared to handle difficulties. I'm more mature, and I take time to consider the cost of my actions. I'll make mistakes, and my stubbornness will still land me in trouble, but I'll not stray from God or the Amish life."

Liza chuckled and opened the door. "We'll all disappoint and upset others at one time or another. I admire the woman you've become, Ellie. I'm blessed to call you dochder."

"You provide a home full of love and warmth, Liza. Danki for taking care of us like you do."

"I have everything I'd ever need or want with my family. I pray you have the same someday with your husband and kinner." She motioned for Ellie to follow her to the wagon. "Let's go visit Mrs. Wenger after work. We need to do all we can to show her she's wrong about you."

Ellie climbed in the wagon and slid onto the bench next to Liza. "Should I tell Joel?"

"Nah. Let's surprise her and Joel."

They picked up Hannah at her haus. "Liza and I are going to visit Mrs. Wenger after work. I'm hoping she'll wilkom us and we can have a pleasant conversation without her animosity kumming through."

Grimacing, Hannah held the rail as the wheel hit a bump in the road and jostled the three of them on the bench. "She might, but her nasty looks at you after church and badgering you when you went to dinner with them upsets me. I don't like you being disrespected over and over again by this woman."

Ellie raised her hands and lifted her shoulders. "I have to make an effort to change her mind about me. Otherwise, Joel and I may as well sever ties. God isn't going to bless our union one day if Mrs. Wenger is so against us being together. The ongoing turmoil for years to kumme for Joel and his parents, over me, would fill me with a mountain of guilt."

"First, let's go to her haus and have a friendly visit." Liza folded her hands in front of her. "If it goes well, then you'll be encouraged. If not, you may need to alter your decision to pursue a future with Joel. I love your daed, and we have a good marriage, but our lives together are not without sacrifices, compromise, and hard work."

Ellie kept her chin to her chest and looked at Liza.

"You wouldn't marry Daed until I approved. Mrs. Wenger's objection to me is similar. I better understand the helplessness you must've experienced when you reached out to me and I rejected you."

"God intervened and blessed us more than we could've imagined. He may do the same for you or introduce you to another man later. Read the scriptures and pray. Seek God's will and be open to it. He doesn't promise life will be easy. He does promise to always be with us and to not give us more than we can handle."

Love had sprung joy in her heart the first time she'd realized Joel was the man for her. The sick ache she'd had each day he'd stayed away from her after she told him about her time in the world had been painful. Losing him for good would be agony. She'd imagined love as a happy and wonderful time when she'd get to experience it with someone. With Joel, she did enjoy the thrill of being in his presence, his woodsy scent, and the brush of his lips on hers when he kissed her. She wanted a lifetime with him. She pulled into the livery and walked to the bakery with Liza and Hannah.

Hannah walked in the middle of them on the boardwalk, halted on the side of the road, and pulled Liza and Ellie back. "Watch out!"

A motorcar came around the corner and the thick-mustached owner shook his fist. "Get out of the way, you simpletons!"

Her hand fisted, Ellie raised her arm halfway, then dropped it to her side. Liza and Hannah would never make such a gesture at the Englischer. A bit of rebellion reared its ugly head at times, and she struggled to control the urge to lash out. Being around Liza and Hannah and living the Amish life had helped. Her fear was speaking before thinking if Mrs. Wenger proceeded in centering on her faults. Not something she could afford to let happen if she wanted to accomplish her goal in winning the woman over. Having Liza with her to go to Mrs. Wenger's was a very good idea.

Ellie sold the last rhubarb and cherry tart. "We sold everything off the shelves today."

"The Englischers are having a social gathering at the inn this evening, with dancing and music. I overheard two ladies saying the event had been advertised and a lot of visitors came to attend."

Ellie lifted a clean cloth from the shelf behind the counter. The piano music had mesmerized her at the dance hall she and Jane had gone to. The piano player's fingers had glided across the white and black keys, creating a rhythm and sound that made her want to tap her foot, clap her hands, and sway to the music. She'd loved being a part of those happy times. The Amish would be appalled she'd learned steps from Jane and participated in such a gathering. Her cheeks warmed. Joel would be even more disgusted than he had before knowing those details. Nothing she could do about her prior poor decisions.

She'd moved on, and she'd not dwell on them. "I like having a steady stream of customers. The day goes by fast."

"Hannah and I have the kitchen in order for tomorrow. The front is clean enough. We'll drop Hannah off and head to Mrs. Wenger's." She held up a plate. "I've got her molasses cookies."

"Your cookies would make anyone smile. Hand her one off the plate first. It's sure to put her in a good mood." Hannah stuffed her dirty apron in a clean flour sack.

Ellie chuckled and followed Liza and Hannah out the door, locking it behind them. "Let's go!" Ellie hurried with them to the livery. She drove Hannah home, and she and Liza went to visit Mrs. Wenger. Her hands shook as they walked to the front door and rapped on it.

Mrs. Wenger cracked open the door. "Ellie, Liza, what do you want?"

"We've kumme to chat with you, if you don't mind." Liza offered her the plate. "I hope you like molasses cookies."

"Oh . . . well . . . kumme in. Danki." Mrs. Wenger accepted the cookies. "Have a seat."

Ellie scanned the room. She assumed things might not be as neat and clean in the home, since they'd caught Joel's mamm off guard. She'd been wrong. The woman had her patchwork quilts folded over hardwood quilt racks in two corners. The maple furniture had stuffed dark blue cushions without one piece of lint on them, and her floors were minus a speck of dust. There wasn't a broom or dusting cloth in sight.

Ellie scanned the haus. The open entryway to the kitchen gave her a full view of the empty counter and organized pots and pans hanging on wall hooks. Their haus always had a pan or two on the stove or Peter's toys or a pair of socks lying somewhere. An empty coffee cup or spoon ready to wash. The cushions or quilts were never as straight as Mrs. Wenger's. The home lacked warmth and coziness. She wondered if Joel had to have everything as tidy and clean as his mamm. She wasn't one to make a big mess, but leaving a cup in the sink or a blanket bunched on her bed, or knitting left out of the bag happened often. "How has your day been, Mrs. Wenger?"

The woman scowled at her. "Very busy. I'm not accustomed to uninvited guests."

"Forgive us for dropping in on you. I'm used to my friends stopping by without notice, and I assumed you wouldn't mind." Liza smiled. "You and I haven't had a conversation yet, and I wanted to get to know you better." She motioned to the patchwork quilt. "This is lovely."

Mrs. Wenger rose and lifted the coverlet. "This belonged to my grossmudder. I didn't repair the tattered pieces of material in the middle. I didn't want to add more handiwork to hers. I find the frayed edges of the material endearing and showing its years of use. We were close, and she taught me to stitch clothes and quilts much better than Mamm." Mrs. Wenger folded the quilt and returned it centered on the rack. "Would you like some hot tea? I made some earlier. I'm sure it's still warm."

"I'd love some. May I help you?" Ellie stood.

"Nah. Please sit. I'll be right back." Mrs. Wenger padded to the kitchen.

Liza and Ellie sat silent.

Ellie tapped her foot on the floor and fidgeted her hands.

Liza covered her knee. "Relax. Everything will be fine."

Mrs. Wenger returned from the kitchen. "Your molasses cookies are delicious, Liza. I've had them at the social. They're quite a favorite among the women." She set the tray with cookies, plates, napkins, and cups of tea on the long, plain oak table in front of them. "Help yourselves." She took a cookie.

"Since Ellie and Joel have formed a friendship which

has blossomed into them considering a future together, I thought we should meet and tell you they have Jacob's and my full support. We couldn't ask for a better suitor for Ellie."

Mrs. Wenger held her cup and threw her shoulders back. "Mrs. Graber . . . uh. . . ."

Palm up, Liza smiled. "Call me Liza."

Blushing, Mrs. Wenger licked her lips. "And call me Naomi."

"Does this go for Ellie too?" Liza tilted her head and wrinkled her nose.

"I suppose." Naomi smoothed her skirt. "Like I was saying, Joel is faithful to God and very committed to the Amish life. He needs a partner he can trust and who shares this desire."

"I do share his same desire." Ellie bit her tongue. Too late. The words had flown out of her mouth. "I'm sorry. I meant to speak in a softer voice." She set her plate on the table. She feared her clenched stomach couldn't handle a bite of food.

Liza sipped her tea and balanced the cup on her other palm. "Ellie's past should remain there. She's done all she can do to make up for her errors in judgment. She grieved her mamm's passing in a way you and I would not approve of, but her daed and I love her and know she's learned from her mistakes. Joel and she want their families' blessing to move forward. I pray you'll give them yours. What a blessing it would be if you would allow our families to become close. I'm here today to help build a bridge between you and Ellie."

"Liza, I have nothing against you. The women in the community admire you. Your reputation is stellar."

"Danki, but I have my shortcomings. The best part

of friendship is accepting each other with our flaws. Don't you agree?"

"Ellie, I can accept flaws like not being a good cook or haus cleaner, but running from the Amish life to seek answers in the outside world is something I can't tolerate." Naomi turned her attention to Liza. "You risked accepting this girl into your life by marrying Jacob. I've heard she gave you a hard time before she gave in to you and her daed. She may run at the first sign of trouble and leave your family brokenhearted. I'd rather Joel not take the chance."

Her throat constricted, Ellie fought to hold back tears. "I promise you, Naomi. I will never turn away from the Amish life again."

"I'm sorry, Ellie. Your actions have shown me what you're capable of doing, and running to the world to solve your problems is not what should enter an Amish girl's mind. I've heard you boasted about what the world had to offer the first time you returned. You had to flee twice before you settled on remaining Amish. Sounds like it was a hard decision to kumme back, due to finding the appealing things you enjoyed. Things that are unacceptable when living the Amish life. Maybe hard to let go."

Liza put down her teacup and crossed the room. She pulled a chair closer to Naomi. She took the woman's hand in hers. "We know about Maryann's departure. I'm deeply sorry for the anguish you must have over her decision. I pray she'll return to you. Please don't punish Ellie because of your dochder's decision. There's nothing more she can do but show you through her actions and words she's being truthful. Your treatment of her is hurting me, watching her yearn for one ounce of kindness from you. As a mamm, I'm sure you can relate to what I'm saying."

Ellie let her tears trail down her cheeks. Liza had loved her unconditionally and worked hard to win her affection. She'd defended Ellie numerous times. Ellie loved Liza with all her heart and soul. She'd do anything for her, and Liza had proven many times she would do the same. Naomi's pinched lips had softened. Had Liza gotten through her tough exterior?

"We're not to mention Maryann." Naomi's lips quivered.

"You can speak of her to us. We'll keep our conversation confidential. Sometimes we need someone to allow us to share our pain and comfort us. Ellie and I are here for you."

Naomi slid her hand from under Liza's. "An Englischer took Maryann against her will. I can't convince Shem or Joel this is true. I'm furious they won't believe me and look for her. They say I can't accept the truth. They say her letter states she's in love with the man and chose to leave with him. He coerced her. I'm sure of it. She'd return to me if she could." She darted her eyes to Ellie and back to Liza. "Ellie chose to leave the Amish life. She came back thrilled about her time in the world, left again, and then returned a second time. I just can't trust her. Not for my son."

Liza remained seated. "Will you please allow Ellie to visit you? Maybe if you open your heart to her, you'll dismiss your misgivings about her."

"We could make a quilt together. Teach me your favorite pattern. Or whatever you would like, we can do." Ellie rose and folded her hands behind her back.

Naomi went to the door. "Liza, you're a kind woman. I don't want to upset you, but I won't do as you and Ellie ask. I'm a mamm, and I will never cease protecting my son. I wish you both the best, and I hope we can remain cordial. Good day." She opened the door.

Liza took Ellie's hand. They left the house and crossed the yard, shoes crunching dry leaves, to the wagon. "I'm so sorry, Ellie. She has allowed the pain of her dochder to darken her heart and close her mind to you."

"Why? Maryann's and my reasons for leaving the Amish life were different. Furthermore, I came back and she didn't."

Liza shifted on the bench and held the reins, keeping the horses still. She swiped a tear. "I believe every time she looks at you, you're a reminder of Maryann. I may be wrong. If I'm right, I don't foresee you and Joel ever receiving her blessing. As hard as it would be, Ellie, you should let him go for both your sakes."

Ellie dropped her head in her hands and cried.

"I'll be with you through this, Ellie, and so will your daed. I wish things had gone better. I'm so sorry. This will be one of the hardest things you'll ever have to face."

"I don't know if I can let him go. I love him so much." She knew Liza was right.

Joel's mamm had dug her heels in the ground, and her determination to shut Ellie out had never been more apparent than today. Ellie could never be the reason for a rift between Joel and his mamm. Nothing good would kumme from it, and Joel might grow to resent her over time.

"God may be shutting this door for you. Pray and search the scriptures. He'll guide you."

The possibility sent a wave of nausea in her middle. They'd had their share of conflicts with his mamm, Abigail, and his distaste for her outside-world adventures. Should their relationship be this difficult? Had she plowed through their field of problems and not given enough thought to God's will? Had God been trying to tell her all along Joel wasn't the one?

Her head ached. "I have forged ahead with Joel and ignored God's signs. I pushed them aside to satisfy my selfish desires. Like I did when I ran away. I have to face the harsh reality that Joel and I aren't meant for each other, or the consequences for both of us will be too great."

Ellie peered over her shoulder. Joel and his daed were kumming down the lane. She had hoped to leave before they returned, to have time to digest her unpleasant visit with Mrs. Wenger.

Joel and his daed pulled up and got out of their wagon.

"Greetings! Did you just arrive?" Joel approached Ellie's side of the wagon. "Mrs. Graber, it's a pleasure."

Liza waved a dismissive hand. "Now I told you, call me Liza."

Joel's daed grinned. "Kumme in for some coffee."

Ellie swallowed the emotion swirling through her mind. Joel's big blue eyes and sweet smile warmed her heart. His beaming face showed he cared. Their connection was so strong.

She forced a smile to hide her disappointment and hurt. "We've been inside chatting with Naomi before you arrived. We should get home and fix supper for the family."

"Understood, although we'd love to have you join us here. I'm sure Naomi can rustle up something. We'll send you home with enough to feed the rest of your family." Shem adjusted his hat.

"Danki for the generous offer, but we've got to get going." Liza waved. "Enjoy the rest of your day." She lifted the reins.

"Wait just a minute." Joel held up a forefinger. "I'll be right back."

Ellie's jaw dropped. What did he have in mind? How long could she disguise her turmoil?

Liza leaned close to Ellie. "Are you ready, Ellie, or do you wish to stay and talk to Joel? I can kumme back and get you, or he can bring you home. I'm not sure what you want to do."

Ellie twisted her lips. "Should I let his mamm tell him what transpired?" Would his mamm tell him everything she'd said to her?

"Nah. You should share with him about our visit and then discuss your thoughts. Communication is important."

She wanted Joel to hear her side of things. She doubted his mamm would keep their conversation from him. "All right. I'll stay and ask him to bring me home."

"I'll save you a plate of food. Take your time. I love you, Ellie." Liza hugged her.

Ellie swallowed the sob fighting to get out of her throat and nodded. She slid out of the wagon and bid farewell to Liza.

"You're not going home with Liza?" Joel came over to her and waved to Liza.

"Nah. I need to tell you something."

He tilted his head and lifted his brow. "All right." He grinned. "I asked Daed to stow the horse for me, and I was going to ask if you'd stay." He brushed her damp cheek. "Something isn't right. What is it? Did Mamm offend you or Liza?"

"Do you mind if we take a walk out of earshot from your daed?"

He nodded. "We'll go on the other side of the smokehaus. Let me get a blanket from the barn."

"I'll wait here. I'd rather your daed not ask what's wrong with me."

"I'll hurry." He left and returned with a rolled blanket under his arm. "You have me worried, Ellie."

She wished she could assure him there was nothing to fret about, but she would be lying. "Your mamm let us inside, and she and Liza started off on a positive path, and then she made it clear she wouldn't accept me and you pursing a future together. She's adamant in her stance."

Joel took her hands in his. "Ellie, I won't let her destroy what we've built between us. You can't either. She's a troubled woman, riddled with anger and fear over losing Maryann. Losing her dochder has muddied her mind and clouded her vision on many things. Let me reason with her."

He'd truly forgiven her. She wanted this whether they pursued a future or not. *What a gift from God.* His determination made this clearer than ever to her. She loved him for his devotion, but he was being naïve.

"Hasn't your relationship with your mamm been strained since she's become aware we care for each other?"

"Jah, but we're not at fault. She is."

He'd blinded himself as she had, to avoid the obvious. His mamm's objection had become a problem they could do nothing about, and they had to kumme to grips with it before they caused more destruction to Joel's relationship with Mrs. Wenger.

"The tension in your haus over me isn't good for your family. You and your daed are suffering because of me."

"Don't worry. Daed and I are used to Mamm's moods since Maryann left. You're not the only reason she's difficult."

"I need to step back from you for all your sakes." She pressed a hand to her throat and stifled the ache of what her words meant to both of them.

He grasped her upper arms. "Nah! Ellie, please! We've climbed mountains of problems to maintain our love for each other. I won't let anyone kumme between us. You're the woman for me. No one else."

She let his declaration linger in her mind and savored the joy singing in her heart. Then the thud of disappointment and grief came over her. She tightened her quivering lips, but they wouldn't cooperate. She pressed her fingers to her mouth.

He pulled her to him and kissed her hair. "I'm never letting you go, Ellie. We've got a lot to look forward to. I'll protect, honor, and love you all of my days."

She took a step back. "We can't pretend your mamm is the reason we must part. I didn't want to admit it, but God may be closing doors we aren't willing to recognize. Are you ignoring them too? Haven't we been fooling ourselves?"

"Nah. You're wrong. We're not responsible for Mamm's flawed judgment and dark outlook. I won't let her bully you or me into getting her way."

The more Joel poured out his heart, the more she knew she was right. Everything he mentioned would cause more dissention and distance between them.

She couldn't let this go on. "I can't live with driving a wedge between you and her. I almost destroyed Daed and Liza's happiness. I won't do it again to you and your mamm."

"She's unreasonable and bitter, Ellie. Please. I believe God means for us to fall in love, marry one day, and have a family. Please marry me, Ellie. We'll show her how in love we are and what a good fraa you are, and she'll kumme around."

She'd give anything to marry him. And he was right. She would be a loving fraa to him. This was so heartrending. "I'm sorry, Joel. I've been selfish in the past, and I won't do it again. The pain it causes others isn't right. Please take me home. There's nothing more we can say or do."

Joel stared at her. His beautiful Ellie was slipping out of his life. Nah. He wouldn't let himself go there. She'd go home and think this over and kumme to her senses.

"I'll harness the mare to the buggy."

"If you don't mind, I'll sit on the bench under the old oak tree until you're ready to leave."

He nodded and went to the buggy, then returned. Daed and Ellie were talking. He didn't approach them but took steps close enough to overhear them. He hoped they didn't notice him.

Daed held out his hand. "God has created a beautiful earth. I never tire of taking in the splendor of the fields, gardens, and wonders of God's making."

"I like the butterflies. I'll miss them this winter."

"You're like a butterfly in Joel's life. Danki for bringing him such happiness. He's got a lilt in his step, and he whistles more often since he's met you. Please forgive my fraa for her behavior. She's chosen to wallow in her pain and suffering. Don't take it personal."

Joel swelled with love for his daed. The man had said the best thing possible to Ellie. He held his breath, waiting for her response. He stayed back, hoping they wouldn't notice him.

"I'm afraid I must."

Joel let out the breath and hung his head. He waved to her. "I'm ready, Ellie."

"Don't rob yourself or Joel of happiness, Ellie. True love isn't easy to kumme by." Daed smiled and walked away.

Joel watched his daed stroll to the horse in the corral. He was grateful to Daed for encouraging Ellie to reconsider severing their relationship. Ellie's damp eyes and her slow steps to the buggy showed she was burdened.

He waited for her to get in and then flicked the reins and headed to her haus. "Ellie, please don't shut me out."

"My decision is not by choice. I'm confident I'm doing the right thing. Hard as it is, it will save us and our families a lot of heartache."

"You're punishing us unjustly. Mamm is angry, frustrated, and taking it all out on you. Ignore her. She'll snap out of it one day or not. Either way, you shouldn't allow her to dictate our lives." He had to dampen his struggle to not show his frustration. "Please, Ellie, let's be happy and plan a wedding."

"Your mamm will make our lives, your daed's, and, possibly, our kinner's, miserable. We can't ignore her. I've tried to appeal to her, and she won't listen. We can't fix this problem, and we must face it may be God's will for us to part."

He couldn't believe her resolve. They'd overcome so much. Nah. He couldn't let this happen. His mamm had made his life miserable long enough. "Ellie, I'll go to the bishop, schedule a date, and we'll get married. Mamm will attend, and all will be well in time." He halted the buggy in front of her haus.

"Nah, Joel. I'm sorry. I can't. Please don't kumme by here or the bakery. It's too hard on me." She sprang from the buggy, sobbing as she ran across the lawn.

He called out to her. "I'm not giving up. I believe

God has put us together, and I'm going to pray God brings you back to me."

His heart jumped as she slowed. Then she ran inside. Falling in love wasn't as easy and enjoyable as he had imagined. Like growing crops, it took hard work and determination. He had the strength and willingness to do both. Anything for Ellie.

He gazed at the road ahead as he headed for home. "Dear Heavenly Father, work a miracle in our lives. Bring Ellie back to me. Heal Mamm's heart. Show her the destruction of her ways. Please, Heavenly Father, please. Amen."

He believed God could do anything, and there was no reason God wouldn't do a mighty work in his life and grant his desire. Joel was a patient man, and he would wait. The day would kumme when he would stand before Ellie in front of friends and family and pledge his love and commitment to her. He knew it.

He arrived home, unharnessed the mare, took her to the barn, and gave her water and food. The animal moved her head from side to side and stepped up and back. "What's wrong, girl?"

The horse neighed, kicked the stall, and turned from him. She finished her water and food and settled down.

He examined her. She didn't appear to have any wounds. She'd finished her food. He shrugged. She must've had a bad day too. He'd let her rest.

He rubbed his aching neck. He'd learned time could heal wounds of the body and the heart. The same way he'd gotten over Ellie's past and made the decision to trust her. He believed God would bring Ellie back to him. He'd wait for as long as it took.

Chapter Eleven

Ellie poured coffee for Dr. Harrison and the sheriff Friday morning. "Dr. Harrison, you're quiet, reading the paper. What's caught your interest?"

He lowered the pages and peered over them. "Hydrox cookies are being compared to Oreo cookies by the writer. They both have chocolate wafers with a white cream filling but taste different. He claims Oreos are much better. Oreos haven't made it to our neck of the woods yet. They're new this year. I'm going to ask Wilbur at the general store if he'll get some in. I'd like to form my own opinion."

The sheriff harrumphed. "You must have a lot of time on your hands if you care so much about cookies." He threw up a thick hand. "Doesn't take much to occupy him. He'll have his nose in any article making a comparison. He yearns for a good argument."

"I beg your pardon. You're the one always wanting to argue. Not me." Dr. Harrison leaned back and stared at his friend.

Ellie turned to hide the grin on her face. She was grateful for their distraction. She'd been broken-hearted over her parting from Joel and hadn't been able to shake their dilemma from her thoughts. Leave it to these two to lift her spirits with their bantering. "Both sound good to me."

"I like all the cookies you make and sell. Cookies made in a factory, in my humble opinion, won't ever compare to yours. Especially Liza's molasses cookies." The sheriff rubbed his round stomach.

"I agree, and those molasses cookies are one of my favorites. I have a hard time turning down any of your goods." The doctor picked up his cookie and took a bite.

The men finished their food and drink and departed, debating if Jeb Stone would purchase a Model T Ford motorcar or if he was all talk.

Ellie chuckled. The two men kept her entertained.

Liza and Hannah carried in trays of tarts and pies to her.

"These look wonderful." Ellie sniffed the apple and cherry pies on the shelves. "Love the aroma, and they're still warm."

Hannah stood next to her and displayed the raspberry tarts. "On our ride in, you mentioned you and Joel couldn't be together because of his mamm. I understand if you don't want to talk about it, but are you sure? She's not a nice woman. You shouldn't allow her to control your life."

Liza held the empty trays. "I agree, Hannah. But Ellie has a point. Naomi would always be a part of their lives. The tension could cause a lot of turmoil. Ellie and Joel can't ignore the potential problem."

"It's so unfair." Hannah crossed her arms.

"Sometimes we want to justify our actions and thinking to have our desires when they aren't God's will for us, and we cause ourselves trouble for being selfish. The result of forging ahead with Joel and not considering his mamm's opinions could be detrimental to our future marriage and their relationship. We're forced to move on."

"Whatever happens, you and Joel will eventually find happiness with each other or someone else." Liza stepped to the kitchen's open doorway. "We like Joel. We would be thrilled to have him as a part our family. I'm sorry it's not working out."

"I'm rooting for Joel. Ellie. You're being unreasonable. God is all powerful. You'll find out." Hannah squeezed Ellie's shoulder and then followed Liza to the kitchen.

Ellie cherished Hannah so much. The girl had a steadfast faith when she was convinced she was right. She prayed Hannah was right.

Ellie rearranged the custard and milk pies again on the top shelf Monday afternoon. A steady stream of customers was what she needed. Too much time to think was driving her mad. She had been extra busy at home. She yawned and stretched. No wonder she was tired. The last three weeks, she'd helped bring in the harvest. She'd dug potatoes from the garden until she had blisters on her hands and fingers, canned more vegetables and fruits than she cared to count, and made applesauce, apple butter, and jams with Liza. Daed had taken care of the corn and bedding the garden down for winter.

She'd cleaned the bakery's every nook and cranny from top to bottom, and she'd gone into the kitchen with Liza and Hannah to start recipes and finished them between waiting on customers. All of this activity to take her mind off Joel. He had darted out after Sunday services like his pants were on fire. He didn't

like to miss a meal. He must be desperate to stay away
from her.

She had hoped they'd run into each other by now.
She stared at the ceiling. What was he doing? Thinking
about her? Did he miss her? He must be terribly disappointed with her to stay away so long. She slapped her
head. What did she expect? She'd told him to stay
away, and she'd given him no hope she'd change her
mind. She'd been reading the scriptures and praying
for God's guidance.

Maybe she'd reacted too fast after having such a
disappointing meeting with Mrs. Wenger. Nah, she
couldn't sugarcoat this. She'd stand by her decision.
Couldn't they be friends and speak? They lived in the
same town and had some of the same friends, and they
couldn't avoid each other forever. She'd go to the
woods where he told her he found peace and tranquil-
ity to pray and ponder what to do sometimes. She
hoped he'd be there. They'd have privacy to talk.

Joel scanned the calendar Monday morning. The
three weeks he'd avoided Ellie seemed like three years.
He'd sat in the back at church services and left right
after the message and hymns were over. He'd wanted
to give her plenty of time to miss him and change her
mind. He didn't want to plead or badger her to plan a
future with him. Staying for the after-service meals
would have made it difficult to avoid her.

He couldn't let another day go by without having
a conversation with her. He went to town. The post
office was on the way to the bakery. He'd stop and get
the mail first. He went inside, stood in line, and
greeted friends.

The postmaster handed him the mail. "Here you go."

"Danki." He strolled out, leaned against a post, and sorted through the envelopes.

He froze. A forwarded letter from Lancaster to Charm from Maryann. It was as if he were in a tunnel, alone. The squeak of buggy wheels, clip-clop of horses' hooves on the hard dirt road, and chatter of the townsfolk grew dim. He clutched the envelope and didn't move. The return address said Massillon, Ohio. *Not far away.* She'd not told them where she and the Englischer were going. Daed had searched for her, but he couldn't find them in the neighboring towns. He had a farm to run, and she'd left of her own free will. They had done all they could to find her. Why had she written now? He'd left their forwarding address with the postmaster in Lancaster, never thinking they'd actually hear from Maryann again.

He tightened his grip on the envelope. Part of him didn't want to know where she was or what she wanted. The other part of him was afraid of what she had to say. Was she hurt? Ill? In trouble? Why had she addressed it to him? He ripped the seal open and unfolded the page, and then he refolded it and stuffed it back in the envelope. He had to read this in private.

He'd talk to Ellie later. Whatever Maryann had written could make his situation worse with Ellie. He couldn't let Maryann or his mamm rob him of Ellie. He got in his wagon and went to his favorite quiet place in the woods not far from his haus. He scanned the acreage. Nah sign of anyone. Quiet, except for the woodpecker working hard on the tree near his spot. He shook the wool blanket he'd brought with him and spread it on the ground. He stretched out on his side and reopened the page.

Dear Joel,

I should've written to tell you where I'm living and how I am. I'm sorry for the worry I must've caused you and our parents over the years.

I didn't address this letter to Mamm or Daed because you're the strong one, and I'm counting on our closeness to appeal to you to help me. I'm living in Massillon, Ohio, in Clara Bee's Boarding House on Main Street, down the street from the blacksmith's shop. It's painted blue with a red sign. My room is number four.

My husband, Gerald Harding, passed a little over a month ago. He got into trouble, and he wasn't a good man. I'm cooking meals at Clara Bee's to earn a living. I'll tell you more if you decide to kumme. Please write and let me know either way if you will help me. If not, I'll need to move soon. Please, Joel, kumme. I need you.

Love, Maryann.

He read the letter three times. His mouth got dry and his heart heavy. Maryann put herself down when she compared her form to other girls growing up. She'd been short for her age and plump, and her pointed nose didn't help. She had blue eyes and striking straight white teeth. A wonderful cook, she did everything to perfection. He loved his schweschder so much. He was twenty-two. She'd be twenty. They'd lost precious years together.

He'd played games with her, and they'd worked alongside each other in the garden. She'd been at his side when she wasn't with Mamm. She was timid and painfully shy growing up. She'd offered to get supplies or food, and he'd been grateful to have more time to complete his chores by himself. He had no idea she'd been meeting a man. He'd trusted her.

Or had he been too busy to notice? He'd found her annoying at times when she'd wanted to tag along with him and his friends. Guilt settled in his chest. He should've paid more attention. What had this man done to her? She'd stayed with him for three years. Why hadn't she asked for help before now? Had he threatened her if she left him? She mentioned he'd passed. He had a bucket of questions. How could he keep Maryann's letter from his parents if he went to help her? He'd have to tell them something, and he didn't want to lie.

He stood. Who was near? He swiveled his head to the open pathway. Someone took heavy steps, their shoes crunching leaves in his direction. Foe or friend?

He gasped. "Ellie, what are you doing here?"

She tripped on a large branch, struggled to regain her balance, and fell into him. She blushed and didn't move from his grasp. "I remembered you told me about your favorite spot. I hoped you'd be here. I wanted to talk to you. It's been a long three weeks."

"What did you want to talk to me about?" His heart pounded as he gazed into her eyes and held her hands. Maybe she'd kumme to say yes to his proposal.

"I said we shouldn't marry. I didn't mean we shouldn't speak to each other at services or if we should run into each other. You've been avoiding me. You don't stay for the meal after the sermons. We live in the same town, and we should at least be civil and speak."

"Ellie, you told me to stay away, and I've honored your request. If I gave you time, I thought you'd miss me and change your mind." He pulled her to him.

"Please, Ellie, tell me you love me and you've missed me as much as I've missed you."

She stepped back. "I'm sorry I've been confusing. And I do love you. And, of course, I miss you." She swiped her damp eyes with the corner of her apron. "As much as it pains me, though, I have to remain strong in my decision, for both our sakes." She turned to go.

He reached for her hand. "Ellie, please stay. I need direction. I received a letter from Maryann. I'm not sure I should do what she's asking."

Her eyes grew wide. "Maryann sent you a letter!"

"I picked it up at the post office earlier. I had planned to kumme into the bakery to speak to you, then I got distracted after receiving Maryann's note." He handed it to her. "Read it and give me your thoughts."

She scanned Maryann's message. "Joel, this is good news. She's reaching out for your help, and she's ready to kumme home."

"Ellie, it's not a simple task. What if I bring her to Charm and she leaves again? My family has suffered enough. No telling what Mamm's state of mind would be if Maryann abandoned us again."

"This is a blessing from God. Your parents have longed to have her back here again. I'd like to go with you. I understand how hard it is to return to the Amish life once you've been away. I want to remind her the majority of our Amish community will wilkom her with open arms and assure her we'll be here for her."

"I can't ask you to go with me. It wouldn't be safe or proper. And she says her husband had gotten into trouble. Who knows what we'd get ourselves into once we found my schweschder."

"All the more reason we should go. She may be in serious trouble and not have anyone else to turn to."

He quirked a brow. "We?" He shook his head. "Nah. I'm not going to jeopardize your reputation by taking you. If I go, I may or may not have to stay overnight."

She hadn't hesitated to put their differences aside to help him. She'd risk the reputation she'd worked so hard to rebuild. She had never met Maryann, and yet she wanted to kumme to her aid. He tensed with guilt for not reacting the same way himself. Another reason he loved her. He'd noticed Ellie's compassion in the way she treated her family, friends, and customers.

She beamed. "We wouldn't go alone. I had in mind to ask Daed to accompany us. He'll go if I ask him. After what I put him through, he'll be happy to bring Maryann back to your parents. I cringe at how painful it must've been for him, wondering where I was, what I was doing, and if I was safe. He and I had a precious reunion. I'd like your parents to experience the same with your schweschder."

Should he ask his daed? Nah. He should find Maryann and gauge the situation before telling his parents anything. "*Caution* is the word kumming to mind. I'm not sure what we'll run into once we arrive and talk to her."

"It doesn't matter. We'll enlist the assistance of the sheriff if we need to. We must make sure she's safe. I couldn't rest if we don't go to her. I want to help you and your family, Joel." She passed the paper to him. "Let's go to my haus. We'll show the note to Daed, and you and he can put together a plan to meet her."

"My parents will be furious I've involved you." He wouldn't be in their good graces for keeping this secret. And when they found out he'd told and enlisted Ellie and Jacob for help, they'd really be upset.

"I believe your parents will be ecstatic to have their dochder with them again. Then it won't matter they weren't told right away or who went with you."

"You're a sweetheart, Ellie Graber."

Her cheeks pinked. "I'm glad you think so, Joel Wenger. Now, let's get going. Where's your wagon?"

"I hid it on the other side, behind those trees." He pointed to the area. "If Daed or Mamm passed by, I didn't want them to wonder why I was here. I needed time to gather my thoughts. Where's yours?"

"Not far from yours." They walked in the direction of their wagons and headed to Ellie's place.

He followed her. Ellie was willing to drop everything and take his dilemma on to help Maryann. His thought process had taken the wrong direction until she convinced him to go to his schweschder. He'd considered ignoring Maryann's plea, to avoid any trouble she might bring with her. Could he have carried this out? He doubted it. He loved Maryann so much, and she'd chosen to reach out to him. She'd always depended on him until she married the Englischer.

He turned down Ellie's lane behind her and pulled his horse next to hers. Ellie offering to go with him was a relief. Her daed was the perfect person to accompany them with his level head and compassion for others. Ellie's leaving had prepared him better than Joel for tackling this situation. He slid off the bench, and his boots hit the ground. He tied up his mare and joined Ellie.

Jacob came out of the barn and clapped dust off his hands. "What are you two up to?" He grinned and shook Joel's hand.

"Daed, we have something important to discuss with you." She gestured to Joel.

"My schweschder, Maryann, left and married an

Englischer three years ago. My mamm hasn't been the same. She's changed from a softhearted woman to a negative and bitter one. She's never given up hope Maryann would return to her someday. To my surprise, Maryann sent me a letter, and she's asking for my help to return." He passed him the note.

Jacob's eyes moved across the lines of the page. "How can I help?"

Ellie beamed at her daed then turned to Joel. "We both care about you, Joel. We'll do whatever we can for you and your family. Won't we, Daed?"

"I'm glad you brought this to me. You shouldn't go by yourself. Together, we can talk with Maryann and assess what we need to do." He handed the note back to Joel. "I could go with you both tomorrow, if it fits into your plans. Since you haven't mentioned your parents, I take it you're not telling them."

Joel lifted his hat and set it on his head. "I chose not to tell them until we speak with Maryann and get more information. I'm not sure what we're facing or what she means by her husband getting into trouble."

"I understand." Jacob motioned to the haus. "Let's go inside."

Ellie said, "I'll go and tell Liza about this, and she can share it with Hannah. They'll be happy we're going." She ran toward the haus.

"I should head home. My parents will be wondering what kept me away for so long. Danki, Jacob. I'm grateful for your help. I realize I'm taking you away from work and your family."

Jacob put a hand on Joel's shoulder. "It's what we Amish do. And we care about you, Joel. Ellie's eyes are full of joy when she speaks your name. It makes my soul happy when she smiles. I'm honored you'd ask me to go with you."

Joel nodded. "Ellie may have given you a rough road, raising her during her troubled years, but rest assured, she loves, admires, and respects you with all her heart. You were the first person she thought of to work this out."

"Danki, Joel. I'm relieved she's home with us. I'm hoping your family will say the same if we bring your schweschder home." He shook Joel's hand. "Be here at five a.m., and we'll head over to Massillon. I'll ask Ellie to pack food and water to take with us."

Joel got in his wagon and went home. He waved to his daed in the field. He padded inside the haus and found Mamm sweeping the mudroom floor. "I'm going to Massillon for some special saw blades at a bigger hardware store there. Is there anything I can get you while I'm there?"

His mamm held the broom handle to her chest. "You could buy about six yards each of dark blue and white fabric for me."

"Will do." He raised his brows and went outside. She'd taken the news of his impending trip better than he'd expected. He met Daed halfway across the yard. "I'm going to Massillon tomorrow and may stay for a day or so. Depends on how much time I spend shopping in town. I'm getting special saw blades I need for the workshop. Mamm wants fabric. Anything for you?"

"I could use a heavier round spade shovel."

"I'll pick one up for you." He took a step toward the pigpen.

"Why did you choose to go now?"

Joel tensed. He didn't want to lie to his daed. "Do you mind if I go?"

"Not at all. You go ahead. Just be careful."

He picked up and clenched the handle of the slop

bucket and poured the feed into the trough for the sows and the piglets.

The piglets and sows squealed and rooted around for the best morsels.

Joel shook his head. They were so ugly they were cute, with their big snouts, pot bellies, and curly tails. This day had brought about one surprise after another. He'd never forgive himself if he brought Maryann to Charm and she caused more dissention for their family. He'd have to decide whether to honor her request once they spoke.

Ellie sat with Liza and told her about their plan to go to Massillon. "I could tell Joel had misgivings about his schweschder. He needed prodding to go to her and find out how she is doing. She needs him."

"Jah. She shouldn't be left alone."

Ellie pressed her elbows to her sides. "I believe she's scared. Her husband was a gambler and not a good man."

Liza tapped Ellie's nose with the tip of the towel in her hand. "All of you should be cautious."

"Daed and Joel will alert the sheriff if necessary." Ellie rose and lifted the lid to the beef and noodles cooking on the stove. She stirred them to keep them from sticking. "Are you sure you don't mind managing the store with Hannah tomorrow? I'm sorry to leave you shorthanded."

"We'll miss you and we'll worry about you until you're home safe. But we'll be fine. You're the perfect person to help Joel and Maryann. This is where your knowledge of living in the outside world will kumme in handy." She shook her head and laughed. "I never thought I'd say those words."

Ellie held her middle and laughed with Liza. "I'm

praying Maryann and her parents can reunite and bring joy back to their family again." She reached for Liza's hand. "Let's say a prayer together." She bowed her head. "Dear Heavenly Father, danki for all you do for us each day. Please prepare Maryann's heart before we arrive. Impress upon her to return to you, and please reunite this family. Give us the right words to say to her tomorrow and guide us to make the right decisions. Protect us from harm. We love you, Heavenly Father. Amen."

Peter came rushing in. "I left Snuggles and Cinnamon out while I played ball. I ran to the barn to chase a squirrel out, and I forgot about them. Now I can't find them! Hurry! Help me!"

Liza threw down her towel and followed him.

Ellie ran out the door after them, raced around the outside yard, and then halted and cringed. Had a coyote gotten to the dog and rabbit? Why were they so still? She took a brisk walk to them. Cinnamon and Snuggles lay close, with eyes closed, under the old willow tree. She didn't notice any injuries. She petted the brown fur.

Cinnamon got on all fours and jumped on her.

Snuggles rolled over and hopped to them.

Ellie yelled, "Liza! Peter! They're over here. They were sleeping."

Liza and Peter came around the corner of the haus.

Peter picked up Snuggles in one arm and knelt to allow Cinnamon to lick his nose. "You two shouldn't run off where I can't find you!"

Liza pressed a hand to Ellie's arm. "I thought the worst."

"I did too when I noticed them not moving." Ellie put her arm around Peter. "Peter, this time the animals were safe. But you'll have to keep a better eye on them or make sure they're in their cages when you can't tend to them."

He murmured, "I will. I promise."

Ellie sucked in her upper lip. She'd been afraid of what she'd find when she came upon the animals, the same way she was worried about what Maryann would tell them. What had this woman been through with her husband? Would she be willing to return to the Amish life? She hoped Maryann wouldn't cause distress for Joel.

Liza grinned. "Supper will be ready soon, Peter. You can play with them a little longer and then put Snuggles away and bring Cinnamon inside. I'll call you when it's time."

Liza and Ellie went inside and cooked a mess of green beans and fried pork cutlets for supper.

Peter and Jacob came in, laughing.

"What's got your tickle bones?" Liza poured pickled beets in a bowl and set it on the table.

Peter scooted out his chair and sat. "I was telling Daed how Samuel gets into trouble all the time at school. He chased the girls with a snake at playtime. They screamed and ran."

"You should've told him to leave them alone." Ellie frowned.

"You didn't let me finish. I did tell him, and he took the snake to the woods and let it go."

"I'm glad. We need to help each other." Ellie wouldn't judge Maryann, no matter what she told them. She'd show her compassion and help her any way she could.

Ellie woke early and hurried through her chores Tuesday morning. She didn't want to delay their departure for Massillon. "Daed, are you almost finished with what you need to do here?"

"I'm done. Liza is fixing us biscuits and ham for breakfast to eat on the way. I'll change and meet you at the buggy."

Ellie went inside and changed into a clean dress. She went to the kitchen. "I'm wide-awake and ready to go. I'm anxious to meet Maryann."

Liza winked. "I'm glad distraction has brought you and Joel together."

"I'm relieved he's allowing Daed and me to go with him. I shouldn't get my hopes up, but I can't help it." She accepted the wooden crate of sandwiches, cookies, and jars of water. She carried a bag of clothes and necessities in her other. "Danki for the food."

"You're wilkom, sweetheart. I'm proud of you and your daed for going with Joel."

Daed came alongside her and took the crate. "He's in a difficult position with his parents and schweschder. I don't mind at all." He kissed Liza. "We'll be home in a day or two."

Ellie smiled. "Give Peter a hug for me when he gets up."

"I will." Liza waved to them.

Daed had the mare harnessed to the buggy. "Got everything?"

"Jah." She pointed. "Here kummes Joel."

Joel pulled up next to them. "I'm ready to go."

Daed took Joel's reins. "I'll put your horse in the barn, and you get what you need out of your wagon and put it in the buggy." Jacob unharnessed the horse and took the animal to the barn.

Joel smiled at Ellie. "Ready for this adventure?" He wore a heavy wool jacket. "I'll get in next to your Daed in case he needs me to drive part of the way."

"I'm glad we're sharing it together." She blushed and fidgeted her hands.

Daed returned, and they rode in silence. Ellie handed Joel the lantern they kept in the buggy to light the way in the early morning darkness. She was ready for the sun to rise.

Joel held up a bag. "Mamm packed food and water for me. I couldn't ask her for more without raising suspicion. I'm sorry."

"Don't worry. Liza packed enough to feed a school-haus full of kinner. We'll have more than enough food to last us on the way there." She gave him a shy smile. She pulled her heavy shawl tighter and tugged at the blanket on her lap.

He smiled at her and then at Jacob. "I appreciate this so much."

"Happy to kumme along. Ellie and I are both look-ing forward to reuniting you with your schweschder." Daed kept his eyes on the road. "Don't fret. I'm no stranger to trouble. We'll deal with whatever we face. The main thing is to keep everyone safe. I plan to call on the sheriff if we suspect trouble, and if it kummes to it, I have my shotgun under the seat. Hopefully, we'll not need it."

Ellie reached in the crate of food and passed a ham biscuit to each of them. "How long will it take us to reach Massillon?"

"I've been there before for supplies not offered in Charm. It's about thirty miles. Our buggies travel about five miles an hour. Depending on the motor-cars, buggies, and wagons on the road, it takes about six or seven hours to get there. You have to take into account how long your stops are along the way."

Ellie ogled the plain and fancy buggies on the way.

Motorcars are fascinating. She'd watched men crank the motorcar, hop in, and drive away. Amish depended on horses to pull their buggies or wagons. She couldn't understand how the motorcars worked. She dare not ask. Joel might get the wrong idea.

"You missed a bountiful meal after the bishop's message Sunday, Joel."

Ellie couldn't believe he'd miss such delicious food. He'd avoided her and gone home after church since they'd parted, but she hadn't expected he'd pass up such a feast at this particular time.

"I . . . uh . . . did enjoy Mamm's dishes at home. She makes the best apple butter and raspberry jam. Daed's corn turned out perfect, and I've devoured so much of it, I'm about to turn into an ear of corn." He managed a half smile.

She shifted her body in the back seat to get more comfortable. "Daed's sweet corn is good too. I understand what you're saying. I've made a pig of myself. I've got to stop, or I'll be as wide as a barn." She laughed.

He laughed with her. "You don't have a thing to worry about."

Daed shook his head. "I tell her all the time she has a hollow leg. The girl can put away food and stay slender. I don't get it."

Hours later, Daed parked the buggy along the road in Winesburg. "We can stretch our legs, use the public outhaus, give food and water to the horse, and have our dinner before making the rest of the trip." He pointed in between the general store and blacksmith's shop. "There's a sign pointing to the outhaus. I'm headed there first. I'll meet you at the buggy in a few minutes."

Ellie got out and waited for Joel. "This small town

is quaint, with its few stores. It might be too small to live in."

"In 1833, the town was first named Weinburg, after a town in Germany. Then they later changed it to a more Englisch name, Winesburg." Joel scanned the storefronts.

She wasn't in the mood for any more small talk. She wanted more from him. She shouldn't be forward, but she wouldn't let this opportunity pass her by. "Joel, it's been a miserable three weeks not speaking to you. I've missed you."

Daed approached them. "Ready to dig into Liza's dinner?"

Ellie's stomach twisted. She'd needed more time to talk to Joel in private. She'd hide her disappointment. Daed hadn't meant to interrupt.

"I'll be right back." She used the outhaus, washed her hands under the outside pump, and returned to the buggy.

Joel and her Daed stood next to it, and they got in.

She slid onto the back bench, reached in the crate, and passed them each meat sandwiches and cherry-jam sugar cookies. She gave them each a jar of water. "Here you go."

Joel took a drink. "Look at the handsome black stallion outside the blacksmith's shop. What a beauty!"

"The town is busy with activity for such a small place." Daed sat back.

Joel ate fast. "I didn't notice a bakery. We'd be lost without Liza's breads and desserts."

Ellie gave Joel an impish grin. "You're just complimenting Liza to get in Daed's good graces."

Joel blushed. "Jacob and I get along fine. I mean what I say. Liza's got the best desserts anywhere. Mamm has her specialties, but Liza kummes up with such unique pastries. And nobody can beat her molasses cookies."

"I'm teasing you. It's true. Liza's got a knack for baking, and she's done well running the bakery. I love working there."

Daed held out his hand. "Speaking of Liza's cookies, I'll take another cherry one."

Ellie grinned and pressed one in his hand.

Around twelve thirty in the afternoon, they arrived in Massillon. There were more crank motorcars than they were used to seeing among the buggies and wagons on the downtown road. A crowd of townsfolk chatted and went in and out of the shops, which were much larger than what they had in Charm. "I've got to go in the quilt shop. Liza said several women have told her about the keepsake pocket quilts sold there."

Joel scrunched his face. "What makes them different from other quilts?"

"A pocket is sewn on the quilt, and a letter is tucked inside for a loved one. It must be a sight to behold to have so many different patterns for sale in one place." She scanned the town. "Liza said one of the Englischers told her Ruth and Becca were schweschders who left Amish life in Berlin, Ohio, and came here and opened their store. Ruth and Becca gave permission to their good friend, Grace King, who remained Amish, to open one in Berlin."

Daed slowed the horse. "There it is. Why don't you check it out while Joel and I head to the livery? Then we'll pick you up to go find Maryann. You won't have long."

"I'll be ready to leave when you are."

Joel snapped his fingers. "I almost forgot. Mamm

asked me to buy six yards of dark blue and white fabric. Six yards each." He pulled coins out of the bag he brought with him and pressed them in her palm. "Would you pick them up for me?"

"Jah, and I'll wait for you both there." She slid out and strolled to the quilt shop. She opened the door and the bell clanged. A beautiful blond woman in a printed crisp blouse and ankle-length skirt approached her. She had a kind elegance about her. "Welcome. I'm Becca Carrington. How may I help you today?"

Ellie scanned the shop walls. The pinwheel, wedding, patchwork, and assortment of patterns in an array of colors made up the pretty quilts on the walls. She put a hand to her open mouth. "This store is full of such beautiful coverlets." Heat rose to her cheeks. "I'm sorry. My name is Ellie Graber. I'm from Charm. We're here for a brief visit. I had to kumme to your store. I'm so glad I did. I need six yards each of dark blue and white fabric."

"It's a pleasure to meet you. Take your time. We also have different sized kitchen towels, table linens, and aprons." Becca pulled the fabrics from the shelves, measured them, and cut them. She accepted payment and wrapped them. "I'll hold these at the counter while you shop. Did someone tell you about our store?"

"Jah, an Englischer told my stepmamm about writing a note and tucking it inside the pocket on the quilt and giving it to someone special. I love the idea."

"Danki. I appreciate your kindness. Did the Englischer also tell her I was once Amish?"

Ellie's breath caught. "She did. I left to explore the outside world twice. I decided it wasn't for me, and I returned to the Amish life. I don't agree that the Amish who leave are shunned by God. A very loving Englisch couple taught me God doesn't just love or live in the Amish hearts, but all those who love and trust in him."

"Yes, it's true. I'm a living example. I fell in love with a handsome and wonderful doctor. We enjoy our children and worship in the church here every Sunday." She clasped Ellie's arm. "I'm glad you are comfortable with your decision. And I'm happy you returned to the Amish life. I miss my Amish friends and family. This path I chose is not easy but right for me."

"You've been kind to share your story with me."

"My sister, Ruth, says I'm to be open with people." She bent and lifted a patchwork keepsake pocket quilt out of an open cedar hope chest. "Today, I'm filling in for the friend who works here on a regular basis. I'm glad I did, or I wouldn't have met you. It's not every day I meet someone who understands our strong belief in God, Amish or not. It's as if I've known you much longer than our meeting here today." She wrapped the quilt and set it in her arms. "This is on me. I want you to have it."

"Oh, I couldn't accept such a generous gift!" The plain colors were appropriate for any Amish friend or family member. Becca had been careful to give her an acceptable quilt.

"Please. I want you to have it."

Daed and Joel came in.

"Ready to go?" Daed waved her to the door but stopped and gazed around. "This is quite a place. These quilts are very impressive."

"I'll say." Joel smiled. "Ellie, did you have a chance to buy Mamm's requests?" He walked to the counter.

"I did." Ellie blushed. "This is Joel Wenger. He came with my daed and me."

Daed tipped his hat and smiled.

"Pleasure to meet all of you. I'm Becca Carrington."

"You have a unique shop." Joel studied the quilts hanging on the walls.

"I can't take all the credit. My sister started the business. I'm glad you like it."

Joel took the package of his mother's fabric. "Nice to meet you, Mrs. Carrington. Ellie, take your time. Your daed and I will wait outside for you."

"I'll be out in a minute." She waited until Joel went out the door, and then held up her package. "Becca, danki you so much. You've made this day very special."

"You've done the same for me, Ellie." She leaned close to Ellie. "Is Joel someone important in your life?"

She nodded.

"Maybe you can save the quilt for him. I gave one to my husband. He loves it, and he reads the letter every few months. It's been good for our marriage."

"Danki for the tip." She held the package. "Danki, again." She turned on her heel and then glanced over her shoulder. "Do you know a Maryann Harding?"

Becca wrinkled her brow. "I met her in church. She's lovely. We haven't had much time to talk. She didn't attend any of the socials. Are you here to visit her?"

"Jah. Danki again." Ellie didn't want to divulge much information. She'd leave it at that. She was here just for a visit.

"You're more than welcome."

Ellie left and joined her daed and Joel. "Becca Carrington is the sweetest woman. She gave me a keepsake pocket quilt."

"What a lavish gift for just meeting the woman!" Joel jerked his head back.

"Jah. I agree. What was her reason?" Daed peeked inside the wrapping.

"She asked if I'd heard she'd left the Amish life. I told her jah. I also told her I learned from living in the outside world for a short time how God loves us whether we're Amish or not, if we love and trust in him." She averted her gaze from Joel to her daed.

"Ellie, you and I believe this, but most of the Amish do not. I'd keep it to yourself as not to stir up any trouble." Daed walked beside her.

"I won't mention it."

Joel patted the package. "She was kind to give you the present. What will you do with the coverlet? Keep it?"

"I'm not sure." She would stow it in her room. Maybe she'd give it to him someday. "You two took longer than I thought. I was glad, as it gave me more time with Becca."

"We went in the hardware store on our way to the quilt shop. I found the saw blades I needed and a perfect shovel for my daed."

Ellie put her hand over her eyes to block out the sun. "Clara Bee's Boarding House is across the road and down about three buildings."

Joel skirted past a huckster shouting out his toys for sale.

Ellie walked between her daed and Joel to the boarding haus. The outside was painted white with a red sign featuring a yellow bumble bee next to the name.

Joel knocked on the door.

A petite and thin woman with rosy cheeks swung open the door. "How may I help you?"

Joel tipped his hat. "I'm Maryann Harding's bruder. I'd like to speak to her."

The woman's eyes squinted. "A Maryann Harding is not here."

Joel took the letter he had tucked in the waist of his pants. "Here's a letter I received from her." He held out his hand and gestured to Ellie and Daed. "These are my friends, Jacob Graber and his dochder, Ellie. They're here to assist Maryann and me."

The petite woman accepted the note and read it. Her cheeks dimpled. "I must be careful who I tell Maryann is here. The poor girl's been through a rough time. I'm protective of her, since her husband got mixed up with some bad men. I'm not sorry her husband is dead and gone. I'm glad you're here to help." She checked the wall clock. "She's getting off work. Let me tell her you're here. Please come in." She gestured for them to follow her. "Have a seat in our sitting room. I'll be right back."

Joel nodded. He folded and refolded the note and paced the room.

Ellie fought reaching out to him. She wanted to comfort him and tell him she loved him, but this was neither the time nor the place.

Daed remained calm and took a seat in the corner.

The woman returned. "I'm Sharon Walter. Maryann's boss and friend. Will you need a place to stay for the night?"

Daed took his money clip out of the hidden pocket in his shirt. "Do you have three rooms available?"

"Yes, and because you're family of Maryann's, I'll not charge you the full price."

Ellie stepped closer to the open doorway to the kitchen. She sniffed in the aroma of beans and corn-bread.

A short and slender young woman standing over the stove smiled at her. The woman was pretty with her dark blond curls, and the sides of her hair were pulled back in a white bow to match her apron. She had blue eyes like Joel's. She smiled at Ellie and joined them. "Joel, you came!"

"Maryann!" He hugged her then stepped back.

"Meet Ellie and her daed, Jacob Graber. They're my friends from Charm."

"Pleased to meet you." She turned to Joel. "You moved to Charm, Ohio, from Lancaster? How did you get my letter? Here I thought you were going to ignore my request to kumme after a month had passed. I'd given up."

"I left our forwarding address with the Lancaster post office. The letter reached me yesterday."

"I'm so glad you're here." She diverted her attention to Jacob and Ellie. "Danki for kumming with Joel, Mr. Graber and Ellie."

"Call me Jacob."

"Only if you call me Maryann."

Jacob nodded.

Ellie hugged herself. "I've been looking forward to meeting you."

"I'm glad you came with Joel. Did you get rooms yet?" Maryann folded her hands behind her back.

"Jacob took care of it." Joel passed Daed money. "Let me pay for it. It's the least I can do under the circumstances."

Daed pushed away his hand. "Danki, but I insist. We're happy to accompany you on this trip."

Maryann hooked her arm through Ellie's. "You and I will share my room. All right with you?"

"Jah. It will give us a chance to get better acquainted." Ellie beamed.

Sharon poked her head out of the kitchen's open doorway. She reached in her apron pocket and handed Jacob coins. "Here's money back for one of the rooms. I overheard Maryann say she was sharing hers with Ellie."

"Danki." Jacob smiled.

Sharon returned to the kitchen.

Maryann said, "Ellie, I'll put your package in my room. I need to go upstairs. I'll take it with me." She took the package from Ellie. "I have someone you should all meet, and then I've got a lot of information to share with you." She held up her forefinger. "I'll be right back. Please wait here."

Ellie raised her brows at Joel. "Who could it be?"

"I hope it's not a new husband." He rolled his eyes. Jacob shrugged. "Don't ask me."

Maryann came down the stairs with a boppli in her arms. "Meet Betsy. She's six weeks old." She cradled the infant. "Ellie, would you like to take her?"

Ellie accepted and cradled Betsy. "She looks like you with blue eyes and dark blond hair. She's beautiful."

Joel stood next to Ellie and put his finger in the boppli's tiny fingers. "You're a pretty one." He was elated to reunite with Maryann and Betsy. He tensed. The need to protect them became stronger. What financial state had her husband left her in? Had he angered men over gambling debts, who would kumme after them? He needed answers and soon. "Maryann, can you sit with us? We've got questions."

Jacob reached for Betsy. "Mind if I take a turn? It's been a long time since I got to hold an infant." He traced the boppli's cheek with his work-hardened finger. "You're a sweetheart."

Maryann sat next to Joel and across from Ellie and Daed. "Yes, I'll be happy to answer them."

The room was simple, with white walls and a small window with the same frilly curtain as the other windows. Ellie sat in the maple chair with a cushion tied to the seat, and Jacob's matched hers. The settee was hardwood with a long cushion on the seat and pillows on the back.

Joel had his elbows on his knees and hands folded. "What trouble did your late husband get into?"

Maryann blushed. "He started to gamble a year after we were married. He'd win, and we'd have enough to pay bills, and then he'd lose, and we were broke. He had a furniture store but lost it in a card game. He was murdered. The sheriff caught the man who took Gerald's life. The murderer claimed Gerald refused to pay a debt he owed. The argument turned into a fistfight, and the man pulled his pistol and shot Gerald. My husband was unarmed. Two men who were there when it happened wrestled the murderer to the ground, and a third man alerted the sheriff."

Joel stole a glance at Ellie. . She'd not interrupted, and let him ask the questions. Jacob was enthralled with the infant, but he knew Ellie's daed didn't miss a word Maryann said. He remained calm and let Joel speak to his schweschder.

"Maryann, has anyone approached you about your husband and his debts?"

Maryann gripped fistfuls of her skirt. "The house where we lived was ransacked a couple of times, when I worked here in the kitchen before renting a room. I suspect they were looking for money. I didn't have the money to pay our rent, and the landlord asked me to leave. The house came furnished. I told Sharon about my situation, and she offered me a room here. She has been very good to me. I told Sharon and Minnie about the break-ins, and they agreed to keep my living here quiet if anyone asked. No one has kumme here asking for the money yet."

"Has the sheriff got any hints as to who is responsible for breaking into your haus?" Joel raised his brows.

"He and his men don't have a clue who is responsible." She shuddered.

Joel narrowed his eyes. "Maryann, do you have the money? Tell me the truth. This is a matter of your life and Betsy's."

Her mouth flew open. "I do not have the money! Please, Joel. You have to believe me. I can't wait to get away from Massillon. I highly doubt Gerald had any money. He was a spendthrift."

"Calm down. I had to ask. I do believe you." Joel covered her hand with his.

Jacob piped up. "We should take Maryann and Betsy to Charm as soon as possible. We'll leave early tomorrow morning."

Ellie settled back in her chair. "Maryann, I'm so sorry you've had to endure all this."

"Gerald wasn't always a bad man. I fell for his smooth-talking ways and thick black hair. He stood tall next to me, and he turned the heads of many women with his perfect smile and confident stature. He was good to me until he started gambling. He couldn't stop, and when he lost money, he'd be angry and miserable. He changed from the kind man I married to a man I hardly knew. He took his worry about gambling debts out on me by being demanding and rude. I kept thinking he'd see the error of his ways and change back to the man I'd married. I was foolish to think so. His love for gambling only grew worse."

"I'm glad he's out of your life and Betsy's." Ellie leaned forward.

Joel heaved a heavy sigh. "Does anyone know you were Amish?"

Maryann shrugged. "I wore Amish clothes when I arrived. Gerald took me to a shop and bought me a dress right away. I doubt anyone would remember."

"All right. Good."

Jacob tightened the blanket around Betsy. "Joel, we should talk to the sheriff and ask him if he's learned anything new about the break-ins."

Joel nodded. "Good idea."

"I'm so relieved you all are with me. God answered my prayer bringing my brother and new friends to me. I'm worried there are more men looking for money Gerald owed them. I'll rest easier when we're on our way to Charm."

Joel stood. "Jacob and I will go to the sheriff's office. We'll be back soon."

Jacob handed Betsy to Maryann. "Pack your things before bed tonight. We will leave at five in the morning. We don't have much room, so you'll have to limit it to one bag."

"Gerald did buy a cradle for Betsy before she was born. I had hoped to take it with me."

Joel circled his arm around Maryann. "Mamm kept our cradle. She can use it."

Ellie stood. "Between our family and yours, we can supply anything you need."

"You're so kind, Ellie. Danki."

"I can't wait until your parents lay eyes on you. It will be a moment to remember."

Maryann squeezed her elbows to her sides. "I hope it's a happy moment. Mamm can be unpredictable."

Chapter Twelve

Ellie followed Maryann up the stairs and into her room. The room had a double bed with a yellow and white circle-pattern quilt. A simple wooden cradle with a knitted blanket inside was in the corner. A weathered side table with a pitcher and bowl sat in another corner. "This is a nice cozy room."

Maryann pulled a clean nappy off a small shelf. "Welcome to my humble abode. You can sleep with me, or I can make you a bed out of blankets on the floor. The outhouse is outside in the back. There's a tub in the washroom. We can heat water on the kitchen stove if you desire a bath. There's a pump for water not far from the back door. We dine together in the kitchen for meals."

"I don't mind sleeping with you." She ran her hand over the quilt.

"You must consider me foolish to marry an Englischer and leave the Amish life. You're right if you do. I was scared, but I was so in love with Gerald. He promised to love, protect, and honor me all the days of my life on earth. He did until he took up gambling."

"Why didn't you write to Joel sooner?" Ellie didn't

understand how she could stay with a man who had been so mean and endangered her.

"I kept waiting for Gerald to give up gambling and turn his life around. I'm ready to put this life behind me and go to Charm, where I can have a fresh start. I'm thankful Joel brought you and your daed and all of you are willing to take me with you. I wasn't sure if Joel would kumme. It's been three years since I left."

"He loves you." Ellie gave her a reassuring smile.

"Are you and Joel serious about each other?" Maryann threw a blanket over her shoulder and fed Betsy.

Ellie stretched her stiff and tired arms. "We have something to work out before we can marry. But we can talk about Joel and me later. Let's concentrate on you and Betsy for now."

"I hope whatever it is works out soon for you and Joel. I like you already."

Ellie grinned. "Danki."

"I hope I haven't shocked you too much with my bad decisions. I could really use a good friend right now."

Ellie lowered her head then raised her eyes to meet Maryann's. "I ran away twice with Englischers to explore the outside world. I was cruel to leave Daed wondering where I'd gone. I returned the second time and asked God, Daed, and my friends to forgive me. I'm happiest living the Amish life."

"Did you leave with men you loved?"

"Nah. I didn't leave with romantic notions about anyone. Mamm had passed, and I was lost without her. My grief brought out the worst in me. We were close, and everything at home reminded me of her. I had to get away. God taught me loving lessons and brought me back to Him and the Amish life."

"I go to church here and worship God. I'm anxious to follow in your footsteps, to ask forgiveness of all those I need to and live the Amish life in Charm. It won't be easy, but I'd like to try."

Ellie hugged her. "God, friends, and family make it all worth it. There's only a few gossips who test you now and then. But don't worry, I'll defend you. I'm glad you're going home with us. You need to get out of this town and leave all these bad memories behind you."

"I've regretted leaving the Amish life, except for having Betsy." She shifted her body to Ellie. "I'm anxious and nervous to go home."

"I wouldn't worry. It's the perfect place for you and Betsy."

"I'm getting hungry. It's time for me to make supper. Maybe Sharon and Minnie will join us. The three other renters moved out last week."

Ellie went out of the room and into the hallway and bumped into a tall, gray-haired woman with crow's-feet around her eyes and wrinkles showing her years. "Pardon me. I should watch where I'm going. I'm Ellie."

"I'm Minnie. I watch this darling little girl every chance I can get." Minnie grinned at Maryann and caressed Betsy's cheek. "Where are you headed? Would you like me to take care of Betsy for you?"

Maryann put Betsy against her shoulder. "Minnie, you're so kind. I'm off to cook supper. Want to join us?"

"No. Sharon made us a big dinner. Let me care for Betsy while you enjoy your brother and friends." She reached for Betsy.

"Thank you, Minnie. She's full and dry." Maryann put Betsy in Minnie's arms.

Betsy cooed and waved her arms and legs.

"Take your time." Minnie took the little one to her room.

Ellie and Maryann warmed some leftover turkey

and noodles, and then went downstairs to the kitchen and served it to the men and filled their own plates. They sat and chatted with Joel and Jacob while they ate.

Sharon stepped to their table about a half hour later. "I'm not going to join you. I fixed a big dinner for Minnie and me, so we're full. I might grab a cookie later." She hugged Maryann. "I'm blessed to have met this woman."

"You've been a good friend to me, Sharon. I'll be leaving in the morning with my brother and friends. Thank you for everything." Maryann dabbed a tear trailing down her cheek.

Sharon bent to hug Maryann. "Be careful going home if I don't see you in the morning. You'll be heading out early, I would guess. Nice meeting all of you. Take good care of them for me." She kissed Maryann's forehead. "I'll miss you."

Maryann stood and held Sharon's hands. "I'll miss you too."

Sharon's eyes had tears pooling in them as she walked away.

Maryann dabbed her eyes with her cloth napkin. "Looks like everyone has finished their meals. Who would like blueberry pie?"

They all nodded.

Ellie popped up to serve their dessert.

Maryann lifted a forkful of the pie. "I wish I had time to take you to some of the shops."

"I went to the quilt shop. It's full of beautiful quilts. The keepsake pocket idea is impressive. I met Becca Carrington. We had a pleasant conversation. I really like her. She gave me a quilt! I was shocked. That's what is in the package I brought with me. I also have fabric your mamm requested."

"Gerald didn't let me get acquainted with many people. I do know her and her sister, Ruth, were both Amish before coming to Massillon. They're from Berlin, Ohio. They both married upstanding gentlemen. Becca's husband is the doctor in town, and Ruth's is a farmer and furniture maker. Becca fills in at the quilt shop and for her husband as a midwife and nurse. She helped me birth Betsy. We talked when she came back to check on me and the baby. She's a kind soul."

"She is someone I'd like to befriend if I lived here. You'll make a lot of friends in Charm. It's a nice place to live."

"Is there room for Betsy and me?" Maryann sucked in her bottom lip.

"Mamm reserved a room for you and arranged it the same as your one in Lancaster. She's been making you things and setting a place for you at the table ever since you left."

"Didn't friends question why? The Amish wouldn't approve of her doing such things."

"Daed shut the door to your room when we had company. He asked her not to mention you to others. She obliged."

"I'm sorry for what I've put them through, and you."

Joel shook his head. "They'll forget all about it, once they lay eyes on you and Betsy."

"When Ellie returned, it was one of the happiest days of my life." Jacob exchanged an endearing glance with Ellie. "I'm worn-out. I'm going to retire to my room."

Joel finished another bite of his pie. "Me too."

Ellie and Maryann bid the men good night, went to Minnie's room to get Betsy, and then went to their room and got ready for bed.

Maryann and Ellie lay in bed with the cradle on the floor. "Are you comfortable? Do you have enough room?"

"I'm snuggled in just fine."

"Ellie, tell me about you and Joel. He can't take his eyes off you, and your face beams around him. I can tell you love each other. You intimated there was some kind of problem. What is it?"

Ellie recounted her past to Maryann in detail. "Gossips have moved on to other subjects for the most part, but they didn't hesitate to share my adventures with your mamm when they noticed Joel and me talking at the after-church meals. She doesn't approve of me, and no matter what I do, she won't give me a chance to befriend her."

"Have you and Joel talked about marriage?"

"Jah, but your mamm would never forgive us for doing so. And I don't believe God would want us to go against her."

"God wouldn't approve of her judgmental attitude toward you. You shouldn't let her shortsightedness get in the way. What does Joel say?"

"He wants to move forward in spite of her warnings about me."

"Then let's plan a wedding when we get home."

She hugged herself. Maryann didn't have a mean bone in her body. She had taken to her the instant they'd met. How wonderful it would be to have her for a schweschder-in-law. "Nah. I don't want to cause turmoil for your family, and for Joel and me. I'm praying for a miracle." She yawned. "Enough about me. This is about you now."

"She'll not wilkom me then. Sounds like she's gotten bitter since I left."

How much should she tell Maryann? Ellie didn't want to disparage Mrs. Wenger to her dochder. She should be truthful but delicate. "No one persuaded me to leave. I wanted to go to the outside world. She blames your husband for your departure and not you. She loves you. I'm a stranger. She misses you, and she has justified your leaving in her mind. I understand why, and I'm glad she is forgiving you."

"My husband was the reason I left, but I made the choice. I'm responsible for my actions. She's being unfair to you."

Ellie stretched the blanket up to her chin. Maryann was a kind and considerate woman.

"I don't dwell on my wrongs. I've moved on and so should you. You have a bright future ahead with your family enjoying you and Betsy. Charm lives up to its name. You'll love the townsfolk, socials, Sunday services, and shops. I can't wait to introduce you to my family and friends."

"You make it sound wonderful."

"I gave Liza, a bakery owner, a hard time when we first moved there. She and Daed fell in love, and she put up with my stubborn and rebellious ways. She wouldn't marry Daed until I approved." Ellie recounted how Peter came to live with them. "She treats Peter and me as if she gave birth to us. Her family is now our family, and her niece, Hannah, and I are best friends. They'll be so excited to meet you and Betsy."

"They sound lovely. Charm has a bakery?"

"I work there with Hannah and Liza. I love it. You'll have to visit. Everything is mouthwatering good."

Ellie bid Maryann good night and rolled over onto her side. It was as if she'd known Maryann for a long time. She loved her already. She hoped Joel's mamm wouldn't keep them apart.

Ellie woke to Betsy's cooing. She rolled over and lifted the little one out of the cradle. The boppli's fuzzy blond hair tickled her neck as she held her on her shoulder and rubbed her little back. She glanced at the calendar Maryann had on the wall. Wednesday. A busy day at the bakery. How were Liza and Hannah doing without her? She missed them. They'd be surprised when she told them what had happened in Massillon. It had been quite a day. They would love Maryann and Betsy. She couldn't wait to introduce them.

Maryann popped in the door. "I brought us some coffee and pastries. I took some earlier to Joel and Jacob. They're almost ready to leave. I wanted to let you and Betsy sleep."

"You're so thoughtful. Danki. I could use some coffee." She lowered Betsy to the cradle, washed her face, changed into a fresh dress, fashioned her hair in a bun, and slipped on her kapp. She picked up her coffee and took a few sips. "My bag is packed, and I'm ready. May I carry something for you?"

"Sad, but all I have is one bag. I'll be wearing Englischer clothes when I get to Charm."

Ellie looked her over. "I've got some dresses we can hem, and then we'll make you and Betsy some new ones."

"Danki. You make going home easier. Your experiences and encouragement make me feel close to you, Ellie. I look forward to a long friendship."

"I feel the same, Maryann." Ellie smiled and slung

her bag over her shoulder and carried Maryann's bag in one hand and her package in the other to the hallway.

Joel met them and took the bags from her. He slung his bag over his shoulder. "Let's go home."

Jacob opened the door, and they stepped outside and walked in the direction of the livery.

Ellie glanced at the shops as they walked to get the horse, but the dress shops didn't hold her interest anymore. She was content with her Amish dresses. The train whistle blew in the distance. She noticed a sign advertising a circus was kumming to town the next week. She would love to go to a circus. The Amish wouldn't approve, so it was out of the question. And sneaking off to one wasn't something she would do. She'd done enough damage satisfying her curiosities in the outside world. "I wonder what the circus is like."

Maryann got in the back of the buggy. "I went to a circus."

"Did you like it?" Joel turned sideways on the bench.

"I loved it. The trainers had taught dogs and horses tricks. There were tiny men and women, who wouldn't get any taller, doing somersaults and cartwheels in clown outfits. They were friendly and sold candy to the crowd. Beautiful women in sparkling outfits did all kinds of stunts while on trapezes hanging from the big tent ceiling. A magician performed tricks and entertained us. The games were fun. I won a stuffed bear from throwing a penny into a cup!" Her face turned crimson. She held a hand to her open mouth. "I shouldn't go on about this. It's wrong."

Ellie shrugged. "I love hearing about the circus."

Joel sat next to Jacob and turned in his seat to address the women. "It does sound exciting, but it's not a topic we should bring up in Charm."

Jacob nodded.

"I won't mention it around our parents or friends." Maryann kept her head down.

Ellie put a finger under Maryann's chin and raised it. She darted her eyes to the men. *Good.* They weren't paying attention to them. She whispered to her, "Don't feel guilty for sharing your circus experience. And you can tell me anything. Understood?"

Maryann lowered her voice. "Danki, Ellie."

Ellie sniffed the air. "Someone's burning leaves." She pulled her shawl tighter around her shoulders and covered her legs and Maryann's with another blanket.

Jacob stopped the buggy hours later on the road in front of the general store. "This is Winesburg, a good place to take a break. We're about halfway there." He got out and stretched his legs. He strolled into the general store.

Maryann changed Betsy's nappy. She then threw a blanket over her shoulder and covered Betsy while she was nursing.

Ellie got out and joined Joel several feet away from the buggy and out of Maryann's earshot. "Are you nervous about taking Maryann and Betsy home?"

"Not anymore, since she has said she wants to remain in Charm. I doubt she'd leave us again. You've been so good with her. Danki." Joel smiled.

"It's my pleasure. She and I have become fast friends."

Maryann yelled to them. "Ellie, will you take Betsy for a minute?"

"Of course." Ellie hurried to her and took Betsy.

Maryann departed from the buggy. "I hope you two are talking about getting married. You shouldn't let anything stop you. I can tell you are in love."

Ellie's cheeks heated. "Maryann, I told you. It's complicated."

"Not really, but we'll discuss it sometime after we get home." Joel winked at Ellie. "I need to make a trip to the outhaus. I'll be right back."

Maryann circled her arm around Ellie. "I need to do the same."

"Go ahead. Betsy and I will be right here." Charm was small, but Winesburg was tiny in comparison. The town had little to offer, but enough for the residents to get by. Ellie studied the boppli's little round face.

Betsy gazed up at her and grinned.

Ellie tickled her stomach. "You're cuddly. Look at your button nose and those petal lips. You're a beauty." She greeted the families passing her, and several women stopped to admire Betsy and then moved on.

Maryann returned. "I'll take Betsy. Stretch your legs a bit."

Ellie found the outhaus then went to the pump to wash her hands. She stood still. Steps crunched leaves behind her. The hairs on her neck prickled.

She swung around. "Joel Wenger! You scared me!"

He laughed. "I'm sorry. I didn't mean to. I had to steal a minute alone with you." He brushed his long, calloused fingers against hers. "I love you so much, Ellie. I won't give up on us, and you and I are going to sit down with my parents when Maryann gets settled there."

"Joel, are you sure?"

"I insist, Ellie. I'm not going to waste any more time without you."

She ached to tell him she loved him and would marry him. He made it difficult to forget they had an obstacle they couldn't control. "We should go."

He heaved a big sigh and then stepped with her to the buggy.

Ellie admired how easy it was for Betsy to sleep with wheels hitting ruts in the road and birds chirping. "Maryann, do you have any hobbies?"

"I like to plant vegetables and to take long walks when I have the time."

"I've developed a love for baking. Liza, my step-mamm, has such a creative mind. She kummes up with the most unique recipes for cookies, pies, breads, and tarts."

"Are you close to her?"

"I wasn't at first, but now, jah. I can tell her anything and not worry it is a subject off limits. Were you close to your mamm?"

"Yes. We enjoyed working together, and we'd knit, sew, cook, and bake. I could only talk to her about safe subject matters. Not controversial topics. She was loving, and I did enjoy doing things with her. But she tended to overprotect me."

"What do you mean?"

"I needed time to myself, and I had to hide to have it. She would accompany me to town, and she insisted we do things together. We argued about it, and she finally let me go to town by myself a few times a week." Maryann cringed. "I met my husband during those times."

Ellie had had a balanced relationship with her mamm, and now with Liza. They'd both given her adequate time to herself. She better understood Mrs. Wenger's unbending demeanor. The woman must have an emotional upheaval going on inside of her with worry, blame, and guilt over her dochder. "If she blames herself for you leaving the Amish life, your

assurance she's not responsible for your unwise choice
will give her some peace."

"I'm worried she'll smother me again. After living
on my own, I couldn't stand it."

"You're not the same person in many ways, I suspect. You can, in polite terms, stick up for yourself
better than when you left. Our experiences, good and
bad, teach us things about ourselves. They're valuable
lessons."

Maryann's shoulders perked up, and she lifted her
chin. "You're right, and I need to stop it if it becomes
a problem."

Joel stretched his neck to look at Maryann. "I'll be
there to help."

Ellie watched the comradery between bruder and
schweschder. She had the same close-knit and protective relationship with Peter. Joel and his schweschder
hadn't been together again but a short time, and they
already acted like they'd never been separated.

Joel reached for Betsy. "Let me hold her for a while."

Ellie watched him talk to her. He'd be a good daed
when he had kinner.

Hours later, Jacob pulled in front of his haus. Joel
and Maryann and Betsy exited, thanked Jacob and
Ellie, and got in Joel's wagon and left to go home.

Joel drove the short distance to their home.

Maryann rocked Betsy. "I'm nervous, Joel."

"Don't worry. They'll be thrilled you're here."

He pulled down the lane and halted the wagon.

The Wengers came outside and then ran to Maryann. Mrs. Wenger cried and hugged her dochder and
granddochder. "I can't believe you're here! You're
home at last! I knew you'd kumme back to me! And

who do you have in your arms?" She put her arms under the bundle and cradled her. "Oh, she's beautiful."

Maryann swiped tears. "Her name is Betsy." She hugged her daed. "Don't worry. I'm here to stay."

Daed's shoulders shook as he wept, holding her close.

Joel stood back and blinked back tears. He bowed his head and whispered a prayer. "Dear Heavenly Father, forgive me for anything I've said or done to disappoint You. Danki for bringing Maryann and Betsy to live the Amish life in Charm with us. Danki for all you provide for us. Amen." He looked up and found his parents and Maryann had bowed their heads and joined him.

"Good prayer, Joel." Daed patted his back.

Mamm carried Betsy and ushered them inside the haus.

Joel recounted the story of receiving the letter and going with Jacob and Ellie to get Maryann.

Maryann told them about Gerald's need to gamble and how the habit had changed him, and not for the better. "I hope you'll forgive me, and I will ask the church to do the same. And if they'll let me, I'd like to live the Amish life here with you."

"Of course we forgive you. I'm certain many of the Amish folks will wilkom you here." Mamm squeezed her hand.

Daed nodded.

Joel's heart pounded with relief. "We have so much to look forward to with Maryann and Betsy here."

Mamm and Maryann fussed over the boppli.

Joel headed to the door. "Daed, let's bring in the cradle you and Mamm used for us. Betsy can sleep in it."

They crossed the yard to the barn, found and cleaned the cradle, and brought it inside.

Joel said, "This will be perfect for Betsy."

"How special that she'll use our cradle, Joel. I had to leave the one I had behind. There was no way to bring it." Maryann clasped her hands under her chin. "I'm glad you kept ours, Daed."

"I had hoped we'd have grandkinner one day."

Mamm showed Maryann around the haus. "I have your room arranged just like it was in Lancaster."

"I'm glad my letter got forwarded. There would've been no way for me to know you'd moved to Charm. Danki, Mamm, for keeping my things. I don't deserve it."

"We left our new address at the post office just in case you would write to us." Joel followed them to get Maryann's reaction to the rest of the haus.

The two women were happy and Mamm's face beamed like he hadn't observed since his schweschder had left.

They went to the kitchen, and Mamm served them potato and bacon soup and cheese sandwiches. She set a pot of tea and coffee on the table.

Betsy slept like a bear in hibernation.

Maryann sipped her warm tea. "If it wasn't for Ellie, Joel might not have answered my plea for help. She's the one who coaxed him to kumme to Massillon."

"Maryann's right. I wasn't sure what to do. I didn't know if it would be good to put you through more hurt should she leave again." Joel stole a glance at Mamm.

She kept her eyes on her plate and didn't look at him. Would she be grateful to Ellie?

Mamm sipped her coffee and remained quiet.

"I'll have to thank her." Daed dipped his spoon in the soup.

Joel waited a moment.

"I'd like to invite Ellie and her family to supper." Maryann reached for the breadbasket. "I want to grow my friendship with her, and she glows when she talks about Liza and Peter. I can't wait to meet them."

"What a splendid idea! When should we do it?" Joel leaned forward.

Mamm's coffee mug shook in her hands. "I'm not sure I agree."

Joel narrowed his eyes. "Why not? How can you object after what Ellie and Jacob did for us? It's the least we can do to thank them."

Her face hardened. "Why didn't you take us instead of them? You were wrong to keep Maryann's letter from us."

Joel gripped his spoon. "I apologize for not telling you about the letter. I wasn't sure what Maryann's situation might be or what I should do. Ellie and her daed offered to go. They were impartial. I thought it best I take them up on their help. I do believe it worked out for the best."

"Joel was protecting you and Daed. He needed to make sure I was serious about living the Amish life and growing roots in Charm. He did the right thing." Maryann put her fork down. "Ellie befriended me without judgment. She's a compassionate and loving woman. I'm blessed to call her my friend. Without her coaxing Joel to kumme to Massillon, I might not be here right now."

"Did she tell you she's lived in the outside world?" Mamm squinted and pinched her lips.

Maryann sighed. "Yes she did. We understand each other."

"Your situation is different."

"No. I'm responsible for my actions, just like Ellie. I left of my own free will."

Joel let his schweschder convince Mamm she should wilkom Ellie into their home. She had a better chance of getting through to her. He assumed Daed had kumme to the same conclusion.

"Did you not listen to a word Joel and I have said? Ellie brought me home to you. Yes, Joel did too, but Ellie insisted he kumme for me. Does any of this matter to you?"

Mamm slid her finger and thumb up and down the cup handle. "I suppose."

Joel leaned back in his chair and folded his arms. "You suppose! Mamm, no one at this table has a problem with Ellie but you. I love her, and I'm going to marry her. I prefer to have your blessing. After what Maryann has shared with you, I'll be flabbergasted if you don't have a change of heart toward Ellie. She's done everything in her power to get you to accept her. To prove she's trustworthy."

Daed crossed his arms to his chest. "Naomi, this woman brought our dochder home to us. She made arrangements with work and her daed. She cared about Maryann, a woman she had never met. All she wants is for you to accept her. Why is it so hard?"

Mamm's cheeks reddened. Tears dripped onto the table. She covered her face with her hands. "I'm sorry, Joel. I'm ashamed of how I've treated her. Look what she's done for us, and I've done nothing but rebuke her."

Maryann got up and bent to wrap her arms around her. "Mamm, it's never too late to mend fences with someone, even if they don't accept your apology. It's good for the soul to ask anyway. I believe Ellie will be thrilled if you tell her you're sorry and would like to get better acquainted with her."

Joel held up his hands. "When should I tell her to bring her family to supper?"

Mamm leaned into her dochder and gave a remorseful smile to Joel. "Friday night?"

"I'll ask Ellie and her family tomorrow." Joel beamed and slapped his legs. "Danki, Mamm."

Daed reached over and covered Mamm's hand. "There's the loving fraa I married."

"Don't worry. Our conversation at supper will go much better than the last time we entertained Ellie and her family." Naomi met Joel's gaze.

Maryann settled back in her chair. "What happened the last time?"

"I've been rude and dismissive of Ellie. I berated and snubbed her. I'm deeply remorseful."

"Mamm! I'm surprised. Why would you do such a thing? You've always been so loving and kind. You took up for newcomers to the Amish community who were disparaged by gossips before this. Why Ellie?"

"I was afraid she and Joel would get married and she'd leave him. I didn't want him to suffer the loss of losing her after the pain he's had over you. I should've given her the benefit of the doubt. God must be upset with me. We are to love one another, and I've rejected her each time she's approached me."

Joel's heart soared. Maryann's return had been a blessing in itself. He didn't realize her presence would have such a positive impact on Mamm's attitude toward Ellie so soon. She spoke like the loving woman she was before his schweschder left. God had worked a miracle in their lives. He couldn't wait to tell Ellie their prayers had been answered. His shoulders stiffened. Ellie might be afraid Mamm would change her mind and give them trouble in the future. He wouldn't blame her for having such thoughts. He hoped she'd be happy to witness his Mamm's sincere change of heart toward her. He had every confidence in his mamm that she would make things right between her and Ellie, and he would assure the love of his life that he believed this to be true. He couldn't wait to bring their families together. He and Ellie had a lot to look forward to.

Chapter Thirteen

Ellie told Liza about their adventures in Massillon. "You will love Maryann, and her boppli, Betsy, is precious."

Peter rested his fist under his chin. "Will she let me hold Betsy?"

"You can ask. I'm sure she will."

Jacob sipped hot chocolate Liza had made for them. "She is pretty. She's got dainty fingers and hands, a cute nose, and a sweet little mouth. Her fuzzy hair tickles your cheek."

"I'd like a bruder or schweschder." Peter stared at Liza.

"You've got a schweschder, and you can enjoy Betsy." Jacob tousled Peter's hair.

"When can we go visit her?" Peter held out his palms.

"We should give Maryann and Betsy time to get settled first." Ellie studied her daed.

His eyes sparkled as he described Betsy's features. He'd smiled from ear to ear rocking her in his arms in Massillon. He acted like he longed for more kinner. She wondered if he and Liza had talked about adding to their family. Liza loved the bakery, and Peter was at the age where he was easier to take care of than an infant. She doubted they would plan a boppli.

Cinnamon came into the kitchen, with Snuggles hopping behind him. Both headed for Peter. He slid off his chair. "Sorry, Mamm. I'll get them out of the kitchen."

Ellie laughed. "Snuggles acts like a dog rather than a rabbit. The two animals are inseparable when they're out of their cages."

Peter petted Snuggles. "While you were gone, Snuggles went up to a mean old dog who came in our yard and tried to play with him. The dog was about to take a hunk out of Snuggles when I swooped in just in time."

Ellie reached for his hand. "Did the dog chase after you?"

Liza swatted the air. "Nah. I was with him. The old dog was hungry and harmless. We fed him, and minutes later, an Englischer came by and apologized. They'd been looking for the dog all day after they realized he was no longer in their yard. They said he started running away after their son passed. The dog might be looking for him."

"Peter, don't approach dogs and other animals. They could be sick or mean and harm you." Jacob waggled his forefinger at Peter.

"I had to rescue Snuggles."

"I'm your protector, and I don't want anything bad to happen to you." Daed stared into Peter's eyes.

Peter picked up his rabbit and nestled his nose in Snuggle's fur. "I'll take them outside."

Ellie waited for the door to close behind Peter then directed her attention to her daed. "He's going to ignore your warning. He loves those animals."

Jacob stretched his arms over his head and rolled

his eyes. "He scares me. He's loyal to Snuggles and Cinnamon to a fault." He winked. "Similar to you. You went after Peter when the woman took him."

"You would've done the same."

"You've got me there. I am proud of you."

"Me too." Liza grinned.

"Danki." She yawned. "Liza, how were things at the bakery while we were away?"

"Slow. Not our usual Wednesday crowd. We missed you, and it wasn't as much fun without you. We're glad you're back." Liza squeezed her arm.

Ellie snapped her fingers. "I almost forgot. I went to a quilt shop." She recounted meeting Becca and told Liza about the quilt she'd given her.

"Some of the ladies here have talked about her shop. It sounds lovely." She lifted a wrapped package off the chair in the corner. "Is this the one she gave you?"

"Jah, it's beautiful. I love how they stitch a pocket on them for you to tuck a note inside." She longed to give it to Joel. She wouldn't have the chance as long as his mamm had anything to say about it. She wouldn't marry him and open both families up to such animosity. "I'm exhausted. I'd better get to bed." She kissed their cheeks and padded to her room. She enjoyed Maryann, and it would be a treat to show her around town and the bakery and do things together. What was she thinking? Mrs. Wenger would have objections. She better put those notions out of her head.

Joel woke up early Thursday and hurried through his morning chores. He wouldn't let anything get in the way of going to town and inviting Ellie's family to their haus. He hadn't realized the burden he'd been carrying while Maryann was gone. He no longer dreaded facing Mamm. She had been moody, sad, and critical. She'd been going through the motions each day to care for them and do her chores. Today she bounced with joy like she hadn't a care in the world. Mamm had let go of her bitterness. What a great day!

He washed and dried his hands and went inside. Mamm held Betsy in her lap. Maryann and Daed were chatting, and he watched them for a moment. Daed beamed, and so did the women. The circle would be complete when he could convince Ellie to become his fraa.

"Joel, I didn't realize you'd kumme in." Maryann pulled out the chair beside her. "Kumme sit."

"I'm going to visit Ellie at the bakery and extend our invitation."

Daed lifted his eyes. "A little anxious, are we?"

"Jah." Joel blushed.

Mamm put Betsy's head on her shoulder. "Ask Ellie to invite the rest of her family. Hannah, Esther, and Abe."

He'd have her extended family here. He had a plan, and this made it even better. "Danki, Mamm. Will do." He kissed Betsy's forehead.

"Tell Ellie I look forward to getting together with her." Maryann stood and opened the door for him.

He nodded to Maryann, shrugged on his wool jacket as he stepped outside, harnessed his horse to the wagon and left. He waved to the townsfolk passing by in their buggies and a couple driving a motorcar. The crisp air, the blue sky, and the sun shining made the cold refreshing. Or maybe it was his heart singing inside his chest. He'd found the woman for him, and there was nothing stopping them from planning a wedding soon.

He'd been saving money for a haus, livestock, and planting hay, corn, and a big garden. He'd need to construct a barn and silo. He had so much to do. One step at a time. He scanned the farms on both sides of the road. Each haus was painted white and they looked about the same. Some larger. Some smaller. The fields and gardens filled acre after acre of land. They were all blessed to have food, water, and homes to live in. Friends to lend a hand when needed. *God is good.*

He tied his mare to the hitching post outside of the bakery. His heart thumped as he strode inside.

Ellie came around the corner of the counter. "Joel! I didn't expect you'd kumme to town today! What a nice surprise!"

He took off his hat and clutched it tight to his chest. "Ellie, Mamm sent me to ask you and your family plus Hannah and her parents to supper at our haus Friday evening."

"What!" Eyes wide, her hand flew to her chest.

"I'm serious. We told her how grateful we are to you and your daed for helping us. Maryann defended you to Mamm, and she got through to her. Ellie, Mamm has let go of her judgmental attitude about you. Please say jah."

She wrinkled her nose. "What should we bring?"

"Not a thing. She's anxious to have all of you. Let her and Maryann do it."

"Joel, I'm astounded. I never thought I'd be invited to your haus again."

"Wait until you're around her. She's a different person. The Mamm she was before Maryann left. We've had tension in the haus for so long. To have it replaced with joy and laughter this morning was an overwhelming change. A good change. Mamm is in love with Betsy." He chuckled. "She's little to have such power over all of us."

"I hope your mamm isn't just putting on an act for Maryann. I'm timid about this."

"She's sincere. I promise." He understood her trepidation.

"Joel, this would mean so much to me. Our lives would change."

"Jah. You wouldn't have any more excuses to keep me at arm's length."

She held his gaze. "Nah, I wouldn't."

Hannah bounced into the room. "Joel! What a pleasure."

"Hannah, you're invited to our haus for supper tomorrow along with Ellie's parents and Peter. Bring your parents too. Will you kumme? Mamm's had a change of heart about Ellie, and she's anxious to show her. She asked if you would all join us."

"What do you say, Ellie?" Hannah tilted her head.

"Let's go. I'd be ecstatic if she's ready to talk to me."

"All right, then. Joel, what time?" Hannah leaned on the end of the counter.

"Six."

Ellie hugged herself and bounced on her toes. "We'll be there."

He put his hat on and opened the door. "This is all going to work out, Ellie." He gave her a reassuring half smile. "Enjoy the rest of your day, ladies."

Ellie clasped her hands and held them to her chin. "Hannah, can you believe it?"

"I do. I've been praying for this day. You and Joel belong together."

"Let's not get ahead of ourselves. I'm not sure I trust her. She might be putting on a good front for

Maryann. I have no doubt her dochder would take up for me. We liked each other from the start, and she doesn't have a critical bone in her body. You're going to enjoy being around her."

"I'm anxious to meet Maryann and Betsy." Hannah pushed a stray hair back in her kapp. "Did you and Joel have time to discuss anything?"

"He believes his mamm has had a change of heart. He and I had the best time together during our jaunt to Massillon. Oh, Hannah, I'm afraid to get my hopes up."

"Let's think good thoughts."

Liza joined them. "What's all the chatter out here about?" She plopped on the stool.

"We're going to Joel's for supper on Friday. She twirled her finger. "All of us."

"Is this Joel's idea?" Liza frowned.

"Mrs. Wenger's." Ellie held up her hands. "She's full of regrets, according to Joel."

"Why, Ellie, how wonderful." Liza sat up straight. "What shall we take to them?"

"Nothing. She's got it all planned." Ellie shrugged.

"Ellie, this could be a big turning point in your and Joel's lives." Liza got up and hugged her. "I'm so happy for you."

"I'm cautious and optimistic. Let's wait until we speak with her."

"I can understand why you'd question her change of heart after the way she's treated you." Hannah sighed.

"She may not want to stir up any trouble with Maryann. Joel said his schweschder supported me to his mamm."

"Give her the benefit of the doubt. God may be working on her." Liza swiped some sugar from her sleeve.

"I'm sure this will be a happy occasion." Hannah

sniffed. "Oh no! I burnt the apple tarts!" She bolted to the kitchen.

Ellie hurried behind her. She threw her a potholder.

Liza stood next to Ellie, grabbed another potholder, and tossed it to Hannah.

Hannah opened the oven door. She jerked the tray out. "I got them out just in time!"

Ellie laughed and then rushed to Liza, who was collapsing to the floor. "Liza!" She knelt beside her. "Liza, wake up!"

Hannah stood over her. "I'll go get Dr. Harrison." She rose and ran from the kitchen.

"Please, please, open your eyes. You're scaring me." She put her ear to Liza's chest. *A heartbeat and she's breathing.* She blew out a breath.

Liza's eyes fluttered open. She raised a hand to the back of her head. "Ouch, what happened?" She lifted her shoulders to get up.

"Nah. Don't move." Ellie tucked a folded towel under her head. "You stay still until Dr. Harrison arrives." She touched where Liza had her hand. "You're getting a goose egg on the back of your head. You fell flat on the floor, and I couldn't rouse you."

Hannah came in. "Dr. Harrison is right behind me. Oh, Liza, I'm so glad you're awake." She glanced at Ellie. "I locked the door and turned the sign to show we're closed."

"Good. We don't need any distractions right now."

Dr. Harrison knelt. "Liza, tell me the last thing you remember." He threw open his black bag and pulled out his stethoscope.

"The room went black, and I'm now staring at you." She winced and touched her head. "Each morning for the last couple of weeks, I've been nauseous."

He nodded, put the tips in his ears, and listened to

her heartbeat. He took the stethoscope from around his neck and returned it to his bag. He examined her injury. "The swollen place on your head may hurt for a week or so, but it will heal. The skin is fine." He closed his bag. "Ellie and Hannah, I'd like to talk to Liza a minute. Do you mind stepping out?"

Ellie clasped Hannah's hand. "Is this serious?" She couldn't lose Liza. They'd formed a special bond, and her family would be devastated. She was the one who gave the best hugs, advice, love, and compassion. The one who brought such happiness to them with her cheerfulness, the lilt in her step, and putting them before herself.

"I suspect not." He offered Liza his hand. "You can sit up now. I wouldn't advise standing. Give yourself a minute."

"They'll listen to us anyway. They may as well stay." She leaned back on her hand.

Ellie and Hannah sat on the floor next to Liza.

"My legs hurt in this position. Let's all sit." Dr. Harrison stood.

Ellie dragged four wooden kitchen stools together.

Hannah and Dr. Harrison escorted Liza to the stools. Dr. Harrison stood in front of Liza. "Are you all right on this stool?"

"Jah. I've recovered. It's as if it never happened, except for the bump." She touched it, made a face, and dropped her hand in her lap.

"Your lack of food is part of the reason you fainted, in my opinion." He asked her health questions, and she reddened and answered she had been absent of her regular monthly cycles the last few months.

Dr. Harrison raised his brows. "Liza, you may give birth this year. You may be carrying your first baby."

"What!" Her eyes and hands went to her stomach. "Me? I assumed I couldn't birth a boppli."

Ellie cocked her head. "Why?" She noticed everyone raised their eyebrows.

"During my marriage to Paul, we never had kinner."

Ellie and Hannah clapped and hugged each other. "We're going to have a boppli in our family!"

"Hold on. The doctor isn't sure." Liza folded her hands in her lap.

Dr. Harrison held up his forefinger. "If I was a betting man, Liza, I'd be surprised if I didn't win big on this one." He sniffed and eyed the nut cookies on the tray. "Mind if I have one?"

Hannah scooped three off the tray, set one in his palm, and wrapped the other two. "It's the least we can do."

Liza walked him to the door. "Danki, Doctor."

"I'm happy for you, Liza. Enjoy this time." He nodded to the girls. "I'll be here in the morning as usual. Have a good day." He walked out the door, whistling.

"Daed and Peter will be ecstatic!" Ellie put her hands on Liza's shoulders. "When will you tell them?"

Hannah whirled around. "I'm so excited to tell my parents!"

Ellie stepped back. "Liza, your frown and worried eyes puzzle me. Why aren't you over the moon about this? Don't you want a boppli?"

"More than anything." She paced the room. "I'm afraid. What if something goes wrong? It's early. I don't want to disappoint Jacob or you or anyone in our family. I should've kept this between Dr. Harrison and myself."

"Liza, you're not to blame if something would

happen. Your family would comfort you, and we'd heal together with God watching over us. This is the time where you trust and look forward to holding your little one and raising him or her." Ellie chuckled. "You may wonder if Hannah, Esther, and I will spoil the infant too much. And jah, we promise to."

"Jah. I'm going home to knit booties tonight!" Hannah mimed having knitting needles in her hands.

Liza dabbed tears under her eyes. "You're right. I shouldn't be predicting the worst. Paul blamed me for not giving him kinner. I need to let those fears go. Jacob would never do such a thing." She curled her lips into a smile. "He's going to want to shout it from the rooftop. Peter will tell his classmates at school. The town gossips are going to love this!" She rolled her eyes.

"Do you mind if we put it in the paper?" Ellie gave her an impish grin and then threw up her hands. "Just teasing you."

"I sure hope this queasiness in the mornings goes away soon." Liza rubbed her tummy.

"Mamm said she had it with me for about three months."

"It doesn't matter." Liza rubbed her hands together. "I'd suffer nine months to have a boppli. I can't wait!"

"What fun this will be!" Ellie bounced on her toes.

Hannah reached for Liza's hand. "Maybe you should go home and take it easy. You can tell Jacob and Peter. They'll want to shout it all over town!"

Ellie bit the inside of her cheek. She would've liked to watch the expressions on Jacob and Peter's faces. They'd beam with happiness. She held her breath a moment. Guilt shot through her. She wouldn't be selfish. Liza's health was most important. She was thankful

Hannah had made the suggestion and she hadn't had a chance to voice her errant thought. She'd have regretted it. Hannah had rescued her again.

"Liza, Hannah's right. Go home and get some rest. I'm sure you're itching to tell Daed and Peter."

"All right. I am anxious to tell them. I'll kumme back and take you both home around five." She untied her apron and hung it on the hook. She shrugged into her heavy wool cape and bid them farewell.

Hannah flipped the sign. "I better get to work. All this excitement has put me behind, but I'm not complaining." She chuckled. "Jacob and Peter will be anxious for you to get home to discuss boppli names, what's needed, and all kinds of plans."

"I'm stunned. It's hard to believe I'm gaining a bruder or schweschder in less than nine months." She followed Hannah to the kitchen. "I'll take these peach and blueberry pies and put them on the shelves."

The door flew open. A middle-aged couple came in. The man was dressed in a dapper brown wool jacket and creased pants with a sharp gentlemen's hat. His crisp white shirt didn't have a wrinkle in it, from what she could tell. The woman had light brown hair and brown eyes to match. She had on an ankle-length black velvet coat and matching hat. Ellie hoped they didn't notice her stare. They were a striking couple.

"What may I offer you today?"

The woman perused the jars of canned fruit on the shelf behind Ellie, and then scanned the goodies in the glass counter. "How about a peach pie, Robert?"

"Peach pie! No! You like peach pie. Not me. I'll take apple pie."

"We'll take the peach pie." She scowled at him and whipped her head to Ellie. "What kind of breads do you sell?"

Ellie reeled from the man's outburst. The woman's reply had taken her aback. Most women didn't oppose their mates in public. She had pegged them all wrong. They weren't a happy couple. "White, wheat, and nut."

"What wonderful selections. I'll buy wheat and nut."

"Nut! Are you out of your mind? I don't like nut bread. Aren't you going to purchase anything for me?"

"Stop being rude. I'll buy you white bread and molasses cookies. Are you satisfied?"

He huffed. "I suppose."

"You're lucky I would buy you anything. If it wasn't for my inheritance, we wouldn't have a motorcar, a nice big house, and the things you enjoy. You're nothing but a lazy no-good spendthrift. I should leave you where we stand."

The man's face reddened and his eyes filled with anger. "No other man would put up with such a shrew. I can always find another woman to take care of me. Go ahead. Leave me if you want to."

Ellie reared back. The woman stood stone-faced and silent.

She pulled out the woman's selections, wrapped them as fast as she could, and accepted payment. How did this couple stand living together? Did they argue all the time? She couldn't imagine the resentment between them getting any better. It made her appreciate Joel. He would be a good provider, and he apologized when he was wrong. She didn't suppose this couple let go of their pride enough to do so. "Danki for stopping in."

The couple departed, and she shut the door behind them.

Hannah poked her head out. "I'm glad they left. His booming voice carried back to the kitchen. They were so rude to each other. They must be miserable. How sad."

"What I can't figure out is why did she marry him?" Ellie shook her head. "She must've known he didn't have any gumption to work."

Hannah clasped her hands behind her back. "It's a mystery. He must've been a smooth talker. It wouldn't be the life for me."

"You and me both."

"I wonder if Liza will let us tell our friends about the boppli?"

"I'll ask her tonight. I'm curious if she'll let me tell Joel and his family when we go to supper. Or maybe she'll tell them."

"Peter will blab the news. He can't keep a secret."

"Oh, you're right!" She laughed along with Hannah.

Ellie waited on customers and Hannah baked in the back room until five. They locked the door and left. Jacob and Peter were outside in the buggy.

"Good afternoon, ladies." Jacob held the reins.

Peter beamed. "We're going to have a schweschder or bruder!"

"What did I tell you?" Hannah giggled.

"No surprise there." Ellie chuckled.

Peter swiveled in the bench. "What do you mean?"

Jacob patted Peter's knee. "They love you, and they're happy about your news."

"Daed, were you surprised?" Ellie watched his face. Daed didn't act as gleeful as she had expected.

"I had an inkling she may be with child when she had an upset stomach each morning. Your mamm experienced the same when she carried you. I didn't want to suggest it since I wasn't sure I was right. I'm thrilled we're having a child. Are you?"

She patted Daed's shoulder. He'd turned to glance at her, and the twinkle in his eye told her he was excited about having a child.

"Jah. I wish it didn't take so long. But it will give us lots of time to knit and stitch things for the little one. What did you say when she told you?"

Peter giggled. "He whistled and picked her up and swung her around."

Hannah tapped Peter's hand. "What did you do?"

"I clapped my hands and turned in circles. It's so exciting!"

Ellie held on to the back of the bench behind Peter. "How is Liza?"

"The pain from the back of her head is better. She put ice on it and took some aspirin powder. She had potatoes boiling on the stove when I left." Daed pulled in front of Hannah's haus.

"I'm glad she's better. Hug her for me! I can't wait to tell my parents the news." Hannah got out of the buggy.

"Don't forget to tell them about Joel's invitation to supper tomorrow evening."

"Oh, I won't forget." She gave Ellie a knowing grin.

They waved farewell and headed the short distance home.

"Are you and Joel courting again?" Daed got out of the buggy.

Peter jumped out. "I'm going inside!"

Ellie nodded to Peter and turned her attention to Daed. "His mamm invited our family and Hannah's to their haus for supper tomorrow evening. She's not been in favor of Joel and me. I'm nervous to encounter her again after the way she treated me the last time I joined them for supper."

Daed unharnessed the mare. "What does Joel say?"

"He insists she's had a change of heart. I suspect Maryann may have spoken to her on my behalf. We liked each other from the moment we met. We understand each other and can empathize with what we've both gone through in the outside world. She's a lovely person. I look forward to growing our friendship if her mamm allows it."

"I like Joel. He's a good man. I hope this get-together will turn into more with his family."

"Danki. You're a good daed." She kissed him on the cheek. "This little one on the way is blessed to have you. I am, and if you asked Peter, he'd tell you the same."

"I love being Daed to you and Peter. I'm thrilled to add another one to our home."

"I'll go inside and help Liza with supper." Ellie jumped to the ground.

"I've got a couple of chores to do, and then I'll join you." Daed took the horse into the barn.

Ellie strolled across the yard, went inside, and padded to the kitchen. "You have a good helper, Liza."

Peter held up his chin and beamed. "I scooped the biscuits off the tray and put them in the basket. I was careful not to burn my fingers."

"He listens and follows directions. I enjoy having him in the kitchen."

Ellie picked a platter of shredded pork off the stove and carried it to the table. "This is a feast."

"We're celebrating our new little addition kumming soon. Our men were funny with their reactions. I wish you could've been here. I laughed until I cried at their joyous whooping and hollering." She playfully flicked the towel in her hands on Ellie's shoulder. "And to celebrate Joel's mamm inviting all of us for supper."

"I'm excited and anxious. She's unpredictable. I hope Joel is right." She pointed to Liza's head. "How are your head and upset stomach?" Ellie stuck a big spoon in the vegetables.

"My head is sore. The upset stomach in the morning is a small price to pay for such a wonderful gift." She held the dishtowel to her chest. "I have an inkling this supper will be a very special one for you and Joel's mamm."

"I hope you're right." Ellie sighed. Mrs. Wenger hadn't had a kind word to say to her since they'd met. She found it hard to swallow that Maryann would have such an impact on the woman. Maybe she shouldn't be skeptical. She'd be pleasant and hope for the best.

Joel went to his workshop Friday morning. Yesterday had gone by fast. He hadn't had a minute to himself with the sow escaping again and repairing the leaks in the roof, along with his other chores. He yawned. Getting up earlier than usual had been challenging. He needed to finish the gift he'd made for Ellie. The box needed a lid. He sorted through the different sizes of cedar and built the lid. It fit the box. He was sure she would like it.

He took out a pencil and piece of paper and started writing. Finished with his note, he tucked his message inside the box and closed the lid. He grinned. They'd been through turmoil, mayhem, and happy times together. He was ready to make her his fraa and share whatever life brought them. He ran inside the haus. "Mamm, do you have a piece of fabric large enough for me to wrap this?" He held up the box.

She reached for the gift. "This is beautiful. Did you make it or buy it?"

"I made it for Ellie."

"Let me wrap it for you." She dragged her fabric basket from the corner of the room and flipped through the pile. She tugged out dark blue fabric. Placing the box in the center, she wrapped the present and secured it with twine. She held it out to him. "You did a wonderful job on the box. She will love it."

"Danki, Mamm." He carried the present to his room and set it on the oak chair. Before now, Mamm would've scowled and made a negative comment about anything he would've made for Ellie. She had put the lilt back in her step, the smile on her face, and she oozed with cheerfulness. His schweschder had such a good influence on her. He hoped her good mood was here to stay.

Chapter Fourteen

Ellie got in the buggy Friday evening with her family. She rolled her shoulders and willed herself to relax. She'd been busy at the counter waiting on customers all day. "I couldn't keep up with filling the orders for our patrons today. I didn't have dinner."

Liza rested her arm on the back of the bench seat. "We had several motorcars and lots of buggies and wagons in town today. The peddler had fresh fryers to sell, and the general store got in chocolate and lemon drops. They've been out of both for a week."

Ellie leaned forward. "Dr. Harrison and the sheriff came in this morning. They said fifteen people were killed and twenty were injured in a railway accident in Irvington, Indiana. One of the trains was speeding from Cincinnati to Chicago when it collided with a freight train! The travelers on the train must've been terrified."

Peter's eyes widened. "I would've been real scared. I don't want to ever ride a train."

Daed said, "Most train rides are safe. Sounds like the engineer of this one broke the law and put people's lives in danger by being reckless. Accidents are more likely to happen when we're in too much of a hurry."

Peter lifted up his pants leg and pointed. "Like when I ran to catch Snuggles and didn't watch where I was going and scraped my knee?"

Daed darted a glance at Peter then back at the road. "Jah, you ignored Mamm's request to put Snuggles away earlier, and then you were in a big hurry and got hurt."

Ellie shuddered. It only took a moment for something bad to happen. The people on the train had no idea their lives would end. She hoped Joel was right about his mamm. She was ready to build a life with him. She bumped Peter's arm. "Are you happy we're going to visit Joel?"

"Jah. I've missed him." Peter crossed his arms. "Is it your fault?"

"I'm afraid so." She smoothed her skirt. "Don't worry. After tonight, I'm hoping he'll be at our haus more often."

"Good." Peter settled back in his seat.

Daed halted the horse at the Wengers, and they all got out. He tied the horse to the hitching post.

Ellie exited with her family, recognized Hannah's buggy, and went to the door.

Joel opened it before she had a chance to knock. "Kumme in. Hannah and her family are in the sitting room."

Mr. Wenger stood behind him. "Jah. We're delighted you're here."

Her face warmed, and she joined the group. "Good evening, everyone." She hugged Hannah, Esther, and Abe.

Mrs. Wenger popped her head out from the kitchen to the sitting room. "Wilkom. Make yourselves at home.

I've got a plate of fresh bread and apple jam for you to nibble on while I finish preparing the food."

Liza went to her. "May we help you?"

"I've got everything almost ready and the table's set. Maryann's helping me." She gestured for her dochder to join them. "Everyone, this is Maryann, my precious dochder. You'll meet Betsy, my granddochder, later. She's taking a nap."

Esther smiled and waddled her ample hips to Liza and Mrs. Wenger. "Let us do something."

"Nah. I insist you visit and let me finish up." Naomi gave them a warm smile.

Ellie hugged Maryann and stepped back for Hannah and the rest of her family to greet her. Her new friend spoke to each one of her family with kindness. She was encouraged by Mrs. Wenger's smile in her direction when introducing Maryann to the group.

Peter greeted Maryann and went to Joel. "Snuggles and Cinnamon miss you. You should visit us more."

Joel chuckled. "What about you?"

Ellie's heart soared. Peter had a special friendship with Joel.

"I miss you most of all." He hugged Joel's legs.

Joel ruffled Peter's hair. "I've missed you too. I plan to kumme over a lot more often. We'll find time to play blind man's bluff."

Peter motioned for Joel to bend down. He got close to his ear. "I'm going to tell you a secret."

"Maybe you should wait and get permission to tell me."

Peter shook his head. "I wanna tell you."

"What is it?"

Ellie tapped Peter on the shoulder. "You should wait and let Liza tell the news."

Her bruder couldn't keep his mouth shut. Anytime

he overheard something of interest, he had to tell the news. She couldn't help but be amused he wanted to tell Joel about the boppli. Peter had been fond of Joel from the start.

"You weren't supposed to listen." Peter narrowed his eyes.

"I couldn't help but overhear you. What you call whispering is too loud."

"Please, let me tell him."

Joel tapped Peter's nose. "Maybe we should wait until after supper."

"I'm going to have a new schweschder or bruder soon!" He brought his hands to his mouth and giggled.

The room grew quiet.

Liza stepped to Peter. "Usually families keep the announcement of a woman with child to themselves for a while. Peter makes this impossible for our family."

Ellie stood and studied her loved ones. They beamed, clapped, and shouted with glee. She held her middle. What would it be like to have a boppli? Joel had taken to Betsy the minute he held her. He had made fast friends with Peter. Did he want kinner?

Hannah approached her. "Everyone is in a good mood."

"Jah, I'm baffled. Joel's mamm wilkomed us with a smile on her face. I don't know what to think."

Mrs. Wenger's smiles were a good sign she'd changed her opinion of Ellie. So why was the hair on her neck tingling with worry?

"Mamm and I will be making all kinds of things for this boppli. I'm excited!" Hannah whispered in Ellie's ear. "And your problem with Joel's mamm may have faded away."

Ellie cupped a hand to Hannah's ear. "We'll find out. I'm hopeful but afraid to trust her."

Mrs. Wenger came into the room. "Time for supper. I borrowed a table from the neighbor. We'll be snug, but we'll have room for everyone."

Joel's mamm glowed with happiness. Ellie couldn't get over the change. She went to the table and sat between Liza and Maryann, across from Joel. Her face warmed as she smiled at him.

He gave her a nod and grin.

"Let's bow our heads for prayer." Shem gave thanks to God for the food.

Ellie lifted her head. "Mrs. Wenger, you must've cooked all day. Everything looks wonderful."

"Call me Naomi. I enjoyed preparing this special meal for you and your family. After we've had our fill of food and the dishes are cleared, I'd like a few minutes alone with you and Liza."

Ellie blanched. She didn't trust her. What did she want to say she couldn't tell them with the others at this table present? "Of course."

Maryann gave Ellie's knee a gentle squeeze.

Joel's schweschder must not share her trepidation over Naomi's request. Was Maryann hopeful? Ellie couldn't help but be skeptical.

Maryann passed her the carrot, pea, and onion mixed vegetables. Steam rolled off them. "Mamm has spoiled Betsy in the short time we've been here. She changes her nappies, and she loves to rock her often."

Naomi beamed. "She nestles in my arms, and I don't want to let her go. I'm thrilled to have them home."

Peter accepted the breadbasket from Daed. "May I hold her?"

"When she wakes, you can hold her." Maryann scooped out a spoonful of cherry jam.

"Mamm, will you let me hold my boppli schweschder or bruder?"

"Of course I will." Liza sipped her water.

Naomi grinned. "Peter, you'll be a big help with the new boppli."

Maryann said, "Your bruder or schweschder will be blessed to have you for a sibling."

Esther blew Peter a kiss. "You're such a sweet lad."

He wiggled in his seat and grinned at her, then he sat up straight. "I won't be the boppli of the family anymore."

Joel winked at Peter. "Does losing your position as the youngest in the family upset you?"

"Nah. I'm excited." He puffed out his chest. "I will be the big bruder and protect her or him." He pushed carrots onto his fork with his thumb. "I want a boy."

Abe picked up his cotton napkin. "Why not a girl?"

"'Cause I already have Ellie, and I'd like to do boy things."

"Like what?" Jacob held his glass.

"Getting all dirty sliding in the mud puddles, building a haus with rocks and wood from the fire pile, and other stuff."

"Will you be disappointed if the boppli is a girl?"

"Nah. I'll have fun with her too." He chuckled. "Can't wait to teach him or her how to do some of my chores."

Ellie laughed with everyone in the room. He had the best attitude about this child on the way. She was glad he wasn't jealous or sad he wouldn't be the youngest in the family. She glanced at Joel. His face radiated joy. He must be happy to have his family whole again. He caught her gaze and winked. Heat rose to her cheeks. She gave him a shy smile.

"I can't put another bite of food in my mouth. I don't have any more room." Peter set his fork on his plate.

"You may be excused. We have board games and puzzles in the sitting room. You'll find them on the side table. They belonged to Joel and Maryann when they were kinner. Help yourself." Naomi rose and pushed her chair back.

"Danki." Peter skipped to the other room.

Liza rose and carried over the empty dishes. "You put on quite a spread. Everything tasted delicious."

Everyone nodded and thanked Naomi.

Shem gestured to the sitting room. "Men, let's join Peter in the sitting room."

Joel grinned at Ellie and then followed the men.

The women cleared the table and washed and dried the dishes.

Ellie enjoyed the chatter about quilts, the weather, and what they'd canned for the winter.

Peter wandered into the kitchen. "Esther and Hannah, will you work a puzzle with me?"

"I'd be happy to. We're all finished here. Danki for the lovely meal, Mrs. Wenger." Hannah took his hand.

"Call me Naomi. I insist."

Hannah nodded.

Naomi faced Ellie and Liza. "Let's sit at the table a few minutes before we join the others."

Esther didn't take a seat. "I'll join Hannah and Peter and let you ladies have some privacy." She padded to the next room.

Maryann sat next to Naomi. "Do you mind if I stay?"

"Jah, sweetheart, you'd ask me what was said. You may as well hear it firsthand." Naomi turned her attention to Liza and Ellie. "I apologize for my previous rude behavior. I listened to gossips, and I misjudged you, Ellie. I held your past against you, and I had no right. I let my sorrow over Maryann turn me into a bitter woman. Liza, you came here and offered me friendship, and I snubbed you. I hope you both can forgive me."

Liza reached for Ellie's hand under the table. "I already did. I'm glad you've changed your mind, and we look forward to more suppers together."

"Ellie, what about you?"

Naomi hadn't said anything about her and Joel. Ellie wished she knew where the woman stood on this matter. Dare she ask? She'd better wait until she spoke with Joel. Maybe they'd get a few minutes in private later. "Of course. I'm happy you're willing to socialize with me. I'd like us to get better acquainted."

Maryann's eyes twinkled. "You can count on it. You've been such a good friend to me already. We have lots to talk about."

Joel came into the room. "Mind if I steal Ellie for a little while?"

Naomi rose. "Not at all."

Joel shrugged into his heavy wool coat. He handed her the shawl she had worn when she arrived. He reached for the lantern. "I've got a fire going outside."

Ellie sat on the weathered maple chair Joel got for her. She stared at the orange flames and inhaled the scent of burning wood. She relished the night, still and quiet, and the shining moon in the black sky. "It gets dark early. I miss the long days."

"I do too." He set the lantern on the ground and pulled his chair close to hers. "Ellie, what did Mamm say to you?"

"She apologized for her behavior. I told I forgave her. I'm surprised and happy she's changed her attitude about me."

"Aren't you glad we no longer have to worry about her approval of us getting married?"

Did he say married? Her heart skipped a beat. "She didn't mention you and me."

"She didn't want to give away what I'm about to do. Ellie, I pulled your daed aside while you were in the kitchen, and he gave his blessing for me to ask you this question. I asked you before, but now I've taken the appropriate steps, and I'm doing this the proper way. Will you make me the happiest man on earth and say jah to becoming my fraa?" He took her hand in his.

"Jah! Jah! Jah!" She swiped tears from under her eyes. "I love you so much!"

"I love you too." He glanced at the haus. "Everyone's at the window." He laughed, picked her up, and swung her around. Then he pressed his lips on hers. A kiss to remember.

They parted and chatted about their special day.

Naomi and Maryann approached them, shivering. "The air is cold out here. Kumme inside."

"We're getting married!" Ellie clapped her hands.

Naomi hugged her. "I'm thrilled! This is wonderful news."

"Congratulations!" Maryann held her arms open wide to Ellie.

Ellie hugged Maryann. "I'm freezing. Let's go tell everyone."

They ran inside, and Joel cupped his mouth. "Ellie agreed to marry me!"

Her family circled them in a big hug. No one had dry eyes. She was glad they were all shedding happy tears.

Liza gently pulled Ellie aside and held her a moment. "Jacob told us Joel asked for your hand in marriage while you were outside. He told Joel that you and he are wilkom to build and live on our land." She swung Ellie's hand in hers. "Our family is growing fast. We're adding Joel, and then later, this little one. What an exciting year we have ahead!"

"I'm sure we will take you and Daed up on your generous and thoughtful offer." Ellie kissed Liza's cheek. "You're right. We do have an exciting year ahead!" Ellie leaned into her.

Jacob took Ellie's other hand. "My little girl is all grown up, and now she'll be starting a family of her own. Of course, you'll always be my little girl."

Ellie rested her head on his shoulder. "Good!"

Peter looked at her. "Can I kumme over and play? Does this mean Joel will be my bruder?"

"Jah, Joel will be your bruder, you can visit anytime." Ellie grinned and gently squeezed Peter's shoulder.

Hannah handed her a handkerchief. "You and Joel are glowing with joy. I hope I find the same kind of man."

"You will, and then we'll plan for your special day. I love you, dear friend." Ellie swiped her wet face with the handkerchief Hannah offered.

Abe blew his nose into his blue handkerchief. "She's kumme a long way, Jacob. I'm proud of her." He kissed Ellie's forehead.

Esther gently squeezed her arm. "You've done well, Ellie. I'm so glad this all worked out for you and Joel."

"Me too." Ellie grasped Esther's hand.

She'd prayed for this day. God had performed a miracle. She would be Joel's fraa, and their families both approved. Ellie went to Naomi. "I love your son, and I promise I'll be good to him."

"I have no doubt. You brought my dochder back to me. Joel told me you insisted on going after her. She has had nothing but good things to say about you. She opened my eyes and made me realize how blessed I will be to call you my dochder-in-law when you wed Joel. The Amish shun their kinner who leave. I couldn't do it. I don't know any other person in our community who would've done what you did for me."

Ellie said, "Maryann is a wonderful person. You raised kind and loving people."

"We're going to start over. You and me. And we'll have family socials often." Naomi put her hands on Ellie's shoulders.

"Would you help me plan our wedding?"

Naomi hugged her again. "I'd be hurt if you didn't ask."

Joel's cheeks heated as the men slapped him on the back and expressed their good wishes. He excused himself, ran to the bedroom, and returned holding a small package. "Ellie, I need a couple more minutes before I dump water on the fire and put it out."

She skipped to the door and stepped outside, pulling her heavy wool shawl close.

He held out the gift. "This is for you."

"Danki, Joel. You're so sweet." She unwrapped the package and gasped. "I love this. How beautiful." She held the cedar box to her nose. "I love the scent."

"Open the lid."

She lifted the top and pulled out a note.

Dear Ellie,
I'm presenting this gift to you as a reminder of our special day. The day our prayers were answered and you said you'd marry me. I'll never forget when we first met. My heart raced looking into your beautiful

*blue eyes. A connection I couldn't explain. I'm excited
to find out what God has in store for us in the years
to kumme. I'll cherish, honor, and protect you all the
days of my life. I love you with all my heart.*

Joel

Tears dripped onto her dress. "This is the best gift
you could've given me. I'll reread this note again and
again over the years. Danki."

"Ellie, your parents have offered us land. I'd like to
accept their offer and build us a haus there. Are you
in favor of this?"

"I would love to build on my family's land. Danki,
Joel."

Peter waved them in. "Daed said to tell you we
better go home. I had hoped Betsy would wake, but
she didn't. I'll have to hold her some other time." He
frowned and snapped his fingers.

Joel and Ellie went inside and she and her family
said farewell and went to their buggies.

"We'll talk more tomorrow. I'll stop in at the bakery.
Safe travels, Ellie." Joel squeezed her hand, and she
went to join her family in the buggy.

Hannah and her parents were heading down the
lane in front of Ellie's family's buggy. They would be
his family soon. He joined his parents and Maryann
on the porch. "What an exciting evening."

"We're happy for you, Son. They're lovely people."
Daed clapped a hand on Joel's shoulder.

"I'm sorry I gave you such a hard time about her. I'm
remorseful as I can be about how I treated her. She's
gracious to give me another chance." Mamm shivered.
"Let's get warm inside by the fire. Joel, you better put
the flames out in the fire pit."

He went and grabbed a bucket. "My mind is clouded.

I'm walking around in a fog I'm so giddy." He went to the pump, filled the bucket with water, and extinguished the fire. The end of a memorable night and the end of Mamm's disapproval of him and Ellie. *New beginnings.* He had questions for Ellie. When did she want to get married? He'd have to build a haus. He was sure Jacob, Abe, and his friend Timothy would lend a hand.

He went inside and said good night to his parents and went to his room. He read his Bible for an hour and climbed into bed. He tossed and turned most of the night. He could rest for one more hour before getting up. He groaned. No use. He couldn't wait to settle the date with Ellie and get their wedding on the bishop's calendar. He raced through his chores and went to the bakery, whistling as he walked inside. "Good morning, sunshine."

Ellie bounced on her toes. "What brings you here this fine Saturday morning?"

"I should speak to you at home later, but I couldn't wait."

"We're not busy. Liza and Hannah are in the kitchen. What's on your mind?"

"What date should we get married?"

Ellie dragged over a calendar and flipped the pages. "February fourth?"

He peered at the weeks. "February fourth is good. I'll get started on our haus, and I'll ask as many men as I can to help. I should have plenty of time to finish it before then."

"The weather might interfere." Ellie wrinkled her nose.

He gently tapped her nose. "Are you making excuses to postpone being my fraa, Miss Graber?" He'd marry her tomorrow if they could make it happen.

He'd work with the threat of frostbite in winter to construct their haus. He'd rather not live with his parents or hers for any period of time.

She swished the skirt of her dress from side to side and grinned. "Not for a minute. I'll leave the construction part of this plan to you." She picked up her pencil and smoothed the calendar out on the countertop. "Liza and Daed will host the service and ceremony."

"I'll ask the bishop if February fourth is a good date for him. Why don't you kumme for supper tonight?"

"I'd love to. I'm anxious to chat with your mamm and Maryann and hold Betsy. What time?"

"Six thirty."

"I'll be there."

Joel smiled. "I'll go home and tell them you're kumming." He looked out the window. "No one's kumming." He kissed her forehead and hurried out the door and headed home.

In the kitchen, Maryann had Betsy in her arms, and Mamm sat next to her, peeling potatoes. "Three beautiful ladies. What a sight to behold."

"Someone's in a good mood." Maryann chuckled. "You must've been to town to visit Ellie. I imagine she puts a smile on your face often."

"I have been to the bakery. We chose our wedding date. It will be February fourth, if the bishop agrees." Joel beamed. "I came home first to tell you I invited Ellie for supper this evening at six thirty."

"Wonderful! Now we can plan." Maryann patted the seat next to her. "Sit a minute."

"I should help Daed. Where is he?" Joel crossed his arms.

"He's over at the neighbor's haus. Their roof has

another bad leak." Mamm smacked her lips and shook her head. "They've had one problem after another with their haus."

Maryann rocked Betsy in her arms.

Joel kissed Betsy's little fingers. "She's such a good boppli."

"I'm fortunate." Maryann stood. "I'll be right back. I need to put her down for a nap." She returned. "Joel, I should speak with the bishop about my situation. I'd rather not do it by myself. Would I dampen the excitement of checking the bishop's calendar for your wedding date if I tagged along and had this conversation with him at the same time?"

"Nah. I wouldn't mind. I'd be happy to accompany you to the bishop's haus. We're all pleased you're staying in Charm. I'm glad you're ready to talk with him about making your home here with us permanent."

Mamm sighed. "You may have to attend meetings with the bishop for a while until he's convinced you once again understand what is expected of you living the Amish life."

"Don't worry. I'm prepared to do whatever is necessary to convince him and the community that I'm sincere." Maryann rested her forehead against Mamm's for a second.

"I don't want anything or anyone to make you change your mind." Mamm wrung her hands.

"No one could. God's will for my life is to live here. Most of the Amish will wilkom me, and a few gossips will prattle on about me like they did Ellie. It won't be easy, but those are the consequences of my past actions. I'll be fine." Maryann gave her mamm a reassuring smile.

"What time is good for you to go with me Monday?"

"Eight in the morning?" Maryann raised her brow.

"Eight is fine with me. When Ellie returned to Charm, she had to meet with the bishop about her leaving, and you can ask her questions tonight at supper. Maybe she can put your mind at ease."

Mamm finished peeling potatoes. "Where will you and Ellie live? I'm hoping you will build close to us."

"Ellie's parents have lots of acreage. They've offered us land to build there. We can have a garden and corn and hayfields. There's enough room for a big barn. I plan to have the haus finished by the time our wedding date rolls around." He was excited to ask men to help him construct the home he and Ellie would spend their future in.

Daed entered. "I'll be glad to help build it. I'm proud of you. How long do we have?"

"February fourth is the date, as long as the bishop has it open on his calendar." Joel stretched his arms above his head.

"We'll have plenty of time. I'm sure Jacob and our friends will join us." Daed opened a drawer and pulled out a piece of paper and pencil. He drew an outline. "Let's get started."

Joel's heart soared. He'd envisioned having a fraa, kinner, and a haus one day. Sitting here with his family, he loved having their input and approval of his decisions. Ellie was right. Having their families' support was important. Their lives would be richer in love and happiness because of their families' approval and joy about their impending marriage.

The time passed quickly.

Knock. Knock.

"Ellie must be here. It's six thirty!" Joel ran to the door. "Kumme in. Daed and I drew out a basic haus plan on paper. I'll show it to you." He took her to the kitchen.

"Congratulations on setting a date!" Naomi clapped her hands.

"Anything you need, we are here for you, Ellie." Maryann squeezed her hand.

Daed held up the paper. "You can change what you don't like."

She scanned the paper. "I love the layout." She looked at them. "I won't be shy. I'll enlist you all for things to do. We'll have fun."

Naomi cooked the rest of the supper and served them. They chatted about the wedding plans, finished eating, and did the dishes.

Joel pulled Ellie aside. "Maryann is going with me to the bishop's haus Monday. Would you mind sharing with her your experience when you first spoke with him after your return to Charm the second time?"

"I'd planned to prepare her. The bishop's a kind man but firm. And I respect him for how he handled my situation."

He nodded to Maryann. "Why don't you kumme with Ellie and me to the sitting room?"

She padded in and sat next to Ellie. "Is anything wrong?"

"Nah. Joel asked me to share my experience with the bishop after kumming back to Charm, to prepare you for your meeting."

Maryann frowned. "I don't want to dredge up any unpleasant memories. Are you all right discussing this with me?"

"I want to. The bishop asked me if I had asked God for forgiveness and if I was truly ready to follow God in my life. I assured him I was committed to God and the Amish life. He required me to ask forgiveness of the church, and I did so following the service one Sunday. Most of the members were kind and gracious. There were a few who avoided me and, later, they gossiped about me. No one's perfect. There will always be some gossips."

"Did you go to his haus for a period of time for instruction?"

"I did, and I enjoyed our meetings. We prayed, and he referenced Bible verses I wrote down to memorize. Some of which I already knew. He was supportive and encouraging. I really like him. You will too."

She pressed a hand to her middle. "I'm relieved. You make the meeting sound much easier than I expected."

"Good. I will warn you, the murmurings of the gossips may get to you. Ignore them. The majority of our community will be kind and thoughtful. Little Betsy will be hard for them to resist."

Joel settled on the high-backed chair. "There's no skirting around Maryann's marriage to an Englischer who was a troublemaker. I'm sure word will get around about him at some time or other. Many of the townsfolk go to Massillon to get supplies not offered here. They're bound to run into someone at some point who will mention him."

"I doubt it, but if the subject kummes up, then you can worry about addressing it. I would recommend you tell the bishop everything about your husband."

"I will." She sighed. "I hope his bad behavior doesn't follow me here by way of gossip or trouble."

"You're safer here than in Massillon. I doubt anyone would search for you in Charm. You and Betsy have a new beginning and family to support you." Joel loved reestablishing his close relationship with Maryann.

She hadn't changed her personality. She was the same compassionate schweschder he remembered.

They visited for another hour, and he walked Ellie to her wagon. "Travel safe, sweetheart. We don't have a service tomorrow. I'll stop over." He kissed her soft lips and watched her go down the lane. After February fourth, they wouldn't have to part. He heaved a happy sigh.

Joel fed the animals and cut firewood and stacked it. He dressed for his early Monday meeting with the bishop. He'd enjoyed his time with Ellie this past weekend. He teased her about him standing in front of the congregation the next time they had a church service and announcing she'd agreed to marry him. At first, she had thought he was serious. They'd both laughed. He loved her laugh. He kept falling deeper in love with Ellie with each passing day. He went inside the haus and found Maryann in the kitchen. "Maryann, are you ready to go? It will take us about ten minutes to get there."

She strode to him. "Ready."

"Don't be nervous. Everything will be fine." Joel crossed the yard with her to the wagon. "The bishop's a gentle soul."

"Ellie said he's firm, and I would expect him to not go too easy on me. He's protecting the Amish community from outsiders. I understand." Maryann shivered.

He'd take her mind off the visit and give her reasons to look forward to her life in this quaint little town. Along the way, Joel pointed out farms and who owned them. "I love this town. It's got what we need without being overcrowded with families. Some communities don't have enough land for newcomers to build and plant. I'm glad we don't have the same problem here." He halted the horse at the bishop's hitching post.

The bishop stood at the water pump filling a pitcher. "Good morning."

Joel gestured to Maryann. "This is my schweschder. She'd like a word with you."

"Wilkom and kumme inside and get warm by the fire." The bishop opened the door.

They went inside.

Maryann sat on the settee. "I hope we haven't caught you at a bad time."

He waved in the air. "Not at all. I'm pleased to meet you."

Joel took off his hat and traced the brim. "Maryann left the Amish life, married an Englischer, and has returned to live the Amish life in Charm with us." He'd ask the bishop about his calendar at the end of their visit, to end on a happy note.

The bishop set the pitcher on a small table. "May I offer you coffee or tea? I've got both on the stove."

"Nah. Danki." Joel didn't know who was more nervous, him or Maryann.

She shook her head. "I'm fine." She cleared her throat. "I've asked God to forgive me, and I'm ready to ask the church members to forgive me. I understand you may require me to attend instructional meetings with you until you're comfortable with my joining the church."

"You're correct. I would ask you to address the folks after our next Sunday service and tell them a little about yourself and ask them for forgiveness. You can tell them what you'd like about your time away." He leaned forward in the chair. "Tell me about your life in the outside world. Where is your husband?"

"My husband gambled and owed money to bad men. One man he owed shot and killed him. The sheriff arrested the man." She recounted the story of what happened during the marriage. She stared at her trembling hands. "I want a fresh start. My parents are happy to have Betsy and I live with them. I'd like to grow roots in Charm."

"Are the other men he owed money to aware you've moved to Charm?" The bishop rested his elbows on his knees and folded his hands.

Joel held up a hand. "Her place was ransacked in Massillon, but she has no idea who is responsible, and neither does the sheriff. Her friends won't offer any information about her whereabouts. Only a couple of people know, and we left town before sunrise. Nobody followed us."

"And you assure me you have no knowledge of the money they seek?" The bishop narrowed his eyes.

Maryann met his gaze. "I do not."

"Part of my job is to protect our community from trouble. It appears we don't need to worry about anyone following you here. This is a relief."

"I can't promise someone won't search for me, but I don't foresee them thinking of me living in an Amish community."

Joel stared at the bishop. He was hard to read. His mouth was in a grim line.

"I'm going to accept your word you had nothing to do with your husband's bad decisions. Let me get my calendar. We'll set up some times for instruction." He got up and lifted his calendar off the small desk in the corner. "We'll schedule weekly meetings."

"Do you mind if they're in the mornings?" Maryann held her elbows to her sides and fidgeted her hands.

"Wednesdays at eight a.m.?"

"I'll be here." Maryann rubbed her hands together.

"I'm pleased you've returned, and I look forward to wilkoming Betsy. Let's pray, and I'll let you get on your way."

Joel held up his forefinger. "Bishop, I proposed to Ellie, and she agreed to marry me. Our families are also pleased and gave us their blessing. I need to schedule a wedding with you on February fourth."

The bishop slapped his leg. "What wonderful news." He flipped the pages to February. I'll pencil you and Ellie in. We should write in your premarital counseling dates. Thursdays at six in the evening?"

"Perfect." Joel held his hat. They had confirmed a very important date in his life. One he'd remember for years to kumme. "Danki."

"The pleasure is all mine. Tell your families congratulations." He turned to Maryann. "I'm glad you're here."

"You've been kind, Bishop. This can't be easy for you." Maryann blushed.

"I'm thrilled to have our people return, as long as they're serious about their decision to follow God and the Amish life. I believe you're being truthful with me, and we're off to a good start. Let's bow our heads for prayer before you leave. Dear Heavenly Father, danki for returning Maryann to her family. Strengthen her and help her to raise little Betsy to follow you in faith and commitment to the Amish life as she grows. Danki for Joel and Ellie's commitment to you and their impending marriage on February fourth. Guide and direct their paths as they plan for this significant day in their lives. We love you, Father. Amen."

The bishop walked them to their wagon and bid them farewell.

Joel held the reins and glanced at Maryann. "How are you?"

"I'm comfortable and happy. The bishop treated me with respect and kindness. He's a good man. I'm glad this meeting is over. I worried about it all night. Ellie put my mind at rest somewhat, but I wasn't sure how the man would take my husband's dealings with bad men."

"He is a fair and just leader. He cares about us, and he wants the best for us."

"You're right, and it's evident. I respect how he conducted our conversation. I'm looking forward to my visits with him."

"Good! Now you can help Ellie and me get ready for our big day!"

"I love her, Joel. She's the best schweschder-in-law I could ever hope for. We get closer each time we're together. She's stronger than most Amish women. I like this trait in her."

"I do too. She'll be a partner I can ask for advice, count on for solving problems together, and not wonder if she's holding anything back from me. She speaks her mind." He didn't have to tiptoe around a problem with her. She could handle most anything. They'd face whatever life threw them, together, with God's help. "Would you ever marry again? You're young and pretty, and Betsy would benefit from having a daed when you're ready."

"She'll have you and Daed."

"Jah, but it's not the same." Joel hoped Maryann would find happiness like he shared with Ellie. A man who would cherish her and Betsy.

"Most Amish men would probably not consider a woman who has a past like mine. They would also choose to have their own kinner and not have to raise

another man's child. I'm not hopeful, but I'm content
to remain a widow."

"God may have other things in mind for you."

"I'm not opposed, but I'm not expecting a line of
suitors out our door." She chuckled.

"Between our family and Ellie's, you'll want for
nothing and be very happy. We'll all see to it."

"I have no doubt." Maryann beamed in the sunshine. "It's cold. If we didn't have the heat from the
sun, we'd freeze." She pulled her heavy wool shawl
tighter around her.

Joel pulled in front of their barn. "I'll secure the
horse. Mamm will be on pins and needles waiting to
find out what the bishop told us. You go on in."

She kissed his cheek. "I love you, Bruder. Danki for
going with me."

"My pleasure. I love you too." Joel watched her cross
the lawn into the haus.

To have Maryann home had been an answer to
prayer. He looked forward to creating precious memories with her. A gift he'd longed for but wasn't sure
would happen. God had been so good to them. He
didn't want anything to spoil it.

Chapter Fifteen

Ellie grinned and hugged herself. Her wedding day with Joel would become a reality. She hoped the bishop had the date free.

A short, stout man with bushy eyebrows and a thick mustache shuffled his feet and used his cane to get to the counter. His black overcoat was too big. Gray hair touched the brim of his collar under his hat. He had sad eyes and slouched.

"Do you have something special in mind?"

"Nope. My wife used to make me sugar milk pies before she passed. Today would've been our fortieth anniversary." He bent to shop the display. "You got any sugar milk pies?"

"Let me check in the kitchen for you." She took a pie off the shelf in the back. "Hannah, I'm taking this one."

"Help yourself."

Ellie returned to the patron. "I have one right here for you. Anything else?"

"Nope." He dragged coins out of his pocket and paid for his purchase. "Thanks."

She slid cookies off a plate, wrapped them, and smiled. "A gift from us to you."

He stood a little straighter, and his mouth curled in a grin. "Thank you, young lady. You're very kind."

The sad little man gave her a weak grin before he left the bakery. She waved to him, and hoped his day got better. She hoped she and Joel would be married more than forty years.

Joel walked in with a big grin on his face. "February fourth is reserved for us!"

"Hooray!" She clapped her hands together. "Let the planning begin." She leaned against the wall. "How did the meeting go between the bishop and Maryann?"

"I'm pleased with what transpired between them. He listened and wilkomed her back. He scheduled instructional meetings for her to make sure she understands what is expected and to convince him she's sincere and ready to commit to the Amish life. She liked him, and she handled herself well."

"I'm relieved. She's been through enough. It's time she enjoyed life here. We'll all help her adjust."

"We have premarital counseling with the bishop. Thursdays at six after work."

"Perfect. What will he ask us?" Ellie raised her eyebrows and shoulders.

"Do we communicate well with each other? Are there any problem areas we foresee at this point? To pray about all matters." Joel took off his hat. "How many kinner do you want?"

"Two or three?"

"I'd like a hausful. How about five or six?"

She held her stomach and bent over. "Are you serious? I couldn't keep up with so many little ones. After our first two, we'll talk about more. Agreed?"

He slapped his hat against his leg. "All right. I can compromise."

"Wait until they cry through the night. You may not want two."

"Betsy's a good boppli. She sleeps through the night."

Ellie chuckled. "Maryann's blessed. Not all kinner are as calm as Betsy."

Liza and Hannah popped their heads around the open doorway. They waved to Joel.

"Is February fourth our date?" Liza swiped a patch of flour on her apron.

"Jah, it is." Joel set his hat on his head and tapped it on top.

Hannah held a plate of cinnamon rolls. "Thanksgiving and Christmas and a wedding! We'll be busier than bees making honey. How fun." The door opened, and she widened her eyes. "Timothy, what brings you in?"

Ellie didn't miss the surprise in her friend's voice or her almost dropping the plate of cinnamon rolls. Hannah was having a hard time hiding her attraction to Timothy. She sucked in her lips to avoid the chuckle wanting to escape.

"I came to invite you, Ellie, and Joel to my home for a game night tomorrow. Mamm will have sandwiches prepared for us, and we'll sit by the fire in the sitting room and play games. My parents are going to supper at the Yoders'." He slapped Joel on the shoulder. "Good to run into you."

"Sounds like a good time. I'll go. You'll go too. Right, Ellie?"

"Jah. I like games. Danki for the invitation, Timothy." Ellie elbowed Hannah. "You love games."

Timothy folded his hands behind his back and

rocked on his heels. "Miss Hannah, you've been avoiding me." He gave her a mischievous grin. "You agreed we'd be friends."

"Um . . . all right . . . I suppose I could. What time?" Her knuckles turned white gripping the plate.

"Six thirty?" Timothy looked at each of them.

Ellie took the plate from her friend and placed the rolls one at a time onto the display shelf. "Do you want me to bring any of our games?"

"Nah. I've got plenty." Timothy crossed his arms.

"What can I bring?" Hannah stood stiff.

"Just you." He held her gaze a moment, until Hannah broke away. He turned to Joel. "How have you been? We've both been working hard to bring in the harvest and then catching up on work at our places. I haven't had time for target practice or anything else."

Joel put his hands together. "Ellie and I are getting married February fourth. Reserve the date."

Timothy grinned and nodded. "I'm pleased for both of you. I wouldn't miss it. Anything you need?" Timothy shook Joel's hand.

"I'm building a haus, and I could use a hand."

"Count me in." Timothy and Joel chatted about where to meet and what Joel had planned.

Hannah held her empty tray. "I'll be there tomorrow night, Timothy. Take care, Joel."

"Looking forward to it, Hannah." Timothy winked at her.

Her friend blushed and bustled to the back.

The men bid Ellie farewell.

Ellie rushed to the back. "Liza, you missed an interesting conversation between Hannah and Timothy."

Liza draped a cloth over the bread dough. "I didn't miss a thing. I overheard the entire conversation."

Ellie rested her palm on the counter and said to Hannah, "Before a customer kummes in, tell me what is going on with you and Timothy. You were tongue-tied and looked like a shy schoolgirl. You like him, and not just as a friend. Your face showed it. You said you were keeping him as a friend. What's happened?"

"We haven't had a decent conversation for a while. He's right. I dodge him on the Sundays we have church and at socials. He talks with all the girls, and I'm not sure what to make of him or his invitation. I've been afraid of getting my heart broken." Hannah tilted her head and smiled. "He's handsome and a tad bit irresistible. I'm throwing caution to the wind and going to his haus. Then I'll go from there. I'm not open to growing a friendship to see if it leads to something more serious if he's never going to mature and settle down."

"He's making an effort to know you better. You two have an obvious connection. Give him a chance." Ellie clasped her hands and held them under her chin. "You've not been giddy over any man. I'm excited about you and Timothy."

Liza measured a cup of flour and poured it in the bowl. "Jah, give him a chance."

"What have I got myself into? I may be sorry." Hannah balanced the tray on her hip. "Don't get too excited yet." The door opened. She leaned back and peeked through the open doorway. "Magdelena and Charity are here."

Ellie went behind the counter in the main room. "Magdelena and little Charity, what a pleasant surprise."

Hannah and Liza came out and greeted them and returned to the kitchen.

"We thought we'd stop in for an apple pie and fruit

bread. This place has the best aroma of sweet sugar. Your shelves are full of colorful desserts, and your canned fruits on the shelves add the perfect touch. It must be a delight to work here. I would enjoy it."

Ellie held out a butter cookie to Charity. "Would you like one?"

"Danki." Charity accepted the cookie and took a big bite.

Magdelena stepped closer to the counter. "I'm serious. Are you hiring?"

Liza and Hannah joined them.

Liza leaned against the counter. "I hope you both don't mind, but I couldn't help but overhear your conversation. Magdelena, you may be an answer to my prayer." She patted her middle. "I'm going to have a child. I'm not far along, but my ankles have been swelling and Jacob's been on me to hire someone. I would like to stay home with the boppli after he or she is born."

Magdelena put a hand to her open mouth. "Congratulations! I'm so happy for you and Jacob."

"What about Peter?" Charity looked up at her schweschder. "We should be happy for him too." She blushed. "He's got pretty eyes."

Magdelena winked at the girls. "You're right. We want to congratulate Peter too, on having a new schweschder or bruder. You like him a lot, don't you?"

"I really do." Charity lowered her chin and put a finger to her mouth.

Ellie held her breath to keep from chuckling.

"Is this a secret?" Magdelena winced and pointed to Charity. "I'm not sure this one won't spill the beans."

"Most women keep their carrying a child a secret

until they show. Peter is spreading the news like a forest on fire. We're overjoyed, so don't worry about it."

Ellie swallowed around the lump in her throat. Liza and Hannah had worked with her in the bakery for a while. They'd formed a bond. A closeness. The bakery provided a place they could talk each day. She'd be getting married and not living in her family home. She'd depended on the bakery to enjoy being with Liza. But she'd been worried about her step-mamm. She needed to take it easy since her fainting episode. She worked too hard here and at home. Magdelena was the perfect answer. "I have noticed the dark circles under your eyes and you are dragging by the end of the day."

Hannah swiped sugar from her arm. "Magdelena, are you sure you want to bake all day?"

"I would need to learn from you. Are you willing to teach me? I'm a good student." She bit her lip and toyed with her kapp string.

"I would enjoy it. Ellie can instruct you too. She'll show you how to wait on customers and record purchases in the sales journal." Hannah circled her arm around Ellie.

Liza darted a look at each of them. "Is everyone in agreement?"

They all nodded.

"I am." Charity raised her little hand.

Everyone laughed.

"When would you like to start work, Magdelena?" Liza unhooked a clean apron.

"I'll need to tell my parents. I don't foresee them having any objection. I've mentioned to them about my desire to work with all of you." She put a hand to her cheek. "Danki for this opportunity. I never thought it would happen. You've made my day."

Liza wrote on a piece of paper and passed it to the girl. "Here's your salary."

The girl's eyes grew wide. "You're generous!" She pressed a hand to her chest.

"Here's an apron. Check with your parents. If they approve, you can begin work Monday, December first."

"I'll be here, and if anything changes, I'll contact you."

Liza held her arms open, and they circled in a hug. "You're going to love being here with Hannah and Ellie."

Charity hugged Ellie's leg. "This is fun."

Magdelena got her purchases and reached for Charity's hand. "What a wonderful day!" She bid them farewell.

Ellie faced Hannah and Liza. "I'm going to miss you. We've been creating memories together here. This is where I first met you two. Don't get me wrong. I'm happy Magdelena accepted the position. The change will just take some getting used to. I love our jokes and conversations and creating scrumptious goodies together."

Hannah dabbed a tear. "Magdelena is a good choice. But I'm sad too. We'll miss you so much." She reached for Liza's fingers.

"Listen, I'll be right next door to both of you. We'll have family meals and social time, and our bond won't break because I'm not in the bakery." She twisted her lips. "I'll miss both of you too. The adjustment will be difficult for me. Although, it's the right decision. And when my little one arrives, I'll be glad we made this transition in advance."

"We'll be together a lot. The holidays are kumming, and we've got a wedding to plan." Hannah clapped her hands.

Ellie's heart swelled with love for them. She had put her past behind her and forged ahead to make her life better. These loved ones had been an important part of the process, and she would be forever grateful to them and to God. Charm had charmed her. The place where she'd gained a family, and soon, a husband. She curled her mouth in an impish grin. "Charity is taken with Peter. I wonder if he realizes it."

"I'm going to ask him. Kinner's innocent comments can make you laugh or turn red as an apple." Liza shook her head. "I have no idea what he'll say. I did notice them playing together after finishing their after-service meals."

"Kinner are adorable." Ellie grinned.

Five rolled around and the women went home. Ellie helped fix supper. "Soon, I'll be doing this for Joel." She stirred the vegetable mixture in the pan. "What do you make of Timothy and Hannah?"

Liza sliced a loaf of white bread. "He's got spunk and loves to make people laugh. He does like to flirt. I'm not sure about him for Hannah. She'll have to kumme to her own conclusion about him. He's been fickle. Talking to one girl and then another. I'd rather he not pursue a friendship with Hannah if he's not ready to consider her for something more serious, should she fall in love with him."

"He has settled down." Ellie grabbed the bread-basket and put it next to Liza. "We'll know more after tomorrow night. She'll tell us if she'll accept another invitation from him."

* * *

The next day, Ellie worked until five, went home, changed, and waited on Joel to pick her up after he stopped to fetch Hannah, since Hannah's place was on the way to her haus.

Joel and Hannah arrived, and she got in the buggy, and they chatted on their way to Timothy's.

"We were busy today." Ellie yawned.

"The men met me over at our property on your parents' land. We unloaded wagon after wagon of lumber and supplies. I've got more men to help than I'd counted on."

"We have good friends in Charm." Ellie held on to her heavy wool shawl.

Hannah snuggled close to Ellie. "Are you nervous about planning a routine to complete all you need to? I'd be a little overwhelmed. There's so much to do."

Ellie sighed. "I'm anxious and thrilled at the same time. I'm embarking on a whole new journey."

"Don't forget. I'll be right beside you. We'll make a good twosome." Joel drove the horse around a rut in the road.

"We do already." Ellie shivered and clung tight to her shawl.

They arrived and Timothy ushered them inside the haus.

Ellie eyed the game boards on the floor and admired the orange hue of the flames in the fireplace. "You're prepared. I'm impressed, Timothy."

"Danki." He gestured to the kitchen. "Let's have supper first, and then we'll play games."

They took their seats at the kitchen table. Ellie passed the sandwich platter to Joel.

Timothy had filled their water glasses at each place setting. "Hannah, Ellie said she was impressed. What about you?"

"Um . . . I am impressed." She kept her eyes on her glass.

"Good. I'm doing my best to get your attention."

Joel covered his mouth with his napkin.

Ellie struggled not to chuckle. Hannah would be upset with her if she did. Subtle, Timothy was not. He teased Hannah to get a rise out of her. Maybe Hannah found it appealing.

As they enjoyed their meal, Joel and Timothy discussed the construction of the haus.

Ellie and Hannah conversed about Magdelena working at the bakery.

"Has everyone had enough?" Timothy scooted back his chair.

They all nodded. Ellie got up and gathered the empty plates.

Hannah took the utensils.

"Don't worry about the dishes. I'll do them before I go to bed. Let's play the games. We don't have a lot of time."

"I'm not going to leave you with all these dishes." Hannah put the dirty plates in the water. "Where would I find a dishcloth?"

Joel and Ellie stood back.

Timothy reached for her wet hands and dried them with a towel. "Now let's go, Miss Hannah. I'm trying to impress you with my skills, and you're not letting me." His cheeks dimpled.

Joel raised a hand. "Timothy, now Ellie is going to expect me to do the dishes."

"You'll do anything for her. Your long, endearing looks into her eyes are hard to miss. She's got you right where she wants you."

Ellie giggled. "Don't worry. We'll do for each other."

"Hannah, I hope you're taking lessons from Ellie." Timothy had a twinkle in his eyes.

She blushed. "You are such a flirt, Timothy Barkman."

They played games, laughed, teased, and chatted.

Ellie had a good time, and she appreciated Timothy's generous and kind hospitality. He'd gone all out to make things nice for them. Hannah relaxed, laughed, and talked a lot with Timothy. She'd be curious as to what Hannah would have to say about him on the way home.

Joel pointed to the clock. "We should be heading home. This was fun. Danki, Timothy."

Ellie picked up the game pieces and placed them in the box. "Are you sure you won't let us clean up the kitchen?"

"Jah. It isn't right for us ladies to leave a mess for you." Hannah stood.

"I insist you go. I peeked out. Snow flurries are flying. The roads might be slick. I'd rather you get home before the weather makes the roads slippery. I really don't mind doing them."

They bid Timothy farewell, got in the buggy, and left.

"Did you enjoy yourself, Hannah?" Ellie sat on her hands to warm them.

"I did."

Joel handed the lantern to Ellie. "Do you mind holding this for me?"

"No, not at all." She held it out where he could see the road better. "Would you accept his offer to kumme over to his haus again?"

"I'm not sure."

Ellie kept quiet a few seconds. Hannah was giving her short answers. Not like her. Maybe she wanted to wait until they had private time to discuss Timothy. Joel had formed a close friendship with him. She'd not question her more until tomorrow.

Joel dropped off Hannah, and they bid her farewell. "Timothy and Hannah got along well."

"She's cautious. Time will tell."

He delivered Ellie to her home. He stopped at the end of the lane and kissed her full on the lips. "I shouldn't, but I had to." He drove as close to the haus as he could for her to get out. "Stay warm, sweetheart."

"I love you, Joel Wenger." She blew him a kiss and went inside.

Liza sipped hot chocolate. "Did you have a good time?"

"We did." She glanced at her daed's chair. "Where's Daed?"

"He went to bed about the same time as Peter. He had a slight headache." Liza frowned. "You're not saying anything about Hannah and Timothy. Did something unpleasant happen?"

"Nah. We had a good chat and laughed all evening. He had our meal on the table, water poured in the glasses, and games ready in the sitting room by a beautiful glowing fire. He flirted with Hannah, and her cheeks pinked each time. She seemed to become more comfortable with him as the night progressed. I asked her about him on the way home. Short answers were all I got from her."

"Joel and Timothy are friends and working together on the haus. She might have found it awkward to share her thoughts in front of Joel."

"I came to the same conclusion." She took off her shawl and hung it on the knotty pine coatrack.

"Wouldn't it be wonderful if they formed a friendship, it grew, and they married?"

"If he's the one for her, it would be ideal. You all get along so well." She traced the top of her mug. "She's always been more mature than her age. Timothy is the opposite. He's playful, full of energy, and a tease. It should be interesting. Time for me to go to bed. How about you?"

"Jah. I'm about to fall asleep right here." Ellie bid her good night and went to her room. She dressed for bed and got under the covers. She had the quilt Becca gave her in Massillon. She'd write a letter and tuck it in the pocket for Joel as her wedding gift to him. On nights like this, this quilt would kumme in handy.

Ellie picked up Hannah the next day. "You didn't say much about Timothy last night. I'm sorry if I put you in an awkward position, with Joel in the buggy."

"Timothy may ask Joel questions. I didn't want to put him on the spot with his friend. I had the best time. He's funny, and I was surprised. He had the food out, games ready to play, and wouldn't let us clean up."

"What man doesn't let the women wash and dry dishes? I couldn't believe it."

"I would take this friendship slow, and I mean slow. Liza's bad marriage to her husband who passed scares me. Paul put on a smile and convinced all of us he was kind and generous. Generous, jah. Kind, nah. I'm so glad she married Jacob and is finding happiness with him."

Ellie nodded. "She said her marriage to Paul was arranged and her parents needed the money. She thought she would learn to love him, and she had him pegged as kind and honorable. Remember, she wasn't in love with him when they wed. You've got plenty of time to learn all you can about Timothy. You already get giddy around him. Your situation would be different."

"I'm intrigued by him, and I'm getting more comfortable around him. We'll see what happens."

Chapter Sixteen

Ellie traced the cape on her dark blue wedding dress. The months had flown by. February fourth was finally here. A day she'd hold special each year for the rest of her life. The holidays had kept her busy, and she'd cherish the memories she made with her family more this year, since it would be the last she'd celebrate while living here with them.

Later today, she'd be Mrs. Joel Wenger. She'd have a haus with Joel where she would invite her and Joel's families to enjoy her meals and goodies. She was glad both families lived close.

She beamed. Naomi had insisted she make Ellie's dress. Her steady handiwork showed in the perfect stitches. She had imagined this day since meeting Joel. Her friends and family would witness them promising to love each other until God took them to Heaven. She was thankful all the planning over the last months leading up to this day had gone smooth. Women had volunteered to make food and do whatever was needed.

She'd learned more about Joel in the counseling sessions with the bishop. He wanted her input on financial decisions, and they agreed on most everything. He hinted he didn't want her to work, but he backed off when she said how much the bakery meant to her. He cared about her opinions and wanted her to be happy.

Peter came in and hugged her legs. "I'm going to miss you. Why can't Joel live here with us? Then you wouldn't have to move into your new haus."

"I'll be close. You can kumme over anytime."

"It's too far for me to walk." Peter pouted and crossed his arms.

"Liza or Daed will bring you, or I'll kumme and get you."

"Promise?"

"Jah, I promise." She sat on the bed, and he climbed up and scooted close to her. "Snuggles and Cinnamon will miss you. You'll have to visit them, or they'll be upset."

"Of course I'll visit them."

Peter got down and clasped her hand. "Mamm told me to fetch you for a special breakfast. Kumme on, before I get in trouble." He gave her a mischievous grin.

Liza and Jacob stood at the stove.

"How's the bride this morning?" Jacob circled his arm around her shoulders.

"I can't believe I'm getting married today. It doesn't seem real." Ellie leaned her head on Daed's shoulder.

Liza flipped a pancake in the skillet. "I'm making your favorite for breakfast. Pancakes." Her voice was weak and her eyes pooled with tears. She slid the pancakes on a plate and set it in front of Ellie's chair. "I'm thrilled for you, but I will miss having you with us each day."

Ellie slid into her seat and put maple syrup on her pancake. "I will miss living in this haus, but I'll be close by. Just a short buggy ride away. Danki again for the land to build our home and enough acreage to grow our crops and room to construct whatever else we choose."

Liza kissed Ellie's forehead. "Giving you the land benefits us. We're guaranteeing we'll see you more often. And there's more land here than we'll ever need. Maybe Peter will get married when he's ready and build near us."

Peter blushed. "I'm going to marry Charity when we grow up. She's pretty."

Ellie covered her mouth to hide her grin. "She's a good choice, Peter."

Liza and Daed's mouths were open and their eyes wide.

Knock. Knock.

Peter slid off his chair. "I'll get the door." He led Magdelena and Charity into the kitchen.

Ellie took her last bite of pancake, wiped her mouth, and stood. "Good morning."

"Good morning to all of you." Magdelena held a package. "We stopped by for just a few minutes. I wanted to give you your present."

Charity didn't take her eyes off Peter, and he stood next to her, grinning.

Ellie untied the twine and peeled back the paper. "I love this apron. I always need one, the way I go through them at the bakery. Danki."

Liza sat at the table across from Jacob. "Magdelena, Ellie has told me what a good job you're doing at the bakery."

"I love working with Ellie and Hannah, and I have enjoyed learning how to bake from them. Danki for the opportunity."

"We're thankful you're with us. I've liked getting better acquainted. Hannah has said the same."

"We should get going. I'm sure you have a lot on your mind today. We'll see you at the wedding. Kumme along, Charity."

Peter waved. "Good-bye, Charity."

Charity blushed and waved her pudgy little fingers at him.

Ellie walked them out. "Danki for kumming." She watched them until they got in their buggy.

Jacob joined her. "I've moved out most of the furniture. Benches are in the front room. Tables are set up in the guest room for food. We're ready for your big day."

Hannah and Esther arrived, carrying baskets with dishes full of food.

Hannah hugged Ellie. "Let's go to your room. I'll brush out your hair and wind it in a bun for you."

Esther kissed her cheek. "I'm ecstatic for you and Joel." She went to the kitchen.

Hannah had a present tucked under her arm. "This is for you."

Ellie sat on the bed and opened it. "Hannah! This must've taken you hours to make. I love this afghan. Danki."

"I had fun making it. Something to keep you warm." Hannah brushed Ellie's blond tresses, then pinned her hair in a bun. "There you go. You look lovely."

"Help me with my dress."

Hannah put the dress over Ellie's head and pinned it together. She put her kapp on her head. "You're ready." She cracked the door open. "The bishop and Joel have arrived. The chatter tells me townsfolk are kumming in. Are you nervous?"

"A little."

"You'll do fine. I'm glad you said your premarital counseling meetings with the bishop went well. You and Joel agree on all the important issues. Finances, kinner, and the rest."

"I had been apprehensive about the meetings with the bishop, but it turned out Joel and I looked forward to them. The bishop is a wise and smart man. We're blessed to have him."

Ellie and Hannah joined the others.

The bishop gestured to her. "You and Joel kumme with me a moment."

She and Joel smiled at each other and went with the bishop.

"Are you both ready to make this commitment?"

They nodded.

"We've had our meetings, and I've been pleased and comfortable with your responses. You both have convinced me you're meant to marry. I'm fond of you both." He said a prayer, and they walked out together.

Joel leaned close to her ear. "I love you, Ellie Graber."

"I love you, Joel. Soon you'll be saying Wenger instead of Graber." She scanned the room and waved to her friends. "Hannah and Timothy are chatting. She's laughing. What's your opinion? Will their friendship grow into something more?"

"He does give Hannah the most attention. And he's toned down his flirting with other eligible women. Maybe he's ready to get serious with someone finally."

Ellie sniffed the air and peeked in the guest room. "Look at all this food. It's quite a feast. The women have outdone themselves."

Joel's eyes widened. "The women have been generous." He faced her. "Ellie, I do promise to love you always. I'm not perfect, and I'm sure I'll get on your nerves once in a while, but I'll work at being a good husband."

"I have no doubt you will. The same goes for me." She grinned. "I may burn your food or chatter too much at times, but I'll work at being a good fraa."

The bishop raised his hand. "Everyone, please take your seats. It's time for the service to begin."

Ellie took her place between Hannah and Liza. She listened to the bishop's message on being kind to your enemies. She glanced over her shoulder and nodded to Maryann, holding Betsy. Maryann was truthful when asked where she'd lived. The gossips would spread rumors about her. She should've warned Maryann not to speak about her past. She loved Maryann. They'd gotten close. It was nice to have a schweschder. She'd defend her anytime she got the chance.

The bishop lifted his *Ausbund*. "Turn to page five."

Ellie sang the hymn by heart. This would be her last service as a single woman. Liza kept a tidy haus, cooked, cleaned, and kept things in order. She was a good mamm and gave them her attention whenever they needed her. She hoped to do the same with Joel.

The bishop closed the book and prayed. He opened his eyes. "Ellie and Joel, please join me and face each other."

Her heart pounded in her chest. She met Joel's gaze. His smile calmed her. She loved him even more for it. He knew what to say and what to do when it came to putting her mind at ease.

They said their vows and turned to face the crowd.

"I now pronounce Ellie and Joel Wenger husband and fraa. Let us pray for the food we are about to eat." The bishop said a prayer for the meal. "Let's eat!"

The crowd headed for the food tables set up in the guest room. Ellie looked around. "It's a good thing Daed and the men moved the furniture out of here. We needed every inch of space."

"This haus has larger rooms than most. Perfect for accommodating our guests. Your daed did build a fire outside, but it's still too cold to sit out there for very long."

"You did a wonderful job on our haus."

"I have a surprise for you there."

"I can't wait to find out what you have for me."

"You'll love it."

She filled her plate. "After we're finished, I have something for you."

"Take the present with us, when we go to our home. We'll give our gifts to each other in private." Joel held her gaze. "Mrs. Ellie Wenger."

Naomi hugged Ellie and gave her a white afghan. "I love you, Ellie. I couldn't ask for a better dochder-in-law. These last few months getting to know you have been wonderful. I'm sorry for being difficult when we first met."

"I've loved our talks, and I'm blessed to have you for a mudder-in-law." She circled her arm around Mary-ann. "I've gained a schweschder, and what a blessing you've been in my life, Maryann. And little Betsy too." She put her forefinger in Betsy's dainty hand.

Maryann wiped her wet cheeks with the back of her hand. "Your kindness and acceptance of me has been generous. I'm thankful for you, Ellie."

Joel pointed to the chairs Liza dragged over in front of the crowd. "Your mamm wants us to sit and open our gifts."

Ellie and Joel sat together. She unwrapped her

parents' presents and held them up. "These towels and the plates, bowls, and utensils are perfect. Danki."

They finished opening the rest of their gifts.

Ellie said, "Everyone has made such special gifts. I'm going to treasure each one of them. Danki to you all." She whispered to Joel, "Look at Peter and Charity."

"He's found a puzzle to share with her, and he's teaching her where the pieces go. Before you know it, they'll grow up and we'll be attending their wedding." He chuckled.

Hours later, Joel had taken one wagonload of presents to the haus and unloaded them. He returned to pick up Ellie and the rest of the gifts. "Ready, my love?"

"Ready." She hugged each of her family and left with him.

He took her home and put the presents in the guest room. He opened the door to their room. "Here's your surprise."

"I love the bedroom furniture. Did you make it?" She loved the long maple dresser, headboard, and side tables.

"I did."

"How did you have time?"

"Your daed and Timothy helped me."

"I have something for you." She handed him the present she'd carried in. "Open it."

He tore through the wrapping and unfolded the quilt. "Is this the one you received in Massillon from Becca Carrington?"

"She suggested I save it and tuck a note in the pocket to you."

He removed the note.

Dear Joel,

From the time we met to this day, we've weathered some storms and had a lot of turmoil mixed in with our happier days, proving we can get through our tough times together. I look forward to our future, and I promise to love, honor, and trust you all the days of my life.

Love, Ellie

He kissed her and held her close. "I'll treasure your note." He spread the quilt on their bed. "It fits and looks good."

"I like it."

He picked her up and twirled her around. "Ellie Wenger, you've made me the happiest man by becoming my fraa!"

Ellie laughed. "God worked a miracle in your mamm's heart, and God brought Maryann home and gave me you. I couldn't be more thrilled!"

Pennsylvania Dutch/German to English Glossary

boppli	baby
bruder	brother
daed	dad, father
danki	thank you
dochder	daughter
Englischer	non-Amish
fraa	wife
grossdaadi	grandfather
grossmudder	grandmother
haus	house
jah	yes
kapp	hair covering for Amish women
kinner	children
kumme	come
mamm	mother
nah	no
schweschder	sister
wilkom	welcome

Connect with Us

Visit us online at
KensingtonBooks.com
to read more from your favorite authors, see books
by series, view reading group guides, and more.

for sneak peeks, chances to win books and prize packs,
and to share your thoughts with other readers.

facebook.com/kensingtonpublishing
twitter.com/kensingtonbooks

Tell us what you think!

To share your thoughts, submit a review,
or sign up for our eNewsletters, please visit:
KensingtonBooks.com/TellUs.

Books by Bestselling Author
Fern Michaels

___The Jury   0-8217-7878-1 $6.99US/$9.99CAN

___Sweet Revenge   0-8217-7879-X $6.99US/$9.99CAN

___Lethal Justice   0-8217-7880-3 $6.99US/$9.99CAN

___Free Fall   0-8217-7881-1 $6.99US/$9.99CAN

___Fool Me Once   0-8217-8071-9 $7.99US/$10.99CAN

___Vegas Rich   0-8217-8112-X $7.99US/$10.99CAN

___Hide and Seek   1-4201-0184-6 $6.99US/$9.99CAN

___Hokus Pokus   1-4201-0185-4 $6.99US/$9.99CAN

___Fast Track   1-4201-0186-2 $6.99US/$9.99CAN

___Collateral Damage   1-4201-0187-0 $6.99US/$9.99CAN

___Final Justice   1-4201-0188-9 $6.99US/$9.99CAN

___Up Close and Personal   0-8217-7956-7 $7.99US/$9.99CAN

___Under the Radar   1-4201-0683-X $6.99US/$9.99CAN

___Razor Sharp   1-4201-0684-8 $7.99US/$10.99CAN

___Yesterday   1-4201-1494-8 $5.99US/$6.99CAN

___Vanishing Act   1-4201-0685-6 $7.99US/$10.99CAN

___Sara's Song   1-4201-1493-X $5.99US/$6.99CAN

___Deadly Deals   1-4201-0686-4 $7.99US/$10.99CAN

___Game Over   1-4201-0687-2 $7.99US/$10.99CAN

___Sins of Omission   1-4201-1153-1 $7.99US/$10.99CAN

___Sins of the Flesh   1-4201-1154-X $7.99US/$10.99CAN

___Cross Roads   1-4201-1192-2 $7.99US/$10.99CAN

Available Wherever Books Are Sold!
Check out our website at **www.kensingtonbooks.com**

More from Bestselling Author
JANET DAILEY

Calder Storm	0-8217-7543-X	$7.99US/$10.99CAN
Close to You	1-4201-1714-9	$5.99US/$6.99CAN
Crazy in Love	1-4201-0303-2	$4.99US/$5.99CAN
Dance With Me	1-4201-2213-4	$5.99US/$6.99CAN
Everything	1-4201-2214-2	$5.99US/$6.99CAN
Forever	1-4201-2215-0	$5.99US/$6.99CAN
Green Calder Grass	0-8217-7222-8	$7.99US/$10.99CAN
Heiress	1-4201-0002-5	$6.99US/$7.99CAN
Lone Calder Star	0-8217-7542-1	$7.99US/$10.99CAN
Lover Man	1-4201-0666-X	$4.99US/$5.99CAN
Masquerade	1-4201-0005-X	$6.99US/$8.99CAN
Mistletoe and Molly	1-4201-0041-6	$6.99US/$9.99CAN
Rivals	1-4201-0003-3	$6.99US/$7.99CAN
Santa in a Stetson	1-4201-0664-3	$6.99US/$9.99CAN
Santa in Montana	1-4201-1474-3	$7.99US/$9.99CAN
Searching for Santa	1-4201-0306-7	$6.99US/$9.99CAN
Something More	0-8217-7544-8	$7.99US/$9.99CAN
Stealing Kisses	1-4201-0304-0	$4.99US/$5.99CAN
Tangled Vines	1-4201-0004-1	$6.99US/$8.99CAN
Texas Kiss	1-4201-0665-1	$4.99US/$5.99CAN
That Loving Feeling	1-4201-1713-0	$5.99US/$6.99CAN
To Santa With Love	1-4201-2073-5	$6.99US/$7.99CAN
When You Kiss Me	1-4201-0667-8	$4.99US/$5.99CAN
Yes, I Do	1-4201-0305-9	$4.99US/$5.99CAN

Available Wherever Books Are Sold!

Check out our website at www.kensingtonbooks.com.